Those Who Were Dancing

From The Rave To The Grave

Those Who Were Dancing

MARK SLEIGH

Copyright © 2020 Mark Sleigh
All rights reserved.

The characters and events portrayed in this book are fictitious. Any similarity to real persons, living or dead, is coincidental and not intended by the author. Obvs.

No part of this book may be reproduced, or stored in a retrieval system, or transmitted in any form or by any means, electronic, mechanical, photocopying, recording, or otherwise, without express written permission of the publisher. But don't worry, I'm very approachable. And look on the bright side, there are no legal impediments to sharing this book by means of telepathic communication. I will also waive my rights if you write it all out by hand or commit it to memory and recite it around a campfire. Anyway, the main thing is that you enjoy it, so enough of this babble. Onwards and upwards to Part One, Chapter One...

Cover design by: Josh Bowe and Antoine Varley

DEDICATION

Those Who Were Dancing is dedicated to Sof, Joe and Lara.

PART ONE

*'And those who were dancing
were thought to be insane by
those who could not hear the music.'*
- ANON

A COMPLETE AND UTTER FOX NEWS ANCHOR

Naturally, at the first of the funerals I was sad.

The second, where we filed past the coffin and outside into the snow, gave me pause for reflection. We drank a lot and sobbed not a little, and Iffy asked me who'd be next.

When the third funeral came along just a month later, the seed of suspicion that Iffy had planted in my mind began to germinate. As had always been the case, my misgivings were a late and pallid bloomer compared to the Japanese knotweed of Iffy's paranoia, and I did my best to ignore his constant nagging, although it went on and on and on, strangling, suffocating and blocking out the sun - until the day when I opened my Facebook account and there was the announcement of the fourth death.

"You're next," whispered a voice in my head as I stared at the RIP messages that were seeping down my computer screen.

My mobile rang. I picked it up, said, "Hello?"

And freaked out when a voice whispered, "You're next."

"Iffy," I said when I could finally breathe again; when my heart was back where it should be after going AWOL for a tiny eternity; when I had checked the caller ID on my phone. "Don't ever do that again, you complete and utter Fox News anchor."

"But it's true, isn't it"? Either you're next, or I am, or it's Clara or the Gaffer or Allan Exit."

"Bullshit, Iffy. Life doesn't work like that."

"Ah, but maybe death does."

I took a deep breath. "What's that supposed to mean?" It was one of those cute little witticisms that sound clever for about half a second, until you thought about it and discovered that, hey, it really meant fuck all. Much as I loved my old pal, after all our years of knocking around together the shifty little git really knew how to wind me up. "'Maybe death does,'" I snorted. "Pffff. Death just is."

"Or maybe it just isn't."

Cradling the phone awkwardly between my shoulder and my ear, I concentrated on not rolling a cigarette and listened as Iffy took me on another journey into the mind of a man whose love affair with illegal substances was as ardent as it was enduring.

"It's like the curse of the pharaohs. Howard Carter and Tutankhamen. We're dying, one by one. That's four of us gone now in, what, a couple of months?"

I inhaled, not feeling the delicious burn of tobacco from the fag I wasn't lighting. "Oh, sure, it's just like it," I said, "apart from the pyramids and the pharaohs." There's a lot to be said for sarcasm during moments of stress. Not as good as nicotine, of course, but it would have to do.

After a second or two, though, I had to ask: "You aren't serious, are you?" Even I, the acknowledged expert in such arcane pursuits, sometimes found it hard to tell when Iffy was joking.

"It's all a bit of a coincidence, you must admit. Four of us all dancing the last waltz in the space of a few months. How you feeling, by the way?"

"Apart from almost going into cardiac arrest when you phoned me? I'm fine. Never felt fitter. Haven't had a puff in three weeks now. Been happily coughing up buckets full of slime from my poor, much-abused lungs. Or is that bucketfuls?" I added, not stubbing out the fag I hadn't smoked right down to the filter. "And you?"

"Great. *Mors certa, hora incerta*, innit." And there he went, dropping one of those wise-sounding classical quotations that he had cribbed from a dictionary of Latin phrases found in one of our squats. "Death is certain, its hour is uncertain," he translated helpfully. "Anyway, I've got the blindfolded base-jump booked for tomorrow. Swimming with the sharks on Friday. Solo ascent of the North Face next week, then a relaxing holiday in Baghdad. What could go wrong?"

I left a pause in the conversation, thinking that maybe my "And you?" hadn't been as heavily decked with meaning as I intended.

"Hello? You still there?" came the voice in my ear.

Sighing, I tried again: "Iffy. Really. How are you?"

"Alright. Really. I'm alright." And I pictured him not snorting a fat line of ketamine in much the same way as I was not puffing on a cigarette. "So are we going then"?"

I knew exactly what he was referring to. "S'pose so. Can't be any worse than the last one, can it?"

Jacek's funeral had been horrible, even as funerals went. (And by this time I was becoming something of a reluctant connoisseur.) His family were raving Catholics and they had repeatedly caught us unawares by breaking into song every few minutes and leaping to their feet at unpredictable times; luckily for us, the clouds of incense billowing through the church had reduced visibility to a distance of a few feet.

The bereaved had been divided into two distinct groups that were separated by three pews and an entire *Weltanschauung*. At the front, the family: suited, booted, sobbing, bobbing up and down and casting tenebrous glances through the haze at us. At the back, a mourning chorus of half a hundred techno travellers from all over the world: dreadlocked, Mohicaned or shaven-headed, bleary-eyed from a lifetime of partying or oily-fingered from a day under the bonnet of a truck, swigging on cans of super-strength lager, standing up when we should be sitting down, sitting down when we should be standing up.

Sobbing, too.

"It'll be in your neck of the woods, I guess. 'Bout time I paid you another visit, anyway. We need to fill that Iffy-shaped hole in your life, amigo. And like that I can look out for you, too."

"Look out for me?"

"In case you're next on the list. For the curse."

One thing about Iffy - one of many - was his stubbornness. His pathological inability to let things lie could be endearing. It could serve him well. It could also piss you off.

A thought struck me. "Why are you so sure I'm next? It could be you. Or the Gaffer or Allan Exit. Or Clara."

"Aha!" he trumpeted down the line. "So you admit that the Curse exists. The Curse of the Sound System."

This was precisely how he sucked you in. I liked the Iffy-boy, despite some of the seedier stories that occasionally drifted my way from our friends. Like the clothes he wore, he was the shades of grey that existed between black and white. "The truth," he had told me once, "lies in the infinite space between zero and one." Sometimes he was hard to grasp and he often left me feeling nettled, but there were usually dock leaves to hand.

"I admit nothing," I said. "Ever. You know that. So what's the nitty-gritty, anyway? All I've got so far is Facebook - a load of RIPs where Udo used to be."

On screen, the messages of condolence and grief were still coming in. 'Can't believe it.' 'I'll never forget you.' 'I hope you can still hear the music.' 'They might stop the party but they can't stop the future.' 'RIP - Rave In Perpetuity.' And at the top of the page, Udo's girlfriend's status update (how ungainly the geek-speak was, I thought; how inapt the digital lexicon was for expressing human emotion): 'Udo left us yesterday. One love.'

"It was messy. You sure you want to hear this? I spoke to Clara before I called you. She'd spoken to Fabrizia. Poor girl's in bits. Of course. As you would be."

Indeed."Go on, then," I said, bracing myself. Not smoking another cigarette.

A BIG MAN, A SHOUTER, A NEVER-IN-DOUBTER

"He fell under an U-Bahn."

"He did what?"

"Where you are - in Berlin. Fell on the tracks in front of a Tube train." There was a catch in Iffy's voice that wasn't down to a bad line. I pictured him back in London. Skinny, pale, rubbing his hands over his balding crown, toying with one of the few remaining dreadlocks that clung on to the back of his head.

I didn't know what to say. A quick death, at least. No time for regrets - but no time to say goodbye either. I hadn't even been aware that Udo was in town. It was strange that after the tidal wave of grief that had drenched me when I learned that he was dead, I still was able to flinch at the thimbleful of hurt caused by the fact that he hadn't phoned me.

Shrugging off the selfish side of grief, I shuddered as I recalled the unholy roaring, rushing noise made by an approaching U-Bahn as it thundered through the underground tunnels beneath the city where I was living. I'd once stayed in a flat that shook each time a train passed below it.

Then I had an image of Udo as I'd last seen him: a big man, a shouter, a never-in-doubter, an oil-stained dog-lover, a gap-toothed sound engineer, a spittle-flecked, ham-fisted brawler, a caner, a crooner, an East German wide boy, a wild and wide-eyed wanderer. And I wondered how he had wound up in front of an U-Bahn.

"Messy," I agreed.

I told Iffy I'd see him when he got to Berlin and came within a midge's eyelash of nipping out to buy some tobacco.

But I hadn't clucked my way through three weeks of non-smoking in order to crack now, so I popped an aniseed sweet in my mouth, dropped to the floor and did fifty press-ups. It was the system I had adopted for giving up cigarettes: every time I really felt the craving, I'd exhaust myself with a bout of physical exercise. As the days went by I found myself having to bang out more sit-ups or hammer out more press-ups or run further before I got short of breath.

At least I was getting fit. Indeed, at forty I was in better shape than I had been since my teenage years. I was trying to make up for more than two decades of enthusiastic drug and alcohol abuse, and I was doing pretty well.

Iffy's impending arrival would be sure to test my resolve, of course. I would have vowed to resist his wiles, but I didn't relish the thought of breaking a promise. Even one made to myself.

Still panting from my exertions, I picked up my mobile again to call Fabrizia. I was far from sure that she would be pleased to hear from me, but I felt obliged to make the effort to show some support. She had never really warmed to any of us, the ghosts from Udo's past. She had hooked up with the big man at the tail-end of our sound system's dog days, and I knew that Iffy for one partly blamed her for the way things fell apart at the end.

Personally, I had been glad to see someone try to yolk the bull-like German giant, and Fabrizia had thrown herself into the task with all the feminine power at her disposal. For his part, I suspect Udo enjoyed his sedentary lifestyle as much he buzzed off occasionally wriggling away from it. Fabrizia had installed him in a remote Sicilian farmhouse where he threw his considerable weight and boundless energy into growing and cooking fine food, and where his combative instincts were curbed by the stories she fed him about what happened when you messed with the locals.

I had been expecting him to turn up at the other funerals, but in fact I hadn't seen him for two or three years, not since the last time he had come through Berlin on his way to visit his parents in Brandenburg. Although we had never fallen out, we had lost contact without realising it.

I hadn't counted on never seeing him again.

Screwing up my courage to phone his grieving girlfriend, I noticed that I had a missed call registered on my mobile. 11.23am on Tuesday the twenty-third of May. Yesterday. The caller had left no message but the prefix was 0039.

Italy.

Udo.

Fabrizia, after much wailing and emotional flailing that flayed my fraying nerves, confirmed that yes, the big fella had been in Berlin, that yes, he had indeed perished under the wheels of an underground train, and that yes, she believed he had come to town to see someone from our old crew, possibly me. No, she didn't know why. No, he hadn't been planning the trip for long. No, he hadn't been drinking a lot lately. Yes, he'd woken up with a bee in his bonnet about something a few days ago - and shit, she wished she hadn't let him go.

The funeral - number four - was to take place in two days' time in a little village tucked away in the forests about thirty K out of Berlin. I offered to pick her up from the airport when she arrived, but she'd see me at the crematorium, she said, and hung up.

Fifty more press-ups.

And fifty sit-ups.

Why had Udo suddenly got it into his head to leap on a plane and charge over to Berlin? I could only presume it was connected to the way the lights of our old travelling sound system were being extinguished, this dwindling of the beacons that led to my past.

There had been nine of us at the heart of our collective - and now we were five. With another dozen or so floaters and flirts who flitted in and out, we had trundled our convoy of trucks and buses around Europe, putting on free raves in abandoned industrial sites and in empty office blocks, in hidden valleys and on exposed mountainsides - wherever we were invited, whenever we could get our shit together, out there on the edges, deep in the underground.

WHELPED ON THE ROADS

It was strange for something that made so much bloody noise to be labelled clandestine, but our underground scene was easy to miss - unless you happened to be within earshot of a party, that was.

Like all good myths, it was lost in the creases of the map, hidden on the dark side of the moon, tucked away where no travel guide could point you in the right direction. It was in every city if you knew where to look, but you could walk past it every day for years and never know it existed. It flourished in the urban wastelands and the unregenerated industrial badlands where night-time vehicular traffic was minimal and pedestrian traffic bold, lost or sociopathic. It burgeoned out in the rural backwoods, under the open skies. It was in constant motion, tatted down in half an hour and loaded in the back of a truck. It was in the middle of nowhere and at the centre of everything we did. Its roots were deep and its branches reached far. It was the darkness of the long night and the dazzling illumination of the soul. It was a spinning spiral, splintering, and it was fractal, constantly fracturing; it was multi-faceted, a negative image, a positive attitude, a parallel universe, a state of mind, a way of life.

What we did, basically, was hold parties - unlicensed, unauthorised and very loud parties. For obvious reasons, we generally chose locations where there was little likelihood of us being hassled, which meant squatting abandoned warehouses or plotting up out in the sticks. Word was spread via photocopied flyers, word of mouth and messages left on infolines. We would roll up in our trucks and install the sound system, and maybe some other rigs would set up alongside us. Some people would come and dance. We'd sell them some drinks, maybe some food, and when everybody had had enough we would pack it all away, tidy up and move on.

Put like that, it was hard to see what all the fuss was about really, but fuss there was. People had been coming together to party and dance since time immemorial, but nonetheless we caused outrage when we did it - possibly because we also took a lot of drugs, and, yes, we did play our music very, very loud.

The press churned out moral panic-inducing headlines about marauding locusts and foul pests. One Home Secretary promised to be "Tough on rapists, tough on armed robbers, and tough on squatters." A junior education minister said people who lived on the road were "No more than a bunch of unwashed, benefit-grabbing, socialist anarchists who deserve a good slap." The Prime Minister himself declared that "Society needs to condemn a bit more and understand a bit less. New age travellers? Not in this age! Not in any age!" After all, what would happen if the movement never stopped growing? Where was the profit in it? Who was in control?

The music we played was hard and uncompromising, fast beats and slamming breaks, basslines that sounded like a rip in the fabric of the universe, screeching top-ends that tore holes through time and space. It was techno music let off the leash, released from the club kennel and allowed to bare its fangs. It was wild and elemental, both the acid techno that came howling out of the squats of London Town and the bastard hardtek sound whelped on the roads of mainland Europe, and it worked for us, the dirty squatters, the free party tribe and the techno travellers.

We were happy to operate underneath the radar of the mainstream musical media. It was about passion, not fashion. It was hard work, a full-time occupation that offered little pay and no job security. Every time we built our speaker stacks and our DJs began to mix, we faced the possibility that the authorities would arrive to seize our equipment - our livelihood - and maybe even the old horseboxes, trucks and buses that we had salvaged and kitted out with beds, kitchens and wood burners and made into homes that ran the full gamut from pristine to ramshackle.

Sometimes the going got tough: when you had run out of money and your truck broke down on a desolate mountain top; when it was minus twenty outside and you had to crack the ice on your water butt to make a brew; when your party had been stopped, your rig impounded, your friends imprisoned and your teeth kicked in by riot cops; when your site got evicted and you didn't know where to go; when somebody you loved died too young.

For me, though, at least when I was younger, there was an irresistible whiff of romance about the nomadic lifestyle that made all the hardships bearable. It wasn't for everyone, but life on the road as part of a travelling techno sound system tribe was perfect for someone who was willing to sacrifice security and stability for adventure and freedom, and to swap the morning commute for the all-night party.

There were laws against that kind of thing.

When repetitive beats in the outdoors were outlawed in the UK, some of us stayed to fight the good fight and some of us left to carry the message overseas. Iffy, Sam Saoule, the Gaffer, Clara, Minnie Mouth, Allan Exit, Jacek, Udo and I plunged headlong into the glorious anarchy. Our time on the road was five years of constant movement, accompanied by the beats of our DJs, a time when we frequently found ourselves in trouble and nearly always managed to blag our way out.

So - we were modern day troubadours carrying our freedom sound to the big cities and the remotest corners of the continent. We were land-pirates, cyber-gypsies, roving, raving renegade techno-punk outlaws with dodgy trucks, packs of dogs and big fat rigs, and wherever we went we took the party with us. We were self-organised, self-financing and leaderless. We didn't give a fuck for the big bucks. We weren't looking for fame or fortune, just the respect of our peers and the liberty to dance the night away under the moon and stars. We believed in what we were doing. We wanted to change the world and we gave it our best shot.

Or - we were a bunch of degenerate, dirty hippies who corrupted the youth with seditious ideas. We encouraged innocent children to take drugs, and we disturbed the peace by making an unholy racket all night long, playing nasty, aggressive music when decent folk were in their beds. We were scruffy social misfits who couldn't hack a real job. We cynically exploited the welfare system, we didn't pay taxes, we robbed and stole. We kept dangerous dogs and lived in unroadworthy vehicles. We squatted innocent people's homes and honest farmers' fields, we failed to educate our children and showed no respect for authority.

Or - we were just an occasional minor irritant, the latest in a long line of kids who thought they were righteous because they challenged the status quo and who believed they were important because they provided newspapers with facile, sensational headlines that titillated the so-called moral majority on dull news days.

And now half us were dead and it all seemed so long ago. Had we changed the world? When I was feeling optimistic, I'd say yes; we'd moved the pieces around a bit, helped create some more alternatives. On a bad day - on most days, these days - I'd look at the legacy we had left behind and wonder if it had all been worth it.

Too many us had gone from being underground to being under the ground. The drugs that should have set us free had trapped too many of us; the alcohol that had loosened us up had rotted our livers and minds; the road to freedom had too often terminated at the doors to prison. Some of us had moved so much, so far and so often that we were lost for ever.

Every new coffin provided another nail.

Fifty sit-ups, and another twenty for the beer I wanted to drink. Unless something happened to cheer me up soon, I'd be the fittest man in town.

I needed action. I needed to move. As homely as it was, I suddenly found my flat oppressive. Too small, too cramped. I glanced at the glowing screen of my computer before turning it off and noticed that Clara had chipped in with an understated lowercase 'xxx' in the tributes to Udo - but I couldn't face thinking about my ex-girlfriend right then.

My thoughts were quite dark enough to be getting along with.

SOME SORT OF GLASS PROSTHESIS

Outside, Berlin was buzzing. The vicissitudes of winter were a memory that still stung, but the heat of the sun acted as a pleasant balm and I would be fully healed by October, when I would no doubt kid myself once more that the next six months wouldn't be so bad.

When Clara and I had our final argument and Allan Exit disappeared overnight with the last remaining bits of our sound system ten years ago, I had jumped at the chance of stability and a cheap flat in East Berlin - or maybe I had just accepted the first offer that came along.

Whatever the reason, I had made my home in Friedrichshain and had been there ever since, and although I observed the inevitable gentrification of that bastion of squatters, punks and hippies with a heavy heart, I was happy there. I'd recently decamped to a new flat, handed down to me by the previous tenant, and the rent was contractually guaranteed against improvident increase. Despite the incremental inflation of the cost of living, I was living proof that it was still just about possible to eke out an existence trading second hand records.

Friedrichshain was like a village in the middle of the city, riven in two not by the Berlin Wall, which actually marked the southernmost point of the district, but by Frankfurter Allee, another remnant of the Soviet era, where Stalinist tanks had once proudly rumbled and the proletariat had gasped at their own power, unaware that the street was just a sham, that the impressively-fronted flats were actually crap, and that only the tanks were real.

The *Sud Kiez*, or southern neighbourhood, was undoubtedly the prettier sister. Colourful, cheerfully floral, crowded with restaurants, host to independent boutiques, she was proving attractive to the yuppie hordes who pressed their suits with pullulating vigour.

The *Nord Kiez*, which ran as far as the old slaughterhouse, was less instantly welcoming. It took more time to get to know her. She refused to flaunt her charms like her southern sister, and it was her rebellious personality that seduced me, not her looks.

After ten years in the village, and a fair proportion of that time spent in bars and gigs and parties, I knew a lot of people. Rarely could I quit my flat without bumping into a few acquaintances, and although misanthropy was growing within me like a tumour, for any given journey on any given day I had to allow an extra half hour for chance meetings, gregarious greetings and the general gathering of gossip.

"Hey! Island monkey! Fuck, eh! You know fucking the news, eh?"

I had almost made it as far as the organic mini-market on the corner of my street. About fifty yards. Willy - small, round, loud, annoying and possibly evil - had learned to speak English while hanging around on the free party scene. Thus, every second or third word he uttered was 'fuck'. Indeed, he had a uniquely venomous way of spitting the word out, and a frankly amusing habit of dropping it in unnatural places in a sentence. He also thought it was witty to call me 'island monkey,' the semi-affectionate term that Germans used for the British. We had known each other for a long time and I had never felt the need to penetrate his façade of bitterness, bile and spite to reach the pure, simple heart that - for all I knew - lay within.

"Hey, Willy."

"You heard fucking about Udo? It's fucking crazy, eh?"

Then he did something I had never seen him do before, something I scarcely believed possible: he put down his bottle of Sternburg beer. I had always presumed that it was some sort of glass prosthesis, glued to his fist.

Freed from his appendage, he actually gave me a hug and I actually enjoyed it, which probably went to show something that I couldn't be bothered thinking about.

"I know, Willy. He was a good friend."

"*Quatsch*, eh," he said, re-armed with his beer and reverting to type. "He never once gave me a free drink fucking when he did the bar fucking, eh."

That struck me as an unfair epitaph, especially as it was certainly untrue. Willy had usually been too pissed at our parties to remember anything after the first few hours. Not wanting to hear any more of his drunken slurs on Udo's character, I started to make my excuses.

"You should go to see Helga fucking, eh," he interrupted me. "She's really cut fucking up, eh. I heard Udo was fucking in her truck the night before the accident, you know. But that's Helga, eh, always wanting fucking to be the centre of everything."

I occasionally wondered if Willy genuinely believed all the bad things he said about the people he spent so much time with, or if he was just fishing for a reaction. If he had such a low opinion of them all, why didn't he fuck just off, eh?

"See you, then, island monkey," he called after me as I left him to down his beer and steep in his own vitriol.

STRUGGLING WITH THE PAST TENSE

I wanted a cigarette, which was handy as Helga's truck was parked on a *Wagenburg* in Lichtenberg and the run would do me good.

When I ran, I opted for the hare's tactics rather than the tortoise's. I'd gallop until exhaustion forced me to slow down to a trot, then I'd pick the pace up again as soon as my muscles permitted. The streets were full of people lollygagging in the sunshine, lazily lapping up the vitamin D.

I dodged around miniature gardens where squares of earth at the base of trees had been planted with flowers. I sidestepped open air living rooms where cafés, bars and restaurants had spilled out into the great outdoors as soon as the weather permitted. In the hotter months the streets in the *Kiez* were truly reclaimed; they became an extension of the home rather than just a dead space to cross on the way to somewhere else.

I ran on until, sweating and puffing, I arrived at the gates to Helga's *Wagenburg*. Hidden from curious eyes by a high wall, the *Wagenburg*, or traveller site, was home to three large trucks, a bus, a couple of long-wheelbase vans and half a dozen *Bauwagens*, mobile building site trailers that had been converted into cosy caravans by Germans who didn't fancy living in a flat. The site was small, peaceful and legal. Its residents didn't bother anybody; they kept a patch of abandoned waste ground in good nick, and in return nobody bothered them.

Two black hounds of questionable ancestry padded over to give me a good sniffing as I entered the yard. I spotted a figure, as dark and dodgy-looking as the dogs, on her hands and knees in the dust next to a truck, measuring lengths of wood against one another. Tattooed filigree scrolls of obsidian ferns coiled around her arms and up her neck and a grey mist of spliff smoked flapped and twisted in the air above her closely shaved head.

Helga opened her mouth and shone her teeth at me.

"It's been a long time, man. Too long," she admonished me after we had both given voice to our sorrow over Udo's untimely death. It was a phrase I had been hearing a lot in the last few months as I caught up with old faces from my travelling days.

"Willy said that Udo'd been to see you?"

"What, Willy? He's quick enough to come round when he smells some misery, that one. Don't see him for weeks if he owes you money. A bit of bad news and he's panting round like a dog on heat."

One reason I kept myself to myself with increasing militancy was my reluctance to put up with all the bitching. Our sound system had gone down in a conflagration of back-biting and infighting and I considered myself well-shot of all the bullshit. I had been quite happy out in the cold, but Udo's death was now inexorably dragging me back closer to the fire - and the smoke was getting in my eyes.

"But Udo was here?" I wanted to move the conversation on, away from wee Willy's manifold shortcomings.

In response, Helga gestured towards the various pieces of wood and upholstery that littered the hard earth around her truck.

She had spent months working on her vehicle. A beautiful forty-year old Magirus Deutz with tyres as high as my midriff, an elongated bonnet like the snout of a Roman emperor and a rectangular box on the back that served as living quarters, it looked ready to circumnavigate the globe. Helga was an artist when it came to kitting out truck interiors and I had assumed that the debris was just another part of the work in progress.

It took me a few seconds.

Then I got it. Udo - big Udo, ants-in-his-pants Udo, boisterous, clumsy Udo - had always had an unfortunate knack for destroying pieces of furniture. Countless times we had watched as he hurled his body down on a chair; we would all wince, the air would be rent by the screech of splitting wood, and Udo would hit the deck in a tangle of arms and legs and a flurry of umlaut-laden swear words.

He might have given up travelling, but I guessed he had still been as clumsy as ever. The broken skeleton of a chair was physical proof that he had recently been in Helga's truck.

"He said he wanted to see you," Helga told me, pointing at me with her joint.

I waited for her to continue.

"But he didn't have your phone number or your new address. That's why he came here first. He tried phoning you yesterday morning, but you didn't answer. I know he'd got another mission here as well, but I guess he was on his way over to your gaff when…When the accident happened."

"He could have Facebooked me," I said, using one of the new verbs that had begun to infest our speech in the Information Age.

It didn't go down well.

"Pffff. Facebooked you? Udo's like me. Was like me. He likes people, the three dimensional kind that you can share a drink and a spliff with. He isn't - he wasn't into all that Fakebook bullshit."

It was true. The concept of mapping all your friendships and uploading personal information would not have appealed to him. I also found it hard to imagine Udo giving a Diana Ross about the dozens of status updates that appeared every day on the social networking site. Instead, I could picture him barrelling into a crowded bar, calling for shots of tequila, bellowing at his dog, guffawing at a joke. In fact, I had often thought Udo was born a millennium and a half too late - he would have made a first-class barbarian warlord.

So no, I guessed that Facebook hadn't been his thing.

"Why did he want to see me?"

Helga shrugged and offered me her spliff. I shook my head, and she said, "Search me. He knocked on my door - shit, he practically knocked it down - at midnight. Came in, sat down, broke the chair, opened a bottle of grappa, drank most of it, roared, rambled and passed out. Shit, that man can snore. Could snore."

Helga was struggling with the past tense, and not because English was her second language.

"Hey, you're going to the funeral, aren't you?" she asked me.

"Seems to be all I do these days. Why? Aren't you coming?"

She scowled. "Don't do funerals. I'll go to the wake, if there is one. But if you're headed there, you can take his bag for his girlfriend."

I agreed. Helga vanished briefly into the darkness of her truck, followed by her dogs. I heard her rummaging around and muttering to herself. Stepping back out into the afternoon sunshine, she lobbed a filthy ex-army backpack onto my lap.

"You want to smoke a joint now?" she asked me, but I wasn't listening.

I was staring at the tatty old bag, remembering the day that I had lent it to Udo. We had been wintering in a squatted factory outside Florence, taking time out to do some essential repairs to the rig. Tarting up some of the faded backdrops, checking power cables for weak points, cannibalising one knackered record deck to repair another. That sort of thing. Udo was moody, itching to get moving again. Finally he announced that he was heading south to hook up with a girl he had met at our last party, the massive multi-rig Millennium mash-up near Bologna. His bus having recently ceded to the ineluctable ravages of time, he stuffed some clothes into my old backpack, snorted a monster line of speed and told us he'd see us later. Went to see Fabrizia. Walked out of our lives.

Ten years later I had my bag back, but I'd rather have had Udo.

THE ONE-FINGERED SALUTE

A dead man's bag is a heavy burden.

I knew I had to give it to Fabrizia when she arrived for the funeral, but that was still two days away as I left Helga to enjoy her spliff and test the splint she had fashioned for the broken chair. Slowly strolling on the wide Berlin pavements, savouring the warmth in the air and the buzzing of the bees as I made my way back home, I passed the old glassworks - just the sort of post-industrial building that would have had Udo salivating at the mouth and reaching for his crowbar a decade ago.

Checking there was nobody around, I dropped to the floor and ground out fifty press-ups. Did them quickly enough to get a lactic burning in my triceps. Did them with the weight of Udo's bag on my back. Did them thinking of nothing but the press-ups, counting them off, feeling the hot tarmac under the palms of my hands, seeing it come nearer, pushing away from it, keeping my back straight. Balancing my weight on the tips of my toes. Rubbing my nose in the dirt.

And I still wanted to look in Udo's bag when I had finished. What did etiquette demand? I asked myself. It didn't seem right just to ferret about in a dead man's belongings, but I was finding it hard to resist temptation - hence the fevered bout of press-ups. Udo was in no position to complain, of course, and I didn't recall him ever being too fussy about privacy.

We all had our own personal boundaries of what was and wasn't acceptable when we were on the road together; consensus was achieved but it was always mutable. It depended on mood, timing and situation. In the end, I think part of the reason we all went our separate ways was simply that we got sick of living in each other's pockets.

I loosened the noose on the neck of Udo's bag and peered inside.

A pair of socks. Unworn, thank Dog. (And, heartbreakingly, now never to be worn. I had an image of Fabrizia reminding Udo to take them with him as he packed for his final trip away from home.)

A tent. (Not really - it was a tee-shirt, size XXUdo. Grey, threadbare, lustre long-since lost, the blanched, peeling logo of an Italian techno sound system barely legible on the chest.)

A bottle of grappa. (Dangerous, home-made Sicilian moonshine, by the looks of it. Meant for me?)

A book. (A copy of the first volume of Robert Anton Wilson's Cosmic Trigger trilogy. Dog-eared, battered, tattered, patterned in oily finger prints. Nothing had remained clean for long in Udo's grubby mitts.)

A marquee. (Actually a sweatshirt.)

A return ticket to Palermo for an Easyjet flight out of Schönefeld. Dated next Tuesday. (Lucky the passenger who now wouldn't have to squeeze into a seat next to Udo's sweating frame and supercharged mouth.)

A passport. (I couldn't bring myself to look at the picture. It was impossible to fit Udo into a tiny photo.)

And that was all. That meagre haul was all that Udo had been carrying to his death.

It was only as I started to re-pack the bag that I noticed a small plastic box tucked away in the bottom.

I pulled it out. Held it in my hand. Smiled. It was an old audio cassette, the kind that technology had long since left for dead, the sort that most people had thrown away when digital gave analogue the one-fingered salute. Only the most sentimental of hoarders still hung onto a dusty few of their most cherished examples: the epoch-defining mix-tapes, the compilations lovingly recorded by old flames, the home-copied albums with hand drawn covers that just couldn't be parted with.

Udo's tape was in a plain black box. I opened it and read the label that was stuck on the tape itself: Millennium Massacre/liveset.

Live recordings made at parties had been a vital facet of the underground techno scene. Only DJs bought vinyl. Everyone else made do with copies of copies of copies of DJ mixes and livesets. The advent of the internet had changed all that, and it was odd to find such an ancient, technologically obsolete artefact when I excavated the depths of Udo's bag.

What made it even stranger was that the Millennium Massacre party was not one that any of our crew remembered fondly.

HEAVY SCENE, MAN, BAD VIBES

Bologna, New Year's Eve, 1999. The site met our minimum requirements for winter festivities: walls, a roof and no neighbours. We stayed there for two weeks, straddling the Millennium.

The party was long, hard and not altogether nice. Heavy scene, man, bad vibes, as our hippy forerunners would have said. The ravers who came seemed to be disciples of the base speed and ketamine diet plan; there was little sign of the loved-up ecstasy eaters and intrepid acid explorers that I remembered from my early years. Crack was smoked openly and smackheads banged up brazenly. There were robber crews who cruised the shadows at the back of the buildings, emptying the pockets and stealing the trainers of anyone who had passed out or fallen asleep. There were fights and threats, and there weren't enough of us to keep the vibe vampires in check. Dogs shat in puddles of human urine on the concrete floor. Humans shat in puddles of canine urine. A dozen sound systems banged out unrelenting hardcore. There were rumours of a rape.

It had all been very darkside, and had no doubt played its part in the eventual break-up of our sound system. We were old school by the time the Millennium came, and having watched the free party scene grow and mutate, none of us were completely comfortable with the direction it had taken, although, admittedly, Bologna had been extreme. There were still wicked parties with good vibes in amazing locations where the tribes came together, danced their socks off, had positive experiences and tidied up after themselves.

Free techno wasn't dead, but in my mind it was gangrenous, and Bologna had been a putrid, cankerous affair of the type for which, had I been a doctor, I would have recommended amputation. We stuck the party out till the end, but it was bitter, and I'm not sure that we ever recovered from it.

Which all went to say that I was more than a little surprised to find a recording of that particular do in Udo's bag. This was no audio version of happy snaps. These weren't treasured memories to coo and gloat over. It wasn't a key to unlock a session of gooey nostalgia. I could only presume that Udo wanted to show it to me; I couldn't begin to suss out why.

Obviously, I'd have to listen to it - and luckily I was precisely the kind of sentimental old fool who kept a tape deck at home, just in case I ever fancied playing any of the shelf-load of dust-gathering cassettes I clung onto.

Try as I might, I couldn't ignore the feeling that the tape held some kind of connection to the deaths of my friends.

But there was no way that all the recent bereavements could be connected, I reminded myself.

Minnie Mouth, sweet, manic Minnie, mother to us all, the first ex-member of our ex-sound system for whom the bell had tolled, had drowned in Amsterdam.

Sam Saoule had died of an overdose.

I had yet to hear the grim details of how Udo contrived to wind up under a train, but I figured that alcohol and a natural lack of coordination must have played their parts.

Only Jacek's exit had been suspicious: although the Polish police had declared a suicide, there were hints of drug deals gone wrong and rumours about the involvement of a crew of Bulgarian heavies which had never been investigated.

So it was a crazy series of random events. A few isolated incidents that pushed credibility to its limits. Apophenia. That was all. No stranger than the man who was struck three times by lightning, and whose grave later took a fourth hit. No weirder than six of the top secret code words connected to the D-Day landings appearing as answers in The Times crossword a few weeks before June 4, 1944. No odder than a pair of twins both suffering fatal accidents on the same road on the same day. Certainly no stranger than Edgar Allen Poe writing a story about four survivors of a shipwreck who eventually ate the cabin boy, a character named Richard Parker, four years before four survivors of a real shipwreck actually ate the cabin boy, an unfortunate kid by the name of Richard Parker.

Coincidence, serendipity and synchronicity abound, I told myself.

I was just meandering through the South *Kiez*, letting my feet lead me where they would. I paused to admire some green-fingered locals' piece of guerrilla gardening in one of the empty lots that 1945 bombs had created. Increasingly, Friedrichshainers were reclaiming these abandoned spaces and turning them into mini-parks. In this one, on Oderstrasse, a dozen or so cannabis plants had appeared overnight. Idly, I wondered what their life expectancy would be.

My phone heralded an in-coming text message. I checked it: Iffy had blagged enough money to pay for a flight to Berlin that evening. I replied, telling him I'd meet him at Schönefeld Airport at eight thirty.

TEMPUS EDAX RERUM

Every time I clapped my eyes on Iffy lately I couldn't help feeling a pang of pity deep within me, and I hated that. The very concept of pitying a friend - more than that, a brother - was foul. That indomitable, incorrigible, irrepressible, inestimable Iffy should inspire such feelings turned my stomach.

But Father Time had finally caught up with the prodigal son. The wit was still there in his regard, but the edge was dulled. The sparkle in his eyes was less evident, the shiftiness more readily apparent. His gait, once so bouncy, had flattened down into a furtive skulk. His healthy cynicism sometimes bordered on bitterness. An appetite for life and adventure still gnawed at his soul, but to my way of thinking he had already consumed too much.

Tempus edax rerum, as he would probably phrase it himself.

Time, devourer of all things.

Of course, I was hardly a blushing virgin myself - but I liked to think that I didn't have the haggard visage of a veteran returning from Passchendaele, either.

Watching him bear down on me in the arrivals lounge, I was suddenly reminded of the time he arrived at a teknival in Italy, having driven all the way from Holland in a car with no reverse gear. That was how he led his life - no going back.

"Hugs, my man. What we need are hugs," he cried, falling into my arms.

He was right, of course.

"Good flight?" I asked.

"Splendid. Arrived early."

We made it safely out of the airport, an achievement which should never be taken for granted when accompanying Iffy.

The only reason he wasn't standing naked watching a sniffer dog go berserk over his clothes was that he looked too skint to be smuggling any drugs.

A short walk brought us to the *S-Bahn* station. Our banter simmered down as we marched arm-in-arm onto the long, empty platform. Long, empty moments ticked by as we stared at the clock counting down to the arrival of the next train. I knew what Iffy was thinking. We didn't speak.

A minute's silence.

I couldn't help myself. I dived down onto the floor behind the bench we'd been perched on. I had done seventeen press-ups while Iffy raised one laconically mystified eyebrow in my direction before we heard the first distant rattle and rumble of the approaching train. I managed another half a dozen repetitions before it ground to a halt. I hadn't looked up, but I was sure Iffy's gaze had been fixed on the lights on the front of the train.

I hadn't enjoyed the thoughts that crowded in on my imagination.

We both let out a "Phew," and got on board.

"That something you picked up from the locals, is it? The press-ups," Iffy wanted to know.

"They're all at it round here," I assured him.

"You wanna watch that."

"It's actually my newly patented anti-smoking technique. I'll teach you how, if you like."

"Don't start."

And I couldn't quite tell if he was joking or not.

DILATING INTO AN ARSEHOLE OF EVEN GREATER DIMENSIONS

A funny thing happened on our way home. Except it wasn't really very funny.

We found ourselves sharing the *S-Bahn* with a small group of British suits who were clogging up the carriage with a stifling fug of unrepentant sexist banter, xenophobia, testosterone and alpha male braggadocio. I noticed Iffy eyeing them up with the pensive and vaguely menacing air of a lion observing a watering hole.

He sprang to his feet, belched, and advanced on his prey, a particularly cocky-looking member of the herd who had been holding forth on the merits of winning two world wars and one World Cup before segueing into a monologue on Teutonic breast size, much to the discomfort of a young girl sitting two seats away.

"Well, look who it is! What you doing here?" Iffy cried, much to the man's open-mouthed surprise, before lurching straight for his jugular and enfolding him in a powerful hug.

The man blinked. I could see the tip of his nose poking out through Iffy's ragged, mangy dreadlocked mane.

"Check it out," Iffy crowed, turning to me. "It's Paul! I told you all about him, remember? Dodgy Paul." The expressions on the faces of the man's companions ranged from mild bemusement to smirking superiority.

I smiled obediently and cringed inwardly. "Nice to meet you, Paul."

"I think there's some mistake," the man said.

"Fuck off, you cunt," Iffy roared merrily, and then briefly hesitated. "It is you, isn't it? Paul Buchanan from - where was it again? Mile End, right?"

A perplexed nod.

"So this is what you get up to when you aren't off your face or in the nick? What is it, a conference or something? You're in banking now, right? Still, got to earn your wedge somehow, I s'pose. Smack doesn't come cheap when you're just banging it up rather than banging it out, eh?"

The man's fellow bankers duly rearranged their expressions from aloof amusement to out-and-out horror, and still Iffy ploughed on: "We had some good times, though, didn't we? Bangkok, Amsterdam...Paul the Dodgy Bastard and His Amazing Bottomless Veins! You, my man, are a complete legend. Respect is due. And managing to hold a job down - I guess they didn't do a criminal records check, then?"

The man's co-workers edged away from him. From top dog to pariah in two minutes. Just as he was mustering his wits and courage in order to reply, Iffy dealt him another monstrous, stinking hug. "Anyway, bruv, this is our stop," he chirruped gaily as the train slowed into some dogforsaken station on the outskirts of the city. "Wicked to see you. And if you ever get any more of them snide laptops, you know who to call, right?"

"Iffy," I sighed as we jumped out onto the desolate platform, "that wasn't very nice."

"Ha. Fuck 'im."

"You might have just ruined that man's life."

"He'll survive."

"So I guess he wasn't top of your Christmas card list? What did he do to you? Rip you off?"

"Nah, he was just a selfish, greedy, arrogant twat with too much money and not enough empathy. I thought I should introduce some doubt into his life. A chaos injection, that's all."

"But you knew him, right? Paul from Mile End."

"Nope. But I know how to read and he'd got a label on his

luggage with his name and address on it. The rest was, er, spontaneous creativity on my part."

I knew how Iffy's reasoning would run if I asked him - that the man was a bully, and bullies needed frequent reminders of their own vulnerability - but I nonetheless found myself wondering what exactly he had just achieved. Spread a little strife and discord, upped the world's unhappiness factor, begot a bit more bitterness. The likelihood of Paul Buchanan seeing the light was low. Having had his credentials publicly questioned, he would probably now try even harder to impress his colleagues, dilating into an arsehole of even greater dimensions.

But Iffy was chortling away to himself as he rolled himself a cigarette.

In the platform lights, his eyes were aglow with something: I was unsure what.

He was, I reminded myself as we awaited the next train, a man with a knack for embroiling others in certainties of his own devising.

THE LAND THAT CLOSING TIME FORGOT

"So what's on the programme for tonight, my man?" Iffy demanded forty-five minutes later as we made our way through the busy streets.

There was some kind of concert on in the new music venue next to Warschauerstrasse station and flocks of heavily made-up vampire teens were milling drunkenly around us.

"And please, please, don't tell me we're gonna do press-ups all night. Big up your clean and healthy lifestyle and all, but this is the town of the all-night drinking hole, the Gaulish village that still holds out against the boring, trendy invaders, where the bars still play punk and the punks still snort speed. This is the city where you can go out at six in the morning and bump into all your mates on the streets and in the gutters. This is the land that closing time forgot. I've been looking forward to this."

Me, I had been looking forward to seeing Iffy, of course - but part of me had also been dreading the siren song of drugs and booze that followed him everywhere he went.

Most of the time I had no difficulty saying no to temptation, apart from the fags. It was the anticipation of the hangovers and comedowns that kept me on the straight and narrow. As I got older, I found that the days after the nights before became harder to deal with, and the maths simply no longer computed. When I had been fresh of face, full of grace, open of mind, eager of disposition and hungry for emprise, the merits of the fun and the discerned benefits of the expanded perception far outweighed the degree to which I felt like shite when it was all over. By the end of the first decade of the twenty-first century, though, I was somewhat of an old git.

"I've got something I'd like to show you," I confided as we made it safely past the open door of a *Spätkauf* stocked with delicious German lager at knock-down prices, just the first of many such obstacles that we would have to circumnavigate. "Let's go back to my gaff."

"I bet you say that to all the *frauleins*. Hey, lend us some wedge, would you?"

I duly dug in the back pocket of my combat trousers, pulled out some notes and slapped a twenty down into Iffy's dangling metacarpus. There wasn't an accountant born who could have tracked the years of loan and counter-loan, of repayment and payment in kind, of transferred and inherited debts, of meals paid for and bar bills settled, of drugs bartered and goods swapped, that had gone down between me and the Iffy-boy. Whichever of us had money, paid. If neither of us had money, we went without. Or Iffy negotiated a five fingered discount.

He doubled back to the late-night off-licence and re-emerged with a bag of Tannenzäpfler beer. I could see their little red hoods snuggling together, peeking cautiously out into the warm night air. I also heard a larger bottle clunking ominously against the others, and I suspected it might be (and hoped it wasn't) tequila.

A miracle happened that evening in Friedrichshain. We made it back to my flat without bumping into a single drug dealer of my acquaintance. I registered the way my companion's gaze strafed the passers-by, searching for a familiar face from one of his previous extended stays in Berlin, looking for someone with whom he could exchange some social niceties and from whom he could purchase some narcotic naughties.

He had never been remotely fussy about what kind of drugs he ingested - his personal motto, he claimed, was *semper excelsius*, or ever higher - but recently downers had started to loom ever larger in his life. Luckily, Berlin remained a largely ketamine-free zone.

Leaper of streambeds, clamberer of trees, scurrier over high walls, dancer on rocky hillsides - Iffy had been all these things in the land of our lost youth. He had been nimble, quick, agile, a mountain goat.

It pained me to realise that now he had to stop to catch his breath after two flights of stairs.

"Just admiring the view," he contended. "Lovely tags you've got here."

The stairwell of my building was indeed coated in layer upon layer of graffed slogans, a written history of previous tenants and passers-through. Gentrification had yet to strike my digs, though the clarion call had been sounded when the buildings on both sides had recently been tarted up, the façades gaudily daubed in pastel hues, the flats centrally heated, the rents doubled, and the old tenants displaced.

"Nice work, that," Iffy gasped, indicating a large spray can rendering of the number twenty-three. "Yours?"

I said it wasn't.

"Hey, but anyway, talking of which... I bet you didn't know that the top speed of an American crow is twenty-three miles per hour?"

A lot of my companions in the free party scene had a great deal of fun larking around with the number twenty-three. Most aficionados agreed that dear old William Burroughs had kick-started the fad, before Robert Anton Wilson and Robert Shea had picked up the baton in their Illuminatus! trilogy in the seventies, and the Spiral Tribe sound system, the nearest thing our underground scene had to pop stars, had lent it new wings in the nineties. If our movement had developed quasi-religious aspects, as I believed it had, then twenty-three was some kind of holy icon, and some people genuinely attached a cosmic, mystical significance to the number.

It was like malaria, the number twenty-three. Once infected, always connected. Walking down a street, you always noticed house number twenty-three. You always checked the time at twenty-three minutes past the hour. The sum of the first twenty-three primes is 874, apparently, which is itself divisible by twenty-three. It is the first number with a prime number of digits, all digits prime, and the sum of all digits being prime. There are twenty-three discs in the human spine. *Homo sapiens* have twenty-three pairs of chromosomes. Nobel Prize-winning mathematician John Forbes Nash, darling of neocon game theorists, had been obsessed with the number.

(Perhaps significantly, he had also been diagnosed with paranoid schizophrenia.)

"And you know something else?" Iffy went on, apparently unfazed by my tepid reaction to his revelation about the American crow. "And this is big. Listen - Udo snuffed it on the twenty-third. Like Sam."

When I had read Robert Anton Wilson's Cosmic Trigger book, the one that inspired the teknival scene's usurpation of the magic number (and the book that I had found in Udo's backpack, I realised), I had taken his musings on the twenty-three enigma to be a mocking reminder about the dangers of selective perception, but Iffy never failed to call every sighting, and he did so in such a sincere fashion that in the end I chalked it up as another of his numerous eccentric beliefs and left it at that.

No-one who pried into the idiosyncrasies of the Iffy-brain came out markedly better off for the experience.

The fact that he was finding connections between the tragic deaths of our old friends came as no surprise. As a man with a natural penchant for conspiracy theories, it would have been out of character for him to do otherwise.

I considered my options. I could try to convince Iffy he was attributing meaning where there was only coincidence. I could bang my head repeatedly against the wall (which would achieve a similar result). Or I could open the door to my flat.

What I mustn't do, I reminded myself, was let Iffy's paranoia override my ability to think logically. Iffy by name, Iffy by nature…

AN EXTENDED EXPERIMENT INTO THE FOCUSED DESTRUCTION OF HUMAN BRAIN CELLS

It was a balmy evening and my windows were wide open. The evening air carried with it the barking of dogs and the shouts and laughter of people on the street. A few weeks earlier somebody had kindly deposited a sofa and two armchairs on the broad pavement below my balcony and the impromptu al fresco living room was generally squatted on a 24/7 basis. I heard beer bottles being cracked open and smelt the pungent odour of skunk weed drifting on the breeze.

"Go on then, Mister Clean, tell me you haven't got any puff," Iffy challenged me.

"Will Sir be requiring the Moroccan or the Afghan?" I wondered, passing him my skinning-up kit. Although I rarely smoked myself, I considered myself a conscientious host.

Iffy set about moulding a ball of squidgy black hashish into an elongated sausage shape and I sought out the tape that I had discovered in Udo's bag.

"What's this? You turning trendily retro in your dotage?"

I've heard tell that face-to-face communication is only forty percent the words you speak, and the remaining sixty percent is down to body language and facial expression.

Haha, good joke. Anyway, remember - I said I had something I wanted to show you. Well, this is it. Take a gander. Be prepared for a surprise, though. It's quite a mystery and I'd appreciate your input, I intimated silently.

But he was busy rolling a joint so he missed it all.

I reverted to old-fashioned oral communication. "Have a butcher's, Iffy-boy."

Well, fuck me: a tape from the Millennium Massacre. Who'd have thought it?... What a fucking nightmare that was. Where did you get it?... Wait a minute; this is connected to the Curse of the Sound System, isn't it?... But you refused to listen to my so-called paranoia about all the deaths in our family. What's going on here?

Iffy had a most expressive face.

"Udo crashed in Helga's truck the night before he died. Helga said he'd been planning to see me. And I found this tape in his bag," I said. "What d'you reckon?"

"Well, by Jove. Yes, indeedy. That's a turn-up for the pigeons. A book amongst the chickens, one might say. The cats come home to roost, if one could be so bold. Yes. I see. Quite."

"Iffy…"

I had been so wrapped up in my thoughts that I had scarcely registered the presence of tobacco in my flat. Only when my guest sparked up his spliff did my olfactory nerves click into action. It smelt good. Not the hash, though that was sweetly pleasing: it was Dame Nicotiana who tempted me.

"'Scuse me," I begged. Sitting on the floor, I curled my feet under the battered old sofa that I had liberated from underneath my balcony last summer and did half a hundred abdominal curls. Iffy gallantly ignored my frenzied activity and continued puffing away.

"My Dog, that party was fucked up," he said when I had finished. "What were we like?"

"As I remember it, you were the one who wanted to stay till the bitter end." Iffy, aka The Last Man Standing.

"Yeah, well, maybe. You know me - *usque ad finem*. To the very end. Nothing succeeds like excess, and all that. I'm always afraid I'll miss out on something."

I just stared. Since when had he engaged in self-analysis?

"Though we couldn't have got the trucks out even if we'd wanted to. It was some party, eh?" Iffy muttered pensively. "The last one we ever did together."

I cast my mind back to the turn of the century. Imagine a pair of long, wide, high rectangular boxes - because that's what the architect of the place we squatted for the Millennium Massacre had clearly done. The architecture of capitalism elevated expediency over elegance and favoured functionality far more than flair. Legacy to the human race be damned! Perish the thought of leaving behind a building that was a monument to beauty and creativity, just knock 'em up as cheaply and as fast as possible.

(Whenever I was confronted by such unlovable edifices, I could not help but wonder how different the world would look if a little more money had been spent on housing projects and industrial centres; how different people's outlooks would be if the panoramas they faced were inspiring rather than depressing.)

The buildings we partied for the Millennium had presumably been left high and dry when the good ship Capitalism set sail for sunnier climes, cheaper workforces, fewer regulations and no bothersome unions.

Like temples to ancient pagan gods they stood vacant and neglected; and like the enterprising builders who ripped apart England's abbeys and monasteries after the Reformation, when we saw the buildings we focused not on their history but on their potential. Dedicated in their youth to the pursuit of wealth for a few and a livelihood that was ground out via wage drudgery and daily alienation for a few more, the buildings outside Bologna had fallen into a dilapidated state in their middle age, sagging in the middle, crumbling at the edges and getting thin on top, until their doors were prised open for one final fling, the two week-long Millennium Massacre teknival -

all sound systems welcome.

Setting up for the party, before the main flood of ravers arrived, the site, the weather and a long, weary period of bickering with Clara already had me in a peculiar frame of mind. We went into the party fatigued by a busted gathering in Milan and labouring under a miasma of internecine squabbles. The halcyon, chimerical days and chemical nights of summer seemed impossibly far away...

I loved summer teknivals. They were ephemeral living spaces, slapdash post-industrial facsimiles of medieval fairs with dozens of dancefloors dotted around brightly-illuminated town squares that heaved with writhing, stomping revellers. Shops sprang up selling food, booze, coffee, clothes, jewellery and records out of the back of trucks. Cafes and bars were roofed over with tarps, and small sound systems in tents and marquees played reggae, punk, disco, ska and dub, while the enormous wall-of-sound link-up rigs blasted out the techno and the drum 'n' bass.

The sites were shifting messes, effervescent, evanescent mazes, fleeting, fugacious warrens, encampments of knights errant and errant nights; they were rough-and-ready townships, temporary autonomous zones, living protestivals - and they were ours. I adored the utopian solidarity of the firepit, the triumph of the dawn, the heat of the sun, the plumes of wood smoke, the lasers reaching up towards the stars, the squelch of mud and the pounding tribal rhythms.

Winter warehouse parties were different. They were a chance to dance in the ashes of industrial civilisation. They were future noir, post-apocalyptic, dystopian. It was us, doing our thing - in their territory. My inner cyberpunk craved Mad Max motors, squalid, derelict buildings, the reek of diesel, rusty iron workshop relics, spray-paint and graffiti on the walls, jagged blades of light bleeding through broken windows - the feeling that capitalism had collapsed and we had survived.

The Millennium Massacre provided the post-industrial setting, sure enough, but it offered little in the way of joyous celebration. It was a long, hard slog from start to finish, an extended experiment into the focused destruction of human brain cells.

Outside the buildings a higgledy-piggledy mass of cars, trucks, vans and buses jammed together in the sort of parking arrangement where nobody could leave until everybody left. In Bologna the space was limited, the perimeters defined by the steel fences of the neighbouring buildings, and the road that led to the venue was swiftly annexed as more and more people turned up.

Inside the buildings, where daylight never penetrated, there was darkness and there was light. Deep, heavy patches of blackness where glass crunched underfoot, and multicoloured bursts of blinding, blazing brightness where the sound system lights swept and pulsed and swirled over the dancefloors.

The noise was everywhere, immense and intense, bass in your face and all through the place. The walls vibrated. A dozen sound systems, each with its formidable black stacks of speakers and its own crowd of dedicated dancers, had set up and were contemporaneously bludgeoning out high-decibel hardcore beats and savage breaks. The cumulative effect was of a mighty throbbing sound, a leviathan booming in the depths, a pulsating, rippling bath of infinite, caustic noise; noise as a physical entity, felt rather than heard.

Brutal.

The crowds ebbed and flowed over the whole fortnight we were there, isochronal waves of Italian ravers every evening, high tides of international subculture flotsam and jetsam washing up at the weekends.

In summer we lived outdoors, but we needed some

protection from the elements at the year's turning point, and in Bologna we had parked up inside, our wall of speakers forming a porous border between our trucks and the dancefloor. Jacek's vehicle was in a state of near-constant siege until he ran out of drugs to sell, I recalled.

More flashbacks followed…

Sleeping a lot, and feeling the bass through my recumbent body, every thundering bassline and every banging kick-drum mainlined directly into my consciousness. Not the classic LSD synaesthesia of seeing music, but the soul-shaking enormity of sensing noise as vibration, sound waves captured in their purest form, bypassing the clumsy filter of my ears.

It was cold. Bitterly, bitingly cold.

Crowds of shambling, dribbling, empty-eyed ketamine drones and fiercely gurning speedfreak automatons.

Packs of scavenging dogs loping through hallways, snapping and snarling at each other.

Crepuscular, monochrome Morrigan figures, cowled in blankets, faces hidden in hoods, stalking the unlit stairwells.

The preternatural paleness of Allan Exit's skin, a sign that he had begun shooting up heroin.

Clara in a foul mood.

Sam Saoule and Udo leathering fourteen excremental shades out of a French raver caught attempting to half-inch one of our crates of beer.

Iffy asleep behind our speakers with his face in a pool of someone else's vomit.

Minnie crying, with her soft, white cheeks disfigured by human scratch marks.

Jacek thinking he was going to die after swigging from a plastic bottle that contained not water but liquid ketamine.

Iffy avoiding an extremely pissed-off Jacek for a few days.

The party as a battlefield. A refugee camp. An asylum.

The eerie silence when the last rig finally turned off. The feeling that something bigger had played itself out.

Maybe the Millennium Massacre wasn't quite as bad as I later came to believe, for memory is a perfidious companion, one that needs regular nurturing with tender words. The parties I recalled best were the parties I talked about the most, and as far as the New Year's party at Bologna went, the less that was said the better.

LOGIC WAS HIS PLAYTHING, REASON HIS NURSE-MAID

Back in my Berlin flat, Iffy and I cracked open a couple of Tannenzäpflers and said, "*Prost!*" to each other. I was on a partial health trip, yes, but not tee-totally.

"It's pretty obvious really." Iffy stated boldly.

"It is?"

"Course. Udo'd sussed it. He was always a smart cookie underneath that bull-in-a-china-shop public persona. He clocked us all dying. Just like I did. First Minnie, then Sam, then Jacek. Too many deaths too close to home to be a coincidence. But Udo must have realised something that I've been missing. I can picture him down there in his Sicilian farmhouse, mulling it all over, a bottle of gut-rot grappa clutched in his giant fist, a candle guttering in the night breeze, the moon rising over the vineyards and olive trees. Then - a flash of inspiration! Fabrizia's in bed, the house is silent except for the ticking of her grandfather's clock. So he tiptoes -"

"Udo tiptoeing? Like a walrus doing an arabesque."

"Okay, so he blunders into the dimly lit living room and breaks open his old box of mementos. Dust in the air. An owl hoots. Like a bear with a beehive, he feverishly sticks his paw into the box. Pulls out dozens of ancient flyers, hurls them onto the floor, scattering them like leaves in a storm. He finds several packets of photos from the old days. Shoves them aside. Finally he comes across his stash of cassettes. Picks one up, glances at the label. Discards it. Chooses another. Tosses it away. Third time lucky - as soon as he sees the label, he gives a muffled cry of triumph. This is it! And yes, there in the moonlight lies the tape from the Millennium Massacre party in

Bologna. With trembling hands, he holds it up. Grabs a candle. Wax drips on his wrist, but he barely notices because suddenly it all makes sense. There it is: the evidence. The tape is the clue he's been searching for."

"Evidence of what? The Curse of the Sound System? There is no curse, Iffy. Get a grip. Yes, our mates are dying. Because of folly, misadventure, bad luck, bad judgement, booze and drugs. That's why they're dying."

"You don't believe that."

"Yes, I do."

"No, you don't."

"Yes, I do. Iffy, mate, I hate it when you try to tell me what I think."

"No, you don't," he smiled, draining his beer.

"So what clue did he find?"

"Ah, well, you see, Udo was a clever man. A thinker. Logic was his plaything, reason his nurse-maid. Me, I've done too many Persian rugs."

There was nothing to say to that, so I decapitated another couple of red-capped Bavarians. And then there was nothing else to do but listen to the tape from the Millennium Massacre.

I hit the power switch on my tape deck, pressed the eject button, and slotted Udo's tape in. Clunk, went the door. I gave the play button an encouraging tap and a familiar hissing noise issued from my speakers. Then came a gentle thumping noise, like an iron-clad horse approaching at speed. Green and red lights began a rhythmic dance on the display of my equaliser. Then came the techno.

"Well, that's my other theory scuppered," Iffy said.

I asked him which one.

"The one where Udo had taped over the original recording and replaced it with a spoken message to us."

"The old voice-from-beyond-the-grave trick?"

"You know, I don't think I've heard this before," was the way he avoided answering my question.

"Me neither," I mused. "Didn't even know it existed, come to think of it."

It didn't sound radically different to any of the other techno livesets I had sat or danced through. It was your bog-standard violently booming, repetitively beeping, nastily squelching, hastily thumping, loopily bumping, twisted, creaking, molten, squeaking, stomping, banging, pounding, throbbing, in-yer-face, up-all-night, on-top-non-stop free party techno, as far as I could tell, the sort that sounded much better ten years ago through the medium of drugs, but which still raised a hackle or two of nostalgic desire to dance and a few goosebumps of pining for a fat rig in a field under a starry sky.

"Sounds like Sam," Iffy said after a while.

A while later: "Or it could be the Gaffer."

More time elapsed as the tape spooled through the deck. "Or the Gaffer *and* Sam."

And then: "Now *that* sounded like Jacek. Got to be Jacek, that."

And later still: "Oh, now that bit could've been Udo. He should've done more music, Udo. I always said that."

And,"And oh, that *has* to be Minnie, that."

And, "Allan. Definitely Allan. Probably."

The fact was that we had all dabbled in making music. Together we managed to scavenge, build, buy, borrow and blag quite a bit of the hardware needed to make techno music, and most of us turned our hand it to it at one time or another. I had reluctantly realised and modestly admitted that my talents did not lie in that direction, Iffy's efforts were not generally appreciated, it had to be (and frequently was) said, and Clara only ever had a go when nobody else was listening, but our rig had been a proper musical collective.

QUOD ERAT DEMONFUCKINGSTRANDUM

"Iffy, you've got to get it into your head," I ventured, my throat nicely lubricated, my head spinning with the sound of silence as the tape finally clicked off. "The Curse, I mean. It's complete bollocks."

"Okay. Okay. Obviously, there isn't really a curse."

"Good. That's settled, then."

"No, the truth of the matter is that there's a serial killer out there, and he's bumping us off one by one."

"Right…"

"And what's more, you think so too."

There he went again, telling me what I believed. It's just that this time, if I acknowledged the thoughts that I had been diligently suppressing, he wasn't so far from the truth. The timing and circumstances of our friends' deaths *were* odd. Curses didn't exist…but murderers did.

"Let's look at the facts, Watson," he told me. "Death number one: Minnie Mouth. Chirpy, on-it Minnie. Organised Minnie. Made-breakfast-for-everybody Minnie. Knew-how-to-bloody-swim Minnie. She drowned. Having a midnight dip all on her Jack Jones. Does that sound right?"

"No, it doesn't sound right. Remember, though, the coroner said it was suicide."

"Not Minnie, no way. She wouldn't fuck up like that."

"She might have done. You don't know. I heard she'd been really down."

"But there were no witnesses. Death number two. Sam Saoule. Heart attack from too much GHB. Now you knew Sammy as well I did. He was nobody's mug. A fierce wee fucker. Hard as a bag of hammers. Canny as a bag of foxes. He knew his drugs and his doses. No way he would have fucked up like that. *Ergo* someone gave him too much."

"Or he was so twatted he didn't know up from down or uppers from downers." I wasn't going to let Iffy have it all his own way.

"Very unlikely. Tell me it's possible that somebody set him up with the overdose."

"Okay. I'll grant you it's possible, Miss Marple."

"Death number three: Jacek. Suicide. Slashed his wrists. That's a load of Jasper Pollocks."

"I dunno. He was no stranger to the sump of despond, either, old Jacek."

"But he had a gun. Remember? Bought it off those Corsicans in Marseilles. He wouldn't have gone for the big bleed - he couldn't stand the sight of blood. Remember when Willy almost cut Allan Exit's finger off? Jacek went as white as a Ku Klux Klan washing line. One shot with his gun would have done it, quick and clean."

"There were rumours about the Bulgarian mafia."

"Nadgers. Jacek never worked with any Bulgarians. Death number four," he continued, barely pausing except to puff on his spliff and pour more lager down his neck, "Udo. Udo who had stumbled across something on this tape, something that made him hot-foot it over to see you here in Berlin. Only they got to him first. Pushed him under an U-Bahn before he could spill his story. What d'you reckon?"

"I dunno, Iffy. There's a few straws being grasped in all that lot, if only you'd give me time to think about it all."

"But you have been thinking about it," he informed me. "Death number five: you. Or me or Clara or Allan Exit or the Gaffer."

"Slow down, compadre. Let's not be getting ahead of

ourselves."

"Mate," he said, stubbing out his joint and tucking straight into the blim of crumbly Moroccan hash, "it doesn't take a genius to spot the connection between Sam Saoule, Minnie, Jacek and Udo."

"They were all born in a month with the letter 'R' in it?"

"Shit, were they? I didn't know that. But why would…No, you can't distract me that easily, Moriarty. We were all in the rig together. Four of us are dead. Five of us are left. One of us is next. *Quod erat demonfuckingstrandum.*"

I was sure there were more holes in his theory than in his socks, and that was saying something, but I needed more time to mull it all over.

"But nobody knew Udo was in town. How could someone have killed him?"

"That, my man, is what we need to find out."

"And how do you slash someone's wrists without them making a scene?"

"Yeah, we need to find that out, too."

"And most importantly, who's doing the killing? And why?"

"The answer is on this tape. I'm sure of it. We need to think about it properly. As soon as we get back from the Hole."

"As soon as..?"

And that's how easy it was for Iffy to enmesh me in his net of paranoia and to drag me down off the wagon and out into a night of booze, drugs and debauchery.

HIS COMBAT TECHNIQUE WAS UNORTHODOX

"Coffee's up!"
"I don't drink coffee. Never have done."
"But I do. Made you some tea."
"Which one?"

The Germans loved their tea. In most of the Berlin kitchens I frequented at least one shelf was dedicated to *camellia sinensis* and all its derivatives, off-shoots, by-products and substitutes. White, yellow, green, oolong, black and post-fermented teas jostled for space with tisanes, herbal teas, roibush and chai. When I had first visited the German capital I had quickly grown ashamed of my claim that a pyramid-shaped bag stuffed with the scrapings off a factory floor was the last word in tea technology, and to some degree I had gone native.

"Brought you some proper English tea-bags from home, mate," Iffy called from the kitchen. "Don't say I never do anything for you."

He had, as a matter of easily proven fact, done rather a lot for me the previous night. He had made me drink more than I had drunk in the previous month, snort more than I had snorted in the preceding six months and feel rougher than I had ever, ever, ever felt. But hangovers always took me like that now. Each and every one was a new nadir.

"What time is it?"
"Time to look lively, princess. Time to get up and greet the day with a song and a smile and a big thank you to your old pal Iffy for showing you a good time. Midday."
"You cunt."
"I'll pretend I didn't hear that."

"Iffy, you're a cunt. You've been here one day - not even - and you've aided and abetted the twisting of my precious melon into a righteous J-shape. A quick beer in the Hole, you said. A little line of billy to pick us up after the booze, you said. A wrap of charlie to take the edge off the billy, you said. A dab of MDMA to level out the charlie, you said. More booze to keep us straight after all the chemicals, you said. Then I don't know what you said."

Many years ago Iffy had announced that he had signed up for the war on drugs. Unconvinced by the tactics of the pusillanimous backroom generals, he himself was prepared to stand on the front line, he told me, and to go over the top. Well over the top. His combat technique was unorthodox, and his was a one-man crusade: its ultimate goal, to rid the world of drugs. His methods: ingestion, inhalation, insufflation, absorption, and intramuscular and intravenous injection. His results: never mind how hard he tried, he had as yet failed to complete his mission. It seemed that the world could produce drugs quicker than he could consume them.

"Fuck, how much money did I spend?"

"Not a shekel, my man. You knew the barman, remember? Some kind soul with an open heart gave us the speed and the MDMA. Oh, you might have got the chang on tick, now I think about it. And the K."

"What K?"

"Ah. Yeah. That was when you started puking."

"I'm too old for this." I lifted the weight of the world off my pillow and regretted it because it spun like a government spokesman after a particularly crass gaffe by his master. "What time is it? When did we hit the hay?"

"Well, it's about thirty seconds since you last asked me the time, so I'd hazard a guess at just gone midday," Iffy said, waltzing into my room with a cup of steaming tea. "You got your head down about an hour ago. I haven't been to bed yet."

"You're too old for this."

"Don't start."

And there it was again, just like when I'd joked about him giving up smoking, an alien hardness in his voice that left me searching in vain for any note of humour.

He plonked himself down on my bed and handed me my tea. To give him his dues, he didn't look much the worse for wear. Our night out had left few traces on his face, but that was possibly because he permanently bore the saggy eyes and blotchy epidermis of a man for whom sleep was a distant memory. A river doesn't look any wetter if you spit in it.

"And right now it's line o'clock. A wee one to clear the cobwebs?" he crooned, pouring an as yet unidentified powder out onto a CD cover. "Turn up for the books about old Udo, though, wasn't it?"

I was struggling to keep up. Shit, I was struggling just to pump blood through my body.

"What about Udo? Line of what? And wait a minute - why does my mouth taste like an ashtray?"

"Coke. From that gram you got on the never-never. And don't go blaming me for everything, your Holiness. I told you you'd regret the fags."

"Oh no."

The booze and the drugs, I could live with. If I was going to be living with Iffy, I'd have to. But the fags…I didn't recall smoking any, but that just meant that I'd suffered a black-out.

Some people I knew stoically accepted short periods of memory loss as the price to pay for having a good time. Personally, after recently experiencing a couple of black-outs in the space of a week, I had realised that I was no longer as capable of enduring prolonged and intense alcoholic punishment as I used to be, and I had toned down my drinking as a result. I didn't like not knowing what I had said and done, a character trait that marked me out as different from the Iffys of the world, for whom a good time was still a good time even if they had no recollection of it later. Occasionally I envied this ability to let go, to abdicate from all positions of responsibility, to surrender to the blender.

But not very often.

"Shit, Iffy, I think I had a black-out last night. Last thing I remember was blagging the MDMA. I didn't do anything stupid, did I? Apart from smoking so much that certain highly placed Philip Morris executives are probably breaking open the bubbly at this very moment."

"Well," he said, sliding the CD case in my direction, "I'm not sure we should go back to the Hole for a couple of days. We might be a bit, er, banned."

Banned from *the Hole*? That took some doing. Absent-mindedly I snorted the line of cocaine that Iffy had prepared. Just like old times, I thought ruefully.

"Anyway, with the news we picked up last night, I think an avenue of investigation has opened up."

"That's great, Iffy. Marvellous. Unfortunately, I feel like shit. And as for this tea you gave me - well, just be thankful that there aren't any Germans here to witness it. Now, I'm going to make myself a decent cuppa. Then you can tell me all about it."

I kept my feet long enough to slump over the kitchen sink, dry heave a little, and pour Iffy's well-meant offering of tea down the plug-hole where it belonged. By the time I'd finished pottering around I felt, if not exactly human, at least like *homo neanderthalensis*, or possibly even *homo rhodesiensis*. Mastering simple stone tools seemed like a reasonable project for the rest of the day.

Iffy was fast asleep on my bed when I looked in on him. A gluey Polo of ketamine encircled one of his nostrils. A tendril of mucus dribbled inexorably towards my pillow. It seemed that while he had given me an energising line of cocaine, he himself had clearly opted for a relaxing hit of ketamine, and it crossed my mind that he was a sneaky little bugger who had wanted my bed for himself.

"Tea's up," I said. Pointlessly.

The concept of pursuing any kind of investigation with Iffy left me completely underwhelmed, but I wanted to find out what had really happened to my dear, dead friends.

And he was, despite it all, my pal.

We passed the latter stages of the afternoon in bouts of snoozing, boozing and musing, ignoring the pulchritudinous sunshine that was heating the streets and softening the dogshit on the pavement outside my windows. We talked a lot of crap - always had done, always would do - but, like coffee through a filter, one interesting new development permeated our cerebral vagueness.

Apparently, during our night of chemical intemperance in the Hole we had had to put up with wee Willy's company, and it was he who had revealed that Udo had met his end on the line S-6 at Kottbusser Tor, a station in Kreuzberg.

Now, Udo might have had difficulties traversing a crowded room without destroying any furniture, but he knew Berlin better than any tour guide, and Kotti was anything but on the way from Helga's *Wagenburg* to my flat. Iffy seemed noticeably keen for us to make a visit to the scene of the accident. Suspecting ulterior motives, I persuaded him that we should save it for the morrow.

The K and the coke ran out some time before darkness fell on our heads, and the bottle of tequila was duly opened and emptied. Iffy suggested tossing a coin to see who got the bed for the night. I suggested that he could fuck right off.

All day I had been feeling at best half-awake, and now, in

my bed, as I was half-asleep, a ragged parade of phantoms came to cavort across the backs of my eyelids, the hypnopompic ghosts of the memories that I had misplaced in the Hole.

I saw Iffy's ugly mug, sweat-streaked, spectral and intensely frowning, thrust right into my personal space. His pupils were black and enormous. A heated exchange. A grubby-nailed finger poking painfully into my chest. Iffy - out of his nut, belligerent, giving it the large. Me - my vision blurred and strobing, telling him to give it a rest. "Never," he was insisting. "You can't just bail out on the lifestyle. Minnie, renting a flat in Shitsville...Udo, owning land in Sicily...Jacek, making dollars...even Sam, working for The Man. Even you, with your easy life and your comfortable routine. Buying into the system, the fucking lot of you, doing your bit to help keep the world the way it is. What happened to you all? Were you just a bunch of kids playing at rebellion? What happened to the rage inside? When push came to shove, you all fell over. Get up! Stand up! For fuck's sake."

Iffy - angry and righteous.

Me - dashing to the bogs and spattering the ceramic in a spray of bitter, acidic vomit.

And only when the phantoms finally fled did sweet, deep sleep deign to join me in my bed.

A POSITIVE SPRING IN HIS SLOUCH

The day before Udo's funeral we confirmed that he hadn't come to Berlin just to see me, and we found out that he had probably been murdered. And despite that fact that Iffy kept harping on about me being the next victim, I found out that my closest friend was further down the road to self destruction than I had feared.

We walked to Kreuzberg, crossing the River Spree at Oberbaumbrucke, the ornate red brick bridge where Westerners used to make the trip over the border to see their relatives and marvel at the empty shops and the funny smell in the German Democratic Republic. It was Berlin's very own Bridge of Tears, where weeping Cold War families had traded sighs and stories from either side of their own Wailing Wall.

We pressed on. One of Berlin's summer storms was brewing, though the sky was still azure where we could see it over the tops of the high-rise apartment block that carved out the curvy part of a question mark and squatted over the road near where the underground and overground trains crossed.

Iffy had a positive spring in his slouch as we approached Kottbusser Tor, and I knew why.

I attempted to take him with me as I went to find some station employees to quiz about Udo's death, but he brushed me off and said he'd meet me in fifteen minutes by the metal punk. I watched him sidle up to one of the shady-looking, pale-faced figures who loitered around the roundabout, and I shook my head in knowing resignation.

I hurried and scurried around the station, nipping at the heels of anyone official-looking and seeking to pry out some information about the death on the tracks. Nothing doing. Lips were tightly sealed. Politely but firmly, all my inquiries were knocked back. Repeatedly it was suggested that I talk to the police, but I figured the authorities would have little they wanted to share with me.

A quarter of an hour later I was waiting for Iffy by the bronze statue of a punk rocker that was one of the landmarks of Kreuzberg. Now sometimes referred to as Little Istanbul due to the large proportion of Turkish immigrants who had settled in the *Kiez*, Kreuzberg had also long been a centre for alternative lifestyles. Throughout the long winter of the Cold War, when the Iron Curtain was drawn across the map of Europe and the threat of nuclear cataclysm hung over it, West Berlin had been an island, isolated in the heart of the GDR with just the airport at Tempelhof and one road reaching out to the rest of the Federal Republic. Because of its sensitive situation there was no compulsory military service for the young men who lived in the ex-capital city. This meant that any German youth who sought to avoid conscription - the pacifists, anarchists, rebels, renegades and revolutionaries - had plotted up a stone's throw away from the Berlin Wall, principally in Kreuzberg and Prenzlauerberg. Their legacy remained and the city had even erected a statue of a punk rocker slumped in eternal ennui against a strange concrete bubble.

The bronze figure was the embodiment of the openness to underground culture that made me love Berlin, a nod to just one chapter of a crazy history that took in everything from militarism to militant homosexuality, from bohemian decadence to state communism, and that vacillated wildly between freedom and fascism. Since the turn of the last century, there had never been a dull decade in the city. It had suffered enormously, but it had always hung on in there. I loved the place, despite its shrinking population and its growing unemployment. I called it home, that fatigued leviathan beached on Prussian sands, that downbeat jungle, that concrete Babel surrounded by lakes and forests, pock-marked with bomb-sites and riddled with sixty-five-year old bullet-holes.

Iffy was late, a fact I would normally have written off along the lines of sylvan ursine excreta and Papal Catholicism, but a churn of concern chewed at my guts as I mimicked the statue's time-defying pose and sat searching the passers-by - Turkish families, ageing hippies, veiled women, teenagers in shell-suits, tourists in shorts and polo shirts - for his familiar face.

I was worried because Kottbusser Tor - Kotti to the locals - was primarily famous for one reason: its junkies.

Somewhere nestled in the nether regions of society's many sub-strata lurked the denizens of international junkiedom, a borderless nation that would open its doors to anyone but was famously reluctant to let them leave. A hidden Free Masonry of the lost-boys; dabblers or out-and-out smackheads, they recognised each other by signs that many of us would miss. In connection to heroin's anti-heroes, I only ever employed the word 'trust' when sandwiched by the words 'never' and 'a junkie', so I hadn't planned on asking any of the waifs and strays around Kotti about Udo's death. To them I was an outsider.

Iffy, on the other hand, could blend in all too well with the confraternity of the doomed.

DOING THE PIN-SPOT BOOGIE UNDER AFGHAN SKIES

"Did you get what you were after?" he asked me when he eventually turned up.

"Nope. Did you?"

"Don't fucking start."

He didn't seem especially hyper or noticeably sluggish. His pupils weren't pinned or dilated. If he had scored some drugs, I reasoned that he hadn't taken them yet.

"Got some news," he said. "Shit, have I got some news. Come on. Let's go for a drink."

We wound up in a bar we had never been in before. Trendier than our usual watering holes, it was light and airy, with shiny, leather-upholstered benches, black and white pictures of skyscrapers on the walls and a clean-looking couple - clearly tourists - sipping mojitos and cooing over their day's haul of photos on a digital camera. They eyed us warily.

Iffy recounted that after he had gained the confidence of one of the skinny dealers who touted for business at Kotti, he asked what the gossip was about the fatal accident that had happened a couple of days earlier. The dealer sent him to talk to another dealer and after Iffy had got that one on side, the story came out.

"He was pushed."

I stared. I hadn't seriously entertained that belief before. Not really. Not quite. Sure, I had lots of unanswered questions about all the deaths, and I could see that each of them was open to interpretation. Iffy had forced me to admit as much. I even partly bought his theory that Udo had spotted something weird about the tape from the Millennium Massacre. But Udo had come to see me, I presumed. Nobody else knew he was in town.

Yet he had been at Kotti and someone had pushed him in front of a train.

Of course, the junkies had said nothing to the investigating police. They had nothing to gain and much to lose by talking to the detectives, but they had no fear in telling Iffy what had gone down. The second dealer he chatted to had seen it happen.

"He was headed off to pick up some more supplies," Iffy said, gulping down the *Weissbier* I had paid for. "If I understood correctly. His English was better than my German, but only just." Iffy had once claimed, I remembered, that only three words of German were necessary to get by in Berlin: *Quatsch*, *Scheisse* and *geil*, which translated as bullshit, shit and wicked.

He went on: "So he clocked Udo - you know how those dealers are always on the look-out for customers or pigs. He saw the big fella talking to someone dressed all in black. He said they had the air of people doing a deal. Then next thing he knows, there's a shove and a shout and a squeal of metal and Udo's just not there any more. And the other geezer's shifting sharpish. The platform's pretty packed and he just melts away. Just ghosts out of the station as everyone's milling around. My man there saw it all. He thought it was some kind of dealers' tiff, but he's sure Udo didn't fall of his own account."

"Fucking hell, Iffy. That's hardcore."

"That it is, sweetheart. That it is."

"It means we've got to check out the other deaths. Sam Saoule, Minnie and Jacek," I intoned.

"And it means we'd better really start watching our backs."

"And we've got to tell the others. Allan Exit, the Gaffer… and Clara."

I barely registered my companion getting up and pushing

through the gleaming steel door that led to the toilets. My world was spinning, its axis tilting.

"It's a good thing I'm here to look after you," Iffy chuntered as he came back, narrowly avoiding a collision with the distressed-looking tourists.

He was clearly mullered. Taking him to Kotti was like holding an AA meeting in a brewery. I knew how he had gained the confidence of the two dealers he had talked to. I knew why he had been late for our *rendezvous* by the metal punk, and why he had been carrying a bag from a chemist's. I knew why he had gone to the toilets in the bar. I knew why he was wearing a long-sleeve shirt on a warm day. I hoped he had disposed of the needle responsibly.

"You fucking muppet."

"What?"

"You stupid little junkie."

"Whoa. Easy, tiger. Wind your neck in. You think those dealers at Kotti would have talked to me if I hadn't thrown a bit of business their way? You should be thanking me."

"Don't give it, Iffy-boy. This is serious. Someone's killing us…and you're gonna kill yourself."

He tried to focus his tiny pupils on me. The girl in her bright summer dress was tutting as she put her camera safely out of sight.

I was pissed off. I had half-expected him to score something at Kotti, had hoped it would just be some jellies, some bargain-basement downers, had thought that even if he bought some gear he would smoke it. I hadn't expected him to bang up in the bogs.

"How much did you score, Iffy?"

"More *quantum sufficit* than *quantum libet*."

"What?"

"Just enough, but not as much as I'd like."

"How much?"

"Just a couple of hits. Chill."

"Where did you get the spondoolics?"

"Borrowed 'em off your kitchen table. Fuck's sakes, it's just a bit of brown. I was feeling a bit tense, what with the fact someone's trying to do us all. And all."

"So it'd be a good idea to have our wits about us. Go and flush it down the jakes."

"No."

"Then you aren't sleeping at my gaff till you give your head a wobble."

"You're so up-tight. But suit yourself, Mother Teresa. You usually do."

We locked eyes. At least we would have done, if his hadn't been doing the pin-spot boogie under Afghan skies.

"I'm serious. I don't want you doing that shit."

"Oh gee, mom, are you worried I won't make my grades at college? Fuck off, will you?"

I considered the merits of his proposal. It was deficient in diplomacy but succinct and unambiguous. I weighed up the pros and cons. Eventually I decided it would be in the best interests of all concerned parties if I took him up on the suggestion.

Off I fucked.

I walked out of the bar and left my pal Iffy to enjoy the feeling of heroin coursing through his veins, sure that he was thinking of little else, hoping that he would come to his senses later.

The storm was nearly overhead.

BETWEEN THE BOLT AND THE BOOM

Berlin does summer storms like the Seychelles do sunshine, Siberia does snow and Dolgellau does drizzle. It does them well.

The wind came first, lugging clouds like a tug-boat heaving great black supertankers into port. Pedestrians started dashing for shelter, their tee-shirts flapping, their feet flip-flopping on the pavements, their gaze flickering upwards at the approaching doom. With the wind came the dust: a fortnight of sun had dessicated the parks and the air was filling rapidly with tiny free-floating particles.

As I quickened my step I found myself entering an innercity sandstorm, a blizzard of grit that stung my eyes and coated my skin. The air reeked of pent-up rain, desperate to hurl itself down on us. The temperature plummeted several degrees in a couple of minutes.

And then the rain came, as if some celestial market trader had slashed a hole in the awning that protected our heads; either that or someone had just emptied the contents of their bath on my head. I was instantly drenched, wet to the core. Puddles appeared as though an enchanter had conjured them into existence. Heavily loaded raindrops ricocheted off every surface. The noise filled my ears as the water filled the gutters, and still the wind blew, driving the rain horizontally before it. The dust on my face turned to mud and then was washed away.

I was alone on the streets of Berlin.

A flowerpot crashed down off a balcony. It missed me by a foot or two, one terracotta shard bouncing painfully off my shin. Iffy would probably have suspected it was an attempt on my life, but I would have to do without the benefit of his wisdom for the moment.

I rarely argued with anyone about their lifestyle choices, but this was not the first time that the Iffy-boy and I had ended up swapping insults. Usually I left people to make their own decisions, for better or for worse, figuring that they must have thought things through (even when deep down I knew this wasn't true), or presuming that they were so bloody-minded and loathe to heed advice that they wouldn't listen. Iffy was remarkably bloody-minded, of course, and he was extremely loathe to heed advice, but I loved the little fucker and I didn't fancy going to his funeral. At his age and with his circle of friends, he knew all about the dangers of smack. I supposed he just feared being straight more than he feared addiction.

Thunder tore the sky to shreds. Thor hammered out his destructive rhythms above the city roofs and made me crave words like 'rend' and 'smite', vocabulary that rightfully belonged in the mouths of Dungeons And Dragons player. I felt a split-second of pure animal fear before I remembered that this was the twenty-first century and I didn't have to worry about disgruntled deities. But for just a moment - the time between the bolt and the boom - I had electricity in my veins, and I knew that Iffy could feel the same rush any time he wanted.

All he had to do was stick the needle in.

AN ASCENT INTO CHAOS

With the raindrops pounding on my head and leeching up through my trainers, with four of my friends recently dead, with Iffy helping himself to my money and injecting smack into his system, with the discovery that Udo had been pushed under a train, with his funeral happening the next day, with the growing suspicion that someone really was killing off the founder members of our old sound system…with all that going on, it was surprising that I still found time to worry my pretty little head over the fact that Clara was arriving in town that evening.

She was not going to sleep in my flat. She had been clear about that. She was going to kip somewhere else. She had been unclear about where. In the email she sent me, she proposed hooking up for a beer and a civilised chat and I agreed. I suggested the Hole. She reminded me that when she had employed the term civilised, civilised was precisely what she meant, so that ruled the Hole out, which was just as well as apparently I was *persona non grata* there after my little night out with Iffy. At eight o'clock I was due to meet her in the Fischladen, the ex-squat right next door to the Hole on Rigaer Strasse.

I dashed a me-shape through the lashing rain and the screaming wind, my figure intermittently illuminated by streaks of lightning. Deftly I dodged heat-seeking detritus, neatly I hopped over fallen bicycles and only occasionally I plunged ankle-deep into uncharted tarns of rainwater. At home, I shed my sodden clothes and towelled myself brusquely dry. Then I reeled off seventy press-ups and whipped up a quick pasta slop, emptying my cupboards of all the veggies which weren't preparing to leave under their own impetus.

I had time to kill before my *rendezvous* with my ex, but while I had the opportunity and the motive, I was not sure what the means would be. I dedicated a minute or two to the execution of chin-ups off my bed frame, which was a suitably solid structure, having been built *in situ* out of stolen scaffolding by the previous tenant. A few more seconds were duly dispatched as I ran my gaze over my contacts' personal headlines for the day on Facebook. Several dozen late-comers had posted their farewells on Udo's page. Allan Exit had even popped up from his off-the-grid lair in Wales, posting 'They broke the mould with you, brother.'

Only the Gaffer from our old crew hadn't left a message on Udo's wall.

I clicked on his page, abruptly wondering if he even knew about Udo's sudden demise. His 'public figure' site had over two hundred thousand people who liked it, although his personal account was limited to five thousand. With all those 'friends,' maybe he hadn't noticed that one of them was gone. I typed him a private message breaking the news, though I couldn't be sure when he would read it. He had not graced any of the other funerals with his presence; indeed, I couldn't remember the last time I had spoken to him.

Long ago, the Gaffer had sold out. Unfortunately the devil who had acquired his services was not the same down-and-dirty bad-ass who did a deal at the crossroads with Robert Johnson. The legendary bluesman allegedly learned to sing and play the guitar as his part of the bargain; for his troubles, the Gaffer got in the charts. The Gaffer was bought by Mammon, a thoroughly modern devil, a devil with a sharp pair of shoes and a limousine, a devil without horns, a faceless chancer, a shameless fleecer, a money-grubber, a bean-counter, a bloodsucking, mother-fucking music mogul who turned the Gaffer from free party lover to corporate whore, and more, who made his life into a mockery of all that I thought he had held dear.

The Gaffer had always inspired strong feelings.

The length and the shortness of the matter was that after our rig crumbled into dust and scattered on the wind, the Gaffer went on to become a popular DJ/producer. He had been popular on our scene first, back when popular meant a few hundred people dancing in a field. Now he was in a different league, or rather he was playing a different game.

His music could be heard on the radio. If you worked in a factory or shop that pumped out Radio One, it could be heard on the playlist twice an hour, every hour. His clips could be watched on TV. His face, still handsome but piggier than it used to be, could be seen on magazine covers and in tabloid gossip columns, and his eyes had jettisoned their friendly smile in favour of a curious, knowing smirk.

The Gaffer was famous, a household name, a force to be reckoned with in the music world. He hobnobbed with the mighty, dined with the great and the good, drank champagne with the movers and shakers, played and partied in glamorous clubs where paparazzi shadowed the doors.

He had gone a long way, the Gaffer low-budget days of our merry travelling circus. Iffy and I had always suspected that the Gaffer had enjoyed being a big fish in a little pond. That he went on to become a shark in the ocean should not have surprised us.

And his biggest crime, as far as we were concerned? Ripping off one of Jacek's finest, fiercest hardtek bangers, skinning it, gutting it, marinating it in cheesy synths, half-baking it in wailing vocal samples, and serving it up as the soundtrack to a TV advert for a soft drink that was as saccharine, artificial and rotten as the reworked song itself.

Personally, I wasn't a fan of his music. Or his lifestyle. Or the message he put across. Or the way he helped indoctrinate pre-pubescent kids into a superficial existence revolving around image and greed, pushing a pre-packaged form of ideological oppression that promoted a culture-ideology of comforting illusion, a hegemonic construct designed primarily to keep the masses from questioning what was really going on in the world, while perpetuating the pernicious cult of celebrity.

But that was just my opinion and I tried not to let it wind me up.

He was doing his thing, ploughing his own furrow, I reminded myself, and frankly it was none of my beeswax. I presumed it made him happy. It certainly made him rich. It could be argued that he made a lot of other people happy, too, and maybe it was just my cynicism that saw their contentment as that of battery chickens at feeding time.

Maybe he had always been searching for fame. The only son of two doyens of the Soho art scene, he had been the star that shone brightest at St. Martin's Art College until he started orbiting the underground parties and subversive ideas of the free techno scene. His eloquence and energy had been what brought our little crew together in the first place. His drive and determination had helped keep us going when times were hard and spirits were flagging.

We called him the Gaffer partly as a piss-take about his habit of trying to organise the rest of us, for whom an ascent into chaos was the best that could be hoped for, and partly because he always had a roll of gaffer tape to hand, just in case. He was the only one of us who tried to patch our collective back together when it came unstuck, but not even his famous gaffer tape was up to the task.

The causes for the dissolution of our rig were obscure and multifarious. Hindsight failed to render the reasons clearer. Maybe the adventure had simply had its allotted time, or maybe we were all just too tired to keep it up. Some of us were disillusioned with the way things had turned out and some of us had other dreams and projects that were born of our years on the road. We were probably restless with each others' company, bored of doing the same thing, party after party, after-party after after-party.

Allan Exit flogging off most of the music equipment hadn't helped, of course, but hindsight made me wonder if his treachery had in fact done us all a favour, finally driving a stake through the heart of a walking corpse.

I was on the verge of closing the Gaffer's page when my glance chanced on his status update. 'Underground Star. Part Four. The Gaffer Is Coming! 25 May, Am Keller, Berlin'.

Well, well, I said to myself. Fancy that. The Gaffer was in town. He was about to DJ at an event…and he had also played two nights ago, I read.

Fabrizia had told me that Udo had come to town to see someone from our sound system and I had taken that to mean me. Now it occurred to me that Udo might have been on his way to meet the Gaffer when he met his downfall.

I checked the location of the club; I had vaguely heard of it, but despite its purportedly underground origins it was no longer the type of place I frequented. It was a West End affair, up-town in Charlottenburg, far from the mad crowd in Fried'lhain.

Mentally gearing myself up to encounter Clara, I knocked out sixty therapeutic sit-ups before leaving my flat, pausing only to remind the washing-up that I'd be coming for it later.

Oh, and to hope that Iffy's smack binge wouldn't lead him into too much trouble.

NOT WAVING, BUT DOWNING HER DRINK

Clara, Clara, Clara.

She had first tickled my metaphorical fancy when I had clocked her in the Healing Field at the Big Green Gathering festival in the mid-nineties. She was squatting in amongst a row of earnest practitioners of alternative medicines, clutching a hand-drawn sign that offered Ego Massage. She became my friend, then my housemate, then my best friend, then my lover, then my friend when we thought we were lovers, then my lover when we weren't really friends, then not my lover, and then not really my friend either. Then possibly my friend once more. And certainly never my lover again. Or something like that. It was a little complicated.

And now? The good memories formed a protective shield around the bad, and although I knew the rough patches were within synaptic reaching-distance should I choose to seek them out, I was content to let them wither. I wished good things for her and I was fairly confident she did likewise for me, but in contemporary talk-show parlance we had both 'moved on'.

Still smarting from Iffy's apparent readiness to stand at the junction of the road to hell, grinning gormlessly and eagerly waving his thumb at travellers going faster than him, still caught by surprise and bowled over by Udo's murder (murder!), I popped my head through the heavy curtain at the door of the Fischladen and realised it was Monday.

Monday had a particular smell to it since I'd moved to F-hain - a bracing cocktail of garlic, ginger, lime, coriander, cumin, turmeric, chilli, cardamom and cinnamon. The staple flavours of Bangladeshi cuisine, admittedly watered down somewhat to cater for the native blandness of the German palate, were the weapons with which Omar's imagination ran riot. A top chef when sober, a whingeing git when half cut and a dangerous hoodlum when totally tanked up, Omar generally managed to keep his head together until the last lentil had been scraped out of the pot and the final paratha bathed in oil, when he would crack open a bottle of whisky and turn into bad company.

But by that time the Fischladen was always packed to the gills with happy eaters. You didn't get a lot for five euros these days, not even in Berlin.

Volxküche, or *Voku* - People's Kitchen - was what German political activists did when they were hungry. A bar, squat, autonomous centre or info-point would open its kitchen up to someone who needed a bit of cash and claimed they knew their way around the spice rack. The emphasis was generally on the cheap and the cheerful as the main ingredients were frequently liberated from supermarket skips, and the atmosphere was usually far more socially interactive than could be found elsewhere. Some cooks gained respect and repute, others fell by the wayside. I'd done it myself, though I hadn't noticed anyone weeping when I hung up my apron.

Good food is great - except when you've already gorged yourself on pasta slop, when just the smell of it makes you feel sick.

A hot bar jam-packed with sweating bodies is a welcome sight on a chill December night - and it's asphyxiating on a clement summer evening.

Good-natured salutations from rosy-cheeked friends will warm your soul when you're lonely - and wind you right up when all you want to do is talk about death with your ex.

Clara - older, thinner, greyer - was perched on a stool at the bar. For a second I thought she had clocked me, but then I realised she was not waving, but downing her drink. Eventually I caught her eye and beckoned her outside. A grimace momentarily added to the worry lines on her face, and I was shocked to see her lumber to her feet with the aid of a crutch. Her feline grace had vanished. She moved like an arthritic stick insect. Executing a series of clumsy pirouettes where once she would have elegantly coiled and curled her way around the chairs and tables and diners, she hobbled out into the cobbled street.

"Don't ask," she instructed me once we had embraced and said our hellos.

But I had always had a rebellious streak. "What happened?"

"Fucking wee wanker in a fucking four-by-four." Her Glaswegian accent came through loudest and strongest when she was pissed off. I remembered that from personal experience.

"What, he just fucking did you, like?"

"Aye. He did, as you so aptly put it, just fucking do me. Like."

My memories of the bad times, so neatly kettled in for so long, began to get restless on the front line. I had done nothing wrong, I reminded myself. She had the right to be miffed and she had the right to express her miffedness in my presence. I should not take it personally.

"You're alright, though?"

"Oh, I'm grand, me. Never been better, me. And you? You're actually looking strangely healthy."

"There's a reason for that. It's because I *am* strangely healthy. Been getting into shape. Sit-ups and press-ups and… that." Better not to mention the old running, I thought. "So did you catch up with the four-by-four? I mean, you know, not physically catch up with it…"

"Aye, that would have proved problematic under the given

circumstances." Her speech taking on the cadence and phrasings of the courtroom was another hint that she wasn't the happiest leporid in the hutch. "He got clean away. Steamed into me on my push-bike at ten at night a hundred metres from my own front door for no reason other than the fact that he must be a complete numpty. Failed to stop. Left me for deid. And as we say in court, 'it is an offence for a person being the driver of a mechanically propelled vehicle and owing to the presence of that vehicle on the road or other such public place an accident having occurred to be a wanker and fuck right off.' And of course, the maximum penalty for failing to stop after an accident is five to ten penalty points, a fine of up to £5000 and a driving ban at the discretion of the court." After the breakup of the rig, Clara had become a lawyer. "Or alternatively a late-night encounter with Big Ian and Mad Sean." Before the breakup of the rig, she had known some fairly lawless types.

"Shit, Clara, I'm sorry."

You didn't do it, did you? So don't be sorry; ah, I know you meant to say you're sorry to hear it, sorry it happened; but it did happen, and I'm fucking crippled so let's dispense with the sympathy and get on with it, shall we? she intimated without saying a word.

And there I was, hearing her words when her lips were sealed, and suddenly I started also hearing Iffy's voice, even though he was probably sitting under a bridge with a needle poking out of his arm (or knowing Iffy, tucked up in somebody's cosy bed with a needle sticking out of his arm). "Doesn't that strike you as a suspicious trifle, old boy?" he was demanding. "Nearly being killed like that, out of the blue and all. Hmmm…"

"We have to talk, Clara."

Well, yes indeed, that's why we've just hooked up; we could always write notes to each other, I suppose; but no, you're right: let's talk.

I was getting pretty fed up with all this unspoken communication by this point.

I told her that the Gaffer was playing tonight and as we headed over to the nightclub in Kurfürstendamm I filled her in on the news that Udo had been pushed, but she used up some of her copious supply of scorn on the idea that someone was murdering us all, dismissing it as pure fantasy.

In the interests of world peace, I elected not to push the point.

IF THE HISTORY OF POP CULTURE HAD TAUGHT US ANYTHING

Kurfürstendamm and the Gaffer had both undergone face-lifts in the Noughties. They had reconstructed themselves and where once they had been rowdy, down-at-heel and shabby, they were now trendy, stylish and media-savvy. Like the Gaffer, Ku'damm was no longer frequented by junkies and spongers; they had been replaced by designer suits and visible brand names. The boulevard, like the Gaffer, was no longer all about blagging ten pence for a cup of tea. Instead, it was all about champagne and the importance of being important.

The venue for the Gaffer's gig was on a side street. It was not one of the super-clubs where our old friend usually plied his trade, but a smaller place that had ventured away from its underground origins and now marketed itself as chic, hip, upmarket and exclusive. Its gradual rise into the overground followed a well-trodden path.

According to Iffy's Unified Theory of Capitalism, it was in the nature of capitalism to sneak up behind every subculture, hit it over the head with a sockful of coins and resurrect it in a cynically diluted version that brought in sackfuls of banknotes. Subcultures, he insisted, had ways of identifying or creating markets that corporate moneymen could never imitate, try as they might. Adverts and gimmicks and new products could start trends, but there remained parts of the population they could never reach, despite the nauseating catchiness of their slogans and the all-pervasiveness of their marketing.

The general public - woolly-thinking, mutton-headed, sheeplike and herd-natured though it may be - generally knew when it was being sold something, continued Iffy's theory. It retained the ability to spot a predator on the prowl, but usually blithely acquiesced, allowing the corporations to play the role of genial shepherd, guiding, directing, chivvying and chiding, and keeping the flock penned in.

But there were always some black sheep who responded to different stimuli. They tended to stray and wander off, out of sight and out of mind. The interactions of these black sheep resulted in the birth of unforeseen subcultures: beatnik, hippy, punk, raver, traveller. As long as the numbers remained small, the shepherds paid little heed. It wasn't worth their while to get involved. It was only when the subculture grew to a certain size and gathered a certain degree of momentum that the attack-dogs were let off the leash.

Sometimes the originators of a scene were happy to cash in their chips, to accept the plaudits, to bask in the limelight, to take the money and run. For them, they were underground simply because they were pioneers. The club where the Gaffer was about to play was one such establishment. Its owners had been happy to see a wider public jump on their German techno bandwagon.

For a movement founded on a non-willingness to pander to the peccadilloes of the profiteers, though, the situation was more complex. The free party scene was hard to prettify. With its very existence predicated on a virulent contempt for the *status quo*, it was by definition ill-suited to the bows and ribbons deemed necessary for true mass consumption. The uncompromising fuck-you attitude, the low-budget, DIY ethos and the heartfelt disdain for law and order were such key elements that if the edges were smoothed off, the product would be altered to such a degree as to be no longer recognisable.

Our scene itself was totally unsellable, I thought as we rode the tram through the Berlin night, but maybe the music was a different matter. It was after all dance music: it made people dance. Especially when combined with drugs. And if the history of pop culture had taught us anything, it was that kids could be manipulated into buying anything; if the pimps of the corporate music industry decided to invest in marketing the free party sound, then sell it they would.

When the Gaffer had started infiltrating the mainstream, I remembered Minnie expressing hope that he would indoctrinate the masses with subversive concepts. Iffy, on the other hand, believed you could only fight the system from the outside: "Once you're in it, you're part of it, and it's in your own interests to serve their interests."

CHRISTIANS, SECURITY GUARDS AND PERFORMING MONKEYS

The way to the door of the Keller on the Kurfürstendamm backstreet was lined with a writhing serpent of eager humanity, a shiny, shouty queue of clubbers waiting to get in. Their tee-shirts clung tightly to their torsos, their glitter sparkled, their high heels clacked, their mouths chattered. The boys' hair was gelled and sculpted, the girls' faces slathered in make-up, the atmosphere one of febrile expectation.

Glances landed on us, lingered and left. I noticed numerous near-sneers and several snide asides as the Gaffer's fanbase registered Clara's casual attire and lack of make-up. I got the feeling that my tatty army fatigues and hooded top weren't terribly fashionable this season, either - and what was more, that something like that mattered to the people in the queue. We all had different priorities, I reflected.

Or maybe we just had different uniforms.

Like generals assessing their troops, Clara and I strolled along the massed ranks of clubbing-fodder - except it was us who received the old hairy eyeball as we got nearer to the entrance. Queue jumping, that most heinous of sins to the well-trained Briton, brought with it the delicious, illicit bliss of guilty pleasure. Despite the dirty looks that spoke a thousand dirty words, nobody said anything until an enormous bonehead lurched into our path.

Upon being informed that we weren't dressed correctly, I explained in German that we were there to see the Gaffer. "Old friends," I added. I flashed the smile that I reserved for Christians, security guards and performing monkeys, and only just refrained from winking.

Another bonehead popped up from wherever they were keeping them. I quickly realised that this one was from a different batch. The first one was muscle, with just enough brain to function in society; the second was the inverse. He was so dramatically skinny that he could have been mistaken for a pencil drawing.

He stared at us and I didn't like it.

"Old friends?" he said in English that contained the merest hint of public school, marinated in mockney. He began to usher us away from the door with all the *joie de vivre* of a funeral director.

"That's right. Heard he was in town. Thought we should say hello."

"He's a very busy man, you must be aware. Perhaps you'd be interested in joining his online fan club? I'm afraid this venue is frighteningly fucking strict about dress codes."

"Is he here yet?"

"I'm sorry," he lied, "I really couldn't say." His expression was as severe as his black silk Nehru shirt, his lips as tightly drawn as the red laces in his well-polished shoes.

"Have you got a number I can reach him on?"

"I'm afraid that won't be possible…"

"S'alright," chipped in Clara. "I've still got his number, I reckon."

She whipped out a third generation mobile and did some hocus pocus on the touch screen. Our host clearly spotted which way the wind was blowing. He switched to a throaty murmur, his sharply-angled face undergoing a sudden transformation, and expressed his delight that we were personal friends of the artist.

"Gaffer, ye wee radge, guess who?" I heard Clara say. "Aye. Aye, it has. Aye, Ah have. Ah ken. Ach, get tae fuck. Aye, that's the hing, though. So'm Ah. Aye, straight up. Right noo.

Ootside this fuckin club hingy. Right. Ten minutes, then. Me, too. Aye." Then, to me with a grin: "He loves it when I talk all Trainspotting to him."

"Old friends, you say?" the thin man breathed. He no longer looked bored by our very existence. "I don't think we've had the pleasure of meeting before...I'm the Gaffer's creative guide and business advisor. Andy." He extended a chalky-white bag of bones, and it took me a moment to realise he wanted to shake hands. Clara was given a brace of air kisses that contained all the warmth and generosity of a chicken pecking for corn. "He's always delighted to see friends from his youth, you know."

"Really?" asked Clara.

"He's said so many times. How exactly did you meet him, if you don't mind me asking? At art school?"

"I can only speak for myself here, Andy," Clara said in what seemed an unnecessarily loud voice after introducing both of us, "but when I first met the Gaffer he was puking his ring up after too much K and vodka. And, oh yes - he'd been for a crap in the woods and his dog must have found the spot and dug it up and rolled around in the shite. The poor beast was pure covered in the Gaffer's crap and was just tucking into the vomit when I arrived. It really was very droll."

"He..? You..? His dog..? Really? That's disgusting."

"Aye, it was quite disgusting now I come to think about it."

"Me, I bought a load of acid off him the first time we met," I joined in cheerfully. "His truck was stuck in the mud at a party and the pigs were circling. They'd already impounded the sound system. The Gaffer was too out of his box to move and he wanted to get rid of his stash sharpish."

"Acid..? The pigs..? Out of his..? Are you sure?"

"Ah, that's a load of bollocks. That wasn't the first time you'd seen him," Clara continued mercilessly. "Don't you remember? He was the naked geezer dancing round the firepit with a feather boa sticking out his arse at the Scumcore party."

"Maybe," I conceded. "You know, it all blurs together after a while."

Before my very eyes, Andy ousted panic-stricken from his features. Cold and business-like muscled in to fill the vacant space. "Well, guys, you sure have some funny stories. The Gaffer has a very colourful past. Sex 'n' drugs 'n' rock 'n' roll."

"Decks 'n' dogs 'n' socks with holes..." I corrected him.

"Ha. Ha. Yes. Of course, the Gaffer's a highly respected member of the music establishment now. He's worked extremely hard to get where he is. And although a wild youth is always to be expected in a real artist, and is even to be applauded, there are some stories that are best kept among friends, don't you think?"

"Doesn't talk much about his days on the road then?"

"The Gaffer mostly talks about the future. The past is for the dead, he says."

"Does he now?"

"But I think you both might be interested in his upcoming album. It's all very hush-hush at the moment naturally, but I can reveal that it was inspired by his life 'on the road'." I could see the quotation marks in the air. "His next album is going to tour the world. His *tour de force*, I call it. London, Rome, Paris, New York, LA, Tokyo, Sydney, Moscow, Ibiza, Rio, Buenos Aires," he recited in hallowed tones. "It will be the album that cements the Gaffer into the firmament of true stars."

"That sounds lovely," Clara cooed - ominously for those who knew her like I did. "Although I'm not sure that cementing someone to the firmament is a well-thought out procedure."

The Gaffer's creative guide and business advisor guided us around the corner and advised us to wait outside the artists' entrance for the arrival of the man himself. There followed a short interlude in which he whispered into his mobile phone like a CIA operative preparing the way for POTUS.

Clara filled in the minutes by talking about her work. I was pleased to realise that she was doing a job that she loved. She was a right-on lawyer, standing up for the dispossessed in their struggles with authority. She had turned out well, I thought, though a few streaks of grey in her hair - no longer dyed crimson - added a new touch of severity to her old feisty charm. She had always been bolshie; now she sometimes seemed overly-aggressive. I wasn't sure if she had changed or if I had.

NO PROCTOLOGIST

I saw a serious-looking middle aged gent waddling towards us. He was portly verging on bulky, with a closely shaved scalp, black jeans and a blacker tee-shirt peeping out from under a really fucking black jacket. Some designer stubble, too, bristling over a heavy tan. Momentarily I took the man for the Gaffer's older brother.

But he was an only child of course.

"Well, well, well," the Gaffer exclaimed as Andy listened in like a Victorian débutante's chaperone. "Thanks for coming, guys." It seemed like he was going to offer his hand for us to shake, but we moved in fast and gave him big hugs. I felt his belly undulate like a water bottle. "It's a long way from home, but I always get a good welcome here," he burbled, releasing himself from our clutches. "I appreciate you coming all this way."

"He lives here, you clown," Clara said, tipping her head in my direction. "And I'm over for Udo's funeral."

"Of course. My condolences. He was a good man, Udo. A very sad affair. I'd go to the funeral, only I've got some tedious press conference bullshit to do that day."

Searching for signs of compassion, I watched his eyes - his piggy eyes - and saw only sententiousness and selfishness.

"I'll send a wreath," he went on. "I think he'd appreciate that."

I did some rapid blinking. Followed it up with a bout of heavy frowning. Wound up with my mouth open.

"Gaffer," I finally asked, "I was wondering - did Udo get in touch with you? I'm trying to work out why he was in town at all."

Shifty. That was the first word that leapt into my mind as I studied my old friend's face. It was swiftly followed by cagey, slippery, furtive and evasive.

"Er...well...I had been hoping to meet up with him, yes."

"At Kotti, by any chance?"

The Gaffer left a hole in the conversation that was big enough Andy to jump into. "Allow me to clear this matter up. I dealt with the logistics of the meeting. That's what I'm here for after all. And the meeting never happened, did it, Gaffer? Your pal simply never turned up to the *rendezvous*."

"No," the Gaffer said. "No. He never showed up." His face seemed to slip temporarily out of focus as though he we were lost in some private thought.

Andy was nodding his approval. "Such a shame," he prompted.

"Such a shame," the Gaffer sighed. "I think he'd have liked what I'm up to at the moment. Still, death always takes the best of us first. What was it Auden wrote? 'As the poets have mournfully sung, Death takes the innocent young, The rolling-in-money, The screamingly-funny, And those who are very well hung.' But don't tell Andy, or he'll be worried that I'm next!"

And so it continued, that one brief moment of strangeness replaced by more politeness, more platitudes, more shameless self-aggrandisement, and the total absence of anything resembling the Gaffer we had known - or rather an amplification of the old Gaffer's worst character traits at the expense of anything decent and caring.

I tried telling myself that it was just the Gaffer's way of dealing with Udo's death, but I didn't believe me.

And all the time Andy was sneaking glances at his wristwatch.

"Thank you both so much for making it over. It means a lot to me, it really does. Andy tells me they won't let you in the club? Don't worry, I'll sort it."

"Er, you're alright, actually, Gaffer," Clara said quickly. "Early start tomorrow. Just wanted to say hello, really."

"Such a shame. Oh well, do give my respects to Udo's nearest and dearest. He'll be sorely missed. And talk to Andy if there's anything else I can do for you."

And then he swept away.

"Well," I said, as well I might.

"Who was that again?" Clara asked me.

"Hey, I'm no pancake expert..."

"But you know a tosser when you see one? Personally, I'm no proctologist..."

"But you know an arsehole when you see one?"

"He's changed a lot in ten years, but then so has the world. Nations have died and been born, revolutions have happened, a billion new lives have been thrown into the melting pot, cities have been destroyed, wars fought, forests burned, seas polluted."

"Bellies extended and egos enlarged."

"Sam Saoule, Minnie, Jacek and Udo have died."

"You're leg's been shattered. Iffy's caning himself to death. Allan Exit's probably worse."

"But hey, the night is young."

My smiles were becoming increasingly rueful of late.

THE DEAD FRIENDS, THE EX-FRIENDS, THE JUNKIE FRIENDS AND THE EX-GIRLFRIENDS

Waking up the next day, the first thing I did was pass wind noisily. Then I performed thirty fast chin-ups off the top frame of my bed.

"Oi, knock that off, will you?" grumbled the mound of sleeping bags piled against the wall.

Only slightly hungover - hardly worth mentioning at all - I rewound my mental film of the last evening. Clara, the club, the Gaffer, the Gaffer's sinister creative guide and business advisor: those images were clear. Clara outside the club saying she would see me at the funeral and limping off on her one good leg, pausing to hawk an unladylike gobbet of phlegm over a parked four-by-four, presumably in the belief that all drivers of SUV's were their brothers' keepers: still a good quality mental recording. Me, feeling sorry for myself (the dead friends, the junkie friends, the ex-girlfriends and the ex-friends all weighing on my conscience). Me, feeling a little lonely. Me, going to Helga's truck with a few beers. Me, feeling a little tipsy. The film started to flicker.

Sitting round a firepit with Helga, poking at embers, cuddling, drinking and smoking. Shit! But only spliffs, no fags. Helga telling me to give Iffy a chance. Helga telling me I wasn't helping him by being a cunt. Me - being a cunt? Helga explaining that asking Iffy to go straight was like asking the sea to be still or Willy to be nice or Udo to be quiet. Helga and I getting rat-arsed and miserable because Udo was finally quiet now and would remain so forever.

And then some very low-quality footage of my walk home

and the big drunken hugs that I gave Iffy when I found him snoozing on the staircase in my building.

"Shake a leg, Iffy-boy. It's the funeral today," I reminded him as I pulled on some clothes.

"Aw, mom, do we have to?"

"I'll make you a coffee."

"Aye, that'll do the trick. That and a monster line of speed. D'you want one?"

The sea would never be still and as long as he lived Iffy would never be straight, it seemed. Who was I to question his *modus vivendi*? Even if it did also prove to be his *modus moriendi*. He was firmly of the 'find what you love and let it kill you' school of thought, and his lover was growing daily more volatile and impatient. My path had diverged from Iffy's, and - though deviation was his byword - I feared that I could see his final destination.

"Oh, why not? But not a monster for me, more of a gremlin."

It was going to be a long day.

"I really can't believe that you let Clara go off on her own like that," Iffy remonstrated as we climbed into the cab of my ex-UPS Mercedes truck ten minutes later. "Someone nearly killed her in London a couple of weeks ago, you knew that the killer's in town 'cos he did poor Udo just the other day - and you didn't offer her the benefit of your protection."

"Didn't really think about it," I mumbled, feeling suddenly guilty. "Anyway, she doesn't believe in the murder theory. And it could just have been a coincidence, her getting knocked off her bike like that," I continued.

"Yeah, right. Sure. Just a coincidence. Of course. But that's why I came back to your gaff last night. Couldn't've lived with myself if anything'd happened to you."

I started the engine and gave him a look. One of those looks that say, 'yeah, right,' with a seventh dan in sarcasm. One of those looks that count for diddly zip if the other person is concentrating on racking up a fat line of speed on your passenger seat.

"And what about the Gaffer?" Iffy asked after he had cleaned up.

"What about him?"

"He was still one of us. And it seems Udo was maybe on his way to hook up with him when he died. The Gaffer might have taken a different road after the rig split, but he was always there back in the day. He was, what's the word? Integral. Right? He must be on the hit list. And he's not exactly publicity shy, is he? Easy to track down. Unlike some of us."

"You, you mean."

"Even I don't know where I am half the time."

I thought about that. Iffy's abode was far from fixed, it was true. He was still squatting back in Babylon-don, but anyone asking around on 'the scene' would soon be pointed in his approximate direction. I didn't know where Allan Exit was exactly; somewhere west of Offa's Dyke was all I could swear to. Clara, a respectable and respected lawyer, was eminently findable. All anyone had to do to locate me was to stroll around the streets of F'hain for a few days and our paths would cross. As for the Gaffer, his every move was publicised.

Reflecting on how we had spread out and grown apart in the last decade made me recall the way the big European teknivals used to bring our tribe together, with trucks rolling in from every corner of the continent to disgorge a stream of smiling humanity. Now that I was older, I no longer felt the pressing need to see everyone - and the only time I was likely to do so was at a funeral, and nobody would be smiling.

THE SAD UNCLES AND THE GRIEVING AUNTS

Out of the kindness of my heart, I will pass over the funeral as succinctly as possible. In essence, it was much the same as Sam Saoule's or Minnie's or Jacek's. A different language was employed but the words were the same. The bereaved parents spoke about their lost child. They choked back their sobs. They broke down and cried. The sad uncles and the grieving aunts asked us, "Who are you?" and, "How did you know each other?" and the silences were filled by the stuttering sighs of the mourning friends. The survivors clasped each other closely as they grasped at what remained of life.

The tears. The regret. The finality.

Iffy and I sat and stood through the ceremony with our arms around each others' shoulders. Clara roosted rigidly next to me and faced squarely front, dry eyed and hardly seeming to breathe. Iffy twitched and shuffled his feet and tapped out broken rhythms with his hand on his seat. I cried like a baby because I had loved Udo and he was dead.

Several old friends from my teknival days did double takes when they saw me. "Don't see you round no more." "What happened to you?" "Nice haircut!" "How's retirement suiting you, then?"

And I did double takes, too, but kept my comments to myself.

Only when we had filed out past the coffin into the gardens did I notice Allan Exit.

We had all found our own ways into the rig, back in the mid-nineties when we had realised that we could actually get out there and do it ourselves. I was drawn to the adventure,

Sam Saoule to the anarchy, Minnie to the family vibe, Jacek to the technology, Iffy to the drugs, Clara to the challenge, the Gaffer to the notoriety, Udo to the travelling - and all of us to all of the above, and the music, and more.

One of the manifold theories that Iffy espoused was that every circle of friends included one example of most human archetypes, pieces of a puzzle that when fitted correctly together formed a tribe. Thus, if Iffy had been our trickster, Sam Saoule our hunter, Jacek our alchemist and Minnie Mouth our mother, then Allan Exit had been our mentor. Like many of Iffy's hypotheses, it sounded better when you had been awake for thirty-six hours and the buzz of the acid you had eaten was only slightly tempered by the vast quantities of alcohol you had been pouring down your throat.

Allan was an old school traveller. He had rolled his bus all around the UK and Europe, even overland to Goa, and he had been tripping his tits off to Hawkwind at illegal free festivals when the rest of us weren't even born. He had dreadlocks down to his knees when we were still at primary school. He had been getting his head caved in by coppers at the Battle of the Beanfield when I had been learning about the equilateral triangle.

He had been our father figure back in the day, teaching us, as all good fathers should, the best ways to bodge generators, break into disused factories, negotiate with the authorities, pull vehicles out of two feet of mud or sand, deal with angry locals, siphon diesel, forage for mushrooms, and many another skill that made life on the road easier. It wasn't that the rest of us were naïve, it was merely that Allan Exit had been doing it for years and he knew just about every trick in all the books.

Unfortunately, he must have skipped the page that detailed the folly of sitting on the bonnet of a Landrover while it was skidding across a bumpy field at a party in the south of France.

Had he read that page, he might have saved himself a broken neck. Had he not broken his neck, he would never have begun self-medicating. Had he not discovered that heroin Cures All Known Pains, he would never have needed so much money, and he would not have fucked off with most of our rig and flogged it to some dodgy Italians. Allan Exit was a good man, an honest, generous soul who would give his last five Deutschmarks to a beggar (I had seen him do it), but he wasn't the first person whose smack addiction proved stronger than his morals.

Blood out of a stone? Pah, that was child's play compared to getting money out of a junkie. A few weeks after his midnight flit, Sam Saoule and Udo, respectively the fiercest and the largest members of our crew, had tracked Allan down to a dirty squat in Milan. By then the money was gone. Sam and Udo had slapped him about a bit for form's sake, but the man was old enough to be their dad, and he had a broken neck and they didn't want to kill him.

We still had some cash in the kitty at the time and we could have cobbled another sound system together, but in the aftermath of the Millennium Massacre we reached a consensus, despite the Gaffer's protestations, and the rig was no more.

None of us had seen Allan Exit since.

I did some quick sums in my head. He had once said he was twenty when he had attended the Windsor free festival in '72. That made him thirty-two when the police had trashed the Stonehenge convoy in '84, forty when thirty thousand ravers had gathered on Castlemorton Common in '92, in his mid-forties when we had first gone on the road to mainland Europe together…and getting on for sixty now.

Blimey.

HE MIGHT HAVE ATTACKED ME WITH AN AXE ONCE

I had a moment of hesitation as I wondered what etiquette required when meeting someone who had robbed you blind many years ago. Was it a) cold shoulder, b) biting sarcasm, c) verbal abuse, or d) physical attack?

I elected to do none of the above. I gave Allan a hug. It was that sort of day.

Iffy came bounding over. (He always reminded me of Tigger when he was on speed.)

"Robbed any nice rigs lately?" he asked Allan, clearly selecting option b).

"I'm sorry, guys. I shouldn't have done that."

"D'you know, pal, you've got a point there," Iffy agreed.

Clara limped past us a couple of yards away. I watched a single tear drip down her cheek. Plumping for option a), she didn't spare us a glance.

And wee Willy, pissed already, made a bad day even worse by choosing both option c) and option d), which was unnecessary as he had never been involved in the story in the first place.

"Fucking wanker, eh," he spat as he wobbled towards the old man. Then he whacked him on the head with his bottle of red Sternburg.

Allan Exit was a big, broad-shouldered man, and his cranium, though calvous, was compact. He slumped for a moment to his knees, then hauled himself up and shook his head. Iffy - all action - bustled Willy away. His strike had evidently lacked force because his victim merely rubbed his shiny scalp, shrugged, and said, "I suppose I deserved that." Eeyore to Iffy's Tigger.

Nobody else seemed to have noticed the altercation.

"Allan," I said. "Sorry about that. You do remember Willy, don't you?"

"Rings a bell. Think he might have attacked me with an axe once at CzechTek."

"That'll be right."

We both nodded pensively.

"So how are you? Didn't really expect to see you here."

"I had to come. Couldn't make it to the other funerals. Obligations. Family. You know."

I asked how his kids were. He had five or six, if I remembered correctly, with three or four different women. If Allan Exit had been charming and fertile back in the tail-end of the hippy era, he had also been careless about safe sex and slack on the fatherhood front. It sounded like he had finally accepted his parental responsibilities.

"They're all sound. And most of the grandkids, too."

"Wow. Most of them?"

"Yeah, well...twelve out of the thirteen are great. Just one black sheep. It's a bit embarrassing, really. Please don't tell anyone. He wants to be a copper."

I commiserated, but there are some aches that are beyond remedy.

Which reminded me: "How's the, er...?" I patted the back of my neck.

"No change. Still can only take eighteen pounds per square inch of pressure. More than that…"

"And how's the, er..?" This time I patted the inside of my fore-arm.

He smiled for the first time. Just a little. "Finished. Five years now."

"Good man, Allan."

"Listen, about the rig. I wouldn't have -"

"Forget it, man. It was years ago. You were a junkie then. You're a granddad now. Twelve times over. Thirteen if you count the you-know-what."

"Thanks, man. I've never forgiven myself."

"It's not your fault, Allan. It was probably just a wrong turning on the tortuous road of life. It'll turn out just to be a phase he's going through. He'll most likely end up as a respectable anarchist like his old granddad, you wait and see."

"No, I meant I've never forgiven myself about the rig…"

"Forget about it. It's done. The thing is, Allan, that I'm not sure you should have come here."

"But you said -"

"Someone might be trying to kill us."

CROOKED FURROWS

We have all been given a death sentence. We are all going to die. The countdown begins at the moment of our birth and whatever we may gain through the gift of life, we also lose our immortality for ever. Being born is the ultimate sacrifice.

But how can we be sure that we only have one shot at it? Every major world religion insists on either an afterlife or reincarnation. Every time we come back our slate is wiped clean, our files are deleted and we appear as *tabula rasa*, but that doesn't mean we haven't been here before or that we won't be here again. Life is movement, time is movement - the constantly mutating dance of molecules and atoms is only the rearrangement of finite matter. It's all cycles. It's like the Ship of Theseus. When every plank and oar and mast and rope has been replaced, it's still the Ship of Theseus. Ashes to ashes, dust to dust - but also ashes to dust and dust to ashes. Every seven years we are a different person. The cells are different but the life is the same. And that continues after death.

What if you don't cut your hair for seven years? The cells are the same then as they were seven years before.

That doesn't count. They're dead cells.

I thought nothing died?

I listened to Clara and Allan Exit and Iffy getting philosophical over their glasses of Paulaner and shots of Jaegermeister. Clara surprised me with her fatalistic attitude, Allan Exit made me smile with his optimism, and Iffy was his usual annoying self, tweaked to a slightly higher level of performance by the speed he had taken.

After the funeral, when I had returned Udo's bag to Fabrizia (minus the tape) and she had left with Udo's family, the four of us had wound up bimbling through the woods until we emerged from the cover of some pine trees onto the shore of a lake, where we installed ourselves on the outdoor terrace of a bar. We lolled in the afternoon sunshine.

And got maudlin and talked about death.

Life is only the bit in the middle. Death comes before and death comes after and death is our natural state. What comes in-between is a tragic game we play, just a way to pass the moments between deaths. We have to try to make it as painless as possible - but it will end, sooner or later. Death is the end of all beginnings, and when it begins it has no end.

Are we minds or are we bodies? Is coma - a mind death - actually death? Can the brain live on without the body? Or are we souls, and do they live forever?

Our souls forever!

I thanked Iffy for giving us the benefit of his wit and wisdom, and went foraging for more beer and shots. When I got back, I steered the conversation around to what I considered to be more pressing issues than the existence or non-existence of the soul.

"We're off to the Dam, me and the one like Iffy," I announced. "We need to have a look into Minnie's death. The drowning. We know that Udo's death was no accident. Now we've got to check out the others. And seriously, Clara, Allan, for the moment I'd recommend that you both lie low. And I'll be saying the same thing to the Gaffer. Even though he seems to have turned into a knob, he was still one of us and his life's in danger, too."

Allan Exit was still locked into philosophical mode. "Seeing as our bodies' cells are completely regenerated every seven years, it's no wonder he seems like a different person. He is. We all are," he said.

Clara was taking a more nuts and bolts approach. "Lie low? You've been watching too many cowboy films. I'm a fucking lawyer. I've got responsibilities. I'm not going to bury myself away somewhere while you and Iffy run round playing amateur detective."

Meanwhile, I was aware of a devilish gleam emanating from Iffy's eyes. I hadn't yet discussed our proposed mission with him, but I knew he'd be up for it - as long as he didn't have to finance it. I had considered going on my own, but eventually I caved in to a suspicion that my old pal's natural paranoia and sheer unpredictability could come in handy. Also, I'd be happier having him with me, where I could keep an eye on his drug consumption.

Although admittedly the fact that our destination was Amsterdam had made me think twice.

"Lie low! Lie low, my bony Scottish arse," Clara was still muttering.

"There. Those kids have got one."

We all looked at Iffy.

"I'm just saying. Those kids in the lake. They've got a Li-lo."

After a long silence, Clara demanded, "And while I'm lying low, you think you two geniuses are gonnae solve the big mystery?"

I confirmed that that was indeed the plan, but I did so sheepishly.

"What about you, Allan?" Clara said, turning in his direction. "Are you gonnae lie low?"

"If I got any lower I'd be subterranean." He had told us he was doing the whole self-sufficiency/renewable energy thing on a bit of land on the west coast of Wales.

"That's the idea," I purred. "Clara, listen, whoever's doing all this has already had a pop at you when you were riding your bike. You could have been killed. They might not fuck it up next time."

"It was an accident."

"Is that what you really believe?"

She shrugged. "Yes."

Then she looked thoughtful and shrugged again, but this time it came with a sigh attached. "Listen. Quite frankly, I suspect you two loons are tripping off on one because you want some excitement in your poxy wee lives. Give me one good reason why someone would want us all deid, especially after all these years. It was a lifetime ago, all that sound system shite. I left it all behind when I went back to school.

"Don't get me wrong. We had a ball 'n' all, but I don't think I'd do it again if I had another bonus life in Clara: The Computer Game. It meant I started my career ten years later than I would otherwise have done. Those ten years that I frittered away getting off my titties, looking for somewhere sweet to park up and nodding along to banging basslines, I could have been doing something worthwhile. That's ten years that I could have spent really helping people who are in shitty situations - people facing prison sentences for their beliefs, for trying to fight the system, for daring to stand up against authority."

"Like we used to do, you mean?"

"Don't interrupt, please, Iffy. There's a dear. And no, that's not what I mean. I mean genuine activists, not party munters. How many of the punters who came to get out of their nuts at our parties truly cared about anything except the drugs and the fashion? How many?"

"A lot."

"Wrong answer. Not fucking many - that's the answer you were racking your addled brains to find."

"Alright then," I countered, feeling Iffy could do with some back-up. "Supposing that's true. At the very least we offered them an alternative to commercial clubs with stupid dress codes, wanker security, expensive drinks and gangster bosses who are only interested in raking in the cash."

"But so what? What did they do with the possibilities that opened up for them? The whole free techno scene became an abomination of the free festival concept. 'All tribes welcome' - as long as they play hardtek and wear baseball caps and hoodies. And tell me - honestly, now - who got the most respect on the scene? The artists? The musicians? The engineers and creators and crew? Or the drug dealers? Hmmm? At what point did the parties cease to be events that dealers came to in order to make a bit of cash while catering to the needs of the dancers, and turn into events organised by dealers in order to get rich? Hmmm?"

I flinched, but not because her remarks had flung their barbs in deep. She was entitled to her opinions, and her point about drug dealers was interesting, but illegal substances were integral to a lifestyle based around dancing all night and just about all of us had sold some drugs at some time. They had always been part of our alternative economy. They provided incomes that weren't dependent on nine-to-five wage drudgery, thus allowing for greater freedom to roam and more time to be creative - and our parties worked best with drugs, and somebody had to supply them.

At first the ecstasy and acid and speed had helped us to explore alternative realities and inspired us to dream of utopian futures. It was only later, as ketamine, smack and crack ploughed their crooked furrows through my crop of friends, that too many of us found doors closing in our faces, and the dreams became dark and depressing.

So, no, it wasn't Clara's line of thought that made me flinch: it was the 'hmmm' that set my teeth on edge. It was that very same 'hmmm' that I knew and feared from times long gone; the one that clenched an icy fist around my heart; the one that she had terrorised me with when we had been a couple. It was an audible smirk, and I found it unbearably smug, and it usually just wound me up and made me want to further argue the toss. As she employed it only when her position was practically unassailable, I suspected that she left it trailing in the air in order to provoke me into digging myself even deeper into shit-filled trenches.

We were all older now. Balder, greyer, plumper, saggier breasted, hairier chested, crow's footed, blotchier, more wrinkled, duller-skinned and possibly duller-brained. Our blood pressure was higher, our muscle mass lower, our strength, speed, energy levels, metabolism, aerobic capacity and bone mineral density all reduced. Our hearing wasn't what it used to be and neither would our eyesight be getting any better. We were past our peak. We were past the halfway mark of our three score years and ten. By my calculations we were all well past the life expectancy of a Haitian in 2010. Clara and I had already lived longer than the average Angolan.

(But then, as Clara had once pointed out to me, those figures were distorted by high rates of infant mortality. Most Angolans didn't actually drop dead in their late thirties, did they? Hmmm?)

But the one indisputable benefit of all those liquid seconds that had passed under our bridges, all those feather-light minutes that had sailed away into the land of used-to-be, all those lost hours that we would never see again, was that I had learned to let things lie.

I was older but wiser.

I ignored Clara's 'hmmm'.

Iffy, on the other hand, went for it like a Senator after a campaign donation.

THE NEEDLING AND THE DAMAGE DONE

"I never noticed you turning down freebies from anyone."

A gentle, soothing breeze was drifting over the Cretan hills, I imagined, and anyone lucky enough to be perched on a sun-warmed rock staring out past the masts into the slowly rolling Mediterranean couldn't help but relax and feel that the world was not such a bad place after all.

Regrettably, I was in Brandenburg, where the skies above us had been darkened by an advance party of rain-clouds. As the drops began to fall into our drinks and onto our heads, we fell to churlish bickering. Older and wiser? Maybe we were just older and wider around the waistline. Or as Iffy would no doubt put it, *barba crescit caput nescit* - beard grows, head doesn't grow wiser.

For ten years the hatchets been buried, hidden away, and now that they were excavated they emerged sharp and shiny and menacing. We sunk them into each other's weak spots.

Cathartic? Pathetic? Or just plain vicious? We turned our reunion into a disaster and raked enough to muck to put the most enthusiastic stable-boy to shame. Not satisfied with our hatchet-work, we filled our shovels with steaming piles of old grievances and flung them at each other. Most of it was petty: off-the-cuff comments from more than a decade ago, promises made and broken in the last century, money owed since the last millennium.

At one moment I suggested that Udo would have been embarrassed to see us at one another's throats like this. I was shouted down for putting words into a dead man's mouth, and then everyone started doing it.

"Udo never forgave Allan for doing the dirty."

"Udo told it like it was."

"And he did his fair share of the work. Unlike some of us."

He had only been dead for three days, but our old companion was well on his way to beatification. There was a certain sly slant to the tributes, though, that meant each big-up for the big man could also be taken as a belittlement of someone else.

"Udo never blagged off anyone who couldn't afford it."

"Always paid his debts."

"He was a much better DJ than some others I could name."

"Handy man to have around if it came to a ruck. Stood up for his mates."

"Loved cooking for everyone. He was never guilty of looking after number one."

"Generous to a fault."

That last piece of praise, from Allan Exit, rang particularly true. Udo, a definite and dedicated epicurean, who loved drinking and taking drugs and would go a long way to avoid pain, both physical and emotional, had displayed a peculiar brand of hedonism: one of his greatest pleasures was making other people happy. This desire - this need - to please all and sundry meant that he agreed to practically every proposition and plan that came his way, and this made things complicated. He frequently consented to be in four different places at the same time, and due to the inconsistency of his timekeeping he was rarely in any of them.

The eulogies continued to roll in.

"You could always trust Udo to keep a secret."

"If you ever need a shoulder to cry on, he was there for you."

"Discovered a cure for cancer."

Iffy hadn't completely lost his sense of humour, and his

intervention saved us from plunging further into the swamp of recrimination and acrimony, although by that time, to misquote Neil Young, I'd seen the needling and the damage done.

Singly and sadly, we separately settled our bar bills and stomped back through the sylvan landscape towards the S-Bahn, with Clara huffing and puffing on her crutch and the rest of us grimly trudging. I reached up to grab a branch and sublimated my desire for nicotine with a few chin-ups. Dropping back down, I started jogging on the spot.

"*Quantocius quantotius*," Iffy urged. "Bit quicker, if no-one minds."

Still coming down from the adrenaline of animosity and the rush of rancour, I presumed he was taking the piss. Clara and Allan Exit also allowed his request to tumble unheeded onto the leaf-strewn forest floor.

"Really. Let's pick it up a bit now. Absquatulate. Pronto."

A penny teetered on the edge of my thoughts. "Who paid for your drinks, Iffy?" I asked.

"Well - I came out with nothing, me, and it didn't seem like the right moment to blag any cash."

The penny dropped. *Resto basket*, as they say in France. Doing a runner, we would say in the UK.

"Okay, let's get our skates on, before the barman decides to go hunting him some hippies in these here woods."

Clara tutted like a hyperactive drummer going to town on the high-hats. Allan Exit muttered something about nearly being old enough to qualify for a free bus pass. We rode the train in silence and bade our farewells stiffly when Clara marched off to collect her bags and catch her plane.

A CHTHONIC OASIS, A CRUSTY VALHALLA

Allan Exit, still grumbling like the murmur of distant traffic, and Iffy, still twitching like the Duracell bunny, came home with me. I phoned the Gaffer. I wanted to talk him into keeping a low profile for the foreseeable future. He was non-committal, pointing out that with his lifestyle he was forcibly in the public eye. I warned him to keep his wits about him. He thanked me for my concern. I mentioned that Allan Exit was at my gaff and suggested he join us on a tour of the squat bars of Friedrichshain, but the Gaffer didn't appear particularly enthused at the thought of hooking up with us.

Allan himself seemed tense, but that was understandable given the circumstances. Iffy, perspicacious as ever, prescribed lubrication and hinted obliquely at intoxication. It was time to go out, he told us.

As far as I was concerned, Berlin had the best watering holes in the world. Before the momentous day when the Berlin Wall was pulled down (it didn't just fall of its own accord) West Berlin was already home to a thriving underground scene, and when the newly liberated *Ossies* began their exodus to pastures greener, the empty houses they left behind were swiftly occupied by legions of squatters. At the same time as techno was making a name for itself in clubs like Tresor, the streets of East Berlin became a haven for radical marginals of the anarchist ilk. One street alone, Mainzerstrasse in the heart of F'hain, saw thirteen squats spring up in the immediate wake of the joyous but muddy confusion of *die Wende*.

On the whole, the squatters were a sociable bunch. They built communities, and with the communities came the bars.

The squatters kept irregular hours and the bars kept pace, their prices reflecting their clients' low levels of disposable income. The bars were haphazardly furnished in cast-offs and salvaged materials, artistically and lovingly assembled. The squats attracted artists, musicians and artisans. The vibe was bohemian and underground.

The eviction of the Mainzerstrasse stronghold, a hard-fought and violent battle, was one of the Berlin alternative scene's most memorable events, but other squats and traveller sites continued to flourish. By the time I popped up there the initial wave of squatting had broken, however, and most of the old squats, with a few notable exceptions, had morphed into legalised *Hausprojekte*. They retained their ramshackle appearances and anti-establishment spirit, but the residents paid peppercorn rent in return for some degree of security.

There were dozens and dozens of house projects scattered around the city, and each of them was distinct from the others. There were arty, hippy houses, hardcore *Autonomen* houses, spiky punk rock houses, gay houses, lesbian houses, techno houses, crusty houses, student houses and houses inhabited by families with kids, and most of them played host to cafés, gigs, parties, cinemas, art shows, plays, political meetings - and, of course, bars.

Of all the improvised drinkeries in town, my particular favourite was the Hole - das Loch - where access was only for the brave and limber, as it involved committing your contorting carcass to the darkness via an old coal chute, the eponymous orifice in the pavement in front of the house, from which tendrils of smoke and gobbets of noise escaped into the night whenever the cast iron lid was lifted.

It was the diametric opposite of the insipidly sanitised, blandly charmless, uninspiringly characterless, mutually interchangeable chains of pubs that clogged up UK high streets. In order to enjoy a drink in the Hole it helped to have tastes that did not preclude punk rock, rebel ska, experimental noise, hardcore techno, cheap booze, graffed-up walls, casual drug taking, dodgy plumbing, smoky air, dogs, nutters, and conversation that lurched with unpredictable volatility from the sublime to the ridiculous. The Hole was physically and culturally underground, and for someone like Iffy it was a chthonic oasis, a crusty Valhalla, a descent into paradise, a gateway to Annwn, the mythical subterranean world of delights and eternal youth.

As for me, it was my local. Getting barred from there was not only extremely hard to manage, it was also proving to be a right regal pain in the arse. But then, as Marcel Proust said, 'The true paradises are the paradises we have lost.'

Iffy, Allan and I trotted downstairs and outside. The streets were no emptier than usual, and this season's well-dressed young Friedrichshainer was sporting pretty much the same outfit as the last ten seasons' well-dressed young Friedrichshainers had. Black was never out of fashion in the *Kiez* where punk was still alive and spitting, though the tone was leavened by flocks of brightly plumed Mohicans, galaxies of twinkling piercings and bodies daubed in swirling tattoos like artists' palettes. There was a smattering of '*ficken, saufen, nicht zur Arbeit gehen*' drunk-punks, but most of the vegan *Autonomen* locals took their political rebellion seriously.

All in all it was a far cry from typical British town centres, where pissed-off boys and pissed-up girls vented their inadequacies on anyone within punching or groping distance.

Which made the fight all the more surprising.

WE DIDN'T LEAVE THE STONE AGE BECAUSE WE'D RUN OUT OF STONE

For old times' sake Allan Exit had allowed himself to be tempted by a line of billy. Rendered suddenly loquacious, he filled us in on his news when he wasn't blathering on his phone, his one concession to modern life. He had always harboured anarcho-primitivist tendencies, and after our rig had split up he had cast off many of the trappings of modern civilisation. "The best way to take the system down," he said, "is by not needing anything it has to offer."

He was living in the Welsh countryside, where he generated his own electricity and drew water from a spring. He grew his own food and survived largely without any money at all. "I do a bit of mechanics when I really need some wedge, or flog some magic mushrooms. Brew my own beer. Cider, too. Gone all permaculture on my smallholding. Grow my own weed."

He believed that the skills he learned would be vital for survival in a world that was headed for man-made disaster. "Maybe we'll make the switch to another way of living of our own accord. After all, we didn't leave the Stone Age because we'd run out of stone, so why are we waiting for the petrol to run out? But the change will probably be forced on us." He wasn't sure which of the various doomsday scenarios that threatened our safe European homes would be the final one to rid us of State control - whether it would be antibiotic resistance or disease mutation and a global pandemic, or over-population and famine, or the upcoming water shortage, or conventional or nuclear war, or nanotechnology and grey goo, or a computer super-intelligence with no need for messy humans - but he was sure that one day each and every human being would be left to scratch out their own survival. "It's not a result of chance that our practical know-how diminishes every day, and that most of us have don't have a Scooby about how to fend for ourselves. Our complete reliance on others has been engineered over the past decades to leave us as helpless as babies, totally dependent on State institutions and, even worse, increasingly on private, profit-making corporations for our continued survival.

"Don't worry, I'm not one of those survivalist nutjobs who think that weapons are the answer," he reassured us. Allan believed that humanity was better than that. He built communities and fostered networks, he told us, sharing his skills and learning new ones. He believed that Man was a social animal, not a selfish one, and he championed a society based on reciprocity, free association and voluntary contract. He was a nice man.

We lost him for half an hour, but just as I was beginning to worry about his whereabouts, I clocked him gabbling away to some earnest, bespectacled young anarchists by the entrance to our third - or was it the fourth? - port of call as we plotted our meandering course towards Carlo's bar near Ostkreuz, where Iffy confidently assured us we would be able drink for free when our cash ran out. Iffy himself was dribbling enthusiastically over a pair of nubile Italian performance artists, and I was having a quiet moment to myself, leaning on the bar, just observing.

Feeling sneakily proud of myself for having turned down the amphetamines that were on offer, and at the same time wondering if my nicotine cravings would ever vanish, I suppressed a sigh when I heard Allan Exit mention the I-word. Israel. Personally, I had long since expunged the state of Israel from my conversations in Friedrichshain, having identified it as a sensitive subject. You didn't have to be either a historian or a psychologist to figure out why Germans tended to shy away from being too critical of anything Jewish.

So when Allan Exit dropped it clanking it into his conversation, there wasn't exactly the type of silence that descends on a cowboy saloon when a stranger announces that he's lookin' for Big Red, nor the quite the sort of hush that falls on a pub in Norfolk when someone makes a joke about in-breeding, but the ambience thermometer descended a couple of degrees nonetheless.

I interrupted Iffy in mid-kibitz with the Italians, who were happily elucidating the finer points of how best to hang off a crane whilst suspended by your pierced nipples, and suggested moving on.

"Where's Allan?" he asked me, glancing round the bar. "He'd love this. Remember his Scottish mucker who used to stick his arm into bear traps?"

"Oooh," one of the girls cooed, "I've never seen that. Does he still do shows?"

Iffy shook his head. "Never did a show in his puff. Just got a buzz out of it."

Ignoring the puzzled look on the Italians' faces, I told him in a fizzing undertone, "He mentioned the I-word."

"Not...he can't have...surely he didn't...Nope. Sorry. You've lost me there."

"The I-word," I hissed. "You know." And I added, "Israel," in a stage whisper.

"Oh my Dog," he exclaimed theatrically. "We've got to get him out of here before it's too late. 'Scuse me, *ragazze*, this is an emergency."

"He's outside. C'mon, our kid, let's boogie."

We were joking, of course. The worst fate that was likely befall our old mate was getting involved in a long and tedious discussion and having to explain that criticising a nation that implemented fascist policies had nothing to do with anti-Semitism.

Then we heard the shouts.

We looked at each other in disbelief and shouldered our way to the door. Momentarily wedged together in the entrance, we popped out into the street like a cork from a champagne bottle. Dogs were barking, voices shouting, a small crowd gathering.

I saw Iffy wade into the melee, swinging his paws.

I saw Allan hit the deck.

"Nobody touch him! He's got a broken neck," I yelled, and repeated it in German.

BRRRR. FFFFP. TCHAK. AYYY. WAAA

I spotted the earnest anarchists hovering around at the back of the group. Maybe it was affection for old Allan Exit or maybe it was a primal cry against mortality that made me charge into the skinny pair and grip one of them up by the throat. Iffy later suggested it was down to the booze in my bloodstream. Whatever the reason, I practically lifted the poor sod off his feet.

A century or two earlier I would have tished the cad's cheek with my monogrammed handkerchief and demanded satisfaction. He would have acquiesced and had the honour of dying an honourable death, neatly filleted by my sabre. At the very least he would have had a damned impressive scar carved across his cheek.

As it was, there was some more shouting, some more barking and some more unchoreographed, frenetic toing and froing that lasted just a few seconds. Hands separated us.

Moments later, I grasped what the poor kid was trying to tell me: I had got the wrong man.

Out of the corner of my eye I saw a black-garbed figure legging it down the street.

And I was running.

Under the street lights. My trainers pounded the pavement and my arms were pumping. My breathing was loud in my ears. Breathing. Running. Sprinting though the night, through my Kiez, through my streets. Pedestrians leapt out of my path, their heads turning to stare as I scorched past. Half of my running was in the arms: get the arms going and the legs will follow. My fingers hung loose. Thighs and knees high. Feet neatly parallel to each other, powering off the pavement. I felt invincible. Unstoppable, immortal. Better than drugs. I was a machine. No - I was Nature. This is what I was born to do and momentarily I forgot why I was speeding hell for leather through the night. Nothing else mattered except for left, right, left, right, left, right, too quick to count the steps. This was life, and I loved it. I would live for ever... my movement was stars colliding and the Universe expanding.

And then I began to feel the inevitable little death of lactic acid gnawing at my muscles and suddenly there wasn't enough oxygen in the world to sustain my dash. I started to lose my form. My head began to rock from side-to-side. My knees lifted lower off the ground and the floor sucked at the soles of my feet as gravity redoubled its exertions.

I remembered what I was doing: chasing the person I thought had attacked Allan Exit. Only he was gone, vanished into the Berlin night, one more black figure among many.

I wound down to a ragged, winded lope and ended in a slumped, panting heap against the bonnet of a car in the road.

With wobbly legs and a spinning head I returned to the bar and Allan Exit's decumbent body. A small crowd was still hovering around the fallen man. I couldn't tell sincere well-wishers from nosy do-gooders and gawking rubber-neckers.

Elbowing my way to the front, I found Iffy sitting in a close approximation of the lotus position. One of his hands held one of Allan Exit's hands and the other was gently stroking the older man's forehead. Underneath the soft, shocked susurrations of the throng, I could hear him chanting: "You're gonna be okay, Allan, you're gonna be okay. You're gonna be okay, Allan, you're gonna be okay."

Allan Exit was white, his face twisted in pain. But he was still breathing, and soon the sound of an ambulance's sirens drowned out all the other noises. I watched in silence as some quietly efficient paramedics questioned witnesses - I watched and then I told them what I knew of Allan's unfortunate medical history. I noticed their expressions grow more solemn. They set about giving Allan Exit whatever treatment was necessary before they could load him into their vehicle. I saw Iffy try to blag his way along for the ride to the hospital, but it was no go. With its lights flashing off the faces of the bystanders, the ambulance spirited Allan Exit away and cop cars began to arrive.

"Well," I said, and left it at that.

"Whatever you're about to order at the bar, I'll have a double."

"I was going to order a double voddie and orange without the orange."

"Well, I'm no mathematician, but I reckon that'd make mine a quadruple."

I had rarely seen him look so freaked out. We made our way round the corner, away from the crowds and cops, and slipped into another squat bar where we would be welcome.

"Pow," said Iffy." "Paff. Poff. Pffff. Tchhh. Whew."

As a general rule, Iffy only very rarely lost the use of language. Humongous lines of ketamine had been known to have that effect on him on occasion, but usually his mouth kept working even when his brain had long since powered down.

"Wheep," he added as I passed him a glass half-full of vodka that the kindly bartender had given me. "Brrrr. Ffffp. Tchak. Ayyy. Waaa."

"Is he going to be okay, Iffy? Is he going to be okay?" I asked, unconsciously echoing the mantra that he'd been chanting outside.

"I don't know. I don't think he was breathing when the ambulance took him away."

I stared at Iffy. He stared into his glass. For the remainder of the evening, we drank until we could think no more.

NUGGETS OF SAGACITY

"They give it the large with the liberalism, but the reality of the deal is that they're a merchant nation. It's in their blood. They saw a gap in the market and they plugged it like a little boy sticking his finger in a dyke. If you know what I mean. This is the home of the letterbox company, where ninety percent of the Fortune 500 filter their profits and avoid paying their taxes. And have you seen suburbia over here? The neat rows of houses, orderly as you like, all with their curtains left permanently open, not because they're so cool that they don't care who spies on their privacy, but so everyone can admire how spotless their homes are. Check out the supermarket shelves, too. Ready-meals and microwavable delights, that's what they're into. Their whole society is processed to the max. This is Legoland. Plasticland. And their idea of countryside is the section of verdantly-challenged wasteland between two dual-carriageways. Your average Dutch person makes your average German look crazy and unconventional. Don't be fooled by the whole 'shmoke shome weed and maybe have shome naughty sheksh for aftersh' bullshit. If it ain't profitable, it ain't happening in the Flatlands, buddy."

He still hadn't slept, the Iffy-boy, and I dearly wished he would. Our train had just sped over the border into the Netherlands and I had personally long since crossed the Rubicon where patience morphed into resignation. It was entirely possible that some of what my travelling companion said made perfect sense. Indeed, he may have scattered pearls of wisdom, gems of wit and nuggets of sagacity in a trail of transcendental treasure that stretched all the way back to Berlin. For all I knew some of his observations might have altered the course of philosophy forever...but I hadn't been listening.

The train was not only modern and practically silent (except for the chuntering of my fellow traveller), but it was also cheap, due to the fact that some people I knew sold special tickets for European train journeys. I had never inquired as to whether they had access to blank tickets or whether they sold complete forgeries. It was quicker, cheaper and far less hassle than taking my van, and that was enough for me.

Unlike Iffy - and much to his disgust, it seemed - was now paying rent to a landlord for the first time in my life, and doing so with barely a qualm. Most of my adult life had been spent in squats and on traveller sites, but these days my van was more of a work vehicle than a home.

There were some great sites in Berlin, some long-established, dating back over twenty years, and although I was sure I could have found space to park up on one of them, my diminishing patience with other people's problems, other people's moods and whims and eccentricities and, well, other people in general, had led to me living in splendid isolation in my own flat. My social butterfly was regressing, squeezing itself back into the solitary cosiness of its cocoon. It wasn't that I didn't like people any more - but the silly row with Clara and Allan Exit, coupled with a hardcore hit of Iffy that was hovering on the brink of becoming an overdose, had reinforced my belief that I no longer needed to live with the fuckers.

The sooner I stopped somebody killing off my friends, the sooner I could return to my quiet life. Not being killed myself would also help me to further my life goals.

"When I spoke to him yesterday, the Gaffer asked if we were going to involve the boys in blue," I mentioned with a smile as we pulled into Amsterdam Centraal, interrupting Iffy's diatribe on the price of solar panels. Or the best way to half-inch bottles of champagne from off-licences. Or the average height of adult male penguins. Or how many pins you could stick in the head of an angel. (I really wasn't listening.)

"Did he? He suggested that?"

"He didn't suggest it. Just wondered if we'd considered it."

"What did you say?"

"That we didn't see the point, of course. That we had no proof whatsoever, apart from the word of a junkie at Kotti who probably wouldn't be too keen on doing his bit for society, and a couple of near misses that the Old Bill wouldn't take seriously anyway. That even if we got the coppers interested, the fact that the deaths were in Holland, Germany, France and Poland would make their investigation complicated and slow, to say the least, and time would appear to be of the essence. That we still adhered as much as possible to our old site policy of PIY. Police it yourself."

One of the basic tenets of the free parties we used to hold was that they were outside the parameters of the law's jurisdiction. The authorities were not welcome. Unfortunately not all the people who turned up were welcome either, but we had no trained, uniformed police with the explicit permission of the community to cart wrong-doers off to the local nick. There was no established system of trial and punishment to cope with whatever sexual predators, tooled-up badboys, blood-thirsty bullies or sharp-eyed thieves came to darken our doors, blacken our name and try to take advantage of our self-proclaimed extrajudicial situation.

So we dealt with it ourselves. No police, no problem, as we used to say. Talleyrand once wrote that 'There is one body that knows more than anybody, and that is everybody'; and thus, who better to look after each of us than all of us? In the absence of any designated authority figure, each and every one of us assumed the mantle of protector of our liberties. Consensus opinion decided what was acceptable and what wasn't. Popping ecstasy was deemed within the boundaries, and so was snorting ketamine (I didn't like it myself, but I was in the minority); banging up heroin wasn't. Transgressors were encouraged to cease and desist from whatever actions were causing problems, and if the trouble-making persisted, they were told to leave, or forcibly ejected - and maybe given a few slaps.

There was no question of who watched the watchers, because we all were all watching out for each other. Generally, we all abided by the tacit rules of behaviour that experience, inclination and common sense dictated, because humans are naturally cooperative when society is seen as just, and because anyone who disagreed with our way of life was free to leave - an option that Thomas Hobbes forgot to include in his description of the nation state. In short, we lived according to our own moral code, and now, even though the crime was murder, Iffy and I felt that we had no choice but to continue to function outside the boundaries of the judicial system.

"What did the Gaffer say?" Iffy demanded.

"Not a lot, as it goes."

"Hey, you don't mind if I just nip to a coffee shop, do you? I need to take the edge off that billy. I'd forgotten how bastard strong the speed is in Berlin. There should be laws against that type of thing. Wouldn't mind winding down soon, maybe getting some shut-eye. You know."

Pleased that he was thinking tetrahydrocannabinol rather than diacetylmorphine, I readily agreed. Not wanting to set foot in a smoky coffee shop, I waited outside. My reservations about bringing Iffy with me to Amsterdam, a city that had far more than its fair share of smackheads and dealers, had been alleviated by the knowledge that we just passing through on our way to Bijlmer.

APOCALYPSE BUNNIES

The last time we had been in Holland was a couple of months previously, when we had said our final farewells to Minnie - poor Minnie Mouth who could no longer hear us; who would never again bollock us for traipsing mud into her truck; never again remind Iffy that he should think about taking a shower some time in the non-too-distant future; never again suggest that we really ought to eat something soon.

Dynamic Minnie. Minnie Maximum. Minnie Mouth. The Miniac - by turns serious and delirious, hamster-cheeked and dimpled, spiky-haired, blue eyed and quick to care, hard to anger and easy to like - had been just as hardcore as any of us, and as we grew closer during our time together in the rig, she had slowly told me her story.

There were her pre-sound system days, before she rocked up at one of our parties in Utrecht and decided she buzzed off our groove. At that time she had been a dedicated clubber, one of that tribe who Iffy dismissively described as apocalypse bunnies: shiny, smiley, narcissistic automatons who cared for nothing except taking ecstasy, hugging strangers, blowing whistles and dancing until the point where their trainers disintegrated; gluttonous consumers who built imaginary fluffy walls between themselves and the spikiness of the world. She had been a right old cheesy quaver, but she soon crossed over to our side of the techno divide. From fashion to anti-fashion. From glamour to grime. From high heels and low-cut tops to siphoning diesel and evading the cops.

In fact many stalwarts of our scene had drifted in from the club tributary, mingling their waters, so to speak, with crusty travellers, punk squatters and disillusioned inner-city youth. Each had chipped in with whatever know-how and enthusiasm they brought with them. There were no employees in the sound systems, just folks who found a place for their talents and passions.

There were location-finders who trawled for likely venues, squat-breakers who opened the doors, electricians who gave us power, hard men who stopped the nastiness, wide boys who dealt with the locals, bar crew who bought and sold the liquid refreshments, drivers with their vans and trucks, drug dealers who made us stay up forever, sound engineers who coaxed the best out of the rigs, arty types who provided the deco, speaker-luggers who carried the tat, speaker-huggers who carried the vibe, and musicians who made us dance, and none of them could have existed without the others.

As for Minnie, I slowly grew to know her better, and came close to comprehending the sequence of events that led to her becoming such a curious cross between a hedonist and a nihilist. The world was doomed, of that she was sure, and nothing meant anything, so why not get off your face and party till the lights went out?

I think she had been lost when our rig split up. It was as though her kids had finally grown up and flown the nest. She had tried to find a surrogate family at first, hitting the road with other itinerant sound systems, but I recalled her saying that it just wasn't the same. She had come to visit me in Berlin several times a year for a while, then once every six months or so, then rarely, then never.

I had been caught up in my own affairs and I hadn't been aware that she was sliding into the depression that her flirtation with clubbing had masked and that I naïvely believed her immersion in our travelling sound system culture had cured.

VAGUENESS, RELATIVISM AND LIKELIHOOD

"Fuck me, I reckon I'd top myself if I lived in a place like this," Iffy squawked with a marked lack of sensitivity as the regional train we had taken pulled into the shiny glass station nearest to where Minnie had lived out her last days.

"If she did, it'd put paid to our theory about the murders," I pointed out, looking out the window at the high-rise flats of Bijlmer, south east Amsterdam's contribution to the world's list of badly thought-out housing projects.

"I thought her parents said she lived in a sweet little village on the outskirts of the Dam."

"So tell me - just how exactly did Minnie wind up living in this shit-hole? I mean, maybe it's not as bad as it looks, but I don't think it'd be top of anyone's list of des reses. I always imagined she'd end up teaching yoga to goats and knitting harp strings from their wool in the Ardèche."

Minnie's death was the one which had caused me the most pain and the most profound soul-searching. It should never have come to this: something had gone badly wrong with her support network for her to end her days in a place like Bijlmer. And in theory I had been part of that support network.

In the quiet times between parties Minnie had confided in me, revealing the roots of her fundamental nihilism that seemed at such odds with her extroverted party-girl persona. Now I recounted some more of her story to Iffy.

When we first met her she had been working in a club, an environment where love was readily available for the price of a pill, but before that she had been truly homeless for a couple of years, drinking herself to sleep every night and passing out wherever she found herself, after leaving her stiflingly strict and suffocatingly sterile home at just sixteen. It was a perilous way of life for a teenage girl in the big bad city. Bad things had happened to her. The Dutch clubbing scene had stuck a plaster over her problems, and our sound system family turned out to be merely another short-term fix.

Her funeral had been attended by hundreds of her old friends, but everyone I spoke to had told me a similar story: she had dropped under the radar. Her middle class parents were rigidly polite and coldly considerate to us, and it was clear that somewhere down the line they had lost all ability to relate to their daughter. Iffy and I doubted the efficacy of noising up them up, so we elected to head over to her last known address and see if the neighbours had anything to tell us.

"This looks like a good neck of the woods to score some puff," Iffy commented as we paced through the dirty streets.

"You reckon? Looks like a great place to be ripped off or robbed, I'd have said."

"Sub us an Ayrton Senna, would you?"

Automatically, I stuck my hand in my back pocket. Located a ten euro note. Paused. Left it where it was. Said, "You just bought something to smoke in that coffee shop by the train station."

"Well, I certainly went in with that very intention foremost in my mind, you're right."

"Didn't they have anything good enough for *Monsieur*?"

"You know how it goes. You're having a gander at the menu, deciding how best to maximise your hard-earned wedge -"

"Or your mate's hard-earned wedge, as the case may be."

"And then your eyes stray to the mushrooms on offer and you say to yourself, hello. Hello, you say, it's been a while. Far too long, in fact. And before you know it, hey presto, you've got a fine bag of Mexican hallucinogens and fuck all to smoke."

At what point do the scales tip? When precisely does a charmingly devil-may-care attitude cease to be a breath of fresh air and become stagnant? When exactly does the moment come for you to face facts and decide that your companion is a liability?

As I wandered further down life's road and the busy, well-lit super-highway of youth became the shady forest track of middle age, I found within myself a tendency to prefer probabilities to certainties, and I increasingly placed my faith in vagueness, relativism and likelihood rather than conviction and dogmatic absolutism.

I wasn't alone in this. Philosophers had long debated the sorites paradox, the question of when *some* sand becomes *a heap* of sand. One grain isn't a heap, and neither is two, nor three, nor four, but at some point we would begin to say, "Yes, that is a heap of sand." But when? How can the addition of a single, tiny grain transform *not-a-heap* of sand into a *heap*?

Fuzzy logic began to appear in the 1920s in order to deal with the concept that something did not have to be either true or false, but could instead be partially true. As Pablo Picasso once remarked, 'If there were a single truth, it would not be possible to do a hundred canvases on the same theme.' In the 1940s, E-prime tried to rid the English language of the dictatorial verb 'to be', replacing rigid assertions with subjective judgements and reasoned presumptions in a bid to remind us of the complexity and chaos of our environment.

This awareness of manifold and concurrent points of view could be traced right back through history to the conditioned propositions of the ancient Jainist religion. According to their doctrine of *syadvada*, they applied the prefix *syad*, meaning 'in some ways,' to divest a statement of dogmatism. Their seven predications were: *syad-asti* - in some ways, it is; *syad-nasti* - in some ways, it is not; *syad-asti-nasti* - in some ways, it is, and it is not; *syad-asti-avaktavyah* - in some ways, it is, and it is indescribable; *syad-nasti-avaktavyah* - in some ways, it is not, and it is indescribable; *syad-asti-nasti-avaktavyah* - in some ways, it is, it is not, and it is indescribable; *syad-avaktayah* - in some ways it is indescribable. It was a formula I sometimes fell back on when seeking to bring one of Iffy's diatribes to an end.

In the digital age, though, binary black/white, on/off, yes/no definitions had once more become the norm, just as the polarising Christian concepts of good/evil, heaven/hell, light/dark and believer/infidel had dominated the thought processes of our ancestors. This omnipresent pressure to categorise and label, to include or to exclude, to approve or to disapprove, to be or not to be, seemed unnatural to me. Cut-off points, when applied by the legal system, as they so frequently were, inevitably became arbitrary and frankly capricious. The amount of pollution a factory could pump into the atmosphere with impunity, the noise level a festival was allowed to reach, the number of people there had to be at a party for it to be designated an illegal rave - these definitions seemed just as nonsensical as saying how many grains of sand constituted a heap.

Applying fuzzy logic, I was still capable of discerning the better from the worse, of liking and disliking, of holding opinions, but I had come to understand that the world could not be divided with surgical precision into saints and sinners. The free party scene was neither all good nor all bad. We were all of us giddy cocktails of strength and weakness, fear and hope, self-confidence and self-doubt, cynicism and optimism, generosity and meanness, paranoia and positivity.

Although Iffy still scored highly on my fuzzy logic friendship meter, when I checked my liability indicator his reading was rising at a steady rate. He wasn't a total liability, not yet - but he wasn't not-a-liability either. I wasn't sure how many more grains of sand would tip the balance.

"Iffy, *mon ami*, we aren't gonna score here. If you wanted some puff so badly, maybe - just maybe - it would have made more sense to have bought some when you went into the shop that sells puff with some money in your hand, rather than now, when you're skint and we're in the middle of the nu-look ghetto. Hmmm?" My 'hmmm' wasn't as good as Clara's, but I reckon it passed muster nonetheless.

He didn't say anything, but I knew what he was thinking. His expression didn't alter and his body language didn't change, but I just knew he was thinking that I wasn't any fun any more.

And I wished I didn't give a toss, because then I wouldn't have had to feel guilty.

We asked directions off a few people and after traversing some wide open stretches of wasteland found ourselves in front of one of the 1950s tower-blocks that neither wayward planes nor crusading town planners had touched. It was grim. A gang of gangling pre-teen weasels, dressed to the nines courtesy of Gangsters-R-Us, slapped on their toughest screw-faces and tried to sell us some drugs, but even Iffy wasn't tempted.

Not relishing the thought of inhaling the piss-fumes in the lift, we set about scaling the stairs. Even the graffiti was naff. Tags scrawled over tags, they were all about staking claims of possession. There were a few badly drawn spliffs, lots of simplistic Uzis, or Mac-9s, or whatever lethal weapons the kids were fantasising about these days, lots of gang names, and not much else.

Eventually we reached the ninth floor. Iffy was gasping for breath. I was light on my feet and trying not to show it.

"Nice," he panted. "If you like utter shit-holes."

The door to Minnie's flat had taken a bit of a battering. The wood around the lock was badly dented. I raised an eyebrow at Iffy and gave the door a gentle push. It swung open.

AS CIMMERIAN AS IT WAS MEPHITIC

The first thing to hit us, as the cliché goes, was the smell. In fact, it gave us an absolute leathering.

Iffy selected a Stan Laurel from his bag of comedic facial expressions. "Piss. Human and canine. Possibly a hint of feline. Shite. Definitely human. Fags, of course. Straights mainly, with just a hint of roll-up. Beer. Cheap and strong. And unless I'm very much mistaken, I can also detect the subtle odours of crack," he announced, his connoisseur's nose furiously twitching.

"Anyone home?" I called into the flat, which was as Cimmerian as it was mephitic. It was clear that *homo rattus* had moved in since Minnie's death, and her home had been given a new lease of life as a crack den-cum-shooting gallery.

At least I hoped she couldn't have been living in such squalor.

"So what do we do now?" Iffy asked. "Don't reckon we'll find much of any use here," he lamented, surveying the filth and debris that littered the floor.

Discarded needles, some empty tins of super-strength lager and a few broken crack pipes decorated the stained and sticky carpet in the front room. A saggy, balding brown sofa, its cushions pilfered, waved its springs at us like Cthulhu's tentacles. Even the light bulb was missing.

"Let's have a quick shufti, seeing as we're here, then we'll go and chap on the neighbours' doors. Shit, this place is depressing. And to think that ours is called a civilised society…"

The little box of a bedroom could best be described as a

good warm-up for death. After seeing it, a coffin would appear cheerful and homely, and an eternity of nothing would seem a positively uplifting experience. I wondered who had chosen the colours of the wall-paper, and whether they had been colour-blind, terminally depressed, heavily psychotic or down-right evil. If poor Minnie had been sound of mind when she had moved in, I feared she couldn't have held out for long in the face of such overwhelming gloom.

There was a mattress on the floor. It was unspeakable. As a matter of fact, Iffy, neither the daintiest nor the most squeamishly sensitive of people himself, made me promise never to speak of it again.

But our attention was quickly drawn to a few pages of a notebook that lay scattered on the floor. I picked one up and examined it. It was covered in handwriting. The letters, like Minnie herself, were tiny, well rounded and perfectly formed.

"Check this out. This is Minnie's," I said, a reverential tremble in my voice. "And it's in English."

Minnie had often MC'd back in the day -whence the soubriquet Minnie Mouth - chatting rapid-fire lyrics over the DJ's beats, and her English had been extremely fluent.

"You'd have thought the *Politjes* would have taken this with them when they came," Iffy frowned. "If there was anything interesting in it. They wouldn't leave it just lying around."

"Maybe they had a glance and decided it wasn't relevant. Maybe it isn't. Maybe they just didn't give a fuck."

"True. They wouldn't waste too much of their valuable time investigating the death of a second-class citizen in Bijlmer. Or maybe Minnie had it stashed somewhere and the junkies who come here found it."

"And used some of it for bogroll, by the looks of it." I had followed the trail of papers into the lavatory, a room that made the rest of the flat look like a luxury hotel. "It's got a date on it.

Woah, Iffy, dude - it's the day she died. These are her last words."

And then we heard voices in the corridor, and froze. Two voices, both accents typical sandpaper Dutch, though one with its roughness leavened by a touch of African velvet. Hurriedly I gathered up the papers - the few pages that remained - stuffed them into my pockets, and said, "Right, that's us then," loudly enough to alert the newcomers to our presence. I wanted to avoid giving any nervous addicts any nasty surprises.

We stepped into the living room at the same time as two other people entered through the front door. One was tall, black, skinny, tracksuited and baseball-capped; the other was equally tall, equally skinny, but white, bearded, long-haired and dressed in an eye-catching yellow and green African boubou. It was as though they had woken up together and - still dopey from the night before - accidentally donned each other's clothes.

The white guy in the African robe was the first to speak. Surprisingly, his was the voice was with a hint of sunshine in it. While I had never really learned any Dutch, sometimes I could understand whole sentences that sounded like a mixture of guttural English and baby-German. Using these language skills and taking the context into account, I deduced that we were being asked what the fuck we were doing there.

TERMINUS

"And you," I countered, waving my wit in their faces, "what the fuck are you doing in Minnie's flat?"

Switching without a moment's hesitation into English, the way a well-drilled relay team might pass a baton, the greasy-haired blond giant ordered us to get out. "Fucking junkies," he added, which seemed a bit rich.

We had nothing to gain by remaining in the flat and were practically out of the door when he added, "Looking to buy something, Englishman?"

I didn't pause. "No."

"What you got?"

I turned and squinted at Iffy. And then I started walking again.

Until I heard him ask, "Hey, did you know Minnie?"

"Sure. She died, right?"

"Right. She was our friend. We want to find out why she died."

"That's easy, Englishman. Because she lived in Biljmer."

"So what you looking for? White or brown?" I heard the other man say as I stood in the filthy corridor outside the flat, mentally running through the lyrics to the Clash song Should I Stay Or Should I Go.

"Bit of both."

"Okay. How much you want?"

"A rock and a ten-bag."

That made up my mind for me. I was content to hang around if the junkies were going to spill some information about Minnie. I was less prepared to watch Iffy purchase some crack and some smack.

I ricocheted back up the corridor, though, when Iffy said,

"But first tell me about Minnie. Was it suicide?"

"Maybe. She used to come and talk to us sometimes. She wasn't very well in the head, you know? Depressed. Lonely."

That hurt me. I should never have allowed Minnie to feel lonely. How could we hope to do anything to help our sorry world if we couldn't make time to help the people we loved?

I had known she was delicate, sensitive, fragile. We had talked so passionately and so frequently about family and tribe when we had lived on the road, but now I wondered if that had been just so much youthful, idealistic bullshit.

I should have chased her up when she stopped phoning me. Gone to visit her when she had stopped coming to see me. Sent a few emails, shown an interest, let her feel the love. Wasn't that more important than earning a crust and paying the bills on time? As I stood in the wreck of Minnie's flat - in the wreck of her life - I realised that I would have done anything, given anything, to have made it better - and I bitterly regretted having done nothing at all.

All she had been looking for, all her life, was love. People shouldn't die for the lack of such a simple thing.

The man was still speaking to Iffy. "Biljmer's the last stop, you know. Terminus. The basement."

I thought about that. When forty years of struggle had steered you to somewhere like Bijlmer, it was difficult to find a way out. Rent was cheap there, and landlords weren't too fussy about where you worked or if you worked, or where your money came from. Sometimes it was only meant to be a first step, or a temporary solution, but it became difficult to move on once other landlords or employees saw your address. You got stereotyped. You got trapped. A lot of kids - like the welcoming committee we had seen outside - got caught up in the crime. What else is there in the way of career opportunities?

Sure, she could have gone back on the road or found a nice

squat to stay in, but Minnie had apparently lost her will to seek out alternatives, and the fastest way out of the estate was homelessness.

Or death.

"She came here first with a boyfriend," the man went on. "When he went, she stayed. It was as simple as that."

"Didn't she have any plans?"

"Plans? Sure. Every day she had a plan. Get pissed. Now, Englishman, you want to buy something or you want to talk?"

I had to make my mind up. If I stayed it would be trouble. If I went it would be double.

"You still out there?" Iffy called. Feeling foolish for eavesdropping, I remained silent. "Lend us some dosh, will you?"

As I sneaked off with Minnie's last words tucked into my jacket pocket, I heard Iffy begin explaining that while he didn't actually have any cash, as such, he might be willing to enter into some kind of exchange deal.

YESTERDAY'S NEWS.
MONDAY MORNING BLUES

the party's over. i sit cross-legged on the pavement and i don't see faces and they don't see me. i watch legs, boots and shoes, that's what i see and all they see is a beggar's hat. i see all kinds of man, and not all are kind. bear this in mind.

i see sly deceivers, so-called winners and arrogant bruisers, true believers, absolute beginners and designated losers, i see them from the pavement, i see what they do for lust and for money, and what they do it just disgusts me. i've seen the winding paths they follow, and what they seek to find is hollow, but it's shiny and it lures them on and draws them on and drags them on and down and under.

fuck that. fuck that shit. bitter? just a bit. i am a beggar, i watch and sit. bitter? i'm the biter...and the bit.

call me criminal? my needs are minimal. it takes a bottle to placate me and three to sedate me. i beg for booze money and search for sleep. at least the booze is cheap, i raise the bottle and i drink deep. a coin in my cap and i'll outlast the day...or not; i do not care either way. i huddle in the underpasses and choke upon the poisoned gasses. i have watched the world, and i watch it still, for all the good it does me.

i sought to do good, i thought that I could, but look where it got me. i genuinely, truthfully, really, with every waking hour, with all my heart and soul and strength and love and power, i tried to make the world a better place, cried to make the world a better place, would have died to make the world a better place...

i lost.

i got lost.

there were other places. i remember some and i've forgotten more. i've forgotten how to keep the score. i could go back - that forest track, that mountain top, that parking lot behind the factory, that old warehouse, that country barn, out on the moors, that falling down farm, that beach where the waves roll in and out and every night the stars come out and the moon makes patterns on the sea...that field, that river, that lake, the empty spaces we used to take and make our own...but none of them - not one of them - would be the same as the ones i've known. i could find them on a map and hike on foot or hitch by car and i would find them changed because any place, be it near or far, without a friendly face is just a place to be and not a place to live. time does not forgive. so here I am and here i stay and i hear no call to get away, because what would be the point? i smoke another joint.

when I was just a little girl i ran away from home and when i found that i was still so cold and all alone, i ran away to join the rig, back when i was young and thought the world was big. i remember when i joined the crew and how they taught me love anew. they came with the chat and they gave it the large, the future was there at that time in those places, those people, those faces, those tunes...we were reading the runes, re-building the world, making it right, a new solution, making it bright, the tekno revolution come to set you free...

our speakers were there and you heard the warning, we lit up the night, the sun in the morning...and all our hopes and dreams faded under the siren screams of yet another false dawning. the noise we made was doomed to fade, the friends that mattered scattered, our dogs are dead, my family fled and everything we did and said was just a lot of noise. make some fucking noise? the kids outgrew their toys. now the trucks are rusting, the records need dusting and i won't put my trust in people again. i'll just swallow the pain. our revolution's come and gone, the lights that shone have all dispersed, the world is as it was but worse, the echoes of our sound have disappeared overground, the revolution's turned right round and we're worse than when we started.

and i'm back in the same place, home in my dark space, and this time no-one's going to come, not anyone, no tribe in trucks, no tekno troubadours, no cyberpunk warriors with roaring black anarchy and wide open doors.

i raise my bottle to the ghosts and know that i am one of them, the forgotten host, the tribe that tried and failed, paled and sighed; those that weren't jailed, died. a footnote on the page of history, the merest mote, its rage a mystery. yesterday's news. monday morning blues. after the party, the comedown.

and now a ghost comes calling, too late to stop me falling, too little, too late, too bad, that's Fate, and i know it shows no mercy. i'm thirsty not for friendship but only for an end to it, oblivion. i give what i got and take what i am given. not a lot.

why come now?

the party's over.

LISTENING TO THE ELLIPSIS

I was glad someone had found Minnie Mouth's final words. I was glad it was us who found them. I wished she had never penned them, but penned them she had and they told her story well enough. The desolate landscape of the housing estate where she ended up had been a mirror image of the emptiness of her last days, lonely days spent drinking and begging.

She had always seen the world in shades of black and white, compartmentalising all forms of human activity into either good or bad, positive or negative. At the time of our rig, she poured so much energy into our little community that I failed to spot the darkness that lay at the heart of her vision. She equated us with the forces of good that would batter down the walls that hemmed us in; after we split up and went our separate ways, the walls grew to block out all the light.

I read her words while waiting for Iffy and fell into a brooding silence. *We* had been the friends who mattered. We had been the tribe who taught her love anew. We were the ghosts. It seemed that after the soaring highs of our years on the road, she had been ill-equipped to deal with a descent into the mundane. Sometimes I, too, came across locked doors in my consciousness where emotions that used to fill my very being now lay dormant in my day-to-day existence, summonable only as faint memories, as though my brain was a child's scrapbook that had no empty pages left. As Minnie had written: after the party, the comedown.

After the best of times, the rest of our lives.

"She was suicidal, then, would you say?" I asked.

Iffy had joined me on a bench outside the train station. It seemed as good a place as any for dissecting our friend's life. It had only taken him ten minutes to catch me up, which was pretty good going for someone who was barefoot, having apparently just sacrificed his footwear at the altar of Morpheus's little helper, heroin, swapping his trainers for a ten bag and a rock.

A sombre silence hung over us as he finished digesting Minnie's last words.

"Maybe. You know, we all need some positive influences in our lives. The place you live, your surroundings, the things you see every day, the people you hang out with, the books you read, the music you listen to. Whatever. Locked inside their own head, some people can't hack it. Look at this shit."

We spared a moment to look around us.

I nodded.

He nodded.

I actually thought he was nodding off, but the rock he'd presumably smoked was balancing the effects of the gear he'd taken, and he went on, "Grey buildings, loveless streets, advertising billboards, the feet of strangers marching past while your paper cup waits for them to toss you a coin and the craving for a drink gnaws at your sanity...phew. She could've made her life easier, she says it herself, but when a delicate soul starts rolling downhill…"

"The oblivion she was looking for - what did she mean? Was it the oblivion of alcohol? Or total oblivion?" It occurred to me that I was speaking to an expert on the matter.

Iffy, though, glossed over my question and asked one himself: "So who was the friend to come calling? In the last part. The ghost that comes too late. Those two Dutch junkies there, they told me that she'd been expecting to meet someone just before she died...and that she'd been annoying the fuck out of everyone in the flats by playing the same techno tape over and over for days on end."

"Really? D'you think it was the same tape Udo had in his

bag? The Millennium Massacre liveset! But why? And her visitor from the old days. It wasn't you, me or Clara. Allan or Udo? They were still alive at the time. So were Sam and Jacek..."

We sat listening to the ellipsis as Iffy waited for me to round off the list.

"The Gaffer," I said. "Minnie used to worship him. She totally bought into his trip. All his preaching about peace and love and people-power. If she saw what he's become, that could have been enough to tip her over the edge. That bit in her diary about the echoes disappearing overground..."

"Or given how much he seems to feel about us now, and given that he was in touch with Udo before was killed, maybe he literally tipped her over the edge. Into the canal."

"Wow. The Gaffer...So do you think she met her ghost?"

"Maybe. Maybe she did. And maybe he gave her a gentle nudge as they strolled along the canal towpath."

"Wow. The Gaffer. Surely not?"

HOMAGE TO PASITHEA

I had always had a soft spot for the sixth century holy man Saint Augustine, he who wrote, 'Give me chastity and continence, but not yet,' and I figured that our successful investigative work had earned me the right to relax and have a good time with my old mucker, even if he was a stupid fucker who had just swapped his trainers for drugs. Weak-willed sinner that I was, I let Iffy talk me into paying homage to Pasithea, the goddess of hallucination. We shared his magic mushrooms as we slunk into the Megacity Four-style train station in Bijlmer.

Riding back into Amsterdam, just as the trip was coming on strong, Iffy gave me a comradely elbow in the ribs and opened up an unexpected line of conversation. "I'm fed up with blagging off you," he said.

Spots. Leopards changing theirs? "Really?"

"Yeah. Really. You've been bankrolling all of this escapade and I feel like I should contribute a bit more."

"Really?"

"Yeah. Really."

Feather. Knock me down with one.

"'Course, I know we go back a long way. Since we were wet behind the ears. Since we were hip hop to a grass-grower, or whatever the expression is. And sure, we could see it as, well, teamwork, with you chipping in with the financial muscle for our investigations and me providing my unique intellectual rigour, my finely-honed deductive skills and my inimitable detective prowess. Not to mention my outside-the-box, blue-sky thinking."

"Goes without saying, geezer."

"But still."

Books. Turn up for.

Iffy had always had a special relationship with money. Apart from one short, memorable period when he had been unfeasibly wealthy after unearthing some criminals' ill-gotten loot in one of our squats, he had always led a hand-to-mouth existence, the type in which he had enough money to last the rest of his life unless he bought something.

He survived courtesy of a haphazard juggling of signing on (or claiming the Drugseeker's Allowance, as he called it), dealing, begging, borrowing, thieving (only from those who could afford it, he primly insisted), busking, and when he truly had no other alternative, the extremely occasional day of cash-in-hand labouring for a pal with a building firm. In a time of mass unemployment, he claimed to be doing his part for the labour market by leaving the jobs for those who wanted them. *Carpe diem* wouldn't begin to describe his attitude to the future.

This innate disregard for the consequences of his actions had naturally led to a few misunderstandings in the past. Friends, for example, who had naïvely lent him money were sometimes caught unawares by the time it took him to pay them back. As far as I knew he always settled his debts, but he settled them when he had the funds and when he saw the person concerned, and sometimes it took years for the two events to coincide, because - according to his own explanation - he ran on kairological time, rather than chronological. Chronos, he claimed, was too absolute and linear; Kairos took a more contextual and qualitative view of things. Iffy went to bed when he could no longer stay awake; he ate when he was hungry; he took drugs when he wanted to get off his face. It was the natural order of things, he maintained.

His dole money disappeared within minutes. Anyone who was with him on giro day was guaranteed a good time; anyone who wasn't would have to wait for his next windfall. Life with the rig, when money from donations and the bar was communal, had suited him well. In an age of rampant capitalism, he was a rare soul who truly didn't give a shit about money.

And so it was with a certain degree of wonder and - if I was honest - an undercurrent of trepidation that I listened to him explaining that he wished to lighten my financial load. Could it actually be that he was maturing?

"Well, Iffy, I must say I'm touched. I don't give too much of a toss about money myself. Not where you're concerned, at any road," I babbled. "All those times you've fucked up - and, yes, there have been many - have been genuine fuck-ups. No evil intentions on your part, just pure stupidity."

"Glad you see it that way."

"You know it, dude. I don't have to tell you. And in keeping with the spirit in which your offer was made, I shall graciously accept your offer to chip in."

The fact was that my own supply of cash was neither bottomless nor indeed particularly deep. The well wasn't dry, but I wasn't sure how long I could on hauling out buckets before they started coming up empty.

"As it goes, I can only see one tiny problem with this whole scenario," I continued.

"And what, pray tell, could that aforementioned tiny problem be, in your humble opinion?"

It was one of our old games, dating from our teenage years, to adopt a pompous and antiquated style of speech when we were out of our boxes. It amused us.

"The aforementioned problem, as you put it, is, if I may be so bold -"

"*Au contraire*, I insist."

"Is that, unless appearances very much deceive me - and I fear that in this particular case they do not - you are, as the much-loved colloquialism would have it - borassic lint. To such an extent, in fact, that you are literally discalceate."

That threw him. "Discalceate, you say? A fine-sounding word, yet perhaps a mite obscure…"

"Discalceate," I said loftily. "Allow me to expatiate. Without shoes. Barefoot. Unshod."

"It could be worse: I still have my feet. But to return to your premise; yes, you, with your idiosyncratic perspicacity, have struck the thingy on the wotsit."

Nail. Head.

"*Justement*, as our *outre-manche* cousins might say. *Justement*," Iffy continued. "You see before you a man who is financially challenged. A man who is in straits that are not un-dire. I am insolvent. I am impecunious. My belt could be little tighter, my means little slenderer. There is something at my door, and that something is a wolf."

The conversation wasn't really going anywhere, but I was having fun.

Iffy sighed dramatically. "And yet my heart yearns to cross your palms with silver. I feel I shall not rest until I can pay my way. I shall know neither sleep nor peace until I find a way to even the monetary pressure that bears down upon us like the celestial sphere on Atlas's shoulders."

"Your sentiments are those of a true gentleman. Let us speak no more of this matter."

"Wait! Be neither too hasty nor too rash. There is a way…"

"Can it be?"

"It can. There is."

"I am nothing but ears."

"There exists a man of my acquaintance who dwells in the very city towards which we are currently hurtling. A man who is many things to many people, but whom to me has long been known as the purveyor of the purest MDMA crystals that I have ever set my nose upon. My plan - for, aye, it is of a plan which I desire to speak - is to approach this man, this acquaintance, this - dare I say it? - friend, and to enter into a business transaction with him. I aim to purchase some of his goods - his very fucking good goods - and hi myself hither across the border to the land of the Germans, there to flog them on at a whopping great profit. And in so doing, make money for the pair of us to invest in a manner we deem fit."

It was at this point that I realised where he was guiding our discussion.

"And how," I asked, "how exactly to you intend to complete this business transaction when you have so little to offer in the way of remuneration? Your smile is, of course, a smile that has launched a thousand deals on tick, but I fear your friend would be a mug to let you disappear over the border with his very fucking good goods. Do you perhaps intend to sell your bonny but bony behind?"

"My smile, dearest friend, is reserved for you. And my arse is reserved for sitting on and shitting out of, so no, that is not a road or back passage down which I intend to go."

"The nub. I sense the nub approaching. Do I err?"

"Do you, er, what?"

"No - do I err? Double Rs."

"Double arse?"

"Iffy, how much do you want to borrow?"

"A couple of grand should do it."

Later I would look back on this bantered conversation with a certain amount of distaste that wasn't entirely due to the mushroom flavour that lingered in my throat. With hindsight, I would question Iffy's motives for getting me tripped out.

The Mexican mushrooms hadn't taken us out the back door for a full-on mental ransacking. They merely buzzed us up and showed the world in a friendly, bendy and mellifluously mellow light. I was happy, just having a laugh with my mate and for once not worrying about murderers or cogitating about death. I remember thinking that it was like the old days again, bimbling around Europe in good company, getting out of my head and merrily talking shite.

It was only later that - however much I tried to resist the sour qualms of mistrust that billowed up from within - I began to ask myself if Iffy had an ulterior motive for feeding me psychedelic substances. I wondered if he had played on my weakened powers of reasoning and taken advantage of the air of genial bonhomie to talk me into lending him the money.

I hated thinking that about him. I couldn't be sure that it wasn't actually a reflection of my own state of mind. I had always trusted Iffy implicitly to do the right thing by me. It was one of the cornerstones of my life. Okay, I wouldn't trust him with my bank card if he was out on the piss, but that was because he was sure to lose it, not because I was afraid he would steal my money. I probably wouldn't have lent him two thousand euros if I had been straight, just because I knew there were an infinite number of ways in which his plan could fuck up.

The idea that while I was grinning, giggling and innocently acting the arse, he was coldly calculating the misappropriation of my funds was a form of mental torture only matched by the other possibility: that he had been grinning, giggling and innocently acting the arse and I unjustly suspected him of coldly calculating the misappropriation of my funds.

LALOCHEZIA

I couldn't draw such a large amount out of the hole-in-the-wall in one fell swoop, but my credit was good in Amsterdam - at least, it was with Nadine, an old school party head who had now settled down and started a family with her Dutch boyfriend. We called on her at home, had a chat, drank some tea, and she lent me the full sum on the condition I would send her the money back via Western Union as soon as I had safely returned to Berlin on the night train that left that evening from Amsterdam Centraal. After all, she needed to put food on her kids' table. Iffy told her that his trainers had given up the ghost on him, and she dug out an old pair of her partner's boots that would have fitted him perfectly, had he been a clown.

Iffy made a phone call and gave me a thumbs-up sign. He borrowed a backpack from our hostess and left. Still enjoying my mushroom trip, I stayed and drank more tea with Nadine. We avoided the subject of the recent outbreak of sudden death in my old sound system. We talked politics, children, trucks, dogs, holidays, work and the weather, and we waited for Iffy to come back.

We didn't wait long. The doorbell rang. Nadine looked quizzically at me. I heaved an eyebrow skywards in response. She buzzed the door open.

Iffy came in, red in the face and clearly flustered. He rubbed his hands repeatedly over his blooming cheeks.

Uh-oh, I thought.

"What's up?" I asked.

"Fuck. You aren't gonna believe this…"

And the funny thing was that whenever people began a sentence with those words my natural reaction was not to believe whatever came next. My fault, perhaps, for having let cynicism grow like a fungus on my core of credulity.

"I got mugged."

"Are you okay?" I asked, because that's what you do when someone tells you they've just been mugged. Nadine enfolded him in a massive hug, because that's what you do when you instinctively believe someone who tells you they've just been mugged.

"Yeah," he managed, the brave little soldier. "Yeah. I'll be alright."

"What did they take?" I asked, even though I knew the answer.

"Everything."

"The MDMA?"

"I didn't even make it that far."

"My money?" Nadine asked, eyes closed, as if to block out the bad news.

"All of it."

"Shit," I said.

"Shit," Nadine said.

"Fuck," Iffy said. "Fuck, fuck, fuck."

Boffins have conducted experiments that show we have a greater tolerance to pain and discomfort when we swear. Anybody would testify to having felt the cathartic effect of a good old bit of bad language when they have just been dealt a rotten hand in the game of life - in medical dictionaries it is called lalochezia - but it has actually been proved that language is apparently so hardwired into our system that cursing really can have a soothing effect. Taboo words - words that provoke a reaction, be it laughter or censure, from adults when used by kids - become words of power, words that prompt not only a deep-lying emotive response but also trigger a corporeal effect. It is the reason we swear when we hit our thumbs with a hammer or when we hear bad news. It is why Iffy fell to monotonously repeating the F-word as he paced around the room, while Nadine went to open a bottle of Goldwasser and I was submerged in what is so accurately described as that sinking feeling.

"Talk us through it, Iffy-boy," I said when we had all drunk from the bottle. I watched the flakes of gold swirl around as the liquid settled. "Tell us what happened. From the moment you left the flat." I listened to my tone of voice and noted the lack of sympathy it contained, and I wasn't proud of myself.

Iffy either didn't notice or he chose to ignore it. "Well," he began, knocking back another medicinal draught, "I s'pose it was partly my fault. What with the shrooms and all, I didn't have my wits fully about me. And Nadine, that red backpack has got 'tourist' written all over it. Anyway, normally I'd have walked to Bart's yard, it's only about forty-five minutes as the Iffy flies," he continued, turning to me and seemingly regaining some of his composure and linguistic dexterity, "but I knew we had to get the train back to Berlin tonight, so I thought I'd better take the Metro. I didn't want you hanging around here on my behalf."

So that was me included in the blame.

"There were two of the bastards. I wasn't paying attention, to be honest. I hadn't scored yet, so I wasn't para about the Old Bill, and, well, my head was full of mushrooms. And Minnie's diary. I couldn't get that out of my brain."

It wasn't his fault at all, in fact.

"So I'm checking the route on the map, and bam! I get a smack in the face. I see stars and feel my arse hit the deck. Then someone's pulling my backpack off and I hear feet running away, and by the time my head clears I'm all on my tod on the platform."

"You didn't go after them?"

"They'd gone. I didn't know which exit they'd taken.

Course, I had a look about, but they were long gone by then. And I couldn't've run after them in these bloody clown shoes anyway."

"What did they look like?"

"Hardly even clocked 'em. Two white guys. Tall, blonde. Sportswear."

That narrowed it down to about forty percent of the Dutch population.

"But you're okay?" Nadine checked. She was after all a thoroughly decent human being, and she was more immediately concerned about her friend than about her money.

"Yeah, I reckon. Might have a bit of a bruise on my boat race, that's all. But I feel like a right muppet. Me! Getting mugged. Fuck."

"It can happen to anybody. The Dam's full of little criminals looking for easy prey."

"I'm not easy prey! Fuck."

"Don't worry. We'll work it out. Roll a joint?"

And there it was again, the same old refrain. Don't worry. We'll work it out. Roll a joint. Stagger along from mishap to crisis to disaster to fuck-up and roll another joint. My fluffy mushroom trip was beginning to veer towards the darkside. I listened with half an ear as Nadine comforted Iffy and fussed over him like a mother hen while he, the eternal ugly duckling, lapped it up, and I wondered if my whole life was turning into a bad trip.

I had bailed out of the free party scene partly because what it no longer excited me and partly because I could see the collateral damage it left behind, the human equivalent of the scorched and muddied grass that was revealed when our trucks pulled off site at the end of a party. Now that I was sticking my nose back into the scene, I was confronted by premature deaths and lurking distrust.

Momentarily, I wanted to sack it all off and return to the quiet life I had carved out for myself in Friedrichshain, never to answer my phone to old friends again - fuck it, to delete them all from my address book. I wanted to start again in a world of sane people, of normal people, of people who didn't have drug problems, drink problems, money problems or mental health problems, of people who didn't bitch or gossip or listen to rumours, of people who hadn't known each other for so long that they were weighed down by ancient scandals, disputed debts and long-finished love affairs. I wanted to tell Iffy to sort out his swinging wrecking ball of a life and leave me the fuck alone. I wanted to tell Allan Exit to take his broken neck back to Wales and leave it there. I wanted to tell the Gaffer to flounce around the sycophantic club scene as much as he wanted and forget that he ever knew us. I wanted to tell Clara to stop whingeing about the past and stay out of my head. I wanted to stop the world because I wanted to get off.

Quite a turn-around from the anything-for-a-pal sentiments that I had felt at Minnie's flat.

"Hey, mister, snap out of it," Iffy said, giving me a poke in the ribs with his elbow. "Skin up, why don't you?"

I recalled my initial jubilation on stumbling across the techno traveller movement, back when it was a phoenix rising from the ashes of the free festival scene. At first I revelled in the freedom it offered and encouraged. I found my home in a society that ran parallel to - and seemingly distant from - a world that I saw devouring itself in an orgy of uncaring and frequently downright malevolent capitalism. Free parties, free festies, free people: it meant liberty from the chains of profit-chasing greed and all the sanitised, commercialised crap that was spoon-fed to those who didn't like to have too much to think.

Back then I took a deep breath and plunged into the tribal

vibe that predominated on the sites and in the squats - and I was slow to notice the drip-drip-drip of filthy lucre that was diluting and polluting the waters in which I swam. I witnessed people make hundreds of thousands of pounds selling ketamine and then spunk it all on crack. I saw kids barely into their teens mugging tripped-out punters of their phones and trainers. I saw innocence corrupted, beauty defiled, respect disregarded, hope laid low, liberty debased, purity crushed, originality mass-produced, inspiration trampled…It wasn't meant to be like that.

By now my trip was seriously gloomy.

I suspected that Iffy was lying about the mugging. I began to doubt the methods he had used to blag the money in the first place, and to question the way in which Nadine's cash had disappeared. The fact was that Iffy was one of the last people you could imagine being mugged. He looked so scruffy, so shabby and so skint that surely no self-respecting mugger (if that wasn't a contradiction in terms) would waste their time on him. I wanted to search his pockets and look for the two grand or evidence that he had Western Unioned the money to himself or an accomplice.

But I was far too polite to do any such thing.

So my suspicions began to fester within me.

Later that evening we said a bashful farewell to Nadine and jumped on the night train back to Berlin. My mind was racing simultaneously along two tracks: one that had set off from Minnie's diary and was taking me to towards a logical but disturbing conclusion about the Gaffer's involvement in her death; the other that had Iffy's possible duplicity as its origin and was leading me to another bad place. My travelling companion soon dropped into a deep slumber. I watched him dribble down his jacket, and I finally drifted off to sleep about an hour before we drew into Berlin.

A BESTIAL GRUNT AND A HIGH-PITCHED SQUEAK

I was hanging by a thread. I was far from my bed. I had a caustic, searing pain in my head and I was doing a hundred and twenty K an hour along the Autobahn, fast approaching the Czech border. White lines vanished under my van like Morse code with a stammer. A brace of low-flying house martins dashed in front of the windscreen, dots against the dark night sky.

I concentrated on blocking out the blah-blah-babble-wibble that was emanating from the passenger seat of my little truck where Iffy - for it was he - was regaling Helga, Jochen and wee Willy Wanker with a selection of tales from his most memorable border crossings.

"…Twenty-four hours. Twenty-fucking-four hours it took 'em to search every crack, crevice, nooklet and bijou crannyette in the trucks. We finally got to the first ever Polish Teknival on Sunday afternoon. Then the trucks got stuck in the mud as soon as we pulled on site…"

I hated crossing borders. I liked going abroad, but borders freaked me out at the best of times.

"…Fucking stupid, really. We didn't notice we'd forgotten to stash one whole kilo of the whizz till we'd done thirty K into Belgium. There it was, just plonked there on the back seat, a big hoofing bag of base. Thank Dog we didn't get a tug…"

This wasn't the best of times. My body was paying the Iffy tax, having eventually decided to call me to account for the punishment I had been giving it since my old chum had turned up a few days earlier. I made a quick mental tally: booze, MDMA, coke, ketamine, speed, shrooms, a few spliffs and nowhere near enough sleep. My head felt as though a lumberjack had split it with an axe. Then ground it under the sole of his boots. And pissed on it for good measure.

Not too many fags, though. I could be proud of that.

"...What a place to break down! No-man's land between Austria and Germany. And you know what it's like trying to get parts for an old Dodge. Ten days we stayed there. Couldn't go forwards, couldn't go back. Almost starved to death..."

I would have felt considerably more relaxed had I been driving a nice, smart Ford Normal with two point four kids and a soppy black Labrador in the back. Instead I was in my Mercedes van (which had actually been quite a tidy vehicle until it fell victim to the local spray-can posse, who had painted a spliff-toking rastaman on one side and a copper-eating punk on the other side) with Iffy and three other reprobates with criminal records waiting inside to greet the Czech frontier police.

"...I almost felt sorry for him, to be honest. My socks were honking pretty badly at the time. But anyone who chooses a job that involves sticking your fingers up strangers' jacksies gets what they deserve, I s'pose..."

The mission to the Czech Republic had seemed like a good idea at the time, but in fact it was the direct result of my banishment from the Hole coming to an end. Allowed back in my favourite bar, I hadn't even been pissed, so I couldn't blame alcohol for the temporary break-down in my ability to make good decisions. Jochen, an enthusiastic young Berliner I knew, had forced a couple of hefty lines of charlie up my nose, however, and it was with that particular chemical fire in my veins that I had agreed that yes, we absolutely had to go to Jacek's wake, and sure, why not, let's all pile in my van.

"...So in the end we drew our own GB sign with a biro and gave it another go. Bastards told us we had to buy an *official* sticker, but how could we do that at two in the morning? We drove seventy clicks to the next crossing but the cunts must have radioed through ahead of us. Eventually we got to the party just as it was being busted..."

Iffy and I had stayed just twelve hours in Berlin after arriving there in a shape that was far from ship on the night train from Amsterdam. I had practically emptied my bank account and Western Unioned two grand to Nadine, before nipping out for a swift pint in the Hole, where Jochen had reminded us it was the night of the party in Jacek's memory in a forest near Pilsen. Willy had wormed his way on board, as he had done many times before, simply by being there at the right time, and we had picked up Helga from her *Wagenburg* after I remembered her comment about preferring wakes to funerals.

"...No messing, they bunged me on the return flight back. Said I didn't have enough money to support myself in Switzerland for two weeks..."

Iffy had offered to take care of the diesel side of the mission. I had wondered for a moment if he was about to produce a wedge of cash, but he had something else in mind. I parked up for ten minutes in Wedding and he disappeared down the road with a length of plastic hose and a couple of empty twenty-litre jerry cans. He returned a little while later, smelling of diesel and schlepping a couple of full twenty-litre jerry cans.

"...And that's when it kicked off with the fash. Right there, in the bar on the ferry. Well, we couldn't let 'em get away with it, could we?"

My headlights scuttled along in front of us, obediently sweeping the way clear and only once or twice getting waylaid by patches of heavy Saxon fog. There wasn't much other traffic at eleven in the evening, which left me weighing up two options in the muddled confines of whatever had slotted into the place where I used to keep my mind: either the border guards would be dozing, or they would be champing at the bit for a spot of hippy-hassling.

"...You see, back then we didn't know that the *Douanes* in France could operate anywhere in the country. We thought we were safe. Anyway, the Gaffer had just piled all this crap in the back of his truck when we quit the party, and he warned 'em to stand back when they opened the doors. Broke one of the fuckers' arms, which was very funny. Though it did complicate things a tad..."

I turned the stereo down with a flick of a shaky finger and PAIN's bass-heavy Rockin' Cross The Border With A Fat Bag Of Weed faded to nothing. "Border in fifteen minutes. I'm gonna pull over in this lay-by so you can sort yourselves out."

"I'm pretty sorted," Iffy told me.

"Me, too," said Helga.

"Fuck, eh," Willy sniffed. "We'll miss fucking the party if we keep stopping. Eh. Fuck."

I remembered that Clara used to call him NBS, in reference to Thomas Hobbes's definition of the life of man in his natural state: nasty, brutish and short. It was a description which fitted the little German much better than his outsize hoodies ever did. ACAB, as Iffy had once commented to me, but not ABAC: all coppers are bastards, but not all bastards are coppers. The freedom, drugs and lawlessness of the underground techno scene unfortunately attracted a fair few wankers alongside the genuinely sound heads.

"Er, thanks, man," said Jochen.

Jochen was younger than us, one of the few Berliners who had come into the free party scene in the third millennium. Most of the other locals preferred dancing to minimal techno or psychedelic trance, musical genres and cultural subdivisions that to an outsider may have seemed barely distinct from our own brand of electronic music, but which to the cognoscenti were worlds apart. Sometimes it depressed me, the way we humans so frequently concentrated on our tiny differences instead of our enormous similarities and found our own definition most clearly when contrasting ourselves to others.

"Last call for the C-Bahn express then?" said Iffy as Jochen hopped down onto the tarmac of the lay-by.

"He means he'd like another line before you stash everything," I translated wearily. C being cocaine, *Bahn* being line.

"Oh. Right. Sure. Why not?"

Jochen was a coke-head, which made him a popular guy around town, a loosely-tied bag of nerves, and a man who had to stuff a big bag of drugs up his Khyber Pass every time he went abroad. People like him made me want to tell them to take a deep breath and chill the fuck out. Jochen himself was frequently so frayed around the edges that his hands weren't steady enough to chop lines out, a state of affairs which only augmented his popularity. There was usually no shortage of connivers, spongers and blaggers willing to help him out.

Iffy hastily racked up, and I watched with thinly concealed disgust as Willy, using elbows of surprising boniness for one otherwise so well-padded, jockeyed himself into pole position. Coke brought out the worst in people, and the worst that was in Willy was pretty bad indeed.

The lines were duly snorted. The bag of coke was then wrapped in a surfeit of layers of plastic and Jochen ducked behind a tree in the darkness, from whence came the sound of a zip being pulled. It was followed by some prime German swear words, a bestial grunt and a high-pitched squeak before we heard the zip again, and Jochen delicately minced his way back to my van.

Ten kilometres later we bore down on the frontier...and

sailed through unimpeded. We rolled on through the night, powered by some of Jacek's old mixes and a few more lines, and guided by a GPS and a series of text messages to Helga's mobile phone. How much easier it was to find parties now, I reflected, compared to the very first events I had attended, when all we had to go on was a dodgy flier or some scribbled down directions.

THE HOST OF GURNING KIDS ON PILLS

Jacek's wake was a night on which to remember our friend, now dead, with whom we had shared so many adventures. It was a pagan knees-up, an ancient ritual, a tribal gathering in one of the far-flung outposts where British travellers had taken their trucks and their music towards the end of the twentieth century, when neoteric genres of music had been introduced, a new, alternative lifestyle demonstrated, and brave new world views propagated. The initial wave of techno pioneers and breakbeat minstrels, the autonomous, free tribes who wandered the highways and byways, had lit a fuse that became a fire as the locals decided that they could do it too. Sound systems sprang into being everywhere that the convoy went, tiny sparks that grew to give their own light and heat, and Jacek's wake was warmed by their glow.

It was a free party deep in the forest, reached by a mile of bumpy, rutted track that curled its way through avenues of towering trees. It was a drug-fucked mash-up underneath the stars, with no laws except the rule of mutual respect and respect for the environment. There was thumping techno music, cheap booze, a huge firepit and a lot of dancing.

It was, as they say, what he would have wanted.

Unfortunately, by four in the morning I was bored - a shameful admission and a surprise to myself even. In theory, I still enjoyed going out partying, although I rarely got around to it any more; in practise, it seemed, I simply wasn't that up for it. What was I doing here? I wondered, lonely in the crowd, the host of gurning kids on pills - until someone tapped me on the shoulder and I turned round to see an old friend grinning cheerfully at me.

The music could be divided into two kinds: there was the type that I had heard a thousand times before, the bang-bang-bang, spine-crunching, brain melting, ear-drum shattering hardtek sound that had predominated on the European teknival scene since its birth in the mid-nineties, and a newer, funkier, less aggressive sound. Of the two kinds, the former still appealed to me, but it did so in increasingly small doses, probably due to the smaller doses of drugs I now took, while the latter seemed to have more in common with what could be heard in clubs than anything that had come out of the underground scene.

There were about a couple of hundred revellers that night in the clearing in the woods, I guessed. A Czech sound system belted out the tunes. A lone backdrop was suspended from the boughs of an ancient oak. A few lights whipped and whirled over the heads of the dancers.

It was a small party, one that hadn't fallen victim to the decibel overkill known as the Jagger Curse: the eternal search for satisfaction, the endless desire for a just little bit more. Its most destructive incarnation was corporate and national lust for growth and expansion, but sound system crews were equally susceptible to the Olympian call of higher, faster, longer - and louder. As the years went by, the rigs got sillier: five kilowatts, ten kilowatts, fifteen, twenty, thirty, fifty. Teknivals were the worst - or best - with rigs linking up and turning it up *ad infinitum*. Who needed seventy K of sound? We did, apparently.

But there in the forest, the little rig did the job perfectly.

I ate half a pill that one old buddy promised me was the dog's bollocks, but mindful of the morrow's comedown and the long drive back to Berlin, I didn't even consider trying to get anywhere near the ecstatic, anoetic, lost-in-music head-state that I used to adore.

I spent most of the night sat in one or another of the trucks that were parked up in the clearing. I would occasionally catch sight of Iffy as he scampered past, or be joined by him for a few minutes as he mixed a cocktail, downed a shot, sniffed a line or swallowed a pill. I wondered where he got his energy from, though with hindsight I linked it to all the aforementioned lines and pills.

Helga, like me, was there more for the social aspects of the do rather than the raving. Willy drank himself into a walking coma, kept upright only by the cocaine that he blagged off Jochen. Young Jochen himself buzzed around like a particularly demented bluebottle, bouncing repeatedly off the stack of speakers but always going back for more. Some of the older heads were noticeably condescending to him whenever he popped his wide-eyed face into one of the trucks to babble some enthusiastic nonsense, but he was armoured in a coke of invincibility and the snide comments floated harmlessly over his head.

HEAD-FIRST UP HER OWN K-HOLE

"That's one of Jacek's tunes," I said thoughtfully as I watched Juliest mixing me a bleeding Mary. Muffled though it was by the insulation of her Renault Midliner, I nonetheless recognised one of the many hardtek tracks that Jacek had written. "Kill anybody?" went the sample. "A few cops." "No real people?" And thump-thump-thump went the kick-drum.

Juliest handed me a tall glass containing two inches of neat vodka, above which a slice of lime was firmly wedged, itself supporting three inches of tomato juice. Taking a straw in my fist, I pierced the lime with one deft jab and allowed the blood-red juice to drip slowly into the pellucid alcohol.

"To Jacek," Juliest declared. She raised her glass of bleeding Mary and poured a dewdrop of the cocktail onto the scarred wooden table-top that separated us.

"To Jacek," I echoed, copying her gestures and repressing a shudder as I recalled the manner of his passing. He had, of course, bled to death.

"So what was the crack, Juliest?"

"What's the crack, Jack? What's the cracek, Jacek? Where's the house that Jacek built? Over the hills and far away."

I sighed and sipped and made a mental note to be patient. I sipped and sighed, and noted that Juliest still acted like a mental patient when she'd had a line of K or five.

Juliest and I went back a long way - we had both been Hackney squatters back in the nineties, when she had been one of London's biggest ketamine dealers - but our friendship had never advanced beyond the someone-you-know-for-a-quick-chat stage. It was Iffy who had given her her nickname, slightly altering her real name - Juliet - when he had first encountered her in the company of two other friends, introduced respectively as Julie and Julia. Adjective, comparative, superlative.

Like many extreme K-users, she no longer even knew when she was fucked, claiming to be straight when her brain was clearly twisted into a fractal matrix that conceivably revealed to her that all of creation, with its accompanying fractal levels, emerged from vortices: the double-helix spiral configuration, where centripetal spirals in the double-spiral vortex pairs created a stable standing-wave structure at their centres - and her linguistic ability was reduced to that of the barely sentient.

Such are the pleasures and perils of ketamine use.

I had sought her out at the party not for the sheer pleasure to be had out of the rapier-like cut and thrust of her conversation (in fact talking to her was like trying to remove a splinter with boxing gloves) but because I knew she had been doing a lot of business with Jacek recently. Despite it being absolutely none of my business, I had become aware that she had been one of the main customers for his fearsome Polish speed.

"I thought I might see you at his funeral," I said.

She shook her head, her tightly curled blond hair waving like pampas grass in a stiff breeze. "Too hot!" she squeaked. "Burny-burny. Burny-burny-burny. Bert and Erny, mate. Ert and Burny." By which I took it to mean that the Polish police were likely to have had a presence at his funeral.

I supposed that Juliest couldn't always be as out of her nut as she was right then, or she wouldn't be able to run tings with any degree of efficiency. She had told me that she rarely took ketamine now. It was just my luck to find her on a night when she was letting her hair down.

I pressed on, a pluckily determined infantryman sticking my

head up over the top of the trenches and hoping it wouldn't all end in tears. "You must have the full story by now, more or less, eh? When I went to the funeral everything was still a bit of a mystery…"

"It's all a bit of a mystery, isn't it? Why do we do this? Why don't we do that? Why don't they do this and why do they do that?"

The effects of the latest little pick-me-down she had snorted - about half a gram, by my estimation - were starting to manifest themselves. I wanted to quiz her for clues as to whether Jacek's apparent suicide was all that it seemed, and I had to do it before she disappeared head-first up her own K-hole.

Bluntness muscled its way to the forefront of my interrogatory technique, shoving subtlety rudely out of its path. "Did Jacek kill himself?"

"Oh là là. Oh là là là-là-là. That's a biggy. That's a big ol' biggy, that is. Fuck me, that's a biggy. Shee-it, mister. Shee-it."

"Juliest, this is really important," I insisted, wondering silently how much time I had before she drifted off into the outer regions of inner-space and the nether parts of ever further.

"Hardly touches the sides, this K," she blathered. "Not like the old days. Got a tolerance, I have. Even though I don't take it any more. Hardly ever. Still got my tolerance. Still got it, baby. Wowee, have I still got it. Not like Jacek."

My hopes of gleaning something of interest ratcheted down a notch as I saw her assume K-position number one: standing, neck muscles limp, head down, arms drooping. The zombie pose.

"Juliest. Hey. Tell me about Jacek."

She switched seamlessly into K-position number two: the same as number one, but with an additional swaying motion, like that of some flotsam caught up in the irresistible swell of the ocean.

"Have a Calvin Klein," I suggested desperately, keen to drag her back onto *terra firma*. "That'll wake you up." A CK was a cocktail of cocaine and ketamine, and I had been given a wrap of charlie by Jochen as his contribution to the cost of diesel. I hadn't bothered explaining that Iffy had siphoned the fuel.

"And why not? That, my friend, is a very very very very very very very very very very very very good thingy-doo-da-wotsit."

I put my idea into action just as she was entering phase three, where the gentle sway morphed into a veritable lurch. I was reminded of Clara's joke that it took five minutes to walk to a K dealer's house and an hour to get back - the difference was staggering. Just in case Juliest was watching, I made a vague pretence of including some of her K in the mix, and presented her with a stonking fat line of coke. I slotted a rolled-up bank-note into her hand and encouraged her to sniff the line.

"Th's's Jacek's par'y," she mumbled. "I mean, h'isn't even 'ere. Ligh'weigh'. Larry ligh'weigh'. Nice par'y. Shame 'bout Jacek. Couldn't make it. Couldn't take it. Never could. Shame."

"There's a line for you on the table," I reminded her. And damn me, if she didn't slip into phase four: the slump against the wall. "Juliest. Take the line. Juliest. Juliest?"

"Hmmm?"

Enough poncing about. I manoeuvred her down onto the padded bench in front of the table. I placed her hand, still clutching the rolled-up note, next to the line of powder. Gently lowering her head, I let old habits take over. I breathed a sigh of relief as she reflexively snorted the coke.

I had to keep her talking and hold the K-hole at bay. "Had you seen Jacek before he died?"

"Poor old Jacek. Too much, too young. Where'm I gonna get my billy now?"

Frankly, I didn't give a monkey's. My old Polish travelling companion, the sometimes secretive, always discreet, softly-spoken, behind-the-scenes deal-maker, had stepped up a few gears in his drug dealing in the years running up to his alleged suicide, and his premature death would leave a gap in the market - but not for long. There would be plenty of other opportunists looking to get rich quick. Jacek himself had plugged the hole in the supply of amphetamines that tighter drug laws in Holland had created. He had converted from being a mid-size all-round dealer into a dedicated purveyor of industrial quantities of fiercely strong and slightly mind-bending Polish speed. He had gone from making quite a lot of money to making a lot of money, and although I knew that most of his customers were old heads from the free party scene, I had heard and not altogether dismissed rumours of an involvement with Bulgarian gangsters.

"Are you gonna work with the Bulgarians now?" I asked.

"What fucking Bulgarians? Uncle Bulgaria? There are no Bulgarians. There never were any Bulgarians. What's a Bulgarian? D'you know any Bulgarians? I don't. Even the Bulgarians don't know any Bulgarians."

"Jacek didn't work with some Bulgarian heavies?"

"Jacek worked with his dad's mate's sister's boyfriend's neighbour's dog's auntie's boss's cousin's Christmas tree, darlin'. Not the fucking Bulgarians."

"Listen. I just want to know what happened and why. Help me out here. When did you last see him? Did he have money worries? Debts he couldn't pay? Had someone ripped him off? C'mon, help me out."

She looked at me through half-closed eyes. "Jacek was a cap'talist. I'm a cap'talist. Ev'ryone crit'cises me for bein' a cap'talist 'cos I make money. Well, I don't care. I'm not 'shamed. Gonna retire soon. Gonna buy a house on a beach, an' I'm gonna sit in the sun and take K all day. Jacek built a house. Nice house. The house that Jacek built. Ask your other mate."

"So he was alright for money? Was he depressed, though?"

"We're all fuckin' 'pressed, us cap'talists."

"Did he slash his wrists, Juliest?"

I supposed that it was possible. Selling large quantities of illegal drugs was a high-stress business. When we were travelling together, Jacek rarely talked about his fear of being busted, although I knew it must have nibbled away at his serenity; he preferred to moan about his day-to-day concerns about collecting money that was owed to him and paying his suppliers back.

His was an ephemeral business. He'd had no pension to look forward to and no state benefits to back him up. If he fell ill, he couldn't work. If a contact vanished behind bars or into a different life, he had to seek alternative business partners, and they weren't to be found in the Yellow Pages. If something went wrong on a deal, he was left to carry the can or sort things out however he saw fit. From what he had told me, everything could be done sweetly on a matey-matey basis, where all parties got what they needed and everyone benefited - until the stakes grew to a certain magnitude and the rules of naked capitalism took over.

A microcosm of society.

"'S dead, f' fuck's sake. Wha' more d'you wanna know? 'S gone where we're all goin' one day, an' the bastard ha'n't e'en sen' me a postcard. Wha' the fuck does it ma'er if he did it or if someone else did it? It's done, innit? Done, dead, gone. Get it? He got it. He got on the early boat. We're gonna get the la'er one. Goin' to the same place, though. Shame he'll never live in his house."

The Colombian marching powder was working, overhauling the Indian crawling powder.

"I didn't know he'd bought a house," I mused, thinking aloud. "Seems a strange thing to do if was going to top himself. C'mon, Juliest, you must have wondered what happened. Don't try to tell me you haven't. When did you last see him? Do you remember?"

"Look," she sighed, "I came here to get off my tits and have a party. You're giving me a hard time about Jacek. And I don't know how much K you put in that Calvin Klein, but I'm in imminent danger of being straight here. Give it a fucking rest, will you?"

Disconsolately I watched as she heaved herself to her feet and began scraping out the contents of the frying pan in which she had cooked up her K. She tipped a pile of glassy, flat crystals onto the table top, prodded them into an approximate line - more of a mound, really - and sniffed them up her nose before I could intervene. It was my turn to sigh.

"Just tell me what I want to know. Then I'll leave you in peace. I promise. When did you last see him?"

"The day he died."

BIKINI OR ONE-PIECE

"Where?"
"At his new gaff."
"Where's that?"
"Near Krakow."
"How was he?"
"Fine."
"Depressed?"
"No."
"Stressed?"
"No."
"What did you talk about?"
"The Jacobite Rebellion. Cod fishing off the Orkneys. Nature versus nurture. Bikini or one-piece. Wave or particle. What d'you think we talked about?"
"Business."
"Bravo."
"The Bulgarians?"
"Repeat after me: the fucking Bulgarians do not fucking exist."
"Okay. The fucking Bulgarians do not fucking exist. How long did you stay?"
"Couple of hours."
"Was he alone?"
"Yes. He was waiting for someone to arrive."
"Was he caning the billy himself?" It was a possibility - he had kilos and kilos of the stuff, so maybe he was taking it every day. If so, then speed psychosis was a distinct likelihood.
"I told you - he was a Larry lightweight. Had an occasional line now and again, just as a tool to stay awake."
"Did he still have his gun?" I remembered when he bought

it, one winter when we had been squatting an old factory in Marseilles and the neighbourhood gangsters had been threatening us. Jacek had hooked up with some elderly Corsicans and bought himself a pistol for protection.

"I think so. Yes."

Like Iffy had said back in Berlin, Jacek had a thing about blood. When Willy had attacked Allan Exit with an axe at CzechTek and there had been an awful lot of blood sloshing around behind the decks, he had gone a paler shade of white and left us to clear up the mess. If he had suicide on his mind, he would surely have bitten a bullet instead of opening his veins.

I was running out of questions. I was also running out of time again as Juliest slipped back into the initial phase of her descent into a K-hole that the line of charlie had merely delayed.

"Did he talk about the future?"

"Eh?"

"The future. What was he gonna do after he saw you?"

She giggled. "No' very much, I reckon."

"Why do you say that?"

"Told you. He was a lightweight. A blue Rizla."

"So?"

"He couldn' take it. Couldn' fake it. Couldn' bake it. I can. I've go' a tol'rance."

She so clearly had no such thing. The ketamine was working its dreary magic on her again. The last line she had taken was the kind that regular users take just before they leave the house. Occasional users, like Juliest these days, would take one that size just before they left consciousness.

"Did you give him some K, Juliest? Is that what you're saying?"

"Did I give him some K? Did I? Did I?"

"Did you?"
"Did I?"
"You did?"
"I did?"
"Fuck's sake! Did you give him some K, or didn't you?"
"No."
"No?"
"Yes."
"Yes, you did? Or yes, you didn't?"

Unfortunately, that was difficult even for me to understand, and I hadn't been slapping my brain around with horse tranquillisers.

"Yes."
"Yes, you gave him some K?"
"No. He bough' some. For your mate who was comin' round later. From your rig."

My mate? I replayed the earlier part of our conversation and pressed pause when I heard her say, "Jacek's got a house. Nice house. Ask your other mate." It had slipped under my radar at the time, but now it threw up an obvious question.

"Which mate?"
"Hmmm?"
"Juliest! Don't wig out on me now. Hold it together. Which mate?"
"Which mate? Rig matey."
"Rig matey? Which rig matey?"
"Which rig, matey?"

Fuck! I screamed. Silently.

"You gave some K to Jacek. For someone who was going to see him after you left. On the day he died. Who was it?"

"Jacek's go' no tol'rance. Bloody ligh'weigh'. Give him a line an' he's anyone's. 'Cept he's dead, of course. Brown fuckin' bread. Where'm I gonna ge' my billy now, eh?"

"Who was it, Juliest?"

"Jacek. 'S dead. Di'n't you know?"

And bugger me backwards if she didn't shift directly into K position five: on her back, eyes open but unseeing, her body in total shut-down while her brain ripped through the night's static to trip the light fantastic.

I racked myself up a monster line of cocaine, mixed myself a bleeding Mary, and watched the bloody drops of tomato juice drizzle down into the vodka.

I wondered who had ordered the K. Jacek, as Juliest had in fact repeatedly hinted, had zero tolerance for ketamine, and as a result would be rendered immobile, useless, helpless and completely at the mercy of anyone in his company if he snorted a line. Lines of K could easily be mistaken for lines of speed. Someone could have spiked him. Said someone could then have slashed open the veins on his wrists and let him bleed to death. And that someone was a mate of mine, someone connected to our old rig.

Unfortunately, Juliest wouldn't be answering any questions for the ensuing half hour or so. I settled down to wait.

And then the music stopped.

UNIFORMED NE'ER-DO-WELLS

The sudden absence of noise - an enormous, gaping hole - normally implied one of three things.

It could have been the result of some soon-to-be-rectified technological malfunction, such as one of the many amps, equalisers, limiters, compressors, mixers or decks going on the blink.

It could have been due to human error: a collective failure to keep the generator topped up with diesel, for example, or wee Willy falling on the decks or accidentally tripping over and unplugging a cable.

Or it could be that the forces of boring order had arrived to shut down the party.

I dared a peek out of the side door of Juliest's wagon. Under the chaotic reel and jig of the lights, under the blinking, blinding glare of the strobe, in amongst the many shaved heads, baseball caps and dreadlocks on the dance floor, my gaze settled on one militaristic peaked cap and a dozen or so shiny black helmets with their visors flipped down.

Dog alone knew how the Czech police had found us, lost as we were in the middle of the woods. I didn't think that there were any neighbours nearby who might have complained about the noise pollution. We weren't actually bothering anyone and we would all have been out of there by the next evening, having cleared up any mess we had made, but there the cops were, seemingly intent on bothering us. The miserable bastards.

I wasn't clued up on the local laws regarding unlicensed musical gatherings - not that the cops would necessarily stick to them anyway. Generally it paid party organisers to be up to speed on the letter of the many laws that affected them. One UK MP had said, when talking about punk, "If pop music is going to be used to destroy our established institutions, then it ought to be destroyed first," and this was the attitude behind Section 63, sub-section 1(b) of the Criminal Justice and Public Order Act 1994. It was the first British law to be passed against a particular type of music: 'sounds wholly or predominantly characterised by the emission of a succession of repetitive beats.' Other nations later followed Britain's lead as politicians across the world reacted to the free party phenomenon. As a matter of interest, back in the thirties the Nazis had passed similar legislation against jazz, music they considered 'conducive to dark instincts.'

I watched as some of the rig posse made a forlorn attempt at negotiation, remembering days past when I had been in their position. I often wondered what went on in the minds of the coppers who were sent to shut down parties. Observation and reflection suggested that they were just following orders - one of the saddest, most depressing and most infuriating phrases in the annals of our history. On some occasions it was possible, via polite social intercourse, to persuade the police that they were better off allowing the party to continue, illegal though it may be. From a logical standpoint it was preferable to keep all the revellers in one place, rather than to have them roaming around, pissed off, with nowhere to go and nothing to do.

When the police turned up already sporting their Robocop gear, though, the chances of anything other than an early cessation of festivities were so anorexically slim that you could lose them down the back of a sofa. Once a high-ranking officer had been dragged away from the comfort of his bed and all his minions had got their party outfits on, the staring match was well and truly underway. The best to be hoped for under such circumstances was that the punters would be allowed to disperse unhassled, without being subjected to drug searches, breath tests or random beatings, and that the sound system wouldn't be impounded.

I ducked back into Juliest's truck and cursed my luck. She was still out for the count. Although I had my suspicions, it looked as though I would have to wait to confirm which one of my friends had called on Jacek and ordered some K on the night he died.

Meanwhile, I had to rustle up the little crew of Berliners I had brought with me. If I read the situation correctly, Iffy would be in the thick of the action, trying to charm the police into letting the party continue. Helga would be carefully weighing up the possibilities and looking for me. Jochen would be panicking (and most likely nipping into the darkness of the tree cover to reinsert his bag of coke up his jacksie) and Willy would either be mercifully inanimate or annoyingly and counter-productively engaged in winding up the gatecrashers.

Reluctant to let Juliest slip out of my clutches when I was sure she had vital information to tell me, I was just deciding to leave it as long as possible before bailing out when I saw the first baton raised in the air. I watched it come down. On Willy's head. As good a place as any, I thought - but I didn't really mean it. Willy might have been a piece of shit, but he was ours, for better or (usually) for worse, and no steroid-pumping, big-bellied, gun-toting, baton-wielding, sunglasses-wearing, trouble-making, mean-spirited, self-obsessed bag of shit Czech police bully-boy had the right to hit him at a party.

There was a scuffle around the decks as things heated up, but it swiftly died down. The older, wiser heads persuaded the younger, less experienced party-goers that on this occasion their numbers weren't sufficient to permit a bunch of pissed-and pilled-up hippies to see off a squad of tooled- and psyched-up riot police.

It was one of those moments that I hated. At the risk of going cheese-core, a little part of me died every time a party was busted. Every time the men in grey suits ordered the boys in blue to stop those colourful people having a good time, the world became a little darker.

When the free party scene had first taken off, alarm bells must have rung in the heads of certain vested interests who saw the advent of free entertainment for the masses threaten their precious profit margins. The ecstasy revolution could have been viewed as a direct assault on the brewers and club-owners who paid for their little luxuries out of the alcohol they sold - and what if the craze really took off and spread to other sectors?

The concept of the youth organising themselves to do what they wanted merely because they wanted to and not in order to make money was anathema to the authorities. Usefully for them, they had an army of thugs on hand to try to stamp out the pests. Eradication would prove to be beyond their means, so a policy of harassment was left in place.

And thus began the end. The wide-eyed people who minutes before had been dancing under the stars were suddenly left facing the unhappy prospect of a long drive home through the Czech night. Now in the forest glade there was only confusion and disappointment where laughter and joy had been. The generator continued to tick over, and the sound system lights only added to the air of disorientation. The scramble started to find sober drivers and to get a vehicle for everyone, to locate jackets and dogs and record bags, and to say hurried farewells as uniformed ne'er-do-wells harried and pushed and shoved in the darkness.

I gave a last forlorn shake of Juliest's recumbent body. No dice. One of her friends clambered into the truck and I ducked out, destined not to learn the identity of her ketamine customer. As the sound system crew set about dismantling their rig, I returned to my van and awaited the return of my little gang of Berliners.

Helga was the first to surface, and while she kindly captured Jochen and scraped Willy up off the floor, I told a sweat-soaked Iffy about Juliest's revelation.

It was difficult to tell if the news sank in. There was a lot of vigorous nodding and a great deal of lip-chewing on his behalf, and he seemed to grasp the details enough to say, "The old friend visiting, the suspicious death - got to be the Gaffer again, right?" which was pretty much my line of thinking too...but Iffy seemed principally interested in the possibility that Juliest might still have some K left to get rid of.

POLISHING MY MEDALS AND FLIRTING WITH HIS GIRLFRIEND

It was mid-morning when we rolled back into Berlin, and I felt I deserved a little R and R. Just one day that didn't involve travel, booze, drugs - or Iffy. I wasn't sure it was a good idea to take a break - time was of the essence - but if I didn't slow down and take a breather I was in serious danger of collapse. I was hankering after my cosy routine of waking up, mooching down to the bakery, taking my time over a healthy breakfast, checking my website for orders, posting some records to their new owners, going for a run in the early evening, following it up with either a sociable *Voku* or an anti-social dinner at home, and finally enjoying a peaceful, mildly misanthropic evening in with a good book.

First on my list, though, was a long-awaited get-together with my old pal Hypnos, the god of sleep, whose divine company I had been missing of late.

"What're *you* thinking of doing?" I asked Iffy innocently after I had dropped the rest of my passengers off.

"Eh?"

"Well, y'know, I was just wondering if you'd got any plans?"

"Why?"

"Why? Well, just, y'know, because I was thinking of heading home. Getting some kip. I'm hanging."

"Sounds good."

I had been hoping he would leave me to my own hebetudinous devices. I had long since rid myself of the habit of sharing my living space with anyone, and although Iffy wasn't the type of house-guest for whom you had to cook or clean, he was the type who made you listen to his stream-of-consciousness crap until he noticed his voice was drowned out by your snores.

"I was thinking of getting my head down for a few hours, that's all," I said. "Need a bit of peace and quiet, I reckon."

"Good plan."

This was proving tricky. My conscience would never normally have allowed me to hint too heavily that Iffy should fuck off for a while, not because I was afraid of hurting his feelings, but because it wasn't a very nice thing to do. Ever since the mugging incident and the nagging doubt it had engendered, however, I had been feeling less prepared to put myself out on his behalf.

"Isn't there anything you want to do?"

"What, me? Nah."

"No little missions you want to go on? Nobody you ought to catch up while you're in town?"

"Nah."

"I see. Hey, there's a circus skills workshop on in Revaler Strasse today. You still into the old juggling?"

"Ah, you know, bit rusty these days. Swapped my fire clubs for an ounce of skunk." He swung his dusty boots up onto the dashboard and closed his eyes in beatific contemplation.

"You haven't even been down to Carlo's bar yet," I persisted. "He does a wicked brunch. And he'd be well chuffed to see you."

"True. Good man, our Carlo. We could bimble down there later if you're up for it."

"I'm cream crackered. But you go ahead."

"Might do. Later."

I began to wonder if he was doing it on purpose. If I had been listening to the conversation rather than taking part in it, I would probably have been repressing a sneaky snigger at his obstreperousness. Now that I was the victim, I was reminded of more than one old friend referring to Iffy as 'that annoying bastard.'

And then the Fates came charging to the rescue in the unlikely form of a phone call from Jochen. He had left his house keys in my van, he told me, and asked if he could nip round to pick them up. He only lived two streets away.

"Iffy," I started, breaking the shell of a plan, "would you do me a favour?"

He opened his eyes and did his thing with his eyebrows.

"Jochen needs his keys, and to be honest I'm not really up for seeing him again."

"Me neither, as it goes."

I pressed on. "I mean, he's sound, our Jochen, but you know what he's like the day after a party…"

"Not really."

"Well, me, for instance, boring fucker that I am, all I want to do is get some sleep. Not like Jochen… he doesn't know when to call it a day. He's always got ounces of coke and he just sits there snorting away like there's no tomorrow, listening to tunes on his big ol' sound system. He only leaves the flat to stock up on beer."

"Oh yeah?"

"You wouldn't do us a favour, would you, and take him his keys back? I'm sure he'll make it worth your while."

"Well, I s'pose I could. If that's what you want, like. I wouldn't mind catching some zees myself. But, hey, if you want me to leave you alone for a bit, why don't you just say so?"

I found myself denying the evident truth of the matter. "No, no, it's not that. It's just…"

"It's alright. I can take a hint. You get your beauty sleep, princess. I'll catch you later. Somewhere. Most likely. If Jochen doesn't kick me out straight away," he sniffed.

I parked my van and located Jochen's door key. In a

momentary flurry of contrition, I also handed Iffy a spare key to my flat.

"Come over when you're ready, eh," I called after his hunched, retreating back, marvelling at the ease with which he sprayed guilt-trips around. He was going off to do the things he liked best - getting twatted and listening to loud music - and yet somehow I was left feeling as though I was sending him to the front line of a war zone while I dozed in an armchair, smoking cigars, drinking champagne, polishing my medals and flirting with his girlfriend.

GETTING ALL THINK-Y

Back on the ranch, I saddled up my faithful old kettle and took some hot water for a canter over Darjeeling way. I harnessed up a couple of houmous-laden hot bread rolls and then hit the hay.

Hypnos, though, perhaps miffed at my lack of attention over the past few days, clearly had the hump with me and refused to answer my prayers. I figured the next best thing to a nap was a natter, so eschewing relaxation for conversation, I decided to give Clara a call.

"*Guten Tag, mein Herr*," she answered.

"And a very *guten Tag* to you, Clara. Are you busy?"

"Are you joking? I'm due in court in an hour's time, I've got two new clients in my waiting room, I've got a report to finish by tomorrow morning, there's a meeting of the partners scheduled for three o'clock, my hair needs cutting, my bathroom needs re-tiling and my fridge needs filling. Is this call important?"

"Oh. Right. I just wanted to run a few things past you, I suppose."

The wonders of modern telephony faithfully transported a sigh across a thousand miles and deposited it directly in my ear like a dumper truck ridding itself of ten tons of sand.

"Go on, then. What's new, Lone Ranger? Are you and Tonto still putting the world to rights?"

"Well, Tonto's starting to get on my tits a bit, as it goes."

"Hold the front page. I'd been wondering how long it would be before the Iffy Effect kicked in."

"I thought you liked Iffy?"

"I like summer storms in the Pyrenees. I like picking blackberries on crisp autumn mornings. I like the sound of rain on the windowpane when I'm curled up with a good book and a glass of Rioja in front of a roaring log fire. I like getting some corporate bastard bang to rights in front of a judge. I like eating pizza in a real Italian restaurant."

I blinked and looked at my phone.

"Are you telling me that you don't like Iffy?" I hedged.

"I'm saying I wouldn't squeeze him into my suitcase if I was packing for a one-way trip to a desert island."

"Well, no, I can understand that. That's fair enough, that is. Don't you ever see him about in London any more?"

"I used to see him now and again. Not for a while, though. Our paths haven't really crossed of late. Which is funny, because until I suffered a rare moment full of charity but lacking in clarity and lent him a grand that he swore he desperately needed to pay off some debt, we used to be in much more regular contact. I did broach the matter with him when you were getting the drinks in after Udo's funeral, as it goes. He made all the right noises - except the noise of bank notes exchanging hands. And you know what?"

I didn't.

"I've been asking myself if maybe it isn't such a bad deal. I pay him a grand, and he stops hassling me with his perpetual stories of poverty, misery, eviction, addiction and woe."

"That's a bit unfair," I protested on my old friend's behalf.

He was happy-go-lucky, was Iffy. He was the salt of the earth, the Weeble who always bounced back up with some sordid tales from the underground and a cheeky smile on his face.

"He can wind you up a bit, of course. But that's just Iffy, isn't it? I mean, that's all part and parcel of his roguish, boyish charm. Right?"

I had phoned Clara in order to grumble about my old mucker. Instead, I found myself defending him.

"If you want to put it down to boyish charm, that's your look-out, buster. Just for your interest, though, I bumped into Serious Lee and Rotten John last week, and they implied that his *persona* is not particularly *grata* in their squat any more, boyish charm notwithstanding. Things started going missing, apparently. Fingers were pointed. Voices were raised. He was sent packing."

"Oh, come on, Clara. That's bullshit. No way. Iffy would never rob off mates."

"I'm just saying. Merely reporting the facts inasmuch as I understand them."

"Since when was he crewed up with Serious Lee and Rotten John anyway?"

"Oh, since around the time that the Saboteur posse got fed up with his boyish charm and asked him to leave. Didn't he mention that?"

"Er, not as such, no. Did Lee and Rotten John have any proof?"

"Not concrete, no. But circumstantial evidence led them to make a logical deduction. I presume that nothing similar has happened while he's been in Berlin? I take it he's still with you. I imagine it hasn't crossed your mind that he's there to sponge off you because he's burnt his bridges back in London and you're an easy mark? Hmmm?"

Dogdammit, there she went again with her "hmmm?" I decided to change the subject.

"Forget about the Iffy-boy for the moment. We've got news for you."

"Have you, by golly?"

"About the murders."

"Oooh. So they're definitely murders now, are they?"

"Well, yes, we think so."

"Is that the latest message beaming down from Planet Iffy?"

"It's a logical deduction."

"Based on…"

"Based on our investigations. Listen, Clara, I wish you'd take this seriously. This is life and death stuff - Minnie's death, and Jacek's and Udo's and Sam Saoule's, and your life, as well as mine and Iffy's and Allan's. I already told you about our trip to Kotti, and what that junkie told Iffy. That Udo was pushed. What you maybe don't know is that Allan Exit's in hospital. Someone tried to kill him by breaking his neck, Clara, right in front of us. Someone who knew about his weak point."

"The way I heard it, he got in a fight when you lads were out on the lash"

"Will you stop doing that?"

"What? Getting all think-y?"

Anyway. "Since then, we've been out and about." I filled her in on our discovery of the pages from Minnie's diary and our trip to Jacek's wake. "Remember Juliest?"

"'Fraid so. How was she? Face down in a puddle or scraping her face along a wall?"

"She was a bit weary," I admitted euphemistically. "But check it out: she told me that Jacek had a visitor on the night he died, and that that the visitor bought a bag of Juliest's favourite tipple." Speaking on the phone, it paid to be circumspect, but Clara would know what I was talking about. "Jacek would never have slit his wrists, never mind how bad things were - and things weren't bad at all. He'd bought a new house, business was good. He had no reason to top himself. But the visitor that Juliest told me about - they could have spiked Jacek up and then done the dirty. What do you say to that?"

"I have to ask the obvious question. Who was this visitor?"

I hesitated. "Yeah, well, she didn't actually tell me who -"

"I see. You didn't think to ask? You didn't think that snippet of information could prove pertinent?"

"Let me finish. It was someone from our old rig! It's got to be the same person that Minnie was planning to meet!"

"But you didn't ask Juliest who?"

"Of course I asked! It's just she was very tired by that point. She kind of nodded off before she could tell me. Then the party got busted. And I can't get hold of her phone number anywhere." It sounded a little feeble, even to me.

"She was so 'tired' that she fell asleep in the middle of your conversation, but nonetheless you'll take her word as gospel truth? I see. And let me get this right. You and your rusty sidekick now believe that someone from our rig is murdering the rest of us? Is that what you're telling me? Have you figured out the motive yet, or weren't you going to bother with that?"

"It's something to do with the Millennium Massacre party in Italy. The tape in Udo's bag, remember? And Minnie had been listening to an old techno set too - probably the same one, though we can't be sure."

There was a pause, during which I imagined Clara raising her eyes to the heavens. I wasn't doing a very thorough job of convincing her of the gravity of the situation, I sensed. She was trotting out too many hmmms for my taste, and she kept asking awkward questions.

"So who is it? Who's your prime suspect?"

"There's only one, isn't there?"

"Go on. But make it quick, I really need to crack on with my life back here in boring ol' Reality."

It was time to lay my cards on the table.

BECAUSE...BECAUSE HE'S IFFY

"Minnie, Jacek, Sam and Udo are dead, so it isn't one of them."

"Can't fault your logic there."

"Allan's been attacked and is at death's door so it can't be him. Same goes for you. You were hit by a four-by-four, weren't you? Like the one we saw outside the Gaffer's gig."

"And like about a million others."

"Oh, come on. You must admit, it's a hell of a coincidence."

"No, I'll admit that it's a coincidence. Which, I think you'll find is not the same as proof of anything."

"Whatever. Whether it was an accident or an attempted murder, the point stands that you aren't out to kill us all."

"How can you be sure?"

"What? Don't be silly, Clara. It isn't you. It isn't me and it isn't Iffy, so that only leaves one person."

"Why isn't it Iffy? Because he's your mate?"

"Because...because he's Iffy. He's sound."

"He's halfway to being a junkie. He's always had a tenuous hold on reality and his barely sustainable lifestyle ensures that every day his grip slips a wee bit looser. I wouldn't trust him as far as I could throw him these days."

"It's the Gaffer, Clara. It has to be," I insisted, refusing to be side-tracked from my monorail of thought. "Don't you see?"

"Well, that's lovely. Thanks for that. I'm glad you've been keeping yourselves occupied. Now, I hope you'll excuse me, but I really do have important shit to be doing. Enjoy your defective investigations, boys."

"Detective," I corrected her.

"Pardon?"

"Detective. Detective investigations. You said defective."

"I know what I said. Anyway, say hello to Tweedle Dee from me."

I would have slammed my phone down, if only it hadn't been a mobile. And if Clara hadn't already hung up.

"Fuck!" I hissed, all alone, my fist clenching tightly around my phone.

THE STENCH OF THE SHIT-PITS

To fall asleep. The vertiginous descent into unconsciousness; the mind-numbing, headlong tumble through darkness into dream. To fall - for a fall it is. Anyone who has ever been shaken awake while sliding down the steep, steep slope to sleep remembers that feeling, that falling, that infinite plunge, that downward, intimate lunge, as the shackles of the here and now evaporate. The weight ascends and the wait ends as Hypnos hugs us and welcomes us home. If that is what dying feels like, then death is nothing to fear.

Anyone disturbed in mid-fall finds themselves halfway across the bridge between worlds, halfway through the door to the soul.

As I lay on my bed, squeezing my eyes shut, I eventually concluded that the bridge was down, I had lost the key to the door, and that Hypnos was still ignoring my calls.

Prior to my chat with Clara, I had just about convinced myself that the Gaffer was offing my friends. Judging by his behaviour when Clara and I spoke to him, he clearly had no love lost for his old comrades from the wild, travelling days of his youth, but nonetheless had arranged to see Udo on the day he died. He was the most likely candidate to have met Minnie in Amsterdam, and to have been the 'rig matey' who Jacek was hooking up with on the night his wrists were cut. I myself had told him that Allan was in town just hours before the old traveller was attacked. Clara had also been hit by a car similar to the sort the Gaffer preferred. I intended to check out the circumstances of Sam Saoule's death, and I suspected I would find clues to the Gaffer's involvement there as well.

So. That was what had been going through my mind before I called Clara. Clara, though, as was her wont, had pissed on my parade. Her scepticism now forced me to pose myself some serious questions.

Had I, as she implied, been lured on board the Iffy-train and taken for a ride? Caught up in the moment and entangled in the excitement of our investigations, had I allowed Iffy's enthusiasm to create a conspiracy when all there was was a series of random events? Was I tripping? And if so, was it Iffy's trip I was trapped in?

I decided to reappraise the situation from what I guessed would be Clara's Cartesian perspective.

Udo came to Berlin to party with the Gaffer. Got completely *rattus rattus gluteus maximus* with Helga on his first night in town. Got up the next morning, not knowing his *gluteus maximus* from his *humerus, ulna* and *radius*, took the wrong U-Bahn, lost his balance - hardly a rare occurrence - and stumbled off the platform in front of an on-coming train. Iffy claimed a smack dealer claimed that he was pushed, but junkies are unreliable witnesses, and anyway there was no physical description of the pusher by the, er, pusher, except that he was clothed in black.

Minnie had become a sad, lonely, clinically depressed alcoholic, begging for booze money and eking out a sordid existence in a pitiful flat in the Dutch ghetto. She drowned one night while out walking next to the canal, probably drunk. She had possibly been visited by an old friend, any old friend, who might have made her realise how empty her life had become since she stopped travelling. Maybe she had lost her will to live - or maybe she had just lost her balance.

Jacek sold vast quantities of amphetamines. Could have cut his wrists while suffering from speed psychosis, or been killed by some heavy gangsters. Juliest, out of her box on K, suggested that someone from our old rig had visited him that night, but a person who can't stand up could also get their dates confused.

Allan Exit: came out of his Welsh lair for Udo's funeral. Went out drinking, snorting speed and talking shit with the boys for the first time in donkey's years. Annoyed someone, got punched. The assailant fled when they saw how seriously he had been injured.

Clara had been involved in a hit-and-run that occurred at night and featured a four-by-four, a car notoriously favoured by idiots.

As for Sam Saoule: until proved otherwise, the techno-punk died because of an accidental drug overdose.

And the Gaffer was simply getting on with his life.

The summary being that it was a tragic but unconnected series of deaths befalling a group of people who were suffering from drink, drug and mental health problems, who had knocked around together ten years ago but had long since gone their separate ways. Which was what I had mostly believed before Iffy bowled up in Berlin, tilting at windmills, barking up trees and generally howling at the moon.

Iffy, who after years of drug abuse and financial chicanery had finally burnt too many bridges in London. Who came to Berlin for Udo's funeral, stole money from me and used it to buy smack, and continued drinking all the alcohol and taking all the drugs he could blag. Kept getting me pretty fucked, too. Took advantage of my mushroom trip to borrow two grand off me. Claimed he was mugged and lost it all.

I recalled one of Clara's private nicknames she used for Iffy. She used to call him the Lurking Doubt. It was apt: he had a fine lurk on him and often left a vague air of doubt trailing in the breeze like the stench of the shit-pits at a free festival.

As my eyelids began to close, I considered my options. Maybe Iffy, suffering the advanced stages of brain-rot, had let his notoriously vivid imagination run wild and dreamed up a crazy conspiracy theory around a series of tragic accidents. And I, perhaps with a brain not entirely rot-free myself, had lapped it up.

As I stepped onto the bridge of sleep, I considered another possibility: that while the deaths were just coincidental, Iffy actually thought so too, the devious git, and was cynically taking advantage of my gullibility to lead me up the garden path and off on a European drug tour.

As I pushed open the door to my soul, I returned to my favoured possibility, namely that Iffy, my best friend, was helping me get to the *gluteus maximus* of the situation in his own inimitable way. Someone was killing my friends and the Gaffer was our suspect.

There was one more possibility: the deaths were murders, alright, but not of the Gaffer's doing.

Hypnos came. Gently, quietly, yet in all his power and glory. And as he pulled me down into his realm, he whispered one final possibility into my ear.

"Iffy's as mad as a mongoose double-dipped in PCP. He's the killer."

I told him to wind his bloody neck in. Iffy was my mate.

UP AND SHAMBLING

I woke up and I wished I hadn't.

I heard Iffy's chirpy voice say, "Carlo's bar, then?" and I really wished I hadn't.

Reversing the time-honoured tradition of things, I put my head underneath my pillow.

An indiscernible but probably all too brief amount of time later, Hypnos relented and relaxed his hold on me, and I slowly, reluctantly pried myself away from his grasp.

For a few seconds I felt like a Star Trek character when the teleportation machine was malfunctioning, zapping between worlds and flashing in and out of existence. I felt so rough that even the special effects of my internal film were of a low quality.

My dreams had been sweet. Clara had been young again, and funny and care-free and colourful. Minnie had been bursting with exuberant life, dancing under skies as blue as they were vast. Sam had been dozy with sleep, feeding logs onto a smouldering burner and coaxing it softly back into life. Udo had been yelling at his dogs to shut up, his cries even louder than their distant baying. Jacek had been spinning some tunes in the back of his truck. Allan Exit had been frying mushrooms. The Gaffer had been laughing merrily at my cack-handed attempts at drawing a flyer.

Iffy hadn't been there. It was only his presence in my flat that alerted me to the fact that he was missing from my dreams.

I didn't bother asking him where he had been.

"There's a line waiting for you in the kitchen. Jochen gave us a wrap on tick."

Life could be relentless. It just kept on coming. All the clues were there to suggest that it even carried on when I was asleep, although I'm not sure I could have proved it. Whatever. As my memory of the previous few days served an eviction notice on my pleasant dreams and made itself at home, ransacking the larder, shoving its dirty laundry in the washing machine, switching channels on the TV and generally acting like it owned the gaff, I realised with a heavy heart that all my problems were still there, and that I had to face them.

Iffy was also still very much there.

Of Hypnos's final whisper, there was not even the faintest distant echo.

I shook a leg, which rather resented the intrusion but nonetheless obediently poked its way out from under my duvet.

"He won't be doing that again in a hurry," I muttered.

"Eh?"

"Jochen - ticking you some charlie."

"I'll pay him back."

"Great. Perfect. Is that before or after you pay me the two grand you lost in Amsterdam?"

"Er. After, I suppose. You're my priority. Hey, I thought you might be in a better mood after a spot of the old kippage. You were on a bit of a dirty come-down this morning."

We sounded like an old couple. In many ways, we were.

"So are we off to Marseilles, then? To find out about Sam?"

Were we still playing that game? I asked myself in response to Iffy's question. I supposed we were. Until we found out something sure and concrete and irrefutable, and actually managed to prove something - one way or another - we had no choice but to press on with our investigations. The consequences of abandoning the mission could prove fatal. If there was a murderer on the rampage, we had to find him; if there wasn't, I'd just have wasted some of my time, and that was a sacrifice I was willing to make. And, I realised, I'd rather have Iffy with me than leave him to his own vices.

So Marseilles it was.

First, though, I had to launch myself out of bed. The leg that I had shaken had crept back under the duvet as soon as my attention lay elsewhere, and had brought with it tales of a cold and unwelcoming place where no sensible limb would ever set foot. I risked a glance out of the window and saw dusk tumbling down over the city streets. I had slept right through the day. Looked like I was on the night shift.

I persuaded not just one leg but both to brave a foray into the outside world, and the rest of me was obliged to follow suit. Iffy performed an irritating little jester's caper, ushering me into the kitchen to where a line of coke sat patiently awaiting my attentions. I duly despatched it. I knew that if I didn't, I would continue to feel like death cooled down, whereas snorting it would increase the temperature of my walking cadaver enough to get it up and shambling. It was as close as I could manage to an act of deferred gratification: I could have called it an act of deferred torment.

"That was the last one of those little suckers to penetrate my nasal cavities for the foreseeable future," I grumbled aloud, smiling inwardly, though, as its caustic, oily teeth sank themselves into my damaged membranes. "Well, maybe one or two to see me through the evening. But after that, I'm cleaner than a terrier's testicles."

"Whatevs, sweet cheeks," Iffy replied. "Let's get down to Carlo's place."

So we did.

TALKING ABOUT CHEESE

On the way, I made a call to my train ticket contact and arranged to meet him in the bar at Ostkreuz. As we strolled through the Friedrichshain streets, Iffy was on good form, witty, philosophical, sensitive to the recalcitrant workings of my dullened mind. I found myself warming to him again, and bristling as I recalled Clara's negativity. By the time we darkened Carlo's bar's door, I was ready to dismiss her bitching as the product of an embittered imagination.

A small part of my brain - the sensible part - was shouting something about the ease with which I let Iffy put me under his spell, but I rarely heeded its well-intentioned advice. It was the part that would have made me pay attention in school, get a degree, move to a sunnier clime, have less fucked-up friends and generally steer along a straighter, narrower path. It meant well, hollering primly away, but I figured that if it really wanted me to listen, it should have made a bit more effort.

"Hey!" cried Carlo on seeing us enter his domain. "It's Batman and Robin!"

Iffy and I swapped a glance. I was wondering who was Batman and who was Robin in our relationship and I presumed he was doing the same. I'm not sure if we both reached the same conclusion.

Iffy made a bee line for the proprietor's open arms. "Carlo, *quid agis*, you old dodger? Who left you in charge of a boozer?" They shared a hug and drummed out some private, primal rhythms on each other's back. "Shift out the way, you old git," Iffy laughed. "I want to get behind the bar before the boss comes back."

"Hehehe," Carlo chuckled, his piscine eyes bulging behind his rimless glasses, his scrawny neck muscles barely seeming to provide a solid enough base for the width of his mouth. "But I am a grown-up now, old friend. I pay rent and electricity and - yes! - taxes. I am maybe the only Italian to do so, but you know how it is in Germany. They do not understand the voluntary nature of taxation. But best of all - and you will like this - I have a pension plan. It's true! I am no more a teenager."

I remembered Carlo, early one morning in a field somewhere in Tuscany, raggacore booming in our ears and the sun's first rays blunting the edge of the lasers' patterns in the sky, regaling us with his theory of how we were all secret Peter Pans. We were extending our care-free teenage years beyond their traditional limitations, putting off for as long as possible the day when responsibilities would weigh us down. Our forefathers' generations had not had this luxury, and it was our filial duty to make the most of it. He predicted that we would remain in a *puer aeternus* state until the patter of tiny feet began to drown out the sound of the rigs. Then our nights would be sleepless due to babies not beats, and the only drugs we would have in our cupboards would be for soothing teething pains.

Carlo liked to talk.

Iffy, who also liked to talk, had shared with us his own theory about teenagers that night. He suggested that our youthful years were in fact the apogee of our existence, and that it was downhill all the way once we hit our twenties. He talked about the depth of emotion that teenagers felt, about the convictions they held so strongly, and the decisions they made so rashly, and he claimed that they should not be dismissed as immature. On the contrary, that particular age bracket saw us hit the peak of maturity, and what we experienced later was merely the slow process of the organism going into shutdown. It was that state of juvenile rawness, when we burned to get things done and to change the world, that life was all about, he said. Throughout most of our history humans had died at an age we now considered young. Our ancestors' life spans were short. They didn't live long enough for their teeth to fall out - or maybe once their teeth began to fall out, they died. The calming-down phase that comes to most teenage rebels never kicked in, and it was never meant to. And Iffy added that he, for one, intended to hold onto his adolescent passions for ever.

Looking at Carlo in his bar, where he had settled down, and Iffy, ever the wild raver, it seemed that both were still trying to prove their own theories true.

"And you, Iffy, my friend?" Carlo smiled, slapping him again on the back. "What's new? You haven't changed - except that you look ten years older! You are back in London, I hear. Such a crazy city. Always - things happening. Good things, bad things - who knows? Here in Berlin, nothing happens. Only the same *merda* in a different shape. You, you are always chasing things. Maybe London is the good place for you. Maybe for me, too. But here you are - in my bar! So what will you drink? I have good whisky - I know you won't say no to that. Or wine? We drink wine from glasses now!"

Carlo had stopped taking speed a few years ago. Nobody had noticed.

"How long are you staying? Why haven't you been in before? I know you've been in Berlin for some days. I know, I know - you have been off travelling too. This is a village, and word travels fast. Zoom! Everyone knows each other's business - it is terrible. Did you know that Jochen farted at half past eight last night? You didn't know? Incredible - it's the talk of the town. No, I'm joking. But all this gossip…London is different. People have things to do there apart from talk, talk, talk. You came here for Udo's funeral?"

Carlo liked to complain about Berlin, and he loved London, but I was sure he would stay in the German capital forever and I knew he had never set foot in the UK. Also, the only thing he loved more than bitching about gossips was to gossip himself. Such was the multi-faceted nature of man. Carlo was no liar, but it was not all always pure and raw truth that sprang out of the trap that he rarely shut. His mouth played top dog over his submissive brain. It said something, his ears reported back, and his brain thought 'that sounds good, it must be true.'

I listened in as Iffy chatted with the periphrastic barman and noted with approval that my sidekick (for I had resolved that Iffy was Robin to my Batman) was holding back from discussing our ongoing investigations. Considering that a stick has only two ends, it was astonishing how often Carlo grabbed hold of the wrong one. I did not want the world and his butler spreading rumours of a killer on the loose.

In point of fact, my friends were talking about cheese.

"I am importing it myself," Carlo was saying. "Well, you have to - these Germans know nothing about cheese. They think if it's yellow and comes from a cow, it must be cheese. I tell them that piss is yellow and comes from a cow - you don't eat that for brunch! No. Really, though, what I need is cheddar cheese. London's finest! More wine?"

We accepted.

"What about the Gaffer, eh?" he continued, and I almost tipped a full glass of Amarone down my crotch.

"What about the Gaffer?"

"You don't know? Where have you been? He was here in Berlin - though why he wants to do a gig here...you can search me. But me and the Gaffer, we are old friends, you know. Of course you know! So I phoned him and I said he can't come to Berlin and not come to Carlo's bar - it is not possible. It is like going to London and not seeing Stonehenge when you are there. Do you live near Stonehenge, Iffy? A beautiful place! They don't make them like that any more, eh?"

"So did the Gaffer turn up,"

"*Si.* He came. He -"

"Do you know what night it was?" I asked, bravely hurling my sentence in front of the on-rushing train of his next digression. If the Gaffer was here in the 'hood three nights ago when Allan Exit was attacked, it would add credence to our theory that he was the killer.

"Two nights ago? Three? And when he walks in, I hardly -"

"Which night, Carlo? Can you remember? Was it two or three nights ago?"

"Eh, what does it matter? One night is the same as another here. No - wait. It was the day I ran out of bocconcini. What a day! I said to him, you must try the bocconcini, it is hand-rolled on the thighs of Neapolitan virgins. A rare and precious thing - both the cheese and the Neapolitan virgin! And then I felt so stupid -"

"And what day was that?"

"Oh, two or three days ago. Who remembers such things? I make brunch, I serve drinks, I see my friends. The sun rises, he sets. No - wait. Two days ago, I think. *Si.* I am sure. It was the day after Allan Exit was hurt. Now that would never happen in London, I said to -"

"Did the Gaffer tell you about Allan?"

"No, no. I told him. What a crazy thing, eh? He is to fly back home soon, I think, Allan. Poor man. I know - he stole your sound system, so maybe it is the justice after all. Who knows?"

Damn, I thought - there was no confirmed sighting of our suspect near the crime scene.

"And how was the Gaffer?" asked Iffy.

"Fat! Fat and very much pleased with himself, I think. I could not believe it - he has changed. How he has changed! But he came to see his old friend Carlo, and for this I am happy. He has done his growing up. It is his choice, his life - and his big belly. And he is famous now. He told me that himself, but I knew it before. He asked about you two."

"What did you say?"

"Only what I could. You were here - though not here in my bar, eh? - and someone said you were off to Amsterdam and Jacek's wake. Always travelling, you two! Moving, moving, moving. Always moving. I need to move, too, but who will make the brunch? Who will order the bocconcini? Who will pay my pension plan? That is the question. Yes."

Having already swapped glances when we arrived in the bar, Iffy and I now returned them to their rightful owners in another silent exchange. If the Gaffer was indeed our man, he could now figure out that we were looking into the matter of the deaths in the rig.

"And do you know what he said? To me, in my bar? 'Carlo,' he said, 'Carlo, I cannot drink your wine and I could not eat your bocconcini.' Unbelievable! Nobody comes to Carlo's bar and refuses wine and bocconcini - nobody. It is the act of a crazy man. A nutter, or what is it you say in your cocky rhyming slang - a peanut butter!"

"He just came to see you?" I demanded sceptically, for when I had seen the Gaffer at his gig I hadn't noticed him pining too wistfully for his old pals. On the contrary, he had given every sign of being a man who was discomfited by his old lifestyle and friends. Hooking up with a chronic gossip like Carlo seemed a strange thing for him to do.

"*Sì*. Sure, he is boring now, and fat, and he has gone over to the other side of the English - the obedient side. You know what you're like - either completely straight or completely fucking mental. I think it is the emotional repression that leads to the madness. Either you conform or you go loopy-fucking-loopy. But what do I know? Anyway, the Gaffer - he hasn't forgotten his old friends! And after we talked about you two, he told me he had been on his death bed before he came to see me. Dying, he said. Poisoned! Something he ate. But that's German food for you...You don't get that with Carlo's bocconcini. I asked if it was the peanuts - you remember his allergy? But no, he says - no, Carlo, no. The peanuts - they would kill me."

Had someone tried to kill the Gaffer too? Was he on the murderer's list?

Or had it been a coincidental case of food poisoning?

Or part of something more devious?

My thoughts were distracted by a sound like steam coming out of a kettle and a hand that landed lightly, like a caress from Nephthys, on my shoulder. Lack of sleep; a line or two of charlie; a murderer on the loose - because of these things, I jumped like a salmon in springtime, though possibly with slightly less gracefulness and rippling athleticism.

The touch belonged to Stephan, my train ticket dealer. Exchanging pleasantries, we padded over to a corner table and he slipped an envelope into my pocket.

"Valid for a month. Two people. Usual price."

I thanked him for his promptness and efficiency. He turned down my offer of a drink and slipped out of the bar, clutching the bundle of euros I had given him.

"I'm gonna head home, pardner," I informed Iffy at the bar. "We've got an early start in the morning."

"Oh no - you are leaving us again?" Carlo interjected as he sloshed more wine into Iffy's glass. "But you will be back soon. I am sure of this. This city, she is the sun - and we, we are her satellites. We go, we come, we turn in circles. Maybe I will leave her orbit one day - to London maybe. Is it true that the bars now they are open all night? Ah, that must be something..."

"Carlo," I grinned, "in Berlin the bars are open all night. Your bar is open all night."

"*Si, si*. But it is not the same."

I smiled. "Excuse us two minutes," I said, drawing Iffy to one side.

"Don't worry about me, our kid, I'll be fine here." Iffy confided. "So we're heading south tomorrow? Marseilles?"

"*Si*," I said, "And maybe London - who knows? Listen, though - what Carlo was saying about the Gaffer…"

"I know. You think he'll work it out that we're on the case about the murders?"

"Could do. Time to double our guard, so to speak."

"You're right. And there's one more big question connected to what Carlo was saying…"

"Yes, I know. I thought the same thing," I replied, feeling thankful that Iffy seemed to be reasoning along the same lines as I was - damn, I was thankful that he was reasoning at all. There was something fishy about the tale of the Gaffer's alleged poisoning. After Carlo had let slip that Iffy and I were headed to Minnie's home town and Jacek's wake, could it be that our suspect had deliberately spun his story to Carlo, knowing full well it would later reach our ears? Did he want us to add him to our list of the nearly-deceased, and thus remove him from our list of suspects?

"Yup," Iffy said in a low voice. "One big question…"

I nodded.

"What the fuck is bocconcini?"

THE MESSAGE

The message arrived just as I was settling down in the train, ostentatiously flourishing a book in the hope it would deter Iffy from launching into one of his soliloquies whenever he returned from whatever he was doing in the toilets.

It was from one of Allan's grown-up children. He had found my name on his dad's phone. He had often heard his dad talk about me.

I began to cry. Tears slid down my face and dripped onto the open pages of my book, tiny splashes that slowly spread across the page.

"Shit," said Iffy as he came back and saw me. "Shit." He hugged me hard and at first I just let him, and then I hugged him back as hard as I had ever hugged anyone.

"Shit," he said. "It's Allan, isn't it? The final exit?"

I nodded.

THE DUTCH VERB '*EPIBREREN*'

The train thundered along high-speed tracks through France.

Memories came just as fast. Increasingly over the last few days I had found myself yielding to pangs of nostalgia, that bitter-sweet homesickness for a place in the past. Wary of the ways in which it could make the old days seem better than the present, I generally avoided the traps it set in my path, but seeing Iffy, Clara, the Gaffer and Allan Exit again, and losing Udo and now Allan in the space of the last few days, had checked my progress and cast me stumbling down Rosy Retrospection Road.

Back home in Berlin, certain parts of the city were still undergoing the unsteadying effects of '*Ostalgia*', a melancholy pining for times that would never come again, specifically for the time when *Ostdeutchland* had been a place a map and not just a page in a history book. My friends who had grown up on the eastern side of *die Mauer* talked about the genuine community spirit they had learned in school, and my more elderly neighbours moaned about modern unemployment and inflation - but they had been living in a police state in the 1980s, and only the vagaries of nostalgia allowed them to forget it.

Neither had my days with the rig been entirely carefree and insouciant. There had been thorns obscured amongst the petals, gravel hidden in the honey, flint lying underneath the velvet, scars concealed by the sun tans.

If I really concentrated, I could recall that Clara had often been moody and sarcastic. Udo had been chronically unreliable. Jacek had been niggardly and parsimonious. Minnie had been cloying and annoying. Allan Exit had been sullen, superior and condescending. The Gaffer had been hectoring and sententious. Sam Saoule had been antagonistic and quarrelsome. Iffy had been Iffy. I may not have been perfect myself. (Minnie had been known to employ the Dutch verb '*epibreren*' in connection with me. Apparently it referred to giving the impression that you are doing a great deal of extremely useful and important things, while not in fact getting much done at all.)

As I stared out the window and watched the world flash by, I recalled fragments of a poem by Housman. Something about 'blue remembered hills', and 'the land of lost content, the happy highways where I went and cannot come again.'

On the train sped, and I could not prevent my memories from racing along with us.

A teknival in the Alps where Minnie and I swam naked in a periwinkle-blue lake, with tiny fish nibbling at our toes and beats booming on the stony shore.

A smaller free party, a family affair in some woods near Macon, where it rained all weekend and Clara and I, swaddled in blankets and cocooned in a bubble of MDMA, hardly left the cosy comfort of her truck.

Another vehicle, Allan's this time, a couple of years and many thousands of miles down the line, breaking down on a steep hillside in the Ardèche, where we waited in a lay-by for a week, smoking our way through a big bag of weed, until Jacek came to rescue us with a new distributor.

A traveller site in Lyons, an old spice warehouse that still smelled of the Orient, where Udo and I almost bought a double decker bus together, until it was burnt out by a smackhead on a revenge mission over a drug deal gone wrong.

Clara's dog, ugly old Che - now long since dead - having puppies in an abandoned farmhouse in the Cevennes as the snow piled up outside the door and stolen church candles spluttered in the icy draughts that came whistling through the gap under the door.

Clara at Avignon bus station, happy to see me, her arms held out wide, her eyes shining, and me descending gingerly from the coach, my buttocks tightly clenched in an effort to keep two hundred pills from slipping out.

We had different things to worry about back then.

Right now, I just didn't want anyone else to die.

'On train to Mars', I typed into my mobile, 'Allan is dead. Gaffer maybe onto us. This is SERIOUS. Think U should go on hols till all sorted. U R NOT SAFE. TAKE CARE. xxx'

I sent the message to Clara's number and watched Iffy picking his nose as I waited for a reply. It was half an hour before my phone beeped. I scanned the text with a sinking heart and a rising sense of frustration. 'So sorry about Allan. He was a good man. But FORGET the murder thing. You are being daft. Going to Mars? Send me a postcard of Uranus and call me when back on planet Earth.'

"Bloody hell. She just won't accept she's in danger."

"Eh?"

"Clara. Fuck's sake, she's the one with the legal training, and here the evidence is staring her in the face. She just won't accept it."

"Middle name's stubborn, that one."

"I know, mate, but I'm worried for her. The Gaffer could be planning his next move at this very moment…"

"Don't stress. We'll be, what, a day or two max in Marseilles."

"Right. I need to pull myself together."

"Keep focused."

"Right."

I averted my gaze as I saw him searching for somewhere to wipe the latest bogey he had excavated. I hammered out fifty press-ups on the floor of our compartment, trying not to think about cigarettes or my ex-girlfriend or Allan and his fatherless kids.

SELF-MEDICATION

That afternoon we were in North Africa, or that's how it felt to me. A scathing, raging desert wind was trying to tear our trousers off, and Marseilles's narrow streets served to concentrate rather than hinder its excesses. Gap-toothed dodgers clad almost exclusively in white and blue sportswear ducked and dived amongst the debris that blew like tumbleweed, and oriental odours squirmed their way insistently up our damaged nasal passages. The sun was hot and high and it was beating down, thawing our weary traveller's bones as we walked out of the train station. There was a different quality to the heat so far south of Berlin. I liked it, even as it made the sweat pour.

I had always marvelled that Marseilles was officially in the same country as Paris. The two great cities were cut from a different cloth, hewn from a different stone, and they danced to a different beat. Where central Paris was posh and predictable, stately, staid, moody and arrogant, Marseilles was washed in the rhythms of the Mediterranean and dried in the wild, herbal scents of the surrounding garrigue. The clothes, the sea, the stone, the sky - Marseilles was a duochromatic delight in white and blue, whereas Paris merely faded from grey in winter to a little less grey in summer. While Paris laboured under its bubble of smog, the southern sunshine ricocheted off the sea in Marseilles and infected everything it touched.

My personal memories of the ancient port, however, were always darkened by an Iffy-shaped shadow.

Nobody knew exactly what had befallen him there. We had gone south for the winter of '98 and were doing a series of big multi-rig parties around the city, most of which went off without too many problems.

Iffy had surprised us all by actually upping his drug consumption. He was in an unusually destructive state of mind for one normally so happy-go-lucky. On the night he got battered, we had been drinking pastis in the square of La Plaine when we had one of our occasional brothers' tiffs. The origins of our contretemps, like much of that period in our lives, were lost in the mists of time. Maybe I had criticised him for not pulling his weight, or maybe he had had a go at me for being boring...I left him alone, slumped against the trunk of a plane tree, rolling a spliff in the oncoming dusk, the camouflage pattern of his combat trousers blending in with the peeling bark.

When he turned up the next morning at the derelict factory where our trucks were parked, he looked as though an entire contingent of hooligans had danced a victory jig on his face. He mumbled that he remembered nothing of what had happened and refused to go to hospital. Minnie did her best to patch him up. Nonetheless, I had rarely seen anyone look as rough as he did that day. We tried to convince him that bed-rest and hot chocolate were what he needed, but he eschewed such comforts in favour of self-medication with the ketamine crew.

The images still haunted me. Iffy rolling around on the floor of a filthy warehouse, fucked out of his brain, blank-eyed and grimacing, dribble oozing out of the corner of his mouth, stale piss staining his combats, his tee-shirt ripped and bloodstained, his cheeks swollen and lumpy with bruises, his nose leaking a stomach-churning cocktail of snot, blood and ketamine-goo.

"It's nice to be back," he surprised me by saying as we checked a map outside the station.

"Really?"

"Yeah. I haven't been here for donkeys'. Not since we did all those parties round New Year's, ages ago."

"Funnily enough, I was just thinking about that."

"Good times."

I stared at him.

"Jacek sussed out how to win on the gambling machines in the bars, remember? And Allan's birthday in that weird restaurant? When we were all so fucked on MDMA and the bill came and we couldn't pay it all. Thirty of us doing a runner! Hardly able to walk! And Sam Saoule going mental, playing a twenty-four hour set on the rig, and everyone too scared to ask him to stop, even when he was totally bollocksing it up at the end. Good times…"

"If you say so."

"You telling me they weren't good times?"

"To be honest, Iffy, I was just wondering if you'd forgotten all about the horrendous kicking you got that one night. Hope you don't mind me bringing it up…"

"Oh, that," he shrugged. "I deserved that."

"Did you?"

"Well, I s'pose he might have got a bit carried away. But I don't remember it hurting very much."

"No. Right. Who?"

"Eh? Oh, Sam. Owed him some wedge. I'd've paid him back, of course, but he got a bit impatient. So he gave me a few slaps and everything was sorted."

I decided to file that away in my Mysterious Iffy section. The man was my closest friend, but it shouldn't have shocked me that he kept secrets from me.

Unfortunately, it brought back some of the doubts I had been having about what had really happened to the money we had borrowed from Nadine. The Marseilles Kicking Incident and the Amsterdam Alleged Mugging seemed to contain two of the same base ingredients: an attack, and money. In Marseilles he had definitely been attacked, but I had only just discovered that money was a factor. In Holland, I knew that money was involved but I harboured lingering reservations about the attack.

ISOLATED COLD PATCHES

But now Iffy and I were in town to check out the circumstances of Sam Saoule's death. Our investigations were gathering pace.

"Been thinking. What happens," Iffy asked me, "when we're sure that the Gaffer's our man?"

"Eh?"

"Logical question. Here we are, chasing all round the continent, poking our proboscises into other people's doings, digging out facts and rumours and building theories, working our way inexorably towards a conclusion and all that. Well...what next?"

"Iffy, I had a chat with Clara the day before yesterday -"

"And how was the weather in London?"

"Eh?"

"Isolated cold patches?"

"You what?"

"You know. That strange micro-system of freezing temperatures that follows Clara's every movement with uncanny accurateness."

"Well, she was a little brusque. Bracing, you could say. As is her wont. She did also mention a grand-sized hole in her finances, now that I come to think of it…"

"Typical."

"Yeah? Well, she happens to think we're tripping off on one about the murders in general and the Gaffer in particular."

"Forget Clara. You always thought the sun shines out her Khyber Pass and the word of God spews from her north and south. Whatway and anyever...like I said, I've been thinking. What if it *is* the Gaffer? Where is that going to leave us?"

"I'm not following you, Iffy."

"Give your head a wobble. When we're really sure that the Gaffer's on a killing spree…what are we gonna do about it? We couldn't shop him to the Old Bill even if we wanted to. They won't listen to the likes of us and our pesky conspiracy theories. So what are our options?"

"Erm. Shouldn't we deal with that later?" I was a long-term believer in getting my procrastination in as early as possible.

"Mate, we're digging to get at the truth, not to make a hole where we can bury our heads and ignore the world. You know what Confucius says: he who buries his head in the sand leaves his arse in a very dangerous position. But the answer's obvious. Once we're sure it's the Gaffer we're after, I mean. It's got to be PIY, innit."

I thought about that. "How? How will we police it ourselves?"

"That, my friend, is the bridge we'll have to cross."

And a pretty daunting bridge at that. Possibly one of those Tibetan jobs that consisted of two parallel ropes spanning the gaping maws of a chasm, with a racing winter-melt river studded with rocks and rapids waiting below to swallow us whole; or maybe a jungle job, with rotting planks winking malevolently at us and alligators snapping at our tootsies.

We would deal with it when we had to, I figured, and not before.

"It's weird being back here again," I said, deftly changing the subject.

We were climbing one of the steeply sloping streets that led up to Cours Julien, a pleasant square where colourful cafés and bars faced each other across a series of fountains. Iffy looked around him, nodded, and took my bait. "This was Sam's city."

Sam and Iffy had got on particularly well. They made an odd pair: Iffy, who was hardly ever serious, and Sam, who was seriously hard. Iffy had never got his own vehicle together, so

Sam had often towed his tiny Sprite caravan for him behind his Iveco truck, like a mother elephant guiding her baby.

"I know what you mean," I said, echoing his wistful tone. "People come and go, they drift in and out of our lives. It's only natural. Some of my mates I'll never set eyes on again. But when they actually die...first Holland without Minnie and then the party in Czech without Jacek, and now coming here without Sam...it's only at times like this that it really sinks in. That they aren't coming back."

Iffy flapped his hand up and down, signalling that we should stop for a breather, but I kept plodding on. "You are familiar, I presume," he called after me, "with my Unified Theory on the Relative Importance of Death?"

I told him I must have been ill on the day we covered that in class.

"Part One," he called after me. "Each and every death is only of relative importance. All life is sacred, they say - though I think that's probably just a typo for scared - but some lives are more sacred than others. Obviously, our personal relationship with the recently deceased is one of the key factors for judging how important a death is," he said. "We all know that. Sure, every now and again the media gets its undies in a lather about some particular death - Princess fucking Diana, Michael fucking Jackson - and declares an outbreak of national mourning, but that's just bullshit. Manufactured grief. I refer you to my Unified Theory on the Pervasive and Invasive Power of the Media for a more detailed study on the subject."

I was waiting patiently for him to catch up. He was momentarily engrossed in cuddling a passing poodle. I watched as he then entered into a *sotto voce* conversation with the dog's owner, the end result of which was Iffy being rewarded with a smile and what looked like a blim of hash.

"Now," he said, returning his attention to me, "what we

sometimes fail to take into consideration are the other two key factors. Firstly: distance. If you read about someone being run over, it doesn't have the same effect as if you see it. Every single day we read or hear about shocking atrocities being committed somewhere far, far away, and we continue with our boring little lives as though it wasn't happening. We think, 'that's sad,' and get on with the washing up. Think how different it'd be if we saw those deaths with our own eyes. We'd be in shock. We'd be devastated, even if the person was a stranger."

I nodded. "Right. Like all the people who'll happily eat any old carcass that's shoved in front of them as long as they don't have to see the animals' living conditions or the abattoirs where they're slaughtered."

He may not have heard my contribution, though, as he was briefly engaged in coaxing a couple of Rizlas and a cigarette out of a passing skater. Blag accomplished, he sat down on the kerb between two cars and began skinning up.

"The third factor is time," he said, glancing up to check I was still listening. "Old news is a wonderful oxymoron, and it's a sturdy barrier that sympathy finds hard to penetrate. Ancient massacres barely register a blip on our emotional meters. Horrific murders that happened long ago become little more than juicy stories as time passes."

The licking and sticking of the papers, the breaking of the fag, the spreading of tobacco in the palm of his hand, the heating of the hash between two fingertips, the mixing of the softened substance with the tobacco, the slapping of the mix onto the papers, the rolling, the final dramatic lick, the flaring of the lighter, the puffing of smoke: all accomplished in about thirty seconds.

"All that doesn't make us heartless bastards, though. It's just part of the human experience. It would be impossible if we felt the same pain for strangers' deaths, or for deaths that happened far away, or before we were born, as we did for friends' deaths. We'd be overwhelmed. It's the same as how our memories filter out most of the insignificant crap - if they didn't, we wouldn't have room for everything. It has to be the same with grief. We'd be crippled by it, if reading about slaughter in far-off places or hearing about historical atrocities had the same effect as actually witnessing them ourselves."

A thoughtful smile danced across his stubbled face, though whether it was a reaction to the taste of his spliff or to the argument he was presenting, I could not have guessed.

"What I'm trying to say," he persisted as we set off again, "is that death is relative. And subjective. We only make a big deal about it when it suits us."

"And?"

"Just saying. Sometimes you have to look at the bigger picture and understand that one person's death may seem like a big deal, but that it's purely a subjective viewpoint relative to your own position in the four dimensions of time and space, and to your emotional attachment to the dead person. D'you want a puff?"

I thought about it, and said no.

THE CHORDS OF REBELLION

Iffy ground his roach out against a lamp post and gazed longingly at the tables outside a bar. "I'll never make it up the hill if we don't stop for a beer."

"But we're going up the hill to get a beer at the top. We're nearly there. So, you know, I never really sussed out if Sam was a spiky anarchopunk or a fluffy hippy at heart."

As a teenager Sam had had his knuckles tattooed with 'love' and 'hate'. (The Gothic script ACAB tattoo on the back of his neck came later.) Often he had been brimful of peace and love and charity. He adored kids and could play contentedly for hours with toddlers. He could be hopelessly optimistic and remarkably kind, caring and gentle on occasion - but most of my memories of him were of a fuming, bellicose, pugnacious pugilist, a hard-eyed, hair-triggered battler who had often been the member of our rig to proclaim, "Yes, we can do it," and, "No, they can't stop us." The Gaffer had usually leapt aboard his bandwagon, but Sam had frequently been the kick-start mechanism that set the rest of us in motion.

He had been there from the beginning of the sound system, his pure anarchist's heart drawn irresistibly to the trouble we frequently found ourselves in. I had met him at one of those London Friday night squat specials where punk bands thrashed out the chords of rebellion downstairs and techno DJs pounded out the beats of escapism upstairs.

We had talked about something, had a line of something and shared a bottle of something, and then he had had a fight with someone twice his size who had done something or other that I never fully understood, but who was apparently bang out of order. I remember dragging him up the over-crowded stairwell to the techno room, despite his protestations that he didn't like electronic music, that it didn't have the rabble-rousing, call-to-arms urgency of punk. I gave him his first E and he soon got into the vibe of things, and that was pretty much where he stayed.

Despite his initial distrust of hedonistic ravers, he grew to love the fuck-you attitude of the free party movement and appreciate acid techno and hardtek as kinds of electronic punk: angry, anti-authoritarian music that inspired seditious thoughts and insurrectionary acts. He became our best DJ.

"Both," Iffy said with convincing sincerity. "Punk and hippy. But much, much, much more of a punk."

Telling tales of cold amber beer, I led the way up the final ascent to Cours Julien. We installed ourselves at a table and let the sun soothe the parts of our faces that the wind had rubbed raw.

"But he had some full-on peace and love moments too, didn't he?" I said.

"When he'd munched a few pills."

I chuckled. "Yeah. You're not wrong. A few vodkas, on the other hand…"

"Ouch."

I figured that that counted as a comment not just on Sam's personality, but also on the effects of two of the most popular drugs of our era, and on the warped reasoning that made the violence-provoking substance legal and the peace-inducing one illegal.

DEEPLY SHUDDERY, WEEPY, JUDDERY

We had been enjoying ourselves despite the gravity of our mission. Our mood was cheerful, beer was sloshing around in our bellies and we were positively aglow with fond memories of Sam Saoule.

It seemed like a good time to break the news to Iffy that we were on our way to see Barbwire Barbara.

"Is that my chain you're yanking?" Iffy pleaded, more in hope than expectation. "That's who Sam was shacked up with? Barbwire? Christ, if I'd known that...And we're going to see her? Voluntarily? Of our own free will?"

I nodded and fired off a text message to which Barbwire replied that we should come straight to her flat. It was just around the corner. The street was quiet and shady. The restaurants and bars wouldn't open until later in the day. Barbwire's door was tucked discreetly between two shop fronts, and when she buzzed it open it revealed absolutely nothing. Once our eyes had adjusted to the darkness, we saw a narrow, sharply winding wooden staircase.

"Third floor," she yelled down to us, before ushering us into her flat and leading us through a room full of cardboard boxes into the kitchen. The lino floor was tacky under my feet. The walls were grubby, the work surfaces grimy, and what little furniture she had seemed to be made of MFI and coated in Formica. Barb's clothing company, named Barbwire of course, had clearly yet to hit the big time.

She had not changed her look since we had last met. She might have got a few more piercings, but - like trying to identify new ants in an anthill - you would have had to pay particularly close attention to notice the recent additions. Her hair was still modelled on Morticia Addams, and her clothes would still have made a dominatrix wince.

She hadn't changed her look, but she looked different. Her mouth, for one, silently told a tale of prolonged amphetamine use. Her stumps of teeth resembled a stack of speakers that was slowly being dismantled after a party had finished. Her hands were tiny, bony, wraithlike and criss-crossed with protruding blue veins. Her skin tone was of a quite remarkable paleness for somebody who lived in the sunny south of France.

I smiled a greeting and delivered a peck on both her sunken cheeks.

If I had been thinking that Carlo, with his greying hair and expanding waistline, and Iffy, with his galloping bald spot, had aged badly, then Barbwire's continuing speed abuse showed me the error of my thoughts.

And to think she had been so young when we first met.

Admittedly, she had never exactly been young at heart. Barbara was born under a bad star, Clara used to say. Black clouds of misfortune dogged her path through life. She had a physical wound or a mental scar from every teknival we had ever done, it seemed. It was always Barbwire who got nicked or lost or poisoned or threatened by gangsters or beaten up by rednecks. She was always the one sitting underneath the poorly-anchored light, or who bought the truck that broke down a week later, or who invested in a hundred E's that turned out to be aspirin, or whose dog caught staphylococcus, or whose wallet got stolen. She had once won the lottery, several hundred thousand pounds, she claimed - and promptly lost the ticket when she got pissed to celebrate the way her luck had turned.

She didn't help herself by making bad decisions, attaching herself to the wrong company and being out of her nut most of the time, and she never learned a lesson from her relentless, unremitting cascade of catastrophe and disaster. On the contrary, Barbwire seemed to revel in her woes, and we all had memories of interminably long nights spent listening to her hard-luck stories when we could have been dancing and having fun. As long as I had known her, a tattooed string of barbwire had encircled her throat, though whether the nickname or the tat came first, I did not know.

Sam Saoule's death was the latest layer on an already well-iced cake.

Shooing a cat off a chair, she swept a slew of flyers into a vague pile on the kitchen table and motioned for us to sit down. Getting the social niceties out of the way, she started making tea and chopping up lines. I saw Iffy begin to leaf through the stack of flyers.

"It's sound of you to come all this way to talk about Sam," she said, offering me a soggy biscuit from what I saw was an almost empty cupboard. "I get the idea everyone's fed up of hearing about him round here."

"I never knew you two were so close," I admitted. "I mean, I know we did lots of parties together when you were with that Italian rig, but it was only when I was down for the funeral that I realised he'd been staying here."

"Funny thing is, I never knew how much he meant to me till he was gone." She took a deeply shuddery, weepy, juddery breath that signified the imminence of tears, and motioned for Iffy to take over the task of racking up the lines of speed. "He was my mate, right? We'd known each for years, since we all used to do parties together. Then I moved down to Mars and we'd see each other about, whenever there was a party. Started knocking around together. It was nice to have someone around who spoke such good English." And he was probably the only other person who could stay awake as long as you, I thought.

Sam had always liked his speed. "I don't know why he had to die." A brace of tears skittered down her cheekbones.

"I heard he hadn't slept for a week."

"I don't think it was that long. It might've been. We got a bit mixed up about what day it was."

"You were there?"

A nod. A sniff. Emotion? A nose full of powder?

"You want to talk about it?"

A shake of the head - but people can lie with their bodies as well as with words.

"Why did you stay awake so long?" I pressed, feeling uncomfortable in my inquisitor's robes.

"Work. Simple as that. He was staying in my flat, kipping on the sofa at first. I needed help to pay the rent and his ex had taken their truck to Spain. And then I got this massive order with a really short deadline. And he offered to help..." Her voice petered out into a sob.

Barbara made clothes, hardcore cyberpunk-cum-bondage threads painstakingly hand-stitched out of recycled inner tubes, seat belts and tyres, but it was more of a passion than a profession. It was a labour of love, time-consuming and badly remunerated.

"It was all for a show in Milan. There was no way I could finish it all in time on my own and I had no cash to pay anyone, so he said he'd help me. I bought the speed. Just as a tool, like. To aid the concentration. You know. We worked day and night. One line led to another, one day led to another. Maybe it was a week, I don't honestly know. It could have been. We actually got it all done in time, so we went out to celebrate. Got drunk. I came back here and passed out while Sam went on somewhere else."

I tried imagining what her wake-up must have been like, but my brain baulked at the prospect. A speed comedown, I could picture all too well. The scale of the comedown after a whole week of no sleep and precious little food was too horrible to contemplate. Finding the corpse of your friend, well…

"The *pompiers* came, of course. God knows what they must have thought of me."

I let her cry for a while, giving her a gentle hug and feeling her bony torso spasm against my chest.

Iffy, meanwhile, had grabbed a flier at random and rolled it into a tube. He sniffed a line himself and then waved the tube at us. I shook my head. Barb had some difficulty snorting her line. Still sobbing, she wiped a black sleeve across her face and smeared snot and speed all up her cheek. More drops fell from the rings that pierced her nose. I grabbed some kitchen roll and dabbed delicately at her face.

When she could speak again, she said, "I found the bottle of GBH later. I didn't even know what it was. I've got no idea where it came from."

"Did he take it often, do you think?"

"Don't think so. He never mentioned it." Dabbing her face with a dirty dish cloth, she tried to steady herself, with no real sign of success. "It's all fucked. I think me and him could have had a future together. And look what happened. It isn't fair," she lamented, reverting to her unfortunate catchphrase, mankind's oldest refrain.

"Ouch," I yelped suddenly as Iffy's para boot connected painfully with my shin. Barbwire didn't appear to have heard my exclamation, but I still pasted my meanest glare onto my face and levelled it in Iffy's direction.

Smugly, he tapped his index finger on the flyer that had been serving as a straw. He slid it towards me across the table top.

I looked at it. Tore off some more kitchen roll and wiped it clean. Picked it up, turned it over, rocked back on the two hind

legs of my chair like a knight about to charge into a joust.
 "Barb, what's this?"

OUR OWN PERSONAL CRUTCHES

"What?"

"This flyer."

Blinking away some tears, she focused on the laminated piece of paper. "Let's have a gander…Oh, that was ages ago. You've missed it."

I checked the dates. March the twenty-third.

"And when did Sam die?"

"End of March. Yeah, the twenty-third, as it goes. That's funny."

I stared at the flyer. It was ultramodern, I supposed, all pixelated grey tones and divergent streaks of colour. A US Army-style font announced 'Underground Star. Part Two. The Gaffer Is Coming!'.

"Did you go?" I asked, a little short of breath.

"Nah. It's your old matey, though, isn't it? The Gaffer, who used to do the rig with you lot."

"That's right. You sure you didn't head down there? Sam and the Gaffer go back a long way…"

She shook her head. "We didn't go. We didn't have time, I told you."

"But that's the day you finished. You said you went out to celebrate, but then you fell asleep and Sam was still up. Could he have gone there on his Jack Jones? "

"S'pose so, yeah. I was out for the count. Eighteen hours. And when I woke up everything was colder and darker and shittier."

"And you don't know what Sam did in all that time? I mean, apart from…I mean, he took the GHB at some point. But he could have gone to see the Gaffer? Or the Gaffer could have come here and you'd never have known, right?"

"You're freaking me out here. What's going on?"

That made me slow my charge to a canter. How could I explain our interest in the fact that the Gaffer had a gig in town on the very night Sam Saoule overdosed without arousing Barbwire's suspicions?

"You don't think it was the Gaffer who gave him the GBH?" she asked incredulously. "Why would you even think that? What the fuck is going on? Why are you two even here? He's dead. Can't you just leave him in peace?"

I noticed her absent-mindedly rolling another flyer into a tube. Saw the way her leg was jitterbugging to its own demonic rhythm. Figured she was itching for another line, for another dose of her chosen medication. Thought about how we all had our own personal crutches that we leant on in times of stress, and wished they weren't always so destructive.

She reminded me of Juliest, mullered on K in her truck, telling me that Jacek was dead and gone, and suggesting that I should let sleeping dogs lie. I couldn't, though. Unpleasant though it was, I had to kick them and keep kicking until something bit.

It was Iffy who moved to smooth the ruffled fur. "Of course we don't think the Gaffer gave him the GHB. Why would he? But maybe he knows something that'll help us out. That's all."

"So give him a ring. Ask him. He's your pal, isn't he?"

He was our pal, I agreed, and we spent the next couple of hours admiring her work, the crazy, beautiful clothes that hadn't been sent to Milan in the end, and reminiscing agonisingly about Sam. Finally we made our excuses and stepped back out into the street, where the demented drivers of tiny, dented cars hooted their horns at each other, where rows of washing dangled from balconies, flapping in the wind, and where life was going on as if we weren't hot on the trail of a murderer.

"What's the address, Iffy?"

He pulled the flyer from his pocket and held it out towards me, only for a sudden gust of wind to snatch it from his grasp and fling it away. With many an exclaimed obscenity we chased after it, scattering pedestrians and careering off parked vehicles. Our eyes followed its progress - up on a draught, horizontal on a thermal, down on an eddy - until it came to rest on the ledge of a first floor windowsill.

"Nice one, Iffy."

"Give me a leg up, will you?"

With all the elegance of a blindfolded bricklayer, I boosted him up and he grabbed the flyer before it could resume its haphazard journey.

"Second *arrondissement*. That's down by the Vieux Port, non?"

A FALLEN ANGELS' CHORUS TO LOST LOVE AND BROKEN DREAMS

Which meant going downhill and uphill, but that was Marseilles for you. We trundled down towards the sea front, admiring the multiplicity of street art and wondering what we would be able to find out at the club where the Gaffer had played. Several times we were offered drugs by random ne'erdowells, and at the third time of asking Iffy cracked. He sidled off into a side street and two minutes later the deal was done.

"Back in a sec," he told me, and dashed into a shop. I watched in silence as he came out clutching a can of Orangina.

"You want a hit?" he asked me.

My continued taciturnity must have been eloquent enough, because he told me to wait where I was and he'd be right back. Off he trotted to find a quiet corner in which to smoke his rock.

I opened my mouth to remonstrate when he rejoined me, but before I could get a word out he said, "Don't start," and to be honest I hadn't really known where to begin anyway.

Down at the harbour, we squinted at the sea and watched the boats for a few minutes. Iffy smoked a cigarette and I sat upwind, munching on a falafel, but I was too impatient and he was too wired to relax.

Plunging headlong into the winding maze of alleys and little streets of Le Panier, we proceeded to get ourselves completely and magnificently lost. The black-shrouded crones who sat in doorways and tottered along the cobble stones replied in an incomprehensible dialect of French when we asked them directions. Finally serendipity waved her wand and the Mediterranean goddess who Iffy stopped told us that she herself worked in the club we were searching for.

"And it is here - see, number twenty-three," she said, her voice an incendiary combination of liquid smoke and delta blues.

Iffy gave a whoop to the world and a meaningful glance to me. I could guess roughly what was churning through his mind: some kind of cosmic shit about the luck that had drawn us to the very woman we were looking for and the involvement of his old favourite, the number twenty-three.

Our interlocutor was somewhat shy of her thirties. A curl of brown hair lazed across her forehead and had me scrambling for better colour adjectives: was it burnished, bistre or bronzed; chestnut, chocolate or cinnamon? It was a shade or two darker than her tan, but paled next to the inky blackness of her eyes. When she leant her shoulders against the wall, her body seemed to ripple and flex like a willow sapling in a storm.

None of this, I reminded myself, would have the slightest bearing on what she had to tell us.

"Are you interested in the club?" she smiled? and she really shouldn't have done so. It didn't help my concentration.

"Yes, yes, yes. Yes, we are," Iffy said, a little too eagerly, admittedly, but it was better than I could have managed. Ochre, I was thinking, or maybe burnt sienna, as I watched the tail of her plaited hair wriggle out from behind the immaculate arch of her back.

"You are journalists? Or DJs?"

I dismissed hazel, but lingered for a moment on mahogany.

"Journalists. Definitely journalists. It's about an old event, actually," said Iffy, fumbling through his pockets for the flyer we had liberated from the flat. "Are you the club manager?"

The woman giggled, sounding like Ella Fitzgerald, Bessie

Smith and Billie Holiday singing a fallen angels' chorus to lost love and broken dreams. "No, no," she said, "I just work there. What event are you interested in?"

Iffy was still rummaging in his pockets, extracting a jumble of odds and ends that would have made William Brown salivate. Luckily nothing remained of the crack he had bought. I immediately seized the opportunity to grin like an idiot.

"This one," he said, thrusting the Gaffer's soggy, crumpled, snot-stained and speed-speckled flyer into her hands.

"Ah," the woman breathed, accidentally created the perfect lullaby. "The Gaffer." *Ze Gaffair*, was how she said it.

"That's right," Iffy confirmed. "We're trying to trace the Gaffer's movements on his latest tour, putting together a timeline of a working artist. Following his footsteps around the globe."

"But it was a long time ago, this event."

"Yes. Yes, it was. Exactly. That's our angle, see. The transience of art and music. The vestiges that linger. What remains when the show moves on, when the last echoes of the noise have faded. The memories, the feelings, the residual emotions. The ghost in the show. The permanence - or impermanence - of the œuvre."

I could only hope the woman was as impressed as I was by Iffy's freshly laid, warmly steaming pile of bullshit. And indeed, I saw that she was nodding as if it actually meant something. The thoughtful frown on her forehead and the delicate curl of her lips met like opposing weather fronts over the ocean of her eyes.

"That's very interesting," she purred. "How can I help? My name is Hélène, by the way."

"Hélène of Troy?" I heard myself saying before I had time to think.

"Troyes? In the north? No, of Orange," she corrected me,

clearly puzzled by my question. I was still half convinced that we were talking to the reincarnation of the woman whose abduction had precipitated the Trojan War.

"Well, Hélène," said Iffy, rushing to fill the embarrassed silence, "you can begin by telling us your own response to the Gaffer's set."

Hélène squirmed. "Oh no. I don't think so."

"Why not?"

"Normally, I am a big fan of *ze Gaffair*..."

"I get you," Iffy affirmed. "Normally, you like his work - but this gig was pony."

"Pony?"

"Yeah, pony. Pony and trap - crap. Shite. Bad. No good."

Hélène blushed deliciously on her cheeks and I found myself thinking of hot chocolate sauce being drizzled over succulent profiteroles.

"Don't be shy," Iffy urged. "Don't worry, we protect the anonymity of all our contributors. You can tell us what you really think in complete confidence."

"I do not wish to have problems with the club manager."

Before I could offer to organise a ten-year siege to defend her, Iffy was able to convince her that she could speak freely. With a nod of her head that set the bottom of her pony tail bouncing like a fish on a line, she told us that she had been sadly disappointed by the Gaffer's latest offering. "But I think his next album will be something special," she offered by way of compensation. "*Ze Gaffair*, he was very excited. Very confident."

"Great," Iffy enthused, while I was busy wondering if tawny was the word I sought to describe Hélène's hair, or whether umber was apter. "Now, maybe you can tell us how the gig itself unfolded. What happened? Who came? Was the club full? What was the public like? Fans, normal clubbers, stars? Old friends, maybe?"

She did something with her mouth and lips that reminded me of time lapse footage of a rosebud opening its petals. On another, less beautiful face, the movement could have been dismissed as a smile, but that simple word completely failed to do justice to what I was observing.

"*Ze Gaffair* himself only arrived in time to play. His manager did most of the work for him - not just the paperwork, but dealing with the press also. It was the grand occasion. The press were here, mostly local, but I think one or two journalists came down from Paris. That's *ze Gaffair* for you. Even if what he played was not, how shall I say…"

"Earth shattering?"

"Yes, that is very good. Even if what he played did not exactly shatter the earth, the club was very busy, so my boss was content. And when my boss is content, it gives me a penis."

That stopped us dead in our tracks.

Iffy was the first to suss it out. "Happiness. It gives you happiness." Hélène's French accent had caused her drop the H and stress the wrong vowel. He carried on, while I struggled to concentrate. "And the Gaffer? Was he happy, do you think?"

The sun (bewildered, it seemed to my over-stimulated imagination, to be outshone by a greater source of light) was creeping across the sky, herding shadows down the wall against which Hélène rested. She shifted her balance with a ballerina's shuffle, and her complexion in the shade was the colour of freshly made toast; where the rays of the sun struck it, it was lathered in a layer of golden butter.

"It is difficult for me to say. He was not unhappy. But always his manager was saying quiet words in his ear, interrupting conversations, saying he must meet this person, that he has to shake this hand. Is it okay if I say these things?"

She clapped a slender-fingered hand over her mouth. Saint Peter barring the gates of Heaven.

"You can say whatever you want. What time did the event finish? What happened afterwards? Where was the Gaffer staying - in a hotel near here?"

A pensive pursing of Hélène's lips persuaded me that perhaps perfection did exist. I silently paid homage to the process of evolution for having created this human.

"We closed the doors at six a.m."

"And the Gaffer," Iffy pressed, "when did he leave?"

"Let me think...He did not stay long."

"Did you actually see him go?"

"He did not say goodbye to me personally. He left with his, er, friend, I think."

That grabbed my attention, even as I was just about to settle on sorrel as the *mot juste* for the colour of her hair.

"Did you meet his friend?" I asked, surprising myself by regaining the powers of speech.

"No," my goddess replied. "But I noticed him." Her nose wrinkled in a show of distaste, much as Cleopatra's must have done when she learned of Caesar's assassination. "He was very...how shall I say?"

"Noticeable?" Iffy suggested.

"Yes. That is the word. He was..."

"Loud? Drunk? Scruffy? Aggressive?" I proposed.

"Well, yes..."

I had a mental of image of Sam Saoule rocking up at the trendy club on the final day of his week-long amphetamine binge. He had always had a brutal face, a face lacking in softness and finesse, a face that frankly scared the pants off a lot of folks. After having been cooped up in the dreary confines of Barbwire's flat sewing bits of rubber together, he would have had the wild eyes of a beast that had broken free of its cage, and he would have fitted in with the fashionable crowd of clubbers like a mad dog amongst preening pigeons.

"Do you remember his name?"

"*Ze Gaffair's* manager dealt with him. Took him into the back room, away from the people. He was trouble, in my opinion. He looked like a *clochard* - a tramp. A punk. An *iroquois* haircut. Dirty clothes."

"Was his name Sam?"

"I think it was, yes. You know this man?"

Iffy explained that Sam was an old collaborator of the Gaffer's fallen on hard times. Hélène said that she had been surprised when the Gaffer and his manager had left the club in his company. "He drank a lot of our champagne, this Sam. He became quite aggressive. It was not a good image for the club. We have sophisticated clients. It was only because of *ze Gaffair* that we did not call the police."

I felt sorry for Hélène. Sam Saoule on the rampage wasn't easy to handle. He had been an insurrectionary anarchist, a hardcore antifascist, always up for the fight, never far from the front line. He had taken his revolution seriously and had gone about it in an earnest fashion, preferring direct action to preaching. Sometimes he used to come back to his truck with a blood stain on his shirt, bruises on his love-and-hate knuckles, and a sly smile slashed across his ugly face, and I would know that somewhere in a gutter a neo-Nazi lay bleeding. He had despised vanity, shallowness and ostentation - things he must have found in industrial quantities at the Gaffer's Marseilles gig.

"To be honest, I was worried when I saw them leave together. Anything could have happened," Hélène sniffed. "They were sure to attract attention and the city centre is a dangerous place, with all those blacks and Arabs who come in from the *cités* - the bad places."

"Pardon?"

"It is not safe for a white person these days. They should send them all back home, of course, but this government is too soft on foreigners. Oh," she added, perhaps registering - but not fully comprehending - the expressions on our faces, "I don't mean foreigners like you…"

And just like that, in a few fleeting phrases Hélène ceased to be a vision of loveliness and became just another casual racist. Her eyes, once so deep and promising, became cold and dull. Her stance, once so lithe and lissom, now struck me as studied and stiff. Her tan, which had hinted at vineyards, olive groves and wind-sheltered, sun-drenched coves on Mediterranean islands, looked like the crisping husk of a lemon left on the dashboard of a car parked on the tarmac outside a supermarket. Her teasing frown lines turned into a glare and her heart-warming smile became a stomach-churning grimace. And I definitively identified the colour of her hair as a mixture of muddy puddle and dog shit brown.

This was precisely the moment for a devastating farewell comment, one of those unforgettable, unanswerable put-downs that hit the nail so squarely on the head that all further conversation is rendered null and void. I knew it was time to hit her with a pithy one-liner that would have left this black-hearted woman to ponder her uninformed racism, maybe even to question her entire outlook on the world, and, who knows, to become a better person for the experience.

The German language has many magnificent words. Briefly, I was feeling *Fremdscham*: embarrassment on somebody else's behalf. And then, as Iffy led me silently away, I couldn't even salvage a *Treppenwitz* - literally a 'stair-joke,' the French *ésprit d'escalier*, the brilliant comeback you only think of when you're already out of the door and halfway down the stairs.

STAY UP FOREVER

"All looks pretty straightforward to me," Iffy announced, raising his glass.

There are many times when a tall, slim glass of bubbling, amber-tinted fermented barley, hops and water, topped with a creamy head, is one of the greatest pleasures known to Man. Not for nothing has the practise of brewing beer survived down the millennia. In China, people were already sipping on rice beer around nine thousand years ago, a time when most of the world's five million inhabitants were nomadic hunter-gatherers. A jar discovered in Iran contained physical traces of beer dating from around 3500 BCE, while the Sumerian goddess Ninkasi, the deity for intoxicating beverages, brewed fresh beer every day to 'satisfy the desire' and 'sate the heart' of the faithful. By around five thousand years ago the Germanic and Celtic tribes of Europe were also knocking it back, and their descendants have never looked like stopping.

Apparently some archaeologists have postulated that beer was instrumental in the formation of civilisations, but Iffy, as so often, had a theory that went further. I remembered him explaining to me how alcohol had not received due credit for its full impact on history. It was after a night out in Hamburg with Sam Saoule and Udo, an evening that had begun at a friendly punk gig in a squat bar and peaked violently near the Reeperbahn.

The gist of his argument was that much of the belligerence that has marked the brotherhood of Man's fratricidal annals was a direct result of too much booze. He contended that the imbibition of water was a hazardous undertaking throughout most of our history, and that kings, generals, warlords and other leaders were in a position to avoid this danger by quaffing safer - i.e. distilled or fermented - liquids. The results, he posited, were plain to see. Maybe, he suggested, the aggressively annoying pair of Austrian tourists who had just been on the receiving end of a mild pummelling were sweet and sensible when sober, but tanked up they were ready to rumble. Imagine, he theorised, that they had an army or a war band to back them up. The same urges, he slurred (for we had been on the sauce ourselves), that nowadays led to brawls at closing time used to lead to invasions, full-scale battles and war.

He had another similar theory that blamed a lot of the most heinous crimes committed by history's vilest despots on toothache, but he had no corroborative evidence for that one.

"All fingers point to *ze Gaffair*," he declaimed between gulps. "Poor old Sam must have moseyed down to the club after Barb hit the sack…"

"Where he met *ze Gaffai*r, who went back with him back to Barb's flat…"

"And even Sam must've been flagging by then. Nobody can stay up forever, though Dog knows Sam did his best..."

"And then the Gaffer gave him the GBH. He could have slipped it into a drink…"

"It's colourless and it doesn't smell, though I do recall a slight salty flavour."

"But Sam was so fucked he wouldn't have clocked it. Not many people have died from taking GBH, I know, but combined with alcohol -"

"And with Sam's body being ready to collapse after the caning he'd given it -"

"It can prove fatal."

"And did."

"Indeed."

Iffy and I noticed that our glasses were empty, so we ordered two more. Not feeling quite ready for the slog back up the hill under the heat that came belting down from the sun like a physical pressure on our heads and backs, we were holding our latest debriefing session in a bar on the seafront, paying a small fortune out of my dwindling resources for the pleasure.

"It's a bit fucking mental, though, isn't it?" I lamented as we clicked our glasses together.

"The cold-blooded assassination of your old mates? It's a bit outside the bounds of accepted social norms, I'll give you that."

I nodded. There are times when a decent bit of understatement hits the mark. "Why d'you think he's doing it, Iffy?" I wondered. "What's he got to gain? I mean, everything we've found out says it's him - but we haven't come across anything that might serve as a motive."

"Remember that tape you found in Udo's bag?"

"Sure…"

"Well…it has to be a clue, right? Especially if Minnie was listening to it before she died too. Maybe something that went down at the Millennium Massacre is the key to it all. If only I had more than the haziest of recollections…"

"I know what you mean. But I can't think of anything at the Millennium Massacre that would drive a man to commit murder. Maybe the Gaffer's just lost the plot. Though he didn't seem particularly barking when I saw him in Berlin. Porky? Yes. Pompous? Definitely. Self-satisfied? Certainly. Murderously insane? No, as it goes."

"Ah, y'see, that's something in itself."

"It is?"

A PRETTY NICHE MARKET

"Think about it, *mon ami*. If he isn't just plain mental, that means there must be another motive. A motive that seems like a good motive to him. The other day when you were catching up on your beauty sleep, I used my time at Jochen's to do some research on the internet. So it turns out most murders are committed because of domestic arguments - we can count that out for starters. Money's another popular motive, but obviously the Gaffer has far more wedge than any of us. Intoxication - booze or drugs - is another frequent cause, but it was the victim who was trolleyed in every one of the deaths, not the killer."

"Maybe that's something? The fact that they were all in altered states when they died?"

"Nah. They were just all caners," came Iffy's dismissive reply. "Now - revenge is another common motive. We can't rule that out, can we? We don't know what he might have been avenging, of course, but it's worth bearing in mind, right?"

"Right." I was genuinely impressed. Ever since I had opened my mouth to Clara about Iffy's shortcomings, he hadn't put one stinky foot wrong, apart from the small crack-stop earlier that day - and even that had proved handy by rendering him loquacious when we talked to Hélène. He had even spent his time researching motives on a computer while I had been sleeping. I was beginning to regret having doubted him.

He continued, "Thing is, the Gaffer's no ordinary murderer. He's what's known technically as a serial killer, a multiple murderer who enjoys a spot of down time between killings. Sex is their usual motive, or financial gain again, but we can safely eliminate those, right?"

"Right. What else was there for serial killers?"

"Visionaries. Could just be that we erred on the side of hastiness when we discounted insanity. Neither of us have seen the Gaffer for years. Who's to say he isn't getting messages from beyond, telling him he has to do the killings. God, demons, aliens, that kind of thing. Stranger things have happened."

I bit my lip pensively.

"Then there are the mission-orientated killers," he went on. "They aren't necessarily psychotic, by the way. They're just on a mission to rid the world of certain undesirables. It's often a race thing, or a religion thing, or it's directed at prostitutes or gay men. Some kind of subculture. This particular brand of loonies think they're making the world a better place."

I gave that some thought. "Maybe the Gaffer's going through a serious reaction against the techno traveller scene. He seems pretty anxious to put a distance between himself and his dodgy past. Maybe he thinks we stole his youth from him, or some bollocks like that."

"Maybe he's cottoned onto the fact that we *are* undesirables."

"Could be."

"Okay, so next up are the lust killers, proper lost-its who like to get in close and go for the whole torture and mutilation fandango."

"Yuck. That's not the case here, thank Dog. All of the deaths were clinical and efficient. Apart from Jacek, of course, but he had his wrists slashed to give the impression of a suicide. Not for a laugh."

"And then there are the thrill killers."

"Who do it just because they get their rocks off killing people?"

"Yup. It's all about the massive adrenaline rush of taking another person's life. Their victims are usually strangers, though."

"Fuck me. This is surreal."

"What else was there? Oh yes, the next one's a good one. The power, or control, killers, who do it to overcome feelings of powerlessness and inadequacy. They buzz off being the ultimate boss, literally having the power of life or death over another person."

"Well, the Gaffer always liked to be in control...that's where he got his name from, after all." I said, then released a snigger I simply couldn't stifle. "Poor sod. Looking back, travelling with us must have been hell with the heat turned up for a control freak."

The free party scene had far more than its fair share of bloody-minded, obstreperous, unruly, non-compliant, wilful, wayward, undisciplined, disobedient, ungovernable, unmanageable, uncontrollable and generally riotous anarchist bastards, and our particular crew had been as out of order as the best of them. The concept of trying to boss us around always brought one of my favourite expressions to mind: it was like herding cats.

"To be honest, though, the Gaffer soon learnt that he wasn't really the gaffer with us," I said. "I mean, his nickname was tongue in cheek, and he obviously appreciated the joke because he kept the name after he left the rig. I thought we'd cured him of his bossiness."

"Or maybe it just really rankled within him. Deep inside. That's what I've been thinking. That it was bugging him for years and it's finally all bubbled to the surface. Know what I mean? Anyway, the last motive I could find was attention seeking, and I thought that could hit the spot with the Gaffer, too. If ever there was a geezer who craved the spotlight, it was him."

"But he's already world famous," I pointed out.

"Think how much more famous he'd be as a DJ-cum-serial killer. It's a pretty niche market when you think about it."

"You think he wants to get caught?"

"Maybe subconsciously. Or maybe he just wants the added fame of being the sole surviving member of his old group of acquaintances. It's worth throwing into the mix anyway."

"So let's sum it up. What are we left with in the way of possible motives? Revenge, but we don't know what for. Messages from a superior being or beings. An attempt to cleanse the world of all traveller scum, starting with those he knew best. Control-freakery relating back to a period of his life when he wasn't really in control. Or some kind of warped bid to achieve even greater fame, either as a killer or as a survivor. Way to go, Iffy."

I reached across the table and shook his paw.

"You know," I continued, "up to now I couldn't get anywhere near a motive for why the Gaffer would do it, never mind how I looked at it. It was doing my head in. He could have been the killer every time - he was probably there, in the right place at the right time - but for the life of me I couldn't figure out why. Now we've got something to work with."

He looked at me smugly, but then I gave him the benefit of the doubt because he could have been trying for modest. "Shucks," he shrugged.

"Shucks?" I repeated. "Do people really say that?"

"Just did, amigo. Just did."

"So what next?" I asked, and it suddenly dawned on me that maybe I was Robin and Iffy was Batman. It was a painful concept, so I didn't dwell on it.

"London," he told me authoritatively. "We get on the Gaffer's case."

"How?"

"By having a look at his life in greater detail. We don't know much about him, if we're honest. We knew him how used to be, not how he is. Remember when Allan was waffling on about everyone being a different person every seven years? The whole *omnia mutantur, nihil interit* thing he was banging on about. You know - everything changes, nothing perishes. We don't even know where the Gaffer's based these days. We should check out his new way of life. Maybe have a wee butcher's at his music studio, wherever that is. See what we can dig up."

He was right. The Gaffer had to be stopped before he could add to his list of victims. I was worried about Clara, back in London. She may not yet have come round to the fact that her life was in danger, but I was convinced it was. With her guard down, she would be an easy target.

Our decision was made. We drained our drinks and stood up. I left a distressing amount of money on the table next to our empty glasses and we set off.

"Oh shit - I think Barb's expecting us to crash at hers tonight," Iffy suddenly reminded me, giving me a painful slap on the arm.

"Arse. I'd forgotten that."

"She's taking it pretty badly, eh - Sam's death."

"Poor lass. Must have been horrible for her, finding his body and all."

"She's still in a state. Probably'd be glad of some company."

"A shoulder to cry on."

"Someone to hold her hand."

"Yup."

"She was really cut up."

"Aye."

"But we haven't any got time to lose."

"That's right. It could be life or death if we don't stop the Gaffer."

"Exactly. Barb'll be alright."

"She's a big girl."
"Been through a lot."
"To say the least."
"It's a matter of priorities."
"That's right."
"London, then?"
"Guess so."

I suspected the shameful truth might have included the fact that neither of us particularly wanted to face another heart-rending session of tears and reminiscences as a distraught Barbwire Barbara-on-speed raked over the smouldering memories she had of Sam and a love she had only recognised when it was too late. With the excuse of having to leave immediately to continue our investigations, we could avoid putting ourselves through that harrowing experience. What was more, we could do so without having to admit it to each other. We were cowards, and I think we both knew it.

Later, when I had time to mull things over, I chastised myself for our behaviour. A few days before, among the debris of Minnie's loveless existence in Amsterdam, I been full of fraternal feelings, but as I texted a message to Barbwire, telling her inadequately to keep her chin up, and we climbed up yet another hill towards Gare Saint Charles and the fast train out of there, I failed to make time for another old friend.

SWAGGER AND STAGGER

"We should get some supplies in for the journey," I suggested, thinking longingly of baguette and cheese. Iffy obligingly offered to go while I waited at the station. I fished twenty euros out of my pocket, said, "See you in a bit," and began to brood over our conversation.

Voices from the gods...mission-oriented killers... attention seekers...

For one whole summer a few years back Iffy had been channelling communications from aliens, or so he had reckoned. Personally, I doubted the veracity of his claims. A couple of the people he most admired, Philip K Dick and Robert Anton Wilson, had reported similar experiences, though Wilson later put it down to a certain over-exuberance with psychedelic drugs and the same charge could justifiably be laid at the sci-fi writer's door. It was noticeable that Iffy's visions stopped not long after Jacek's batch of home-made LSD blotters ran out. (It was Jacek's first experiment at transferring liquid acid onto paper and the end result was that some of the tabs were pretty poky and the rest were ridiculously fucking hefty, and Iffy munched a lot of them that summer.)

Long before that, there was his Candid Camera Paranoia, during which he seriously entertained the possibility that the world as he knew it was a giant set-up for a candid camera show, with him as the victim. He insisted on shaking all new acquaintances by the hand in order to reassure himself that he was not talking to Jeremy Beadle in disguise.

Then there was his visceral Fear of Moustaches, inspired by their popularity amongst members of the constabulary, dole office workers and customs officials.

For years I naïvely believed that he always took the stairs

because he enjoyed the exercise, until one day he revealed his Escalator Phobia and his unshakeable suspicion that they concealed the entrance to the underworld. He countenanced that it was unlikely to be true but nonetheless refused to take any chances, just in case.

For a few months, back when we were squatting in Finsbury Park, he claimed that the woman who ran our local corner shop could read his mind, and I actually gave momentary credence to the theory when one day we walked in together and she greeted us with the words, "It *is* a lovely day for a drink in the park. Yes, the scrumpy's still on special offer. And of course I'll put it on the tab and you can pay on giro day. Packet of blue Rizla and ten Silk Cut too, is it?"

On the subject of his more obvious eccentricities, Iffy himself liked to point out that it wasn't a sign of good mental health to be well adapted to a sick society. He often quoted Philip K Dick ("Sometimes the appropriate response to reality is to go insane.") and Hunter S. Thompson ("I hate to advocate drugs, alcohol, violence, or insanity to anyone, but they've always worked for me.").

And just then, as I sat wondering what was taking Iffy so long, I was rocked by a memory from our night out in the Hole - the semi-visible ghost memory that had come back to me the day after my black-out - of Iffy ranting, really ranting, scarily ranting, about how we had all sold out. I recalled the disgust he had voiced, the venom in his words, the fanatical sincerity in his face and the naked hatred in his eyes as he banged on about the way we had betrayed our scene, our beliefs, ourselves, each other - and him.

As for attention seeking - well, apart from the obvious fact that he always loved being the star of any party, there was something about Iffy's incessant scrapes with authority and his dizzying dance through the underground that hinted at a profound need to be spoken about.

It seemed that several of the motives he had listed for the Gaffer could actually apply to him. Switch a hatred of travellers for a hatred of sell-outs and you had a possible mission-orientated killer. He was more than partial to being the centre of attention. And it wouldn't totally surprise if he was hearing voices again - after all, there weren't many situations or possible mental health issues that were improved by smoking crack cocaine for breakfast.

But my judgement couldn't be so awry that I was hanging out with a serial killer. Iffy was a nutter, but he wasn't crazy, I told myself, as he slipped into view in the shimmering air, his last few dreads writhing around his shoulders, his arms noticeably unburdened by anything resembling either bread or cheese, his stride marked by that inimitable combination of swagger and stagger that told me just what he had done with my twenty euros and reminded me that he would always be trustworthy, right up until the moment he wasn't.

PART TWO

"Two roads diverged in a wood, and I -
I took the one less travelled by."
- ROBERT FROST

THE EMPTY PRODUCT

Perhaps as a punitive measure for putative misdemeanours - or, fuck it, felonies - in a past life, in this one I had spent a long time in Iffy's company, ever since Day One of our friendship when our paths had first crossed at Junction One of the M1, a suitably prime numbered location for a beginning. (Though I had read somewhere that one is also called the empty product, as any number multiplied by one is itself, which is the same result as multiplying by no numbers at all.) We had both been trying to hitch a lift out of the big bad city, and Iffy had continued with equanimity to take the rides that life offered him, and not to grumble when it ignored him and sped on by.

He had by turns vexed, perplexed, dumbfounded, confounded, confused, bemused, amused, amazed, fazed, frustrated, fascinated, irritated, entertained, enchanted, disgusted and disappointed me, sometimes all within the space of twenty-four little hours, and I had facial expressions to match each and every one of these diverse sentiments.

Now, as we sat in a London pub, having a few minutes before raised our glasses and said "Cheers!" to each other for about the fifteen thousandth time, I stared at him blankly. My mind, too, froze. I was trying to assimilate the sentence he had just oh-so-casually uttered.

"Did you just say that?" I finally asked, watching as he sipped at his pint and deftly flipped a fifty pence coin between his knuckles.

"Pretty sure I did. Or at least I thought it at top volume."

"Right," I said. "Just checking."

And he carried on sipping and flipping, as nonchalant as you like. To an outside observer he was as unremarkable as a plane cruising through clear skies over a city; to me, having heard what he had just said, the plane was the Enola Gay and the city was Hiroshima.

Struggling, I decided to take his statement word by word in order to avoid any possibility of miscomprehension. "'We' - that would mean us, I'm guessing?"

"None other, old friend."

"Okay. And 'have', well, as it's followed by 'to', that makes 'have to', as in 'it's necessary', or 'we're obliged to'?"

"Spot on. We have to -"

"Whoa! 'We have to'. Okay. Got it, so far. Now, next, I couldn't help being struck by the enormity - the severity - the violence - of the next word. So let me run it past you again. Just to be sure that I heard correctly. All those years of listening to banging techno music haven't done my hearing any favours, you know. But as far as I could make it out, the next word, the one that followed directly from 'We have to' - well, I think you said 'kill'. Correct me if I'm wrong. Please."

"No, no, you got it first time."

"'Kill'. As in..?"

"As in 'kill'."

"As in terminate? Or exterminate?"

"For example."

"As in exterpate?"

"Or liquidate."

"Assassinate."

"Eradicate."

"All right, mate. I'm getting the picture. Would murder also hit the mark?"

"A bit emotionally charged, that one, I'd say."

"Yes. Yes, it is. Lots of negative connotations there. What would you prefer? Rub out? Bump off? Slay?"

"You know," he said, still sipping and flipping, flipping and sipping, "I think I'll stick with 'kill'."

"Fine. 'Kill' it is. And then the end of the phrase, unless I'm very much mistaken, was 'the Gaffer'"

"Oh, well done. Nothing wrong with your lug-holes, mate. Twenty-twenty vision of the auditive kind."

"I'll run this past you one more time, then. A final recap. Just to be sure. 'We have to kill the Gaffer.'"

"Bingo."

"Bloody Nora."

"Language, Matron."

So it seemed that there was nothing wrong with my hearing, despite having repeatedly and sustainedly assaulted my ears with extreme noise levels throughout a fifteen year period of my life. That was unfortunate, because it meant that Iffy was suggesting we commit murder. I would have been more at ease, though somewhat puzzled, had he instead been implying that we should *bill* our ex-travelling companion for the time we had spent chasing his trail around Europe, or that we should *thrill* him with the devastating wit of our repartee. But no, the word had definitely been *kill*.

"What?" Iffy said in reply to the look I was sending his way.

When I found some words, I was dismayed to discover that they were straight out of my locker of mildly amusing understatement. "Bit harsh, don't you think?"

"Think about it." He flicked his coin up in the air and let in land in his fist. Plop. "Be logical. Be reasonable." He wiped a paw across his mouth and narrowed his eyes. "And don't tell me you didn't know where this whole investigation was going to lead us."

I did one of those sighs that I kept in reserve for emergencies, filling my mouth with air and puffing my cheeks out like a greedy hamster, before letting it all out in a trumpeting torrent of vibrating lips.

The truth was that I had been existing in a state of denial.

Iffy, whom I regularly accused of living a *carpe diem* lifestyle, had been thinking ahead, while I stubbornly refused to project myself into the future. I had been following the clues and the trail of bodies, gathering information assiduously - and just as assiduously, I had been brushing off Iffy's attempts to settle the matter of what we would do when the evidence had stacked up.

And now, ensconced in a Hackney boozer at five thirty on a drizzly summer afternoon, watching the after-work crowd pour in through the door and pour beer down their throats, sat in the same room as all those boys and the girls who had their own little worries, who bitched about their bosses, gossiped about the new boy, martyred themselves for their mortgages and drowned it all out in a dose of comradeship and an alcoholic daze, I came very close to facing up to reality.

I tried the idea on for size.

We had to kill the Gaffer.

It didn't fit me.

Iffy finished his pint in two or three massive gulps, released a muffled belch, and leaned across the table. Raising his voice over the increasing din of the other drinkers, he told me to give his proposal some thought, and added that he was open to any other alternative solutions I could come up with.

"How about another pint?" I suggested.

BAD NEWS FOR CLARA'S TEE-SHIRT

Upon our arrival in the UK, we had scoured the internet for information about the Gaffer, and we found that he had been in Rotterdam just after Minnie had died and in Warsaw on the night before Jacek ceased to be, performing at Part One and Part Three respectively of his 'Underground Star' mini-tour. Parts Two and Four had been in Marseilles and Berlin when Sam, Udo and Allan had died.

While we were catching the internet waves, we also located the Gaffer's home base. We had toyed half-heartedly with the idea of simply phoning him and saying we'd like to pay him a visit for old times' sake, but quickly cast a veto on that. Carlo, the chatty anglophile whose inertia and masochism condemned him to seeing out his days in the comfort of his Berlin bar, had alerted us to the possibility that the Gaffer knew we were on his case, and that wasn't a very comforting prospect. Eventually, after many a digital dead-end and labyrinthine link, we had found an address for the Gaffer's studio. It was just off Mare Street in Hackney - grounds where Iffy and I had had many a stomp when we had been squatting together back in the nineties.

Enthusiasm for our investigation into the deaths of our friends had superseded my initial scepticism, but now that we had convinced ourselves of the Gaffer's involvement I was having to force myself to continue. Despite my reluctance, or rather in order to quell any lingering doubts, we planned to put our suspect under close observation and, should the opportunity present itself, have a nose around his place of work. Maybe we would at last find our hard evidence.

I subtly guided the ship of our conversation away from where it drifted in the dangerous swells and eddies that Iffy currently favoured, and we cruised gently along on a tide of reminiscence. Our minds' eyes watched younger versions of ourselves on the distant shore of the hazy past. The buildings we had squatted, the techno parties and punk gigs we had attended, the demos we had been on, the summer days spent chilling in the park, the winter days gathering fire wood and the winter nights when we huddled under blankets and passed endless spliffs back and forth.

Finally Iffy seized the rudder of our discussion and ran it aground. "Right then. Let's go and have a gander at the Gaffer's gaff, shall we?" he said, banging his empty glass down on the table.

"Oh, I think we've got time for another pint," I hedged. "Haven't we?"

"We can't sit on our honeyed buns guzzling beer all day, matey mine. Come on."

While I've said before that Iffy was a man who did surprises like most folks performed their daily ablutions, there were one or two things that I took for granted. Accepting the offer of a drink was one of them.

"Just a half?" I tried.

"There's work to be done. Come on, get a wriggle on, Sheila."

This was what I had wanted, I reminded myself: that he should party less, be more serious, get a grip, shoulder the burden, remove his nose from a wrap of powder and put it to the grindstone. Now that it seemed to be happening, I wasn't so sure that I liked it. In our little team of two, I was responsible for being responsible, and Iffy was in charge of the light entertainment. I was the steady bassline and he was the swirling 303. I did the chivvying and chiding, the reflecting and deciding, and he took care of the frolicking and joking, the drinking, snorting and toking. It was his role to lighten the atmosphere and always to tempt me with another beer; it was mine to tell him to wobble his head and to remind him when it was time for bed. I was Batman; he was Robin. I was the Lone Ranger; he was Tonto. He was the waster, the caner, the dosser *extraordinaire*, the loafer *par excellence*, and I had always been secure in the knowledge that compared to him my shit was well and truly together.

Now, as I cast a final, longing glance at the dribble of beer left in my glass and stood up to leave the pub, I indulged in a moment of brutal self-analysis. Maybe my shit wasn't quite as together as I liked to believe. Okay, I had successfully reduced my alcohol, nicotine and drug consumption to part-time activities, rather than having them as the cornerstone of my existence, but really, at the end of the day that was hardly anything to be too proud of. Looking down the barrel of my fifth decade, I was living alone in a flat that was cheap but also shitty, paying rent and keeping myself mildly amused with the money I earned buying and selling second-hand records.

At least Iffy gave every impression of loving his dissolute life, of milking it for all the joys and pleasures it could yield. He didn't pay taxes to prop up a system of which he disapproved, nor rent to settle someone else's bank debts. He had made no concessions, had never backed away from the front line. Me, I had begun to ask myself questions about old age. Carlo's self-mocking comments about his pension plan had actually ruffled a few of my feathers. Iffy was still living his life and loving it just as he always had, while I was caught precariously between two stools, trying to escape from the lifestyle of the eternal teenager but reluctant to land my skinny arse in the realm of the armchair anarchist.

"Iffy," I began hesitantly, "don't you ever get tired of

scratching an existence out of the dirt? Don't you ever want a bit of comfort in your life? Just the tiniest degree of security?"

He stared at me and said, yet again: "Don't start."

"I'm not starting... I'm just asking."

"You're kidding me, right? Security? I take it by security you mean possessions?"

I supposed I did, when I came to think about it.

"So what do I own in this world?" he asked, rubbing his paw over his scalp. "I'll tell you. These trainers, these socks, these trousers. The tee-shirt's Clara's and the hoody's Cousin Dave's. I've got a bit more tat back in his squat - a few more clothes, a saucepan, a couple of paperbacks, a few records that I've been given. A bag of carrots, some garlic and a few tatties left over from my last skip-shopping mission. A dozen capsules of MDMA that Danny the Builder ticked me. A sleeping bag. A mattress.

"It's all ephemeral. I'll wear the clothes till they rot and drop off my body." He wasn't exaggerating. It was bad news for Clara's tee-shirt. "Then I'll find some more stuff to wear. The food came from the earth, and unto the earth it shall return. I'll end up giving the records to someone else. The books, too. I'll flog the powder and spunk the money at the next party. I'll lug the mattress and the beeping slag from squat to squat until some cowboy landlord locks me out in my absence - and when he does, it won't matter 'cos I'll just blag some other ones somehow."

"Isn't it hard work, though? You're not getting any younger, my friend."

He shook his head angrily. "You used to get it - what's happened to you? You think that cunt there," he said, jabbing his finger towards a random passer-by in a suit, "you think he's *happier* than *me*? You don't think he's worried about what would happen if his boss handed him his P45? If someone slashed the tyres on his motor? Or if the pound collapsed, or his yard got robbed, or the revolution came, as come it must? Everything in his life costs money. His life is expensive - and if it's *expensive*, it ain't *free*."

"Surely there's a happy medium?"

"No. That's precisely where you're wrong. All of you - you and all the other ex-teenage rebels. You know the story about the Buddha-dude and the cows, right?"

"No…"

"The Buddha-dude's chillin' with his bredren. They see an unhappy farmer who's lost his cows. The farmer needs money from the cows to pay the rent. But in order to feed the cows he needs land to grow food. Basically, he needs cows to make money to pay the rent on the land he needs to grow the food he needs to feed the cows he needs so he can pay the rent on the land he needs to grow the food he needs to feed the cows. The Buddha-dude says: the happiest people have no cows to lose."

"Yeah, but…ah, forget it."

"You're the one who's forgotten it, sweet cheeks."

Silently asking myself how many cows I had rustled up in the last ten years, I followed Iffy as he weaved his way through the crowd towards the door and out into the East London evening.

BORN TO SLOPE OFF

A few desultory raindrops fell from the orange sky as we did a walk-by on the Gaffer's studio. We performed a slow pavement-cruise, our hands firmly and deeply in our pockets, our lips releasing a duet of tuneless whistles into the humid atmosphere, our eyes straining the limits of their peripheral vision. It was an old routine, tried, tested and never bested during the half dozen years we had spent squatting in London.

And as chance would have it: "Thought so!"

I looked at Iffy, wondering why he had upped the smugometer to smarty-pants factor eleven.

"Sweet," he whispered, showing me his jaundiced teeth. "Saboteurs used to squat the unit next door, and yours truly helped crack it in the first place. And it's empty again by the looks of it."

We were on one of the streets that branched out off the trunk of Mare Street. Like much of Hackney at the time it was an indecisive mix of wealth and poverty. Its residents, I guessed, ran the gamut from under- to upper-middle class, from the long-term unemployed to gentlemen of leisure. The buildings went from dilapidated council flats with boards on the windows to carefully restored properties with cascades of red geraniums tumbling from flower pots. The flower pots were chained down, of course.

The Gaff, as the Gaffer had wittily named his studio, was a flat-topped old industrial unit built on two floors. A fearsome fence crowned with menacing spikes deterred unwelcome visitors. Next to the steel front door I clocked a box of tricks that was clearly linked to a sophisticated alarm system. I had expected nothing less; the Gaffer's top-of-the-range studio equipment must have been worth a mint.

The drizzle turned to rain as Iffy and I nipped into one of the ubiquitous beer, fags and mags shops that littered British cityscapes. We bought a couple of bottles of Polish lager and then sedately strolled past the Gaff for a second time.

"If you happen to know someone looking for a nice place to squat, I think it's only your mately duty to tell them of any empty properties you happen across," I reminded Iffy as he paused to untie and re-tie his shoe laces.

"I agree," he said, all the while giving the buildings a thorough undressing with his eyes. The Gaff's empty neighbour was protected by sheets of metal Sitex on the downstairs windows and front door. "As a purely unselfish and altruistic action. We should probably even check that the move goes smoothly for them, which would mean visiting quite often. It's only polite."

By the time we were back on the main drag we were thoroughly soaked, and our thoughts turned to the matter of where we would lay our weary heads that night. Nobody yet knew we were back in town, but there were plenty of doors that would open for us if we asked. At least, I presumed there were; I recalled Clara's words about Iffy having pissed some people off of late.

As for me, I was sitting on a cerebral fence, tossing imaginary coins up in the air. On the one hand, I was tempted by the idea of hooking up with some of my old London posse, close friends like Danny the Builder, Eltham John and Cousin Dave, so I could have a good old drink up and forget for a moment about our current problems. I wanted to call this the Iffy Option. My other choice was to give my little grey cells a work-out, presuming of course that Clara could spare me the time.

I phoned her from Iffy's mobile and was transferred to her voicemail. Accepting the increased charges, I tried again from my own German phone and was rewarded with a brief and heavily tut-laden conversation, the begrudging outcome of which was an invitation to stay over at her Crouch End flat.

Promising to find some squat-hunters who would be happy to become the Gaffer's new neighbours, Iffy sloped off into the night. I watched him go, thinking that if ever a man was born to slope off into the night, it was him.

THE TOE-TICKLING CARPET COW

I hopped on a bus and went for a top-deck trundle through the contrasting architectural styles that jostled each other for prominence, and after many glimpses of the past and a few glances into the future, I alighted in Crouch End and made my way to the quiet residential street where Clara had plotted up.

Her front door was plain and simple, and when it opened it revealed a Clara whose crow's feet had been marching with a noticeably heavier tread of late, and whose dusting of grey hairs were in danger of out-numbering the brown ones. Her smile drooped at the edges and her hug was limp, and as she hobbled on her crutch towards the sitting room, I remarked that the injury to her leg didn't seem any better. I sank gratefully into the wide-stretched arms of a well-padded chair and accepted the offer of a herbal tea.

I couldn't help counting the cows that Clara had amassed: the flat-screen TV cow, the nice stereo cow, the toe-tickling carpet cow, the matching sofa and armchair cows; and in the kitchen the dishwasher cow, the washing machine cow, and lots of little gadget cows. Her flat was clean without quite having the scarily antiseptic properties that control freaks revel in. A few books and CDs, some clothes, some unopened letters and an unwashed wine glass and dinner plate provided a healthy degree of clutter.

"Go on, then," she sighed, handing me a steaming mug of something that smelt of ginger and, unless my nose was deceiving me, lychees. She poured herself a glass of red wine, I noticed. I saw her go to fold her legs up beside her on the sofa, then correct the action and prop her damaged leg up on a foot stool.

"Go on, then, what, then?" I wondered, confused.

"Go on and tell me how my life's in danger. Then proceed forthwith to tell me how you reached that conclusion, i.e. trot out all the same bullshit as when last we spoke, plus some tenuous so-called evidence that you and your loveable side-kick unearthed about Sam Saoule. Then, depending on which way the wind's blowing today, either moan about what a useless, fucked-up twat Iffy is or back him to the hilt for being a stand-up guy, a misunderstood genius and an example to us all."

"Clara, why have you given me ginger and lichee tea?"

"Look," she said, softening slightly, "I know what Iffy's like when he gets on a mission. His mind closes to all other possibilities. He's like sound systems at a teknival. Must play techno, can only play techno, will only play techno, techno, techno, forgetting that anything is possible. He flies head-first into something and he doesn't check out the other angles of approach. Now he's got you convinced that there's a killer out there, and you're sure that the Gaffer's your man. Let's take a step back for a moment. Now, you're pretty sure that when I got done by that four-by-four -"

"Aha. Yes," I interrupted, leaning forward and brandishing my mug of herbal tea. "That was so dodgy. What are the chances of you almost getting killed at the same time as all the other deaths?"

"Well, the fact is that I found the car."

"You did? Where? Was it the Gaffer's?"

"Of course it wasn't the bloody Gaffer's. Its owner appears to live two streets away. I clocked it a couple of days ago, recognised the reg plate."

"So it wasn't the Gaffer. It was just an accident. Just a coincidence."

"Yup."

"Damn."

She squinted at me from under violently corrugated brows.

"No, sorry, that's not right. I mean...good?" I faltered, thinking that wasn't really I meant either.

"Aye, well, anyway, I superglued a couple of sink plungers to the bastard's bonnet, spray painted 'tosser' on both sides and rammed a sweet potato two feet up the exhaust pipe."

"As you do," I remarked blandly, silently wondering what particular properties the humble sweet potato laid claim to when it came to fucking up a car's engine.

"So, bearing that in mind," Clara went on, "and returning to your deluded fantasies about the Gaffer, can I just check that you do actually know the difference between deductive reasoning and inductive reasoning, don't you?"

I looked insulted. "Do I know the difference between deductive reasoning and inductive reasoning?" I spat sardonically. Then I said, "Er, maybe you could remind me?"

"Deductive reasoning is what clever people do. It's top-down logic. You start with the concordance of multiple premises that are indisputably true and follow them through to a true conclusion. All men must die. Socrates is a man. Socrates must die."

"Sounds reasonable. Shame for Socrates, of course."

"Inductive reasoning, on the other hand, is bottom-up logic for idiots. When I drink white wine, I use a wine glass. I have a wine glass in my hand. Therefore I'm drinking white wine."

"But that's Rioja you're...Ah."

I experimented in my head: four of my friends have died; they all probably saw the Gaffer just before they died; therefore the Gaffer killed them. According to Clara, this would appear to be inductive, not deductive, reasoning.

"And also," Clara continued, "you should ask yourself - but please, don't ask me - if you're really sure there is a nutter on the loose - whether it might just possibly be someone else. Check out all the options. Question everything. Always.

Especially Iffy. *De omnibus dubitandum*, as he'd no doubt put it himself.

"I'm sorry if you think I'm pissing on your chips," she said, sounding anything but. "I accept that you mean well. I know your heart's in the right place; I just wonder where your head is. But I'm overworked, stressed out and really, really tired and I don't fancy another evening going over the same old ground. You should do what you think's right - if you can make your mind up - and we should have a quiet evening in. We should share this bottle of wine and have a roast dinner, and you should cook it."

Which didn't leave much for me to say. Clara had always been she-who-knew-me-so-well, and no amount of time apart would change that. And never mind how much it could wind me up when she held a mirror up in front of me and I saw a sucker staring me in the eye, I was grateful for her friendship.

"Is there anything else you'd like to add?" I asked humbly.

"Don't forget to roast some garlic in with the tatties. And you?"

"Erm, yeah. Please, Clara, please look after yourself. Keep your wits about you, if only to humour me. I've lost a lot of the people who were dear to me. I don't want to lose you."

She had the grace to dip her head in agreement.

By the time that clocks all throughout the land were chiming twelve times, my belly was full and I was mildly drunk. I courageously took on the sofa-bed in a no-holds barred, first to three falls bout. It had me temporarily in a Vulcan death grip but I deftly extricated myself and wrestled it into sullen submission.

As Clara no doubt knew, the devious sod, while she was noisily brushing her teeth I was busily questioning Iffy's motives. She had set me off on a trail of thought (deliberately, I suspected) and I had followed it for such a distance that I left sleep far behind. I called a distracted "Good night," when I heard her close the door to her bedroom and ploughed on in the darkness.

The journey had started with Udo's death and Iffy's phone call. Iffy had popped up at Schönefeld Airport that very evening, claiming to have blagged the air fare off a nameless donor. I had since found out that his credit rating was low in London. I hadn't seen him come out of the arrivals lounge; rather, he had popped up in the lobby, telling me that his flight was ahead of schedule. Was that even possible on such a short haul trip? In other words, it was feasible that he had already been in Berlin when Udo died. I only had his word for it that a junkie had seen a mysterious figure push Udo onto the tracks. What if Iffy had been buying his silence rather than hounding him for information?

He had definitely been in Berlin when Allan was attacked. He was outside the Friedrichshain bar where it happened. Fists had been flying in all directions and nobody was very clear about who had hit whom. Iffy could have landed the blow himself. He certainly knew about Allan's weak neck.

Minnie, whose diary we had read in Amsterdam, had only spoken of an old friend coming to visit. Iffy, of course, would fall into that category as easily as he would fall off a bar stool at four in the morning.

Similarly, at the party in the woods Juliest confided in me that someone from our old rig had ordered some of her K and paid Jacek a visit on the night he died. She had passed out before telling me who. It could have been Iffy.

He could conceivably have been in Marseilles when Sam Saoule overdosed. I had no way of knowing.

He could have been accompanying me on my investigations not because he wanted to help me, but because he sought to steer my suspicions in a direction that suited his own ends.

Mulling it over, over and over again, I didn't know if Clara had really intended me to consider Iffy as the murderer, or if she had gone for the old lawyer's gambit of presenting the jury with another possible culprit in order to plant a seed of reasonable doubt about the prime suspect's guilt.

Sure, Iffy was a bit mad, given to delusions, and fully capable of creating alternative realities. Sure, in Marseilles he had listed several motives that could apply to himself just as much as to the Gaffer. And I knew for a fact that he was now seriously contemplating killing the Gaffer, seemingly with few qualms. Had our escapades around Europe been an elaborate way of suckering me into helping him commit the latest in a string of murders?

Eek.

I shook my head. The Gaffer was still our prime suspect - but I'd have to keep a beady one on the Iffy-boy, I decided.

I was deep asleep when my phone woke me. Apparently Iffy had summoned a posse of prospective squatters who were keen to occupy the empty building that shared a wall with the Gaffer's Hackney studio.

OUR PIE-EYED PIPER

We met at ten the next evening in the Royal Sovereign, the best pub in Hackney, and once I had verified that Iffy wasn't too drunk - he had gone for just a drop or two of Dutch courage - I took the opportunity to size up his volunteers.

I was pleased to find a genial crew of Spanish layabouts. They were old enough to know what they were doing, yet young enough to be brimful of enthusiasm for the underground London lifestyle that attracted so many of Europe's party-heads. If one wave of British techno travellers had exported the scene to Europe, the crews who stayed behind in perfidious Albion continued to draw Europe to them, attracting all sorts of bright-eyed fun-lovers to the well-established party network. I reckoned this particular posse were still in their first bloom of drug-taking and hadn't had time to succumb to the more squalid substances that sometimes took a hold on people's lives. They were experienced enough to know their rights as squatters, and still motivated enough to want to exercise them.

I heard them ask if the building was large enough to host Sunday after-parties and mid-week cafés. Feeling a touch trepidatious about breaking my first squat in many moons, I envied them their dynamism.

Six-up, tooled up with a crow-bar, a torch, some bolt-croppers, a screw-driver, a spare lock barrel, a printed copy of a 'Section Six' and - on Iffy's insistence - a length of rope, we set off towards our destination. Iffy led the way. He told us that he had already broken the place once, back when it had first been occupied a couple of years ago, and claimed to know the best method for effecting a quiet, unobtrusive entrance.

Mooching down the road, we passed eight belly-bouncing

builders, all clutching packets of chips and cans of lager and merrily effing and blinding their way back home from the boozer. We passed seven saggy-trousered rude boys, six stilettoed screechers, five teenaged mums, four turbaned Sikhs, three suited office drones, two hirsute Greek Orthodox priests and a bedraggled, bearded beggar. One of the Spaniards handed the beggar a coin.

And then we passed the insurmountable spiky railings in front of the building we were aiming to squat, and carried on going.

"No lights next door," Iffy commented contentedly as we strolled past the Gaffer's studio.

We followed our pie-eyed piper round two corners and onto a parallel road. Once we were directly behind our target location, he slipped up an alley into a secluded little private car park. No-one was watching. We crept after him.

FORTUNE FAVOURS THE BALDING

"Leg-up, *por favor*," Iffy whispered, standing in front of a low-roofed garage and cupping his hands in front of his stomach to show what he wanted.

Soon there were six silhouettes crouched on the roof of the garage, the last man having been dragged up by his upraised arms. Most of us had opted for black hoodies that night. I felt the old buzz of excitement coursing through my body as we ninja'd bent-backed across the flat surface, to be faced by a windowless brick wall. Another series of bunk-ups made short work of the obstacle, and we were soon on the roof of the soon-to-be squat.

"This is the tricky bit," Iffy murmured, lying prone on the roof and peering over the edge. "There's nothing to tie onto so you lot have to make sure and certain you've got a good grip on your end of the rope. It's a two-storey drop onto concrete and I'd rather not know what it feels like."

A skinny girl with messy black dreads, pierced eyebrows and a voice so husky it could have pulled a sled translated for the rest of the crew, who in turn had the good sense to question the wisdom of Iffy's plan. He assured them that he knew what he was doing. I could only admire his audacity as five of us took a firm hold on the rope and dangled the free end over the edge.

We braced ourselves.

Still standing on the flat roof, Iffy coiled the cord once around his waist and leant back with all his weight. We staggered forward a few rapid paces, then backed up again. I watched as he slid the rope between his hands, and then he was balanced on his heels right on the brink - and then we were grunting and groaning and scrabbling for a footing and for a long moment he was slipping a bit too fast and I felt my muscles straining and I forgot that he was probably a bit of a twat and might even be a killer, and I saw his head disappear and I heard his boots slithering down the wall, I heard him say "Oh my Dog!" - and then we held our ground and held him up.

"Oh yeah," his voice floated up to us, "if an alarm goes off, pull me up - and then we leg it."

We felt him abseil inch by inch down the wall. A series of small jerks almost sparked off some wobbling, but we held firm and were rewarded by the sound of glass breaking. Legally, squatters aren't allowed to force entrance into a building, but nobody would be able to prove that the window hadn't been broken before we arrived on the scene. We heard the wonderful noise of the window sliding open and the next thing we knew we were all falling over backwards as Iffy's weight vanished from the rope. There was no alarm.

Bruised but happy, we untangled ourselves from each other and the rope. There was a lot of grinning, a dash of back-slapping, a few hugs and one or two high-fives going on, but the girl with the locks just rasped, "Now what?"

I saw her point. Iffy was safely inside, which was good. He would be on his way to cut the cables that held the Sitex in place on the side door and to change its lock. (It wouldn't take him long; he probably changed locks more frequently than he changed socks.) The door opened onto the little courtyard above which he had affected his entrance. But unless he intended that we should sneak up an alley, bunk up two roofs and descend on a rope into an open window every time we came and went, there remained the problem of the intimidating metal fence that ringed the front and side of the building.

Luckily, Fate - or the random workings of an unpredictable

world - was on our side. Inside the building, Iffy found a key to the padlock on the gate.

By the time the gates to paradise swung open, Iffy had turned on the electricity and water supplies. The Spanish squatters flew past me into the building, keen to check out their new abode. Iffy and I explored at a more leisurely, measured pace.

I had always loved empty buildings. Getting into them could be scary and tricky, but once inside there was something exciting about them, as though they were made of pure potential. They were like the first dawn after a revolution, or the first day of a child's summer holidays. The sky was the limit and the only things holding you back were the boundaries of your imagination.

Sometimes, generally at around four in the morning, I wondered if I liked that feeling of *tabula rasa* too much. Maybe it was what had prevented me from mastering any one trade or selecting any clear path in my life. Once the furniture was in place, even if you chose it yourself, the possibilities were diminished.

"Nice work," I congratulated Iffy as we moseyed through the building. "Don't think I'd have done that abseil myself."

"I fucking loves it." He said, apparently buzzing so much on adrenaline that his accent went all Welsh. "Never yet saw a building that I couldn't break. You know me - says what he's going to do, does what he said he was going to do. *Dictum factum*, if it pleases you. It just needed a clinical eye, a strong heart and nerves of steel."

"Couldn't have done it with you, dude."

"Ah," he shrugged modestly. "Fortune favours the balding. And you know what they say: there's no I in team."

I grimaced. "No, you cheesy bastard, but there's a U in fuck off."

"And an I C in dickhead. Anyway, now we're the Gaffer's neighbours."

"At least, our Spanish friends are."

"And who knows, we'll maybe to get to have a wander round his studio one of these days."

"It'll be Fort Knox, Iffy."

"I prefer to think of it as Opportunity Knocks."

MARK SLEIGH

THE VOICE FROM THE OUTER EDGE OF DARKNESS

With a mercifully minimal display of reluctance, Clara consented to letting me crash in her flat during my open-ended stay in London. She proved to be just as busy as she so frequently complained about being, leaving early in the morning and returning home at eight or nine or ten in the evening. I kept a low profile and ensured there was always food in the cupboards and wine in the fridge. She might have knocked the party lifestyle firmly and definitively on the head, but I couldn't help noticing that she set great store by her evening tipple. Every night she toppled into bed slightly the worse for wear. She needed to relax after a hard day's lawyering, she told me, and wisely I kept my counsel.

I didn't know and tried to act like I didn't care where Iffy passed his nights. London was his city, his home, his manor, the base from which he launched all his missions, the bolthole to which he always returned, but I no longer knew where he was sleeping; he had failed to share that detail and I had elected not to inquire. He was good at compartmentalising his life, distributing information on a strictly need-to-know basis. It was a useful mindset for anyone who juggled debts and dabbled in illicit activities the way he did, and I had long ago accepted that there were parts of his life I was better off not being privy to. Clara had told me that he had been asked to leave a couple of squats before he had rocked up in Berlin, but I took that with a pinch of salt - and anyway he was never going to be short of a crash-pad in London.

Iffy was keeping out of sight, and I had no idea where the Gaffer was either. Marta, the dreaded squatter with the voice from the Outer Edge of Darkness, had promised to text me as soon as there was any sign of activity in the Gaff, but my mobile remained mute and unilluminated for twenty-four hours. I rested, relaxed, recuperated…at least, I did when I wasn't stressing, worrying, fretting.

THE YOUNG ONES

One afternoon I called in at a charity shop near Clara's, and was browsing listlessly through the vinyl section in one, trying not to smile at the touching spectacle of four doddering senior citizens nodding happily along to a Cliff Richard song called The Young Ones, when my gaze fell on a small metallic silver box that was perched on a high shelf, tucked away almost out of sight behind a royal wedding souvenir mug and a Rubik's Cube.

Abandoning a box of mass-produced hideous pop nightmares, I reached up and plucked down the scuffed, scratched relic - a genuine Sony Walkman - and thought how such a once-ubiquitous, banal and everyday object must already be hard to identify and mysterious to people younger than I.

Sure enough, as I handed over a couple of quid to pay for it, a teenager tossed me exactly the same kind of look that I had given to the elderly folks just seconds before, and for a very similar reason. Undeterred, I popped into the newsagents next door to buy a couple of batteries and congratulated myself on a wise investment when I felt the machine begin to hum and saw the little black cogged wheels start to spin.

Back at Clara's, I did some tidying, cleaning and cooking. When I could hold out no longer, I pulled the Millennium Massacre cassette out of my bag and slipped it into the Walkman. Ever since I had found it in the bottom of Udo's bag, and then heard that Minnie might have been playing it too, my mind had kept returning to the tape. I remembered reading that Einstein had been enthralled by a compass he was given when just a child; the way its needle always swung irresistibly towards north, never mind how much he tried to point in other directions, had set him wondering about what invisible forces lay behind it.

The Millennium Massacre tape exercised a similar fascination on my imagination, and it had gradually grown to represent not just a possible clue in our hunt for the person who was murdering my friends, but also to serve as doorway to my past.

Out through Clara's door I walked, and into the already nippy evening air on the North London street. Soft light oozed out from some of the terraced houses, and their brown bricks and white-painted window frames were cast pink under the auspices of a pale setting sun. As I walked along the pavement, the music on the Walkman came with me and my steps subconsciously began to synchronise with the rhythm of the techno...

The music had never really left me, and here it was again, banging away somewhere in the centre of my being. They say that writing about music is like dancing about architecture, but the Millennium Massacre liveset was much more than just organised tone, sound, rhythm, melody and harmony.

I made a conscious effort to disassociate the tape from the party where it had been recorded, and to listen to it for what it was: a prime example of the free party sound, something catalytic and mystical, a vehicle for conveying the environments, emotions and experiences that were particular to our way of life as a travelling techno sound system; indeed, the music and our lifestyle were so interwoven, so interconnected, so intimately spliced and braided together that the two were mirror images, and to think about one inevitably led me to thinking about the other.

Those ninety minutes of music by Minnie, Sam, Jacek, Udo and Allan were a postmortem testimony to my dear departed friends whose lives I'd shared for five ensorcelled years; to my brothers and sisters of the open road; to my comrades of the wild road; to all my companions of the endless, twisting road where the stars shone bright and the breath of night was raw and pure and sweet upon our skin.

I was getting into the music, the lines in my forehead hardening, my jaw clenching, my lips tightening, my heart galloping, my chest swelling, my skin tingling, my stomach fluttering, my mind slipping further and further away from the suburban streetscape that penned me in on every side...

Our convoy of trucks and buses was rolling through Europe once more: through Britain, France, Spain, Portugal, Germany, Holland, Belgium, Switzerland, Austria, Italy, the Czech Republic, Poland, Romania, Bulgaria, Croatia, Slovenia and Slovakia. It was snaking along motorways, nosing up country lanes and crawling along unmarked tracks; we were parking up and partying in office blocks, warehouses, factories, cement works, film studios, underpasses, farms, airfields, quarries, meadows, forest clearings, beaches, mountainsides and moortops.

The buzz of helping to create a successful free party came back to me as I paced through the darkening city listening to the old liveset.

I found myself reliving the old times. The excitement and satisfaction of finding a site. The adrenaline hit as we rolled our trucks on. The overwhelming rush of relief, elation and anticipation when the first beats came hammering out of a newly installed rig. The massive sound of our speakers as the mixes of our DJs spun quixotic dreams of rapturous abandon. The smell of acrid human sweat and bitter skunk and sweet, hot, wet mud. The sight of clouds of dust rising up through angled beams of sunlight and lines of pounding feet. The gift of pure, innocent, unadulterated bliss that we shared with anyone who cared to come to dance to our sound. The knowledge that we had created something beautiful where previously there was nothing...

Our network had stretched across the continent - we were never far from a friendly face, from someone who knew someone. In every city we could make contact with an extended family who shared our vision, who operated on the same level as us, and who would take us in and make us feel welcome.

I felt a throb of sorrow and genuine pity for anybody who had never experienced life on the road like we had.

I knew it was silly. Presumably most of the people on Clara's street were happy, or at least were giving happiness their best shot. They must enjoy the routine of their existence, and they must either appreciate the safeness and peace of mind brought by regular employment, or be seeking it. They must like living in a house in a street in a city, and probably had absolutely no interest in taking up a rootless, nomadic existence, I thought.

I, too, had settled down into a static, urban lifestyle - but my memories of days and nights I would neither forget nor regret still burned as brightly as comets within me, and as I marched on and the techno roared through my headphones and into my ears, I was reminded of the Kerouac quote that you won't remember the time you spent working in the office or mowing your lawn, that you should climb the goddamn mountain...and I was back in the cab of my truck, and my speakers were blaring a Crystal Distortion liveset, and I was grinning with the knowledge that the road would go on for as long as I wished, and that I could go in any direction I chose, and that whenever I wanted to I could pull off into a lay-by or back lane, and there I could slide open the side door of my truck and make my home.

And my crew, my magnificent, wonderful, fucked up crew, they were with me, too, as the dying sun leaked a final blood-red stain across London's blackening heavens; they were living on within me, destined to be part of me for the rest of my days. I had seen them happy and sad, seen them laughing until they literally pissed themselves and sobbing without shame. I had seen them naked in the morning, I had seen them stripped of all pretension by LSD, I had witnessed them acting selfishly in the grip of terrible comedowns and selflessly in moments of real adversity. I had listened to them as they poured out their traumas, and they had listened to me and mine. I had seen them blinded by tears, speechless with fury and delirious with joy; I had offered them silent love in times of grief and cautious advice in times of confusion and heartbreak, and they had done the same for me.

I had seen them as few people ever see got to see other human beings. I had seen them as they really were, I had known them for what really were, and I had loved them. Years and miles had come between us, and each and every one us had changed after we abandoned the rig, but the moments we had shared - the mist-enshrouded mountain dawns, the wagons encircled around smoky forest firepits, the drunken nights out in a hundred different towns - had tightened the ties of affinity that bound us.

When we had been together, the earth itself had been sufficient to us, and all the fortune that we needed was the fortune we carried in our trucks and in our hearts as we roved the rolling, reeling, mazy, merry highways, and the hillroads wet with rain, and the lost roads where long-forgotten goddesses watched wistfully as we passed by and hoped that we would halt.

Now that my friends' travels were over and we would be apart for ever more, and they would never kiss a lover again, nor shiver in the morning chill, nor bask in the midday sun, nor laugh nor weep, now that they - Minnie, Jacek, Udo, Sam and Allan - were dead, this tape contained more magic than a million years of a million people working in offices or mowing lawns ever could.

I WASN'T THE BUDDHA-DUDE

At last my phone brought me the message that I had been awaiting. 'Lights on next door.'

I phoned Iffy, donned a cavernous hoody that cloaked my face in shadow, and headed Hackney-wards.

The empty building had changed radically since it had been squatted. It was filled with noise, energy and activity, good cheer, good beer and bright colour. It was what squatting was all about: turning dead space into living space.

Iffy popped out of a doorway when I arrived and hustled me into the kitchen, where Marta was smoking a cigarette and painting her toenails black. He helped himself to a beer from the fridge and the leftovers from a frying pan. I said that I'd already eaten; I was more interested in finding out who was next door.

"Marta, did you see a fat geezer with trendy specs at all?"

"*Si*," she said, or maybe somebody outside was tipping a load of gravel down a steel chute. "Two men. The fat man and a thin man. Both with skinhead hair, you know? Both wearing black. Expensive clothes. The thin man, he had red string in his shoes."

The Gaffer and his manager. What was his name? Andy? I remembered talking to him at the Gaffer's gig in Berlin. He hadn't been particularly welcoming at first, but had soon switched into fawning mode when alerted to the fact that we were his milk cow's friends. When he then discovered that we had known the Gaffer during his time on the road, I felt that our standing had fallen again in his estimation. A long way. When I thought about his probable reaction to the arrival of squatters on his doorstep, a nasty, vindictive smile came to my lips. I wasn't proud of it, but, hey, I wasn't the Buddha-dude.

I asked Marta if it would be okay for us to hang around in the squat for a while. Growling like Cerberus after forty Woodbines and a bottle of potcheen, she inquired as to what the fuck was going on. "You know, we are very thankful for the help with the squat. Of course you can stay here. But why are you interested in the men next door?"

Iffy responded. "It's a private thing. Personal. Very complicated - but very important. They can't know we're here. I can't explain any more, I'm sorry."

To my relief, she accepted his justification with a moue and a shrug and a comment about the British love of secrets, and then pointedly left us alone.

"Where d'you reckon the Gaffer's been till now?" I wondered.

"New York."

"Well, maybe…"

"No, really. He's been in NY City, baby. What have you been doing with your time? All you had to do was check the internet. He was doing some interviews over there, bigging up his up-coming album."

"Right," I said. "Well done." I had been spending my time listening to my Walkman and reliving my glory days.

"And before you ask, I phoned Allan's partner. We missed the funeral, it was family only. They scattered his ashes in his weed plantation."

"Right." I hadn't been going to ask about Allan. Not that I didn't care; it was just that my head had been otherwise engaged. Had the Gaffer killed all my friends? Had Iffy killed them? Was the Gaffer going to kill Iffy? Was he going to kill Clara? Or was Iffy going to kill the Gaffer? Was he going to kill Clara? Was I going to kill the Gaffer? Was anyone going to kill me? And on and on and on and round and round and round.

THE PANTOMIME COW

For the first time in my life, I was happy to see Venetian blinds. As a rule I hated the things with a depth of emotion that I generally reserved for companies like Monsanto, Shell, McDonalds and Coca-Cola. The misery that Venetian blinds engendered in the world was less than that generated by the multinationals, of course, but every time I had tangled with them I was left harbouring a similar feeling of helplessness in the face of pure evil. They never stayed up when I wanted them to, invariably refused to close on demand, and the cord always got stuck on one side. Utter bastards.

In an observation post, though, they were ideal. They were a vast upgrade on standard issue squat curtains - sheets held in place by nails - because we could peer through them without fear of being seen from outside.

"So how are we going to do this?" I asked, hunkering down and poking a finger into the slats of the blind.

Iffy was slumped on the dusty floorboards, his back against the wall, his knees tucked under his chin. He scratched his ankles, and spoke quietly. "Well, we need to find out more about the Gaffer's life. If he's turned into a nut-nut psycho killing-machine, there must be one or two little tell-tale give-aways that hint at it. We watch him, see what he gets up to. Try to find out what he's all about these days. We follow him when he leaves the studio, study his habits - ready for the day when we decide we have to…you know."

I frowned. "You don't think he'll be a bit suspicious when he starts seeing us following him around?"

"Ah. That's where the disguises come in."

I laughed, and then, when I realised I was the only one to do so, I sighed. "Disguises?"

"I've thought it all through."

"Oh. Great."

"Yup."

"Care to share?"

"We have to be unrecognisable. These hoodies are fine to hide our faces while we nip in and out of the squat, but we need something much better for out on the streets. Proper disguises."

"I've always fancied a pantomime cow."

"Me, too! But that won't wash in the inner city. So, I got to thinking, right, and I reckon I've got the perfect disguise for walking round Hackney without him spotting us. Don't want to blow my own trumpet, but I'm pretty chuffed with myself. Wait here a sec."

When he came back into the room he was carrying a large plastic bag. He began pulling out items of clothing. "Did a tour of the charity shops yesterday," he explained. First out were four black flat-soled shoes, their shine now a thing of the dim and distant past, their shabbiness and scruffiness very much in evidence. Next came tatty black suit trousers and stained white button-down shirts.

"City gents fallen on hard times?" I wondered.

"Better than that. Much better than that."

He pulled out two long black overcoats.

"Flashers?"

And then he revealed two black wide-brimmed hats and, as so often when I was with Iffy, I didn't know whether to laugh or cry.

"I think I preferred the pantomime cow," I said, watching as he opened another bag and held up two false beards for my approval.

"It's a stroke of genius is what it is. There's a synagogue around the corner. And wait for the *pièce de la résistance*...

Marta?" he called. "You can come in now."

"*Mazeltov*," she said as she came in, giggling like a tractor backfiring and clutching two severed dreadlocks in her hands.

I told Iffy he was on his own for this one, and he shrugged.

FULL OF BEANS

The game we played was a waiting one. Patience was the order of the day, which was unfortunate. Iffy paced, Iffy prattled, Iffy tattled, Iffy wittered, Iffy waffled and Iffy tittered; Iffy littered the room with cigarette ends and began to get on my nerves. Should I have been pleased that my efforts to give up smoking had rendered the smell of tobacco, once so inoffensive, now quite disgusting? I should. Was I? No.

I did a lot of sit-ups.

On the second day of our stake-out Iffy didn't show up at all. That evening as I sauntered along Mare Street I noticed cars and buses honking their horns and drivers winding down their windows to shout abuse at a shambling figure weaving its way dangerously down the middle of road. The staggering, scruffy derelict ignored them all, lost in a world of his own, mumbling away to himself and waving his arms in the air.

From a distance, he bore a superficial resemblance to Iffy. A crusty Ghost of Christmas Yet To Come, I thought sadly.

From less of a distance, he bore a marked resemblance to Iffy.

Up close, I saw that it was Iffy.

My heart shattered.

And I opted for discretion over valour and jumped on the nearest bus.

The following morning Iffy came to the squat bright and early, but he was shaky and trembling and his hands and forearms were criss-crossed in scratches. I noticed a leaf and some twigs trapped in the dreads he had not washed for over twenty years. He was moody and brooding all day, strangely uncommunicative. He asked to borrow a tenner to tide him over and I handed it over without a comment.

It was frustrating to dwell on the fact that the Gaffer was probably just a few feet away from us, but that we had no way of knowing what he was doing. We watched as a succession of take-aways were delivered at irregular times. I presumed the Gaffer was adding the finishing touches to his new album, the one that he would soon release upon the world, the one for which he had such high hopes. For the sake of his precious career, it had to be a hit. He had a lot at stake.

On the fourth day, Iffy was full of beans.

Magic beans, I presumed...

"The Gaffer, the man who's what's left over when you take the Shorpe out of Scunthorpe, used to say our scene was sublime," he announced *à propos* of sweet Fanny Adams save the ramblings of that infernal confusion engine known as his mind. "And I've been mulling that over."

"For the past ten years?"

"Yup," he said, leafing through the pages of a dictionary that he appeared to have brought with him in a worrying act of preparedness. Having found the entry he sought, he cleared his throat and began to read. "'Sublime: lofty, grand, or exalted in thought, expression, or manner; of outstanding spiritual, intellectual, or moral worth; tending to inspire awe usually because of elevated quality (as of beauty, nobility, or grandeur) or transcendent excellence.'"

The Gaffer had been a true believer back in the day, I recalled, which made his total defection even harder to comprehend.

"And he was right, ye ken," Iffy said, suddenly and dramatically banging the dictionary closed with both hands. "Our scene *was* sublime. Ecstasy and LSD naturally lead to blissed-out levels of consciousness, especially when they're combined with music designed to make you rush like a motherfucker, a setting that challenges your perceptions - either due to its sheer natural beauty or to the feeling of empowerment engendered by the swords-into-ploughshares act of reclaiming, recycling and reattributing a *raison d'être* to a space that capitalism no longer needs - and the family vibe fostered by a common sense of purpose created by like-minded individuals coming together in a self-regulating community."

Iffy really talked like that sometimes: times when he was undergoing the effects of a particularly hefty dose of amphetamine sulphate. At least I knew what drugs he was on that day.

"But I've found a better description for what we used to get up to with the rig," he told me. And it required a longer explanation, he announced in a threatening manner. Realisation dawned on me that I was about to be subjected to another one of his Theories, and a thin sheen of perspiration broke out on my forehead.

"It was *liminal*," he smiled, looking every bit as pleased with himself as a dog with four testicles.

Panicking, I admitted that liminal was not a word I was familiar with. Iffy actually licked his lips, visibly slavering at the mouth at having the opportunity to lay out the carcass of another one of his pet theories on my doorstep.

He had stumbled across this latest concept in a book scavenged from a dustbin. It was amazing how much a man could learn by simply reading whatever tomes the gods left lying around, he informed me. In this case, it was a work of anthropology.

"Some sociologists would have labelled us marginals, or maybe outsiders," Iffy went on as I shifted uncomfortably in my seat. "Both terms have been used since the mid-1960s to denote individuals and groups who display 'deviant behaviour', the difference between the two being that marginals are forced to the edges of society, and outsiders are there through choice;

either, like Sam Saoule, as a protest against a system they seek to change, or, like Minnie, as a refusal to function within a system they see as unchangeable. In theory, outsiders have the luxury - one that is refused to genuine marginals - of being able to return to the fold if they so choose, although missing out on an education, picking up an addiction, or undergoing a process that could best be described as noninstitutionalisation could render the return to societal norms problematic."

Clara had managed her reinsertion with aplomb, Iffy pointed out, but Minnie had failed spectacularly. The Gaffer, it seemed, had followed the lead of many of our hippy predecessors, turning his back on alternative subculture and embracing a life of relative conformity.

I wondered if one reason that Iffy himself still remained an outsider was because he was noninstitutionalised. He wouldn't know how to live as the majority of people did, for some of the same reasons that many homeless people had difficulties coping with a move into permanent accommodation. I just couldn't imagine him jumping through all the bureaucratic hoops without stubbing his toe, hitting his head, scraping his knee and eventually fucking it off as a stupid idea. He would struggle to open a bank account without any pay cheques to deposit, and whoever wanted to employ him would first ask for his bank details. Who would rent a flat to a person without any employment history, and who would employ someone of no fixed abode? In all his life, he had never paid utility bills, nor rent, nor even had a permanent address, and settling debts on time was hardly his forte.

A lot of travellers found it genuinely unsettling to live in a brick box, and although Iffy had plenty of experience in flats and houses, I knew he valued the sense of rootlessness that squatting permitted. The freedom to up sticks and move on a whim was dear to him, just as straight society was alien, even on a purely social level. Every single person he communicated with - apart from the most fleeting interactions - was another outsider: travellers, punks, protesters, ravers, squatters and drug users, the lot of 'em. He was a merry prankster, and the trips he had taken - of both a physical and psychedelic nature - had left him with precious little to chat about with the man on the Clapham omnibus.

Maybe, I suddenly thought, his pathological contempt for anyone who had, in his opinion, reneged on their youthful ideals was a manifestation of some inner doubt. Maybe his own inability to adapt to the needs of straight society was transformed into scorn for anyone who managed the process.

"Liminal," he continued. "It's all about 'twixt and 'tween. It's dusk and dawn. It's the seashore. It's marshes, crossroads, springs and caves. It's edges and borders. Twilight. It's New Year's Eve, Samhain, Beltane, Imbolc, the equinoxes and the solstices. It's neither fish nor fowl nor meat, neither naked nor clothed, neither indoors nor outdoors. It's delirium. Burning fever. Altered states. Adolescence. The middle of the book. Ambiguity and disorientation. It's *threshold*.

"Now, Van Gennep, the anthropologist who first hit on the theory of liminality, was talking specifically about rite of passage rituals in small-scale pre-industrial societies. As he described it, the initiate was first deprived of their habitual position in society, before going into the liminal state of transition, and finally being welcomed into their new social status. The intiand was there through necessity, not choice."

He was nodding furiously away to himself as he spoke.

I suspected my own eyes were developing a glassy sheen.

"Obviously that isn't true for a raver at a free party, though it is true that there is a certain well-documented, quasi-religious element to the type of festivities we know and love. The congregation, the sacrament, the hebdominal gatherings. It's got pagan overtones, and there *is* something ritualistic about the proceedings."

He got to his feet at this point and began to pace up and down the little room. All he needed was a pipe, a tweed jacket with elbow patches, a blackboard covered in semi-legible griffonage and a telescopic pointing stick.

"Turner, one of the later anthropologists who popularised the theory, used the term liminoid when talking about a similar experience undergone in a voluntary context, which would apply to us. He also banged on about permanent liminality, when the transient state becomes a fixed state. This is where it gets *really* interesting," he promised. "It all begins with the sloughing off of the dead skin of expected roles. It's *that* moment at *that* party from which there's no going back. Remember that? Your first proper free party moment in a transitory space, where anything and everything is possible. Allow me to elaborate."

Short of knocking him senseless or turning on my heel and dashing out the door, I had little choice in the matter, though I did briefly consider both options.

"The liminal period is a temporary autonomous zone. It's the time when you're on the threshold, you're inside going outside and outside going inside. Social hierarchies become irrelevant. Traditions are abandoned. The future you had always imagined dissolves before your very eyes and the past you thought you knew mutates beyond recognition. It's the moment when Eris appears and offers chaos in place of order. It's the total collapse of structure. It's destruction and reconstruction. It's Shiva, it's supernova, it's world's dying and being reborn."

"Gosh," I said. "Actually, it sounds like an acid trip."

"Wrong is precisely what you aren't, my friend. It can be sparked off by LSD. What does acid do? It dissolves.

Assumptions, biases, prejudices and standard perceptions are melted down and stripped away. A metaphorical death of the old self takes place and a fluid, malleable openness rushes in to fill the space. Spatio-temporal dislocation and distortion lead to the possibility of a complete redefinition of self, surroundings and circumstance. You stare into the abyss. You shout into the void. You fall through the cracks. You shift your identity. You reprogramme your biocomputer. It can be exhilarating - but also unsettling, scary and distressing. You discover that everything you knew is wrong. The structure of society as you know it is suspended. The potential for disorder is infinite - everything you took for granted is thrown into doubt. The chances of emerging with a new sense of purpose are high. *Sic infit* - so it begins."

"Golly," I said. "A serious acid trip."

"But - and this is where it gets even more interesting - for the free party crew it's more than an acid trip. The trip is the party is the lifestyle is the party is the trip. The liminality of the trip extends to the liminality of the party where the trips are taken, and ultimately to the lifestyle that surrounds the party. It isn't just the psychedelic experience which makes you question the received wisdom of society's normative behaviour, beliefs and constraints. The environment you're in also defies preconceptions and redefines your place in the world and the world itself. The rules that previously governed your thoughts and actions have been permanently altered and subverted. In the party, standard concepts of class, wealth, ownership, position, rank and status disappear. The laws that bind us are held in suspension, and the whole differentiated, hierarchical system of politico-legal-economic positions is of no importance. There is no authority to shackle you. The where and when are sublimated by the here and now."

"Crikey," I croaked. "Is that right?"

"You must remember that feeling. The music is crunching, the bass is pounding, and you're off your tits and loving it, wishing it could go on forever and feeling that it will, that it simply has to, that something this good can never end…and you know deep inside you that everyone else feels it too. The soul-destroying drudgery of alarm clocks, matching socks, final exams, traffic jams, bullying bosses, profits and losses, nice neck ties, little white lies, microwave meals, two-for-one deals, game shows, shiny shoes, the evening news, tidy haircuts, labour markets, subservience, form-filling - all that dull, tedious, mundane, ultimately pointless and unnecessary crap - is just so monumentally, massively, completely fucking irrelevant as you look around and all you see is just so good - good people dancing to good music - that you think, *I'm gonna make this my fucking life*. And every week you plan and prepare for a party and every weekend you party and the liminal moment turns into a liminoid culture, and why the fuck not?"

"Blimey," I whispered. "Who'd've thunk it?"

"The withdrawal and escape from normal modes of action expands and extends exponentially from the trip. Seclusion and reclusion from accepted paradigms can only lead to the conclusion that, yes, another way of life is possible outside the parameters, perimeters, restrictions, constrictions and configurations of the concatenation of constructions of contradictory contracts that confine us and condemn us to an eternal continuation of concessions to their condescending consensus conception of corporate conformity."

"Well now, that's easy for you to say," I said finally, when he had ground to a halt. "Listen, Iffy, I've known you for a long time. I love you like a brother. But I have no bleeding idea if what you said makes any earthly sense."

"I think you'll find it makes perfect sense."

"I think you'll find I can't be arsed."

"Let me put it another way," he replied, and before I could persuade him otherwise, that's exactly what he began to do. "Let's do the nutshell thang. I'm talking about *liminal* techno here. The initiate is removed from the security and predictability of his day-to-day existence. He is immersed in a space where a spiritual, moral and ethical transformation ensues. The transcendental state is induced by the ingestion of psychoactive substances in a *Gesamtkunstwerk*, non-hierarchical environment where the priority is not the hoarding of wealth, but rather the enjoyment of life, spontaneity, creativity, sharing, equality, fellowship and freedom of thought and expression.

"Even the locations we use are liminal. The squats and sites and the buildings we party lie empty for years until we open the doors - the liminal gateways - and they'll be empty again when the party's over or the eviction is served. Thresholds are crossed again and again. An office or factory becomes an illegal nightclub. The nightclub becomes a home. Buildings mutate and new hybrids are created. The post-industrial boundaries between living space and working space are eradicated. You sleep where you play, you play where you work, and you work where you sleep. Your life consists of crossroads and roads that never end. You live in no man's land, *terra nullius* where everything is *res nullius* - up for grabs. The ephemerality of the travelling life, the way it refuses permanence and stability, the ways in which it differs from the static existence that most people experience, is liminal in itself. Not criminal, but liminal."

I opened my mouth to speak. Then decided not to bother.

"Now, as I'm sure you're aware, Turner thought that the liminal phase often ended up with the intiand returning to society to occupy a new role, and that the liminal state was unsustainable due to its instability. That its volatility and intensity meant it would of necessity be short-lived. But it has also been posited that liminal communities can develop, with their own internal social structure. This has been called communitas - a communal group in which all are equal. And this, *mon ami*, is what we created in the techno traveller scene."

"That's nice then," I said. And went back to staring out the window.

I hated it when Iffy was on speed.

MAN AND MULE

Dressed as an Orthodox Jew, Iffy did not look like an Orthodox Jew. He looked like Iffy in a false beard, an old mac, a fourth-hand suit, a black homburg that hovered slightly above his head due to the fact that his dreadlocks were rolled up underneath it, and somebody else's dreadlocks framing his face.

"Are you sure this is a good idea?" I asked him when he was togged up.

"Yup."

"You don't think you might, well, offend anybody?"

"Who?" he said, just as one of Marta's severed locks fell off.

"Orthodox Jews?"

"I don't see why," he grumbled, safety-pinning the hair back in place, only for the other one to come loose. He stumbled a little and giggled like a schoolgirl.

I had resolved not to hassle him about his heroin use. I knew he liked the opiate hit, and seeing as how he took just about every drug known to Man and mule, I just had to hope he had the strength of mind to keep it under control. He was all clued up about the perils of addictive narcotics, and me getting on his case would probably have had a detrimental effect, so stubborn and contrary was his nature.

But I couldn't help myself: "Are you pinned, Iffy?"

"Not really. Don't suppose you've got a belt I could borrow?" he added - not because he wanted to fashion a tourniquet, but because just then his trousers spooled down around his ankles to reveal a pair of Bart Simpson boxer shorts and all the knobbly-kneed glory of his skinny white chicken legs.

"Ah, forget it," he muttered. "I'll use that bit of rope that Marta drags her dog round with. Sure you don't want to come?

Last chance."

It was just then that I spotted the Gaffer stroll out into the street below. Pausing only to grab and relight a spliff, Iffy legged it downstairs.

From my position behind the Venetian blinds I saw him come hurtling out of the squat. He caught sight of the Gaffer and dashed after him, holding onto his homburg with one hand, the other clasping his false beard in place. Unfortunately, the spliff in his mouth was still burning and I saw wisps of smoke begin to rise from the false beard. He drew a lot of puzzled frowns from other pedestrians, but the Gaffer appeared oblivious and the pair soon disappeared around a corner and out of my view.

I did some sit-ups. And waited. And wondered what the chances were of Iffy actually finding out anything pertinent. Slim, I figured. So I did some more sit-ups. And waited.

Four hours later Iffy was reporting back for a debriefing.

"He still likes Indian food."

"You followed him to an Indian restaurant?"

"Yup."

"And?"

"And then I lost him."

"You lost him. In an Indian restaurant."

"I was waiting outside, you see, and then I bumped into Eltham John and he took me for a pint in the pub and a smoke back at his yard and then I sort of lost track of time a bit."

"I don't see what we're hoping to gain by following the Gaffer round anyway," I grumbled, "unless he goes round Clara's flat with a manic glint in his eye and a bottle marked 'Poison' grasped in his claw-like fist. Maybe we should just sack the whole idea off."

Iffy looked downcast. "Just one more day?"

"If you have to…"

But the next day played out in a similar fashion. The Gaffer, Iffy informed me at nine in the evening, also seemed to like Italian food, and our old mate Danny the Builder was now renting a flat just round the corner, and he had some extremely potent red Lebanese hash, and then someone else had turned up with half a litre of K.

WITHOUT RUTH

I was still sleeping in Clara's front room, but since the Gaffer was back in London my shifts at the Gaff tended to finish late and my path rarely intersected that of my hostess. Out of respect for her privacy, I would do my mouse impression in the evening when I returned. Every night the disarray in the kitchen and an all but empty bottle of wine proved that she had supped and sipped, and the muffled drone of the TV in her bedroom suggested that she slept.

(Nighttime TV or radio had been a bone of contention between us when we had been a couple. She loved to drift off with noise in the background; I hated it. I had argued that it defied our primitive nature. For millennia, I said, our ancestors had gone to sleep when it was dark and quiet, and that was the way it was meant to be. She had countered by telling me that in fact the opposite was true: babies had felt protected and safe when hearing the murmurings of the tribe and seeing the flickering flames of the campfire. Hmmm?)

As I tiptoed into her flat, I was surprised to find Clara using my bed as a sofa. It was nearly midnight. She was up late.

"Hello, stranger," I said, entering the room.

She smiled at me blearily, and wearily waved a wine glass like Sir Simon Rattle on Temazepam. "Hope you don't me mind me squatting your bedroom," she drawled.

"Make yourself at home."

"Couldn't sleep."

"Shame. It's the best cure for insomnia."

"There's a glass in the kitchen, dear boy."

"Then fill it, dear Clara, dear Clara, dear Clara. Well, I can do that myself, actually." I found a clean glass in a cupboard and tipped some red wine into it.

Stepping over her outstretched leg, I settled down next to her on the sofa. "So what's a-bothering you?"

"I'm fighting a losing battle. I'm not even a grain of grit in the shoe of the Establishment. More like a stain of shit. I feel we're passing into a new age, and isn't the fucking hippy-dippy Age of fucking Aquarius. The wealth and power of the few is exceeded only by their greed and ruthlessness. They are completely without ruth and they are so without reck that they hardly even seek to hide it. The sociopaths are running the asylum. The majority of the oppressed cry out, not in pain, but in favour of more oppression. They are hoodwinked and brainwashed and distracted by crap."

"Bad day at the office?"

"Bad times are here to stay. When I was younger, I used to watch sci-fi films and read futuristic books and comics. Most of them were dystopian, and what I didn't understand then was that they weren't nightmare scenarios - they were blueprints. You know, those films where the select few live inside the bubble, and outside it's chaos and brutality, slums and poverty and filth. The world is divided between the blessed and the damned and it's the blessed who do the damning. Well, that's exactly what we have now."

"Really bad day at the office?"

"Do you remember the scene in Monty Python's Life of Brian when Brian's thrown in jail? And there's the old geezer chained to the wall? Saying that crucifixion is the best thing the Romans ever did for us? He's delighted to be unchained for twenty minutes every day, and that's what the majority of us are like. Daily Mail readers. Remember when we used to go to see Chumbawamba? They had that wicked line: 'They break our legs and we say thank you when they give us crutches to walk with.'"

This wasn't like Clara. Minnie used to babble like that on

occasion, but Clara had always claimed that the way things were wasn't the way they had to be.

It saddened me to hear her sounding so negative. I told her as much.

"Don't get me wrong," she insisted. "I'm still all for fighting the good fight. Just sometimes my energy runs low. That's all. Sometimes my anguish overcomes my anger. I got called a do-gooder today."

"Ouch."

"Aye," she said, perking up, sitting up, her eyes lighting up, "and you know why that pissed me off? Because the knob-head who said it - some self-satisfied, I'm-alright-Jack twat - meant it as an insult."

"Yeah, I can see how that'd wind you up. Shall I open another bottle?"

She nodded absent-mindedly. "One of those Italian ones."

As I turned my back on her and located the bottle, I heard her quietly say, "There's something else too."

"Oh yeah?" I pierced the cork with the corkscrew, twisted it in.

"The Gaffer phoned me today."

I pulled, hard.

"He wants to come and see me tomorrow."

Pop, went the cork.

FAITHFUL TO HIS WYRD

"What did you say?"

"The Gaffer wants to come and see me."

"I meant, what did you say to him?"

"I should be home by nine."

"Wow," I said, filling our glasses. "Is he going to bring his own weapon or will you be providing him with a kitchen knife? Clara, are you sure this is wise? I know you aren't totally convinced by our theory that he's the killer, but I did ask you to be careful - and you did agree. And now you're inviting him over?"

"Aye, well, he sounded like he needed a chat. Said it was important. I couldn't say no, could I?"

"You could easily have made an excuse."

"But I'm a do-gooder, aren't I?"

"At least let me and Iffy be here, too, then. And don't drink or snort anything he offers you. Watch he doesn't spike your wine. And don't get drunk and do keep your wits about you."

"Aye, fair enough."

"Really? Promise?"

"But I won't have Iffy here in my flat."

"Because you think *he's* the killer?"

"Because he's an annoying wee bollocks."

"Aye, fair enough."

We sat in a silence that seemed companionable and drank our wine. Clara made no move towards her bedroom. Eventually I said, "He's still doing it, though. Iffy. Still living the life. True to his beliefs. Faithful to his wyrd."

"Or just plain weird. D'you think he'll ever change?"

"I can't see him ever living in a place like this, if that's what you mean. Working, paying rent. He wouldn't know how. You think he's trapped?"

"Do you? Why are you so fascinated by him?"

"I'm not. He's my mate, that's all."

"I think you admire him for 'still living the life', but you can't be arsed doing it yourself. It gets to be hard work, fucking the system, because the system's big and you're small. Or, if you prefer, it's a massive cunt and he's a little prick. On the whole, the system's the fucker that does the fucking and you're the fucker that gets fucked over. And I don't even think that Iffy's fucking the system any more. Okay, he doesn't contribute to its success, but neither does he do much in the way of impeding it. He's hardly what you'd call an activist these days, you know. He just takes shed-loads of drugs."

But at least he isn't contributing to the continuation of the unsustainable consumer society that prevails at the moment, I thought to myself. That's got to be something to be proud of when it comes to the final reckoning. Hasn't it?

MIDNIGHT IN SICILY TO FIRST LIGHT IN FINLAND

A baseball bat was not a piece of sporting equipment with which I had a great deal of experience. I always kept one, a lightweight aluminium job, in my van when I was travelling, but had never had occasion to swing it in anger. There had been a game of baseball with some kids in Portugal, and another time after a teknival in Poland when Sam Saoule and I almost came to blows with a gang of sparrow-legged boneheads we took to be neo-Nazis until we clocked the red laces in their boots that marked them out as anti-fascist Skinheads Against Racial Prejudice, aka sharp skins.

In the zen tranquillity of Clara's bedroom, I hefted the bat in one hand and attempted to quieten my beating heart. The room seemed to be designed as a refuge from the harshness of life outside its confines. It was draped in hangings that reminded me of fishermen's nets and painted in hues of blue that ran in a sliding scale from midnight in Sicily to first light in Finland. Clara, so blunt and grounded, clearly felt the need to relax in a space where she could float free from the problems that filled her working hours.

I gripped the bat hard when I heard the Gaffer greet her. He had a voice like a bittern trying to get served when last orders are called, with just a tinge of braying equine. I would have no difficulties eavesdropping on their conversation. I wouldn't be able to see much, however: with my eye pressed to the keyhole like some voyeuristic teenager, all I could see was the sofa.

I heard Clara open the door, saw her legs, crutch and crotch cross my line of sight, and moments later the rotund protuberance of the Gaffer's belly appeared.

I tensed, ready to spring to Clara's aid, wondering if she had just invited a killer into her home, but she calmly offered him some tea and he said, "Yes, please, milk and two sugars."

If he was planning murder most foul, at least he was starting the evening by respecting the social niceties.

"It was good of you to come to my little event in Berlin," I heard the Gaffer say as Clara banged around with kettles and cups in the kitchen.

"Gaffer, do I have a reputation for letting people talk utter shite in my presence?"

"Er, no, Clara."

"Good. We spent a lot of good times together when we were on the road, and you said you had to talk to me, so I've made time in my hectic schedule to meet you. And that's fine. But I won't waste my valuable time listening to your self-congratulatory drivel. Do you understand what I'm saying?"

"Er, yes, Clara."

"Good lad. Now, please, just for the record, can you say something about Berlin that doesn't massage your fragile ego and has some vague semblance to consensus reality?"

"Erm, thanks for dropping by to say hello while you were in Berlin for Udo's funeral?" Crumbs of humble pie tumbled to the floor around him.

"Aye, well done. See - you can do it when you try."

My own fragile ego was comforted to find out that Clara wasn't just hard on me. She was hard on everyone. She was the hardest dogdamn do-gooder in town.

"So how're you doing, big man? We didn't have time to chat in Berlin as you were busy with the sycophants and the arse-lickers. Your music's shite, I have to say."

Was she trying to provoke a reaction out of him? Or was she simply being herself, throwing hurtful truths around like black confetti at a Satanists' wedding? I was developing a theory in which we all became caricatures of ourselves as we grew older.

The Gaffer's belly inflated momentarily as he filled his lungs with air. I prepared myself to hear a self-justifying rant, an impassioned defence of his work and his standing in society.

Instead, a monumental sigh blew through the room, a lonely, wounded breath. "Never one to mince your words, you. But don't fret, my next album's going to knock them dead."

An interesting turn of phrase, I reflected.

"I'm not fretting. I really couldn't give a toss."

"Right. Well, that's pretty clear, then. I thought you might be on my side."

"I'm not on anyone's side, except the poor and needy, and I just can't shoehorn you into that category these days," Clara said, and she even managed somehow to convey a sense of exasperation in the way she slurped her tea. As agreed, she was avoiding alcohol. "So what's the big deal, big man? Why the sudden need to have a blather with your old pal? Feeling lonely? Only, if it's a lawyer you're after, you've come to the wrong place."

"Clara, joking aside, we really need to talk. Christ, this stuff's hot." I saw him place his cup on the coffee table in front of the sofa.

"How long have we known each other?" he asked, starting again just as the silence was growing oppressive.

"We first met about twenty years ago. But we haven't really seen each other for the last decade, so I'm not sure that the present perfect is the tense you're looking for. Oh, we *knew* each other, alright, but how well do we *know* each other? The Gaffer I knew had dreads to his waist, oil on his hands and a spliff in his mouth. The Clara you knew had a dog called Che, a motorbike chain around her wrist and a Crass tee-shirt. Now what've we got? A beer belly and grey hair. The belly's yours, by the way."

"Do you miss it, Clara? Our time on the road?"

"No."

"That's what I want to talk about, in a way."

The Gaffer had never been so into the ol' listening. Talking was fine, but he considered it more blessed to give than to receive in the noble art of conversation. Considering that like most humans he had two ears and just one mouth, it was a pity he used them in inverse proportion.

"We didn't really get to chat in Berlin," he began again, omitting to mention that the fault was entirely his, "but there's so much I need to say. Clara, I take it you heard about Allan? Poor sod. The thing is, there aren't many of us left now. From the old days, I mean. Doesn't that strike you as odd?"

Clara's face was obscured by her foot, propped up as usual on a low stool, but I imagined her rolling her eyes. "What we had then," she said, enunciating slowly and clearly, "was an unsustainable lifestyle. I got out of it, you got out of it, both more or less with our faculties and health intact. Neither of us even went to prison, come to think of it. But the others - well, you know what happens when you burn a candle at both ends."

Where did I sit in her summary? I wondered. Faculties intact, or waiting for the flames to reach each other?

"Is that all you think it is? Live fast, die young?"

"Don't you?"

"I don't know, Clara. Udo, Jacek, Sam Saoule, Minnie - all of them dead in the last couple of months. And now Allan, dead after a fight when he was in Berlin for Udo's funeral. Don't you find that all a bit too much to be a coincidence?"

I was flummoxed. Where was the Gaffer going with all this? Was it leading up to a confession? I clutched the doorknob with one hand. The baseball bat hung heavy in my other fist.

"Conspiracy theories? There are enough real conspiracies

going on in the world, more than enough cartels and agreements and cover-ups and dissimulations being perpetrated by our great leaders - political, social and economic - to worry about. There's no need to invent any more. The real problems of the world are created by the types you hang out with, pal. They're real people, doing real bad things."

That at least went some way to explaining Clara's attitude. She was angry at her old friend for cosying up to the rich and famous.

"I came here tonight because I need to talk to you," said the Gaffer, dashing light-footed over the minefield of Clara's disdain. "I already wanted to say something in Berlin, but I didn't want to talk in front of Andy."

"Andy? Is he your lovely manager? The one who stepped out of a Lowry painting? He certainly seemed happy when we made a move to go."

"Andy's very protective of me, but he means well. He can come across as a bit of a prick, I know, but his heart's in the right place. Don't know where I'd be without him. He'd do anything for me."

"And what would you do for him?"

"I pay his wages."

Now, that, I knew, would totally fail to impress Clara.

"But listen," he said, making like Sid James, Kenneth Connor, Charles Hawtrey, Joan Sims and Kenneth Williams and carrying on regardless, "I have my doubts about all the old crew just dying like that. Doesn't it make you wonder?"

"Not even the slightest bit."

"Well, it made me wonder. And now I think I'm being stalked."

"That's the price you pay for celebrity."

"No, of course. I agree. The whole fame thing. But that's not what I'm really all about anyway...nobody knows what's going on in my head...and nobody sees the work that goes on behind the scenes."

I wondered if he would have made similar comments about our days in the rig...Nobody saw the hard work that went on behind the scenes. There had been a sort of arrogance connected to our *mode de vie*, or perhaps a degree of self-confidence that was necessary to ensure the scene's survival. There had been big egos a-go-go. The difference, at least in our own eyes, was that we were fighting the *status quo*, not perpetuating it. But still, a certain elitism had evolved; a love of name-dropping, a pecking order, even, dogdammit, a dogma and a hierarchy of sorts. Originators of the movement had talked about taking the focus of a musical event away from the musicians and giving it to the music itself, but inevitably we had created our own stars, our own heroes, our own big names.

Allan Exit liked to point out that human beings are social animals, but that meant that as well as seeking acceptance within the group, some of us hankered after status, and perhaps that was why we insisted on making organised religion out of pagan beliefs, and why every movement that started out as something vibrant, organic, free and beautiful ended up becoming commercialised, dogmatic and rigidly structured. It had happened again and again throughout history, and the free party scene was but one example.

Maybe the lesson was that moving into someone else's house could never be the same as building your own, I reflected.

And I also wondered where the fuck the Gaffer was steering the conversation.

"If you're after a lawyer to take out an injunction on your stalker - well, like I said, you've come to the wrong place," Clara reiterated.

"No," the Gaffer barked. "What I'm trying to tell you, Clara, is that I think the person who's stalking me could have killed all the others. And it's someone you know."

I heard Clara asking him how long he'd been living a realm of rampant paranoia and if he'd considered seeking professional help, because there were people out there who were trained in dealing with mental health problems, but she wasn't one of them. And at the same time, I was trying to figure out what kind of a game he was playing.

His next phrase almost made me drop my baseball bat.

"I'm pretty sure it's Iffy."

NO WHY IN THE A TO Z

After a small pause and a loud slurp, Clara said, "Now that's just daft, Gaffer. What drugs are you doing these days?"

"Hardly any. But I'll swear to it, I've seen Iffy following me round. Dressed as a tramp or something, with some kind of melted growth on his face."

"You have got to be kidding. Iffy's an oddball, I'll be the first to admit, but why on earth would he be stalking you - dressed as a fucking tramp?"

"He's in disguise. He doesn't know I've seen him. But think about it. It all makes sense. I know for a fact that he was out with Allan on the night he got killed. He's killed Allan and all the others and now he's coming for me."

"Why?"

"Why? Why? This is Iffy we're talking about here. You don't need a why. There's no why in the A to Z of Iffy. He doesn't need a reason. He's always been one leg short of a table. He's got a screw loose. An essential part missing. He's never been right in the head, and now something's finally gone click inside him and he's totally lost the plot. I don't know why. All I know is that five people from our rig have all recently met untimely deaths, and now I'm being stalked by Iffy. Dressed as a tramp - I mean, is that normal behaviour? And you know what? I think he's trying to set me up to take the blame for the other deaths. Every one of the others died just after I'd seen them."

He sounded genuinely panicky as he spoke, I thought - but then, I had never had any talent for spotting lies. I had often read of characters in books who had the capacity to sort truth from untruth, and maybe such people existed. I wasn't one of them.

"Alright, I'll grant you that Iffy's a touch eccentric -"

"He's mental."

"A touch eccentric. Unfathomable. Ineffable. But I'm sure if he's dressing as a tramp and stalking you, he's got a good reason."

I noticed that Clara, too, fell to defending Iffy when others attacked him, and it made me feel slightly better about myself.

"You're joking."

"Only a bit. A good reason in his idiosyncratic world view."

"That's what I'm saying! The reason is that he wants to kill me."

Poor Clara. She must have been undergoing a massive feeling of déjà vu. She had reluctantly put up with me spouting my theory that the Gaffer was the murderer. Now she was confronted by the Gaffer telling her the same tale about Iffy.

She confirmed my suspicions, saying with a degree of ferocity that mounted as she spoke, "Do you have any idea how ridiculous this sounds? Listen carefully, big man. I'm only going to say this once. Take notes if you're so inclined, so you can check the text next time you get vexed. Sam Saoule overdosed on GHB. Minnie drowned. Udo got hit by an U-Bahn. Jacek committed suicide by cutting his wrists. Allan Exit got in a fight and someone broke his neck. These events are only connected inasmuch as all the unfortunate dead people used to knock around with us ten years ago. Iffy's a bit mad, but we all knew that. If you see him again, dressed as a tramp or not, go and ask him what the fuck he's doing. And for God's sake, leave me out of it. Let me get on with my life in relative peace. Please."

"You don't believe me? You think I'm making it up? I thought I could count on you to see reason. I've no-one to turn to. No-one I can talk to. I tried to tell Andy, but he's touchy about anything connected with my time with the rig. Clara, I'm begging you, you've got to take this seriously! I came here to talk to you. There's so much I want to say. That I need to share with someone. About my life - what I've been doing and why I've been doing it. The loneliness I've felt."

Oh, I thought - the poor little rich boy.

Clara wasn't falling for it either. "Let me guess. You're worried about my safety?" She slurped loudly from her mug.

"Eh? Oh, sure. Of course. Didn't I say that?"

"Maybe I just wasn't listening. Like I won't be listening if you ever try to tell me this bullshit again."

The Gaffer seemed all worked up. I could see his belly contracting and expanding like the nitrous oxide balloons we used to suck on at parties. One leg was twitching as if he had been snorting pervitin all evening. His voice was cracking like a man who had been smoking rocks for breakfast. Maybe he was a consummate actor.

"Gaffer. Leave it. Just leave it. Go home. Go to work. Produce some more crap. Sell some more crap. Make some more money out of numpties with more money than sense. Or use your wealth and influence to promote young artists and musicians, genuinely creative types with talent and commitment who struggle to pay their daily bills. Do whatever you want. But don't do it here."

"I'm not going to let it happen, Clara," he stuttered. "I'm not going to stand by and act like nothing's happening. I'm not going to let Iffy ruin everything I've worked so hard for. You'll see."

From my vantage point behind the door I watched as his stubby legs hoisted his belly up in the air. He was huffing and puffing. The atmosphere was tenser than a Tory in Tower Hamlets.

"I'm telling you, Clara," he cried, his voice muffled now as he strode out the other door, "you lot have all got a big shock coming your way. All of you. Just you wait and see."

I heard the door slam behind him.

"Bloody Nora," Clara sighed to herself. "They're all as bad as each other."

Slurp.

THE WAY HE DIDN'T TRY TO KILL ME

Stepping into the living room, I tried to look like a man who knew what the hell was going on. Clara told me where to find a bottle of Chilean Shiraz. I uncorked it, sloshed two generous servings into some glasses. Sat down in the seat the Gaffer had been in. Swiped away a passing thought that asked why, when sitting down where someone else had sat, the seat always felt hotter than when returning to your own chair. Or was it just me? Was I a cold-arsed bastard?

"I swear to fucking God, you're all as bad as each other," Clara repeated, drinking deeply from her glass. I heard the gulps as the wine raced down her throat.

"He's a devious git, alright," I said, matching her swallow for swallow.

"Aye. The psycho - did you clock the way he didn't try to kill me?"

"Got him running scared," I agreed.

She looked at me, probably trying to figure out if I was being sarcastic. Eventually she was defeated by my poker face. "Running scared?"

"Uh-huh. Do I need to explain it to you?"

"Need is a powerful, emotive and yet highly subjective word. Don't feel obliged on my behalf."

"It's like this. He's trying to win your trust and pin the blame on Iffy. Now he can go and kill the ol' dodger and you'll think it was self-defence. He practically admitted as much just before he huffed out the door. 'You lot have all got a big shock coming your way.' His very words."

In fact, the Gaffer's visit had only served to further

complicate my life. Was he genuinely convinced that Iffy was the murderer and was he really in fear for his life? Either the Gaffer had been on a killing spree and was getting Clara on side for when he offed Iffy - or Iffy had been on a killing spree and was getting me on side for when he offed the Gaffer.

"The stakes have been raised," I declared dramatically.

Clara drily responded, "I'm off to bed," and I was left to do some sit-ups and press-ups and watch the flickering light of her TV creep out from under her bedroom door.

A BIT SQUEAMISH ABOUT THE WHOLE VIOLENT DEATH THING

"The fence won't take your weight any more, comrade," Iffy told me. "It's decision time, dearest."

He had been mightily miffed to hear that we had allowed the Gaffer into Clara's flat, and had settled into a state of ominous calm when I filled him in on the veiled threat with which the visit had terminated. Tucked away in our eyrie, squatting in the squatters' little room, he was now doing his best to persuade me to help him kill the Gaffer. It was a subject I had been avoiding since our chat in the pub when we had arrived in London.

Also of note was the slowness of Iffy's speech. He was drawling the way he did when he had been taking nasty drugs. It didn't inspire confidence. The bags under his eyes had grown to the size where he would have had to pay extra to take them with him on a Ryan Air flight. His skin, which had briefly shone with a glow that bordered on healthy after our trip to the Mediterranean coast, had reverted to its normal papery pallidness. What came across as ominous calm might have had its origins in the fact that he was off his tits again.

"I know decisions aren't your big thing," he mumbled, just like that.

"Since when?"

"Since, like, forever. Duh."

"Is that what you think?"

"It's what the world thinks. Don't tell me nobody's ever commented on it."

They hadn't.

"I make decisions. If I never made a decision, I would have

starved to death," I said, trying and failing to keep a petulant tone at bay.

"Well, yeah. Obviously, you make some decisions. But only when you have to. And it's not exactly your strong point, now, is it? I'm not having a go at you, mind. I can see your reasoning - if you don't make decisions, you won't make bad decisions. There's a certain zen beauty to it as a way of life. The path of least resistance."

Maybe he was being slyer than the Family Stone, placing me in a position where I would have to decide that he was right about the Gaffer, if only to prove that his appraisal of me being indecisive was wrong.

Or maybe his appraisal was right.

I couldn't decide.

"Let's leave that for the moment," I suggested.

"Sure. Whatever. You'll be telling me next that nobody's ever mentioned how small your head is."

"Pardon?"

"You know."

I didn't. Whatever nasties he had been caning seemed to have involved a truth serum.

"What we have here is a major moral dilemma," I said, moving on from the revelations that Iffy seemed intent on making. "We're talking about taking someone's life."

"Happens all the time."

"People listen to the Gaffer's music all the time. Doesn't make it right."

"Fair point."

We lapsed into a silence so long and so absolute it would have made a Trappist curse.

"Do you believe in the death penalty?" I asked, when I could take no more.

"Nope."

"Then why are you ready to sentence someone to death?"

"This is different."

"Because…"

"Remember what you said in Marseilles about meat-eaters and how they should be prepared to slaughter the wee beasties themselves? It's the same with the death penalty. The judge or jury or whoever makes the decision should be made to pull the plug - to flip the switch - themselves. You shouldn't say you'll eat beef so long as someone else kills the cow; you shouldn't say that someone has to die if you aren't ready to do the deed yourself. And another problem with the death penalty is the risk of a miscarriage of justice. 'Ooops! Sorry about that, old man. Better luck next time' - except there can't be a next time."

"Yeah, but that's it precisely - what if we're wrong about the Gaffer?"

"But what if we're right?"

A couple of seconds ambled past, and I realised he expected an answer. "Well, if we're right…shit. Bollocks, Iffy…If we're right, then he'll probably go on to kill you, me and Clara."

"Good point."

"Wanker."

"It's like the trolley problem," he continued.

"The trolley problem?"

"It's a bout a tram, actually - called a trolley in the good ol' U S of A. There's a runaway tram. It's headed for a platform where five people are waiting, and it'll kill 'em all. You can divert the tram onto another track and save their lives. Do you do it?"

"'Course."

"What if there's a worker on the other track? You'll save the five people, but you'll kill the worker. Still do it?"

"Guess so. Would you?"

"Yup. So there you go. Sorted."

"But wait a minute. I've read about this before. You're oversimplifying. What if there are two workers on the track? Or three? Four? Or what if the five people are all over eighty years old and the worker's a young man with two kids? Or the worker is a pregnant woman? Or your friend, or your brother? Or what if the five people are war criminals? Or they're the board of directors of Blackwater? Or what if there's only a seventy percent chance of the tram killing the five people?" I was getting into this.

"Or alter the details a bit," I went on. "You're a doctor and there are five people in vital need of new organs. Do you let another patient die and harvest their organs? Kill them, even? The trolley problem's been used to justify the fire bombing of Dresden, you know, and the bombing of Nagasaki and Hiroshima."

I had him there, I thought. And then I decided to flourish my trump card: "Remember - *syad-asti-nasti-avaktavyah*, my friend. In some ways, it is, it is not, and it is indescribable."

"Buddha on a bicycle, you don't half like to complicate matters, don't you?" he said. "Trust me, in this particular case, the worker is a murderer and the five people are three people. You, me, and Clara."

Outside, the sun was burning, simultaneously sustaining life on Earth and hastening its end.

I nipped out to buy us some falafels.

They weren't anywhere near as good as the ones I got back home in Berlin.

Back in our fortress, I found that Iffy had cooked up another argument, no doubt culled from another book he had found somewhere: "Look at it from a Utilitarian perspective. Bentham's theory of the greater good. The greater good here is for the Gaffer to die, and everyone else to live. 'If a judge sentence you to be imprisoned or put to death, have a dagger ready, and take a stroke first at the judge.' Bentham's words, not mine."

It was my turn to launch another sally. "Taking a life, though, Iffy, I mean…"

As sallies go, it wasn't the best.

"Needs must when the devil drives. *Si vis pacem, para bellum* - if you want peace, prepare for war. Don't you think we're all just a bit squeamish about the whole violent death thing these days? Not everywhere, of course, but your average Joe on the street in this neck of the woods."

"A bit squeamish?" I wasn't sure that I had ever really been aghast before in my life. Taken aback, dismayed, shocked, stunned, horrified - but never aghast. I didn't like it.

"I see it's time for Part Two of my Unified Theory on the Relative Importance of Death," Iffy announced. "As I'm sure you recall, Part One of my Theory dealt with the way a particular individual may respond to death according to their own relationship with the death-ee, and their own position in space and time relative to the one who has died. Part Two deals with how people place relative importance on death according to the predominant local cultural mores and norms, and how that varies through history and geography.

"You've read history books. How many of your ancestors went from cradle to grave without getting caught up in a war? Or never had their village raided, their town besieged, their city sacked? How many of our forefathers died in their beds and how many had their lives taken away by greedy, bloodthirsty bastards in power? And capital punishment used to really bring the crowds in, you know. You think the circus in Rome used to feature clowns tripping each other up and girls in spangly costumes spinning round on ropes? It was leopards not leotards in those days. History is drenched in blood. Life has always been cheap."

He was beginning to freak me out.

"Are you trying to freak me out?" I asked.

"I'm trying to give you some perspective, sweetheart. What difference does one more dead bloke make? You think our respected and venerated leaders give a tom tit about people living or dying except as a means of control, or to create positive or negative publicity? They don't. They'll go to war if it suits them. They're happy for *us* to die for what *they* believe in. To sacrifice millions of lives. You think the bosses of Shell or Blackwater or Union Carbide or Merck care about the sanctity of human life? Do they Jemima Puddleduck as like. But they've got us, the herd, to believe that killing someone is beyond the pale. Not the done thing. Because otherwise they'd be in danger. We've got to break their conditioning. Take away the state monopoly on violent death. Think about it. This could be just the beginning."

"Do you realise you're sounding like a nutter? A psychopath?"

"Break the conditioning. Would you exchange the complete works of Shakespeare for Adolf Hitler's life?"

"Of course. But that's purely hypothetical."

"It's a way to demonstrate my point. The value of life is relative, not absolute. It's just a matter of where you draw the line. And whose line is it anyway? It's all about whose trip you choose to live in. The arbitrary one imposed on you or the one you create? You could have gone to sleep in 1977 in the UK with a bag of ecstasy as a decent member of society and woken up the next morning as a criminal because the law had changed. Then you could have had the same bag of drugs in the US and not broken the law till 1985. You can cross a line on a map and become an illegal person. Or take the five thousand Enclosure Acts that effectively fenced off eleven thousand square miles of land in Britain - pieces of paper that changed reality, just because Parliament could call on their gang to back them up, and their gang was the biggest and baddest. I'm sure one day in the future I'll wake up in an old abandoned house I'm living in and be told I face a prison sentence because squatting has been outlawed."

I frowned. "But the thing is - you said it yourself - our gang isn't as ruff 'n' tuff as theirs. They've got the monopoly on violence. What they says goes. Their word is law."

"And it's up to us to challenge it. I'm not talking about the law. I'm talking about what's right. Sometimes the two intersect, but not always, and certainly not in this case. We have to kill the Gaffer. Simple as."

I took a deep breath. "Did you kill the others?"

I GAVE HIM SHEEPISH

There. I'd said it.

"What? Of course I didn't kill the others. Never killed anyone, me. Not yet. Never had reason to before."

"Minnie wrote in her diary that she was waiting to see someone from the rig. Could have been you," I heard myself saying.

"But it wasn't."

"Juliest said some old matey from the rig ordered some K off her before hooking up with Jacek. Was it you?"

"No."

"How do I know you weren't in Berlin when Udo was killed? I didn't see you get off the plane. I only have your word for it that that junkie saw someone else push Udo."

"It wasn't me."

"How do I know you didn't break Allan Exit's neck in the fight in Friedrichshain? You were right in there."

"I didn't."

"Who can prove where you were when Sam overdosed in Marseilles?"

"Nobody. But I wasn't there."

"Says you."

"Says me."

If it sounds convincing and it looks convincing, I thought, it must be convincing. Right? I was pretty convinced.

"Did you really think it might have been me?"

"Dunno." I gave him sheepish, and I gave him a lot of it. Then I gave him a hug.

"With friends like these…" he sighed.

I needed a little time to myself to assimilate his denial. The funny thing was that I was just about prepared to consider the possibility that he was a murderer, but I refused to entertain the idea that he would lie to me about it when I confronted him.

The sun was still on fire when I went out to buy us some beer. I guessed we were a little nearer planet death, and there was nothing I could do about it.

A THREE-HOUR DISPUTE ABOUT THE DATE OF MY BIRTHDAY

Using his cigarette lighter, Iffy flipped the top off a bottle of lager. He fished a half-smoked fag out of one of his pockets and lit it, and asked me if I had decided whether I was with him or agin him yet, blithely carrying on as though I hadn't accused him of several murders; as though it was just another bridge we had crossed on the long and winding road we walked together.

"As I think I've made clear, this is a major moral dilemma, Iffy. I need some time to think about it."

"There you go again…You and decisions…"

This time I gave him peeved.

"Actually, old buddy, this isn't a moral dilemma at all," he told me through a fog of smoke, the nauseating, stale kind that comes from re-lit roll-ups.

"It isn't?"

"Nope. It's a simple matter of practicalities. Him or us. Okay, so maybe we're wrong, but like you said, if we're right and we leave him free to finish us all off…"

"There must be another solution."

"Not this time, Josephine. We can't call the police in, even if we recognised their moral authority to arbitrate in our personal disputes. Which we don't, of course. They'd just tell us to run along and stop telling tales, and then nick us for a blim of puff."

"And if we warn him off?"

"If he's gonna do it, he's gonna do it even if we ask him not to."

"I just don't think I'm capable of killing someone."

"Shit of a bull, man - we're all capable of it. It's an act like any other. Like I said, humans have been doing it to each other forever. The big cheeses decree when and under what circumstances it's socially acceptable as part of their agenda for total control. It's okay if you're a soldier at war. It's okay if you're a cop. It's okay if you're a landowner and the victim's a thief. It's okay if it's self-defence - even you have to agree with that, surely."

"Well, yeah."

"Well then. This is self-defence, *n'est-ce pas*? Slightly pre-emptive, admittedly. But better to strike first than to give a sucker an even break and wait till he's bearing down on you with a meat cleaver in his hand. Or pushing Clara in front of a truck. Or whatever."

Iffy had always presented a good argument. We once had a three-hour dispute about the date of my birthday, and I only narrowly won.

"Supposing I was capable of it..." I allowed. "I'd still insist on just a wee bit more proof," I said, feeling the roads of my own life diverging, and preparing to take the path less travelled.

"Then you shall have it, my buttercup. For I have a plan."

MOSTLY WITH LUMP HAMMERS

The Gaffer was the first to leave. He looked properly pooped after a long day farting around. We watched as he swivelled his head from side to side, no doubt checking if Iffy was following him. I almost felt sorry for him. He crossed the road, re-crossed the road, changed direction, pretended to look in a shop window, crossed the road again, and finally scuttled away round the corner.

Andy, his skeletal manager, emerged three hours later. He didn't look the whistling type, but we saw his lips pursed and tried to guess what tune was issuing from his mouth. Something cheesy, like the music he promoted, or something sinister, like the vibe he gave off? He pulled some car keys out of his pocket as he walked and was soon lost from our sight.

"Here we go, then," Iffy said, clambering to his feet. "Time to have a shufti round the Gaff."

"So what's the plan, Stan? How're we going to get in there? After all, there's a helluva lot of money's worth of equipment in that place. They're going to have some serious security. We're not breaking into some old abandoned building this time."

Both of us had cracked our fair share of squats, either houses and flats to live in or factories, warehouses and old offices to park up and party in. The Gaff was fish in an altogether different kind of kettle.

"Trust me," Iffy said, knowing full well that I hated it when he did that. "I've got it all worked out."

I tried to gauge how fucked he was. By the same logic that decreed Eskimos should have a plethora of words for snow, in our scene we had developed a multitude of expressions that covered intoxication. So - was Iffy out of his box or out of his nut; off his head or off his tits? Cunted, munted, fucked, wankered, bollocksed or twatted? Spannered, hammered, shit-faced, mullered, battered or trolleyed? Wasted, caned, trashed, mashed or cabbaged?

A combination of all of the above, I decided regrettably. He had been snorting speed and K all afternoon, and occasionally nipping off to the bogs, which was what bothered me. I hoped he hadn't been sticking needles in his arm.

I followed his thinning head of hair down one flight of steps, then down another. Our Spanish hosts were having a party, their first and only party in the building we had helped them squat. It was an eviction party. To the chagrin of Marta and her crew, the owners had come up with a fast-track eviction because the place had only seen the back of its last group of squatters a month before. I wondered if the Gaffer or his manager had tipped them off to its re-occupation.

The Spaniards' plans for running a weekly squat café would have to be put on ice, along with the proposed free yoga classes, language lessons, art sessions and weekly martial arts training. Such was a squatter's luck - some you won, some you lost. Maybe their next place (they had already secured an empty pub in Whitechapel) would stay open for years. Tonight, though, they had brought in decks and a little sound system and invited their mates around for a knees-up. Acid techno boomed through the building.

Nobody paid us any attention as we slipped down into the basement. Iffy flicked on the light-switch and a single bulb illuminated a room with low ceilings, damp walls and concrete on the floor.

"You might want to mask up for this," Iffy told me, tying a tee-shirt to cover his mouth.

"Bandito-style? I like it."

"Gloves, too."

"Oh, good stuff."

He went to a bag in the corner of the room. "Good old Danny the Builder. If you're ever looking for a lump hammer or two, he's your man."

"Any particular reason why you were looking for lump hammers?" I asked.

"Now that you mention it...I was thinking of hammering lumps out of this wall."

"I see. And I like."

It was an old classic, much loved by bank robbers. To be honest, it was something I'd always fancied trying my hand at. The Gaff was alarmed on its windows and doors and our rudimentary breaking and entering skills didn't stretch to the disabling of alarm systems. Our skill at simply breaking things, on the other hand, was quite advanced.

We attacked the bricks in the wall that divided the cellar of the squat from the cellar of the Gaffer's studio with gusto, vigour and main force, but mostly with lump hammers.

Bang, wallop, thump, whack, smack, crack, and repeat. Grunt, sigh, pant, gasp, heave, puff, wheeze, and repeat...

Until clouds of dust began to billow around us. Clearing away some of the rubble that had piled up around our feet, we enlarged the hole in the wall until it was just big enough to crawl through. Iffy went first.

Then: "Get off me! Help! Aaargh!" I heard him cry, his voice muted by the wall that now separated us.

A JOB-LOT OF CHEAP WHITE EMULSION

I wasn't falling for that one. "Alright there, mate?"

"There are some bloody big spiders in here. Come on."

I stuck my head through the gap and dragged the rest of my body through. The beam of Iffy's torch was dancing over the walls, but there was nothing of note to arrest its swinging terpsichorean promenade. The cellar of the Gaff was indistinguishable from the cellar of the squat.

It was only a few days ago that Iffy had mentioned Howard Carter's penetration of the Great Pyramid. Although the time since then had been but brief, it had seen me cover more kilometres, experience more emotions and peer deeper inside myself and the convoluted soul of Man (and Iffy) than I could possibly have envisaged on that sunny Berlin afternoon.

On that occasion, Iffy had referred to the supposed curse that fell on Lord Carnarvon's doomed treasure hunters. Now, here we were, having breached a wall, trespassing in the underground realm of the Gaffer. No pharaoh, he, but a prince among men. If you believed the hype.

Which I didn't really.

Nonetheless, it was with bated breath and whisp'ring stumbles that we mounted the stairs to where the air grew cleaner and fresher. We reached a blue-painted metal door that led out of the cellar. I watched as Iffy's torch showed his fingers grasping the handle and I smiled in the darkness as he pulled and the door swung open. We were in.

Why do people speak in hushed tones in empty, unlit buildings? Maybe for the flipside of the reason that they shout on mountaintops. Outdoors in the elements you know you're alive and that life is worth living; darkness and silence are a foretaste of the grave.

"Should've brought two torches -" I began *sotto voce*, but canned the rest of the sentence when Iffy turned the light on.

"No point creeping around like thieves in the dark, eh?"

"Right. You'll be telling me you can turn your torch off next."

"Eh? Oh yeah."

"C'mon then. Let's see what we can find…"

From floor to ceiling the place was predictably white and minimal. As homely as an operating theatre. As cosy as a lab. The Gaff's interior decorators were presumably inspired by Hoxton art-chic, or maybe they had just got a job-lot of cheap white emulsion that they wanted to get shot of.

There was nothing in the corridor except us, and we weren't there very long. Opening another steel door, we began our search for the eye of the Gaffer's creative storm, the control room where he plotted world domination…

Penetrating intrepidly further into the dark heart of the Gaffer's lair, we opened and then closed the door to a room that resembled an airport lounge, then briefly poked our snouts into another space that had presumably been modelled on a Silicone Valley start-up's recreation room, dedicated with dismal earnestness to 'fun'. Pool tables, table football, air hockey games and dart boards; that kind of crap. Another door opened to reveal an office.

I followed Iffy's bony body inside, momentarily wondering if he had always been quite so thin. Back in our youth there been an intangible air of hunger about the boy, a questing insatiability, a yearning for the type of knowledge that only experience could provide. These days he just looked malnourished.

"Check this out," he called from across the room. "I think

I've found some kind of masterplan."

He was leafing through a pile of A3 print-outs. I took the first proffered page, and as I took it in I wondered if the Gaffer was taking the piss or if he'd lost the plot.

"This, my friend, unless I'm very much mistaken, looks like a mock-up of a free party."

"Uh-huh."

The pages that we were perusing were labelled 'Rio', 'New York', 'Sydney', and so on through many of the world's major cities. Each one showed a floor plan. The placements for backdrops were marked, along with sculpture installations. There were other pages with printed out pictures that showed the kind of thing Iffy and I had seen before, a hundred times and more, a thousand times, under lights that flashed, vibrating to the bass, strung between tree trunks or slung across the sides of trucks, rained on, snowed on, 'neath moon and sun and stars, trailing in puddles of piss in post-apocalyptic warehouses, splattered in vomit, stained with beer, hung high, hung low, hung wherever we could hang the fuckers: techno backdrops. There were images, too, of metal sculptures, the type that the Mutoid Waste Company used to specialise in, cyberpunk humanoids and replicant hell-hounds; bastard, mongrel robots welded together from scrap.

It was the typical decor for a free party.

"I mean, I s'pose, well, it's not bad," I admitted.

"Yeah, 'course, it's pretty good, and all that."

"Would've looked wicked at one of our parties."

"Blinding, yeah. But it's not exactly…"

"Commercially viable?"

"Yeah. Not exactly…"

"Going to take the world by storm?"

"Not at all…"

"What you'd expect from the Gaffer these days?"

"Not really..."

"Going to save his career?"

"What's he playing at?"

Returning to the plans, we also identified impressive lighting rigs, DJ tables and meaty speaker stacks. The plans were nice, alright, and maybe there were cities that hadn't yet experienced the joys of free party raves, but why would the Gaffer, who as far as I knew sought to expunge any record of his involvement in the scene, even going so far as to disown his old friends, and indeed quite probably kill them, want to turn his upcoming worldwide tour into a homage to all that he now despised? Was it ironic? Tongue-in-cheek? Even, Dog forbid, post-modern?

I was thoroughly mystified. I said as much, though the exact words I used were, "I don't fucking get it."

"C'mon. Let's have a gander upstairs. There's got to be some kind of explanation to all this," Iffy suggested, and it was hither we hied ourselves, and with anticipation that we were agog.

Finally we reached the music studio itself. It was state-of-the-art, of course, a set-up worthy of a chart-topping musician.

"Funny, really," my crusty companion opined. "All these amazing hi-spec, top-end bits of kit, and what does the man produce? Bland, generic crap. Remember how it used to be? When underground techno first hit the road in the early nineties, you needed loadsa money to get a working studio together. That was doable, I suppose, but only for the truly dedicated. A little while later, thanks to advances in technology, any fucker could make whatever sounds they liked. Electronic music was taken out of the hands of the professionals and gifted to any chancer who wanted to give it a crack. Part-timers, amateurs, experimenters. True innovators. People with genuine passion, who weren't concerned about sales and profits. A studio in your bedroom, a liveset in your backpack. And now the Gaffer's got all this stuff in here and it must weigh a ton. This, my friend, is one heavy bag. This is some serious investment. This beast has to be fed."

"Aye. So -"

"The Gaffer's in deep, man. His toes are curling, his nuts are freezing and the water level's rising. He's no longer just having a laugh, he's involved in *business* now. All the publicity and hype, all the lifestyle, all the minions and managers, they've all got to be paid for. What are the chances of him producing some interesting music? He can't afford to take risks. He wouldn't be allowed to. Remember that ad he did for TV? He can't have actually wanted to do that. He had no choice. His label would probably have sued him for breach of contract if he'd kicked off about it. So what does he do? He comes here, shoots a game of pool, checks out the sound of the latest hit tunes and shovels another turd off the production line. He hates it, but what can he do?"

"Stop!" I shrieked. "You're breaking my heart."

"I do hope you're joking. He made the decision to sign the contract. He took the King's shilling, he accepted the devil's dollar, and he has to live with the consequences. Don't pity him. Despise him, by all means. Deride him, scorn him, revile him and disdain him - but never, ever feel sorry for him and his like. Poor little rich boys! Fuck 'em. There's no excuse for the wealthy and privileged not to do their bit. It's about free will - everyone *does* have the ability to escape from their pre-ordained roles and to choose their own path. Let them use their money and positions of influence to do some good. To do *something* good. At the very, very least, to make some decent fucking music!"

I meekly suggested that we, too, should start doing something: "Like unearthing evidence of the Gaffer's evil plot. Or even something that would allow us to make sense of all those plans downstairs. Er, what are you doing, Iffy?"

"Eh?"

"What are you doing?"

He had turned on the energy supply to the formidable banks and ranks of instruments and machines. Masses of LEDs burst into spontaneous life like the birth of a galaxy. Somewhere, I imagined, a bespectacled watchman on the night shift in a power station was staring in goggle-eyed stupefaction and crying, "She cannae take it any more!" as needles flipped, dials spun and alarms hooted.

Iffy hunched over a computer screen. He busied himself tapping some keys. A few minutes later the sound of music came roaring out of the studio monitors…

The production was slicker. The sound quality was smoother. The effects were cleaner. The drums were crisper. The basslines were fatter. The top-ends were trimmer. The breaks were sharper.

But what we were listening to was basically the liveset from the Millennium Massacre party we had done together in Italy all those years ago. The tape that I had found in Udo's bag. The tape we thought Minnie had been listening to before she died.

"That's strange," I said.

"Isn't it just? Know what's stranger?"

"A penguin in a tutu?"

"Well, yes. But pretty damn strange, nonetheless - the title for this 'ere music what we is listening to."

"Oh my Dog. Hit me with it, Iffy-boy."

BOGGLIN'

"Work In Progress. New Album."

Right about then was when a whole heap o' bogglin' started goin' on.

Apparently the Gaffer's new album was a re-working of the tape that had been recorded at the Millennium Massacre party as the year 1999 rolled into 2000. Iffy and I went through the complete sound file methodically, from its first thunderous bassline to its final cackling echo, and as far as we could tell - and I had listened to it repeatedly over the course of the last few days - all the Gaffer had done was tidy up the original recording by eliminating the errors and beefing up the production values.

It certainly tied in with everything we had already uncovered in the Gaff. We had been baffled when we came across the blueprints for a free party set-up. Now that we knew what our one-time partner in crime was cooking up in the way of music, it all made sense.

"This explains everything," I said breathlessly.

And then paused and added, "Doesn't it?"

"Yeah. It must do."

"Because now…"

"Because before…"

"Because…fuck it, Iffy - what's going on here?"

When I had played the tape in my flat, Iffy had tried to identify the creative talent behind it. He claimed to have recognised the Gaffer's input, so maybe it was one of the cheesy pop-tart's own livesets, in which case he had every right to release it as his next album.

But Iffy was also convinced he had clocked contributions from Minnie, Sam, Jacek, Allan and Udo, all of whom had recently celebrated their back-to-the-earth-day.

So was that what it was all about? I winnowed my theory through the threshing machine of my vocal chords. "Have a chuff on this: the Gaffer, running desperately short of ideas and faced with a difficult deadline, resorts to good old-fashioned plagiarism. He's got form there. Remember that awful TV ad soundtrack? He knows that neither Andy nor anyone else at his record label will spot what he's doing, so he simply rehashes a favourite old set. But it wasn't his set - or not exclusively in any case. Faced with the possibility of the other musicians tapping him up for a share of the royalties - which will be enormous - he decides to kill all the collaborators."

Maybe it would even work for him commercially. Before his gig in Berlin I had concluded that, given enough of a push by the music industry, the free techno sound could be made profitable. But I had also reasoned the rest of the scene was unmarketable, and yet here was the Gaffer seemingly going the whole hog.

Iffy was nodding. "Not bad. Not bad at all. I like it. But have a go on this one, just for the hell of it: Udo and the others somehow got wind of the Gaffer's project and were blackmailing him for a share of the profits. That's why Udo had the tape with him in Berlin. Proof."

I thought about it for literally milliseconds before dismissing the idea as axiomatically anathematic. "Not their style, mate. But look, it's all falling into place. For whatever reason - probably a lack of any new ideas - the Gaffer has plagiarised the Millennium Massacre liveset for his new album. As some kind of gimmick, he's after copying the look and the sound of free party techno on his next big tour. To avoid sharing his royalties, he's killing off the people who worked with him on the music. If only there was some hard evidence of his involvement in their deaths…"

In a small upstairs room, the twin of our look-out post in the squat next door, in a locked cabinet that didn't stay locked for long under Iffy's energetic ministrations, we found what we were looking for.

TIMES LIKE NO OTHER, TIMES LONG GONE, FRIENDS NOW DEAD…

"'Ello, 'ello, and indeed, 'ello," Iffy murmured, opening a cardboard folder. "'Death Of A Travelling Sound System.' This looks interesting."

Minnie Mouth. Jacek. Big Udo. Sam Saoule. Allan Exit. Photos. Sketches. Drawings. References to video clips. Potted biographies. Newspaper cuttings.

Our friends' faces. Smiling, laughing. Young. Alive.

Minnie, Sam, Udo, Jacek and Allan.

Silently we faced our past.

Minnie in a shocking pink afro wig and a spangly silver dress, sporting a grin so wide it would have strained the muscles on anyone who hadn't had so much practice.

Udo up a stepladder next to an improvised lighting gantry, his builder's bum, a fleshy half moon, boldly on display in front of a daub of clouds that spanned the sapphire heavens like a child's drawing.

Jacek behind the decks, head cocked to sandwich his headphones between one shoulder and an ear, his hands a blur above the mixer, his brow creased in a frown of concentration.

Sam Saoule alone, eyes closed, two steps from the bass bins, his shoulders hunched, his fingers splayed, his Mohican rain-flattened, his boots forever caught in mid-shuffle.

Allan Exit sprawled over a battered, balding armchair on a barren, rocky hillside, waving a spliff, brandishing a bottle of vodka, laughing.

Minnie in a red miniskirt and a black bomber jacket, swinging her fire chains in an alley made between two buses, her eyes to the skies, up to her ankles in mud, smoke escaping, rising high.

Udo in shorts, beached on a sandy seashore, sleeping with his mouth open and the gaps in his teeth on display, dribble oozing down his jowls, his torn tee-shirt - bearing the slogan 'Do no harm - but take no shit' - tugged taut over his bulging belly.

Minnie in a bikini top and baggy trousers, down on her knees, the only obstacle in front of an endless line of baton-wielding coppers.

Sam Saoule and Jacek's ugly unshaven mugs in close-up, sweat cutting swathes through the dirt and dust on their faces, their pupils as big as planets, who knows what crazy war cry issuing from their screaming mouths.

Minnie and Sam rolling down a hillside, legs and arms and hair sticking out in every direction, destined never to reach the bottom.

Udo wearing a white tank top and a tartan farmer's flat cap in the back of his bus, tossing a pancake, dusted in flour, performing an ungainly pirouette, losing his balance, not giving a shit, a fragile looking chair about to break his fall.

Allan hunkered down in front of a heavily graffitied wall, his locks trailing all the way down to the floor, with six dogs of differing sizes standing to attention, all slobbering and staring at the tiny biscuit in the palm of his hand.

Udo and Minnie in matching blue overalls high-kicking a cancan next to a smouldering firepit in an empty field as dawn breaks over a distant, undulating line of grey-blue hills.

Sam Saoule on a deck chair, naked except for a pair of pants and his boots, his ACAB tattoo clearly visible on the back of his neck, reading a newspaper, smoking a pipe, sipping a cup of tea, the only still point on a dance floor where a hundred bodies gyre and gimble.

Iffy and I passed the photos to each other - grains of sand trickling through our hands.

Walls of sound, dodgy vehicles, squatted buildings, open skies, happy faces, decks, dogs, food, booze, convoys, dancing crowds, cables like tentacles, times like no other, times long gone, friends now dead…

"*Ubi sunt qui ante nos fuerunt*," Iffy whispered. "Where are they, those who have gone before us?"

Was that a tear I saw, a drop of pure emotion, rolling down his cheek?

I couldn't be sure because my own vision was blurred. "'Death Of A Travelling Sound System?' This was The Life Of A Travelling Sound System. This was our life. These were our lives. And it was dead long before the Gaffer came along to read the last rites and apply the *coup de grâce*. It died when it ceased to be new. It died when it started conforming to its own non-conformity. This is just the autopsy."

Iffy gave me a slow round of applause. "Way to go with the Oscar speech, man," he said, the chopsy little bastard.

And then he picked up another cardboard folder.

More photos.

Iffy.

Clara.

And me.

"Time to bust a move, buster," Iffy's voice came from a place that seemed far, far away. "Our work here is done."

I let the photos fall from my grasp. Drops of water on the surface of a lake.

"Did you break the lock on the cabinet, or pick it?" I asked, returning to practicalities.

He looked offended. "Picked it." Looked pleased with himself.

"Then un-pick it. We don't want the Gaffer to know what

we found here."

"And the rest of the stuff? What d'you reckon? Make it look like a robbery?"

"You mean rob it? Nah, that'd be too hot for Marta and our friendly Spanish posse. Don't want to bring it on top for them. What say we give it a bit of mild trashing and leave it at that?"

"You don't think breaking a hole in a brick wall seems like a lot of effort for a bit of mild trashing?"

"Well, yes, I do. But so what? If nothing's missing it wasn't a burglary. They'll decide that whoever broke in must've been disturbed or got cold feet and fucked off empty-handed."

Now, a bit of mild trashing might sound like an undemanding kind of undertaking, but it's easier said than done. I had always been well into the old R-E-S-P-E-C-T, be it for my brothers and sisters or for the planet on whose crust I walked. We had always tidied up the places we partied, improved the buildings we squatted, tried to talk to the people we pissed off. Sure, I had helped trash McDonalds outlets, bankers' offices and other similar dens of cupidity on demos and during actions, but that was targeted property damage, a venting of righteous anger, the only way of getting a message across to the faceless institutions who understood no other language but the language of violence and financial cost.

I felt bad as I ripped cables from the Gaffer's machines and tipped them over and toppled them onto the floor. This was not the Luddite's act of sabotage against the machines that sought to enslave him. It was just wrecking some stuff. Even though I had lost all respect for the Gaffer as a human and could no longer call him a friend, I tried not to imagine his face when he saw the damage. But I did it because it had to be done.

And then we crawled back through our hole in the wall and re-surfaced in the party. According to his Facebook page, the

Gaffer, and hopefully his manager, were due to be schmoozing it up in Vienna for the next forty-eight hours, so there was time enough for the party to wind down and the anonymous squatters to decamp to their next new home before the our break-in was discovered.

We mingled, drank, danced, did some drugs, chatted, danced some more. But the people around me weren't the ones who danced before my mind's eye.

MARK SLEIGH

GET OLD TESTAMENT ON THE MOTHERFUCKER'S ARSE

What's the best way to take a life; the best way to kill? The slither of a knife? Poison in a pill? A blow to the head, a gunshot at night? A rock in a forest, far from city lights?

Strange thoughts.

A speeding car and the crunch of flesh. A rope around the neck. A cliff top and an unexpected shove. A hammer. A head, water, bubbles. The roar of fire, the stench of smoke. The boom of explosives. A crossbow's twang. Blood.

Strange times.

The English word talion, meaning punishment identical to the offence. The Latin, *lex talionis*: an eye for an eye. Get Old Testament on the motherfucker's arse.

But like a wise man said, that road leads to nothing but blindness for all. And it wasn't the path that our moral GPS was sending us along: our killing was a preventative measure, not an act of retribution. It was, as Iffy had reminded me, a case of *aut cum scuto aut in scuto,* which he had translated as meaning that we would either do it with our shields in hand, or our bodies would be carried from the battlefield on our shields. And by taking out the Gaffer, we would be giving the gift of life to others.

Or so I told myself.

Lying in bed, back at Clara's flat, I fell to thinking about these matters.

To the best of my knowledge, our criminal justice system was based around the triple tenets of punishment, deterrence and rehabilitation.

I had seen little evidence of the latter. Dear old Dr Timothy

Leary had seemingly had some success in reducing the figures for recidivism back in the fifties, but his LSD therapy soon fell out of favour with the power-trippers who made the rules. The reality was that in the early twentieth century the majority of ex-prisoners in the US and the UK soon found themselves prisoners once more. There was precious little sign of any successful rehabilitation.

Theories as to the correct degree of punishment a crime merited had changed as often as the lengths of women's hemlines, I knew. The old Anglo-Saxon *wergild* system placed a monetary value on the living soul. A debt of blood was repaid in coin. The American tort law still totted up the cash equivalent of a human life. Some cultures adopted the vendetta approach, the one that makes the whole world blind. Nearly four millennia ago, the Babylonian Hammurabic code said that retribution could be no more serious than the original crime, although offences against members of a higher social class were dealt with more severely. Of course.

Meanwhile the threat of prison as a deterrent probably worked for the majority of people, who were scared of going to jail, but figures for incarceration continued to rise around the globe. The States went from having 800,000-odd prisoners in 1985 to over two million twenty years later. The number behind bars in the UK had also more than doubled in the two decades since the beginning of the nineties. That was a serious amount of people who presumably reckoned that doing the crime was worth risking the time. And by a happy coincidence, the privatised prison business was flourishing.

I had never had much truck with the criminal justice system. Too many of my friends and associates had suffered at its hands, mostly for drug offences - which shouldn't even have been offences in the first place, in my book - or for getting nicked in a riot. Judges thought nothing of banging people up for a year or two for being found in possession of a couple of hundred grams of hash or a handful of pills, or for breaking a pane of glass on a corporate store front. No matter how I looked at it, I couldn't make that balance on my own personal scales of justice. And surely the forty-odd grand per prisoner per year that was spent could be used to achieve something more positive.

Nobody I knew came out of prison a better person for the experience. No reformed characters. No lessons learnt. Just an added layer of surliness. Less willingness to smile, less *joie de vivre*, more fear of showing 'weakness'. A lot of bitterness. However much of a cliché it may be, however much men may preen and strut in the company of women, a man starved of female company inevitably shrinks into a hardened carapace of something less human.

All of which nocturnal musing about crime and punishment was inspired by two dominant thoughts.

Firstly, that Iffy and I had passed a death sentence on the Gaffer. Yes, after seeing the inside of the Gaff and the Gaffer's heart I had hung my colours on the good ship Iffy. I had thrown my hat into the ring where he was ringmaster. I had placed my hand in his paw, set my qualms aside, and agreed that for our own safety, the Gaffer had to go. The decision was as final as it was fatal.

And secondly, my other preoccupation was that we had to get away with the murder. I had no intention of going to prison for twenty years. My own death was preferable.

It seemed like a good moment to start smoking again. I wondered briefly if Clara's flat contained a secret stash of tobacco. It didn't, so after a hundred sit-ups and fifty press-ups, I shuffled into the kitchen and settled for a cheese sandwich. A pickled onion, too, and a packet of crisps. A cheeky glass of red wine. Was this how assassins lived?

How would Clara react to the knowledge that she was harbouring a would-be killer under her roof? Not very well, I figured, bread knife in hand. Best to guard it as my little secret with Iffy. And later, when she read in the papers or heard on the TV that the Gaffer was an ex-Gaffer, how would she take it?

Eventually, my hunger placated and my belly sated with cheddar and bread, and with the tang of the onion and the tawny taste of the wine lingering on my lips, I fell asleep. It was surprising, given the circumstances, but I would have had to be awake in order to register the surprise. And if I had been awake, I would have had nothing to be surprised about. One of life's many paradoxes.

METAPHORICAL STRAPPING DUTCHMEN

Have no motive. Use no weapon. Make no physical contact. Leave no corpse.

One bottle of red wine was all it took Iffy and I to come up with these basic guidelines for how to get away with murder.

The wine had been my idea. My new theory was that as long as Iffy was drinking, he wouldn't be doing too many opiates. The two substances didn't mix well, even for a notorious drug-cocktailer like Iffy.

My other suggestion, that we should do some research into how to get away with murder, had been mockingly dismissed by my accomplice. He had pointed out that by definition there would be no record of any perfect murder. We settled instead for some good old fashioned brainstorming, otherwise known as even more old fashioned getting pissed in the park.

We figured we were pretty safe as far as the motive went. As there had been no official investigation into the Gaffer's own killings, it stood to reason that nobody would look in our direction when the Gaffer's clogs went a-popping. We were nothing more than peripheral figures from the great musician's dim and distant past, and as such were unlikely to draw any heat as perps. (Despite ourselves and in spite of the serious and dour nature of our position, we occasionally liked to enliven our conversation with some Hollywood vocabulary.)

The murder weapon, though, be it a smoking gun or a bloodied blade, a dented bonnet or a knotted cord, often marked the first step in a trail that led from cadaver to killer. Evidence could be bagged, links established, ownership traced, suspects identified, charges pressed, guilt proven, sentences handed down, time served.

Not that we anticipated getting in close and striking our man down anyway. The only blood we wanted on our hands was of the cleaner, less sticky, metaphorical kind. We were leaning towards the use of poison as our tool of choice. A woman's method, so we had heard, but we had always been committed to equality of the sexes and had fought against gender stereotyping, be it at home, at school, in the workplace, or in the choice of murder weapon.

We also had to make sure that we didn't leave any little telltale fibres, specks of dirt, saliva-coated fag ends, loose hairs, errant eyelashes or flakes of skin at the scene of the crime. Whilst Iffy's increasing baldness slightly reduced the chances of him leaving a hair behind for diligent forensic scientists to find, the specks of dirt could prove problematic - unless the killing took place somewhere heavily contaminated by other people's DNA.

Making the Gaffer's corpse disappear would be a tall order, we realised. We didn't own a pig farm, and neither did we have access to any meat processing plants. Danny the Builder might not be too keen to have his old mate's body buried in the foundations of his current work site. Our friends at the bronze foundry definitely wouldn't be up for an illegal cremation. We ran through a few other possibilities - weighing the body down and dumping it in deep water, digging a hole in a forest floor - but came up with nothing that seemed to guarantee foolproof, discreet and permanent disposal of a body.

We were engrossed in our reflections, calmly and rationally discussing the previously unthinkable. The sun was shining. I could almost feel the grass of Clissold Park growing beneath my bum cheeks, lifting me infinitesimally higher. Two terrapins were trying to stare Iffy out, or perhaps they were just doing their natural thing and Iffy had elected to see it as a challenge.

A couple of rastas cycled past, disseminating whiffs of pungent sensimillia. Occasionally a Frisbee whistled over our heads. A chalky-white bonehead swung a branch round and round in circles, his grimly determined Staff hanging on by the skin of its teeth. Mothers with pushchairs, kids with hoods, granddads with legs that didn't go as fast as they used to...life's parade rolled on.

And then, after a long silence, just as my eyes were beginning to close, Iffy suddenly said, "Mate. I've got a confession."

I jerked fully awake so fast that Iffy snatched his gaze away from the terrapin duo. I just had time to clock them looking triumphant before they plopped back into the murky waters of the pond.

Hello, I thought, and, "A confession," I repeated.

"Aye."

So, I thought, and, "Oh?" I encouraged.

"Here goes..."

Go on then, I thought, and, "Go on then," I said...

...thinking - murder? But no, he had already denied it, and I had believed him...

"It's about our trip to Amsterdam. I'm afraid I wasn't quite totally straight up with you and Nadine about the money you borrowed off her."

I mentally threw a lever that switched the tracks under my train of thought. Iffy wasn't confessing to murder - of course he wasn't. He was confessing to a far less serious crime. I may actually have been foolish enough to smile. I hardly even noticed that now it was me who had borrowed the money, not Iffy, or even us.

"I could see at the time that you didn't really believe me about the mugging, you know. I'm not stupid. And that hurt me - that you, my best mate, would doubt me. That hurt me a lot."

It was true: I could see the hurt on his face.

"I'm sorry, Iffy. But...wait a minute. I was right, wasn't I?"

"That's not the point, though, is it? The point - the big point, the point of life - is to look after our loved ones, right? So they don't end up like Minnie. And sometimes that means saying things that aren't necessarily true in the strictest sense of the word, but that convey a deeper, inner truth instead."

Was that really the point of life, I wondered? Maybe it was.

"Thing is, I think I might have given poor old Nadine the impression that I was mugged, and though that wasn't really so true in a, well, a literal, nuts and bolts, old-fashioned kind of sense, it was definitely true in a kind of metaphorical, philosophical sense. A meta sense, if you like."

I parsed that through the Iffy sentence-grinder. "You weren't mugged."

"I'd honestly have to say that depends on your definition of mugged. If I told you I got carried away, I wouldn't literally mean that someone had picked me up and carried me away, would I? And so when I said I got mugged, I might not necessarily have literally meant that two strapping Dutchman punched me and robbed me."

"No?"

"No. If you'd listened properly, you would've seen that I might actually have been saying that two metaphorical strapping Dutchmen metaphorically punched me and metaphorically robbed me."

"Two metaphorical strapping Dutchmen metaphorically robbed you."

"I knew you'd understand."

And the crazy thing was that I did, sort of.

"Thing is, I didn't want to hurt Nadine, she's so lovely, and she lent you that cash out of the kindness of her heart. If I'd told her I'd just lunched it out, she'd have been angry, and anger is such a negative emotion. She'd have been angry at you for asking for the wedge in the first place, angry at me for leaving her backpack on the seat of the Metro when I got off, and worst of all she'd have been angry at herself, and she didn't need that in her life. So I thought it would be best for her if I could turn that anger, that negativity, into something more spiritually uplifting, something better for her soul, something that wouldn't weigh her karma down. I wanted to propose a scenario that would allow Nadine to access a truer, kinder aspect of her nature, the sympathetic part, the part that feels love. If I'd told her the standard version of the truth, she'd probably have lost the plot with us, and can you honestly say how that would have benefited anyone?"

I couldn't.

"Why didn't you tell me before, though?"

"I just presumed you'd figured it out yourself. I clocked all those suspicious looks you were giving me at Nadine's and I figured you knew the score. After all, you can't have thought that I'd stolen the money, right?"

"Mmmm."

"Don't worry. I forgive you. Even though I would've appreciated a bit more support at the time. It's a pretty shitty experience, getting mugged like that."

"Metaphorically mugged."

"Exactly. You know that I'd be there for you if it happened to you."

"Thanks, man."

"And as soon as I've got some spare spondoolics I'll even chip in to help pay off your debt."

"My debt."

"I know it's put a hole in your finances. At least you squared it with Nadine. Poor lass, she hadn't seen you for donkey's, and then you turn up out of the blue and blag a load of money off her. My explanation about the mugging, though, I think it stopped her being too pissed off with you. I couldn't see your reputation trashed over an innocent mistake, could I? It's not like you deliberately sent me off to score while I was tripping on those shrooms. It's not fair to blame you, and you shouldn't be too hard on yourself either. Shit happens. You couldn't have known."

"Er."

"Anyway, I'm glad we've got that sorted. You're my mate, and I thought you deserved the truth."

I was still trying to work out what I thought about all that when my phone rang.

A PLEASANT WEE RIVERSIDE RESTAURANT

"Clara," I said, turning on the loudspeaker on my handset so that Iffy could eavesdrop. "What can I do for you?"

"Ask not what you can do for Clara; ask what Clara can do for you."

"Sounds interesting," I said, upon realising that raised eyebrows cut no ice telephonically.

"I don't know where you and Captain Chaos are up to in your *sois-disant* investigations…"

"Oh, you know, we're kind of easing off on that front," I said casually, with a glance at the Captain, who tipped up the wine bottle and poured the last drops down his stubbly chin. "Why?"

"'Cos I've been thinking. I don't like it, seeing yous lot all at each other throats. You should have a powwow. Pass the pipe of peace. Hug and make up. Ye ken? And next weekend would seem to be the ideal opportunity. We're all gonnae be there - the Gaffer, me, lots of old faces. Allan's partner's been invited, and Fabrizia from Sicily, though I doubt they'll come."

"Come where? You're gonna be where?"

"Where d'you think? A pleasant wee riverside restaurant in Timbukfuckingtu? The launch party for the Gaffer's new album, of course."

"It's next weekend?"

"Aye."

"You're going?"

"Aye."

"And the Gaffer'll be there?"

"It is customary, I believe."

"And you've been invited?"

"You have, too. And lots of the old crew, apparently. Though Captain Caveman'll have to come as 'plus one' on someone else's invite, I reckon. So? What d'ye say? Are yous in? Bury the hatchet, and all that?"

"Aye," I said, looking into the eyes of the man who stared at terrapins, trying not to focus on the red wine that coated his chin, trying not to see it as blood. "Bury the hatchet. We're in."

"And then you can get back to Berlin, where your pals must be missing you." And allow my sofa to give up its nocturnal service as your bed, and leave me to get on with my life in peace, she didn't add, because she didn't have to.

"What do you call it," Iffy began Clara when had rung off (as always, just half a second before I expected her to, leaving a sentence of mine to dangle forlornly in the air like a windsock in a vacuum), "when you have one of those moments?"

"Epilepsy?"

"No. Though the word's similar. One of those moments when your brain goes 'ping.'"

"A stroke? A microwave?"

"A stroke of genius. Or a brainwave. One of those moments when it all comes together. When you see the future laid out before you like an eagle sees the ground. When all the parts slot into place. When you've been scrabbling around on your hands and knees in the dark and suddenly the light comes on. One of *those* moments."

"Rare?"

"Epiphany."

"Oh yeah. Why?"

"We're going to kill him at his launch party. I've got it all worked out. Nothing can go wrong."

Clearly that was fundamentally untrue. I let it ride.

"I've got it all mapped out," Iffy insisted. "Every step of the way. And you know the first steps?"

I didn't.

"They take you out of the park, along the street, into the offy and land you in front of the tequila section."

THE AUTHORITY OF THE BOOTMAKER

They say that organising a funeral keeps the mourners' minds occupied after a loved one has spun off the mortal coil. Well, Iffy and I were one step ahead, keeping ourselves busy organising the death. And personally I had already begun mourning - not for the Gaffer, the household name, friend to the stars, star in his own right - but for the man I had known and loved like a brother so many years before.

He had been one of us, maybe even the best of us, a man on a mission, genuinely dedicated, I thought at the time, to the overthrow of capitalist society and the inception of a freer, fairer, sustainable, non-profit based way of life. The way he chose to do it wasn't through campaigning politics but through playing loud music and demonstrating that having a good time while being naughty could be educational. He liked to quote Oscar Wilde: 'Disobedience, in the eyes of anyone who has read history, is man's original virtue. It is through disobedience and rebellion that progress has been made.' There were other sound systems on the scene who made no secret of the fact they were all about getting fucked and having a good time, but the Gaffer aimed at setting an example of how things could be done.

He wasn't our leader, but he was motivated, active, brave and imaginative. He was a prominent figure on our scene, one of those who were given more respect than others. We had no leaders, but we certainly had experts to whom we deferred in certain matters. As Bakunin wrote, 'In the matter of boots, I refer to the authority of the bootmaker; concerning houses, canals, or railroads, I consult that of the architect or the engineer.' Following the same logic, we turned to Jacek when we needed to tap into a power source, we looked to Udo to coax the best sound out of the rig, and we listened to the Gaffer when the conversation turned ideological - usually at around ten in the morning at a party.

He had been a militant radical. We had all believed in what we were doing, of course, but with varying degrees of zealotry. Out of all of us, it was the Gaffer who preached the finest sermons. There was something of the guru about him back then, a certain fiery, fervent fanaticism that, when you listened to him, elevated our deeds out of the mud and onto a higher plane.

It was frequently stated by those outside the party scene that there was nothing political about squat partying, and it was true that some of the people who showed up only came because they wanted to have a dance and get off their faces. The Gaffer contended that even these simple pleasures became political acts in a time when big business and little politicians sought to exercise control not only over what went on in public and private space, but also in people's minds. Free techno parties were not obviously, overtly political, he claimed, but they were anti-authoritarian non-conformist illegal gatherings where people could be truly free.

According to the Gaffer - the old Gaffer, the one who always held your gaze just that little bit too long, the one who loved to lecture, the one you couldn't help listening to - we weren't just hosting illegal raves. We were involved in nothing less than the overthrow of free market capitalism. Our thriving black market economy was living proof that another way was possible.

How he ended up where he ended up amazed and saddened me.

Maybe I was mourning the loss of my own innocence, I

thought, snapping out of my recollections, as well as the loss of my friend. To kill a man is to step outside the parameters that define society, to cast yourself out and set yourself apart. I said as much to Iffy, but he stuck to his hard-line beliefs that it was only our modern, civilian existence that saw it that way. In other places and in other times, killing a man made you a man yourself. It brought you respect; glory even.

This was the blue-sky thinking he had boasted of possessing when we were in Amsterdam, I realised with a shudder.

Since my teenage years I had sought to make my own mind up about matters of morality and ethics, but the seventh Commandment was a tough one to shake off. I bore no love for violence, seeing it as a mutually damaging action that proved nothing and settled no point apart from who was better at violence. I had been a pacifist for a while, until I discovered that allowing someone to hurt me or my friends was beyond my power.

From pacifist to killer. A tale of innocence lost. But if innocence was just a flowery moniker for ignorance, maybe Iffy was right and I was better off without it. I had been shedding its shackles for years, but each chain that fell left me not just freer but also more exposed.

Iffy's plan was a simple one, he assured me. He told me to relax. He had everything under control. I laughed, of course, but it wasn't very funny.

NIPPERS AND SLIPPERS

Iffy and I approached the venue for the Gaffer's album launch party, the event we planned to turn into his farewell do. Iffy was scurrying eagerly ever onwards with half a spliff extending from his lips like some kind of antenna. I moved with a more trepidant gait and a more hesitant step. Unlike the music-biz stars and 'journalists' who had also been invited, we had an inkling of what to expect, having unearthed the plans when we broke into the Gaff, and having already attended hundreds of real squat parties.

Ever since my very first taste of clandestine raving, my arrival at a squat party had always triggered a flotilla of fluttering butterflies in my belly as the music drew us in like moths to a flame. It was always a thrill to discover the lay-out of the once-abandoned building, to be where we weren't supposed to be, and to be doing what we weren't supposed to do.

Squat party gatherings were at the same time both ancient and futuristic, part pre-historic and part post-apocalyptic. In an age where Big Brother was practically omnipresent, where nearly every facet of human interaction was regulated, circumscribed and profit-based, where cameras tracked the streets and TVs dominated living rooms and lives, where an average of fourteen new laws were passed every day in the UK (all but two percent without a full parliamentary debate), where health and safety ruled, where the right to remain silent and the right to make some fucking noise were denied, here, among the throbbing basslines and open minds, was the heartbeat of the nation. This was what made us human and what made me think that maybe humanity was worth saving. This was people searching for alternatives, finding hope not death in new technologies, and having a fucking blast while they were at it.

Tonight was different, though. The event was legal and licensed. The tension I was feeling was more than my traditional keenness to see what treats lay in store for me (accompanied by a slight nagging doubt that maybe the cops had already arrived).

Tonight we intended to kill a man.

We heard our taxi change gear and watched it disappear. Having sussed out that a run of the mill club was no place to hold what was essentially a mock-up (or perhaps a mockery) of an illegal rave, the Gaffer had hired an uninspiring, strictly functional empty warehouse in Acton for the occasion.

It was around midnight - early for a rave. We knew that the Gaffer had been sending invitations to some of the old heads who used to turn up week in, week out back in the day, and from a distance we clocked a few familiar faces in the queue at the entrance.

If the Gaffer was attempting to re-create the atmosphere of old school London squat parties, what we saw at the door left me unconvinced. Predictably, indeed logically, in fact inevitably, the average age of the punters was about fifteen years older than it had been fifteen years ago. The Gaffer didn't know any of the younger generation who had followed on our heels and trodden in our footsteps, but he had clearly put some considerable effort into unearthing so many old-timers.

Although some of us, like Iffy, still clung like barnacles to the scene, many of us, including Clara, had pried ourselves loose. Others, like me, remained semi-detached, surfacing now and again for a special occasion, nurturing some of our old friendships and letting others wither and die. Geography and physical distance had come to separate us, families forced us to narrow our horizons, work kept us busy in the daytime and sent us to sleep weary at night. Nippers and slippers, as Iffy put it.

Of our own little crew, Udo had ended up in Sicily, Jacek had plotted up in Poland, Minnie had wound up in Holland, Sam Saoule had gone back to Marseilles, Allan Exit had retreated to Wales, and I had settled in Berlin. It was a diaspora, a family spread far and wide, and tonight was some kind of reunion.

We said some hellos, shuffling our feet as the night air grew cooler, but I was distracted. There was a lot of the usual banter flying around, but mine was half-hearted at best. Iffy seemed to be on top form, slapping backs, cracking jokes, weaving and bobbing, but I couldn't help noticing that the general vibe outside the party was cynical. This was a crowd who had seen it all before, who had hand-printed the tee-shirts and flogged them out the back of a truck in ten different countries. They would be hard to impress.

I listened in as Iffy chatted with someone I vaguely recognised, a Greek woman who used to have long green dreads but now sported a neatly-trimmed black bob.

"I just came for the laugh," she admitted with a shrug. "You know, I got this invite on Facebook from the Gaffer saying my name's on the list. I don't see him for years but I know he's the big man nowadays and I think maybe it's interesting. It's his new album, so why not? It's good of him to think of me after all these years. We're still one big family."

We inched closer to the entrance, catching fierce blasts of acid techno every time the door swung open. I heard the Greek girl - Anna? - ask Iffy if he'd got any drugs, and directed my eavesdropping elsewhere. Behind me were a pair of forty-something media darlings. They were probably big fish in their own pond, but seemed out of their depth here among the sharks and crustaceans.

"Not bad, as gimmicks go," I heard one of them saying *sotto voce.* "You know, the whole retro thing. But who are all these people?"

"Actors," the other one replied coolly. "Got to be. Though they are rather convincing…"

A CHRIS LIBERATOR SPECIAL

We arrived at the door. The presence of two glowering giants dressed in leather jackets with walkie-talkies clipped to their lapels instantly dispelled any lingering possibility that this was a genuine old school squat party. They had chewing gum in their mouths, contempt in their gaze and potential violence in their bulging muscles. One of them set about fondling me intimately.

Back in the day, we only ever asked for donations, or a two- or three- or five pounds entrance fee, at the door - just enough money to cover our expenses, bung the musicians a few quid and maintain the sound system in a reasonable state of repair. The kitty was split between however many rigs turned up. We really hadn't been in it for the money, though the beguiling, tempting presence of cash had occasionally led to disputes. One big family, for sure, but sometimes a dysfunctional one.

Finally the bouncers opened the door for us. We stepped into a hallway. I gave my name to a smart-looking young gentleman with a clipboard, and indicated that Iffy was the 'plus one' on my guest list.

I was already nervous before we pushed through another door and were immediately engulfed in a cloud of sweaty air, and getting searched for drugs on arrival hadn't helped. The dull thud of the music crystallised into a towering party favourite from the late nineties, a Chris Liberator special, all pounding beats and blistering 303s, and the air was drenched in the odour of dancing humans. Smoking was against the law in public places, I remembered. As a newly converted non-smoker I should have been happy with this development, and indeed I could see it made sense in a restaurant. In a massive warehouse where people came to drink and take drugs, it struck me as annoying.

I had loved squat parties because of what they stood for; the freedom they represented. Despite the entrance tax, they were known as free parties, and for me the name referred to the feeling of liberty they engendered. I adored the lack of rules and regulations, the absence of bouncers, dress-codes, drinking restrictions and smoking bans. I hated the way that clubs had to comply with stupid laws. I had always agreed with the Gaffer that partying shouldn't just be about listening to loud music and taking drugs.

"Don't do that," I said to Iffy. He had taken his tobacco pouch out and was fishing around in his sock for some weed.

"What?" he said, pure as the driven snow.

"You can't smoke here."

"Bollocks to that. The Gaffer wants a squat party, that's what he'll get."

"Iffy. Chill. We mustn't get kicked out. Remember? A low profile is what we agreed."

"I thought we agreed to act normal."

"We agreed not to draw attention to ourselves. That's not the same thing. And you shouldn't even be here. C'mon, let's have a mooch."

Huffing but not puffing, he did what I least expected. He did as he was told.

The place was laid out according to the Gaffer's instructions that we had stumbled across in his office. The event was happening in one big room. Twin stacks of speakers stood like sentries on either side of the record decks. The music was booming, the windows vibrating. A hundred or more people were dancing under flashing lights. The backdrops and robot statues were in their places.

At first glance it bore a close resemblance to a squat party.

Closer inspection revealed the speakers to be brand new, the massive sound system rented for the night. I didn't recognise the DJ. And something else struck me as strange. There were no dogs, no bastard hounds loping through the legs on the dancefloor or galloping after empty beer cans and growling at each other, chasing the patterns cut by the laser lights on the concrete floor. And the works of art, I discovered, were all protected behind thick sheets of glass.

"We can have us a wee line, though, can't we?" Iffy whined, tugging at my sleeve like a toxic two-year old.

A quick glance around told me that we could do no such thing. While a genuine squat party was dotted with crouching figures snorting lines, this was the kind of place where you had to queue for a toilet cubicle and watch out for the bouncers who hovered menacingly outside the door while the owners and VIPs merrily hoovered powder up their nose in comfort backstage.

I knew that Iffy shared my aversion to legal clubbing. Lamentably, he lacked my discretion. Whenever he went to a club, the chances were high that he'd be forcibly ejected before the night was out. The degree of violence involved varied but the end result was always the same. I understood his refusal to compromise, but tonight was not an occasion for him to be whimsical. With him straining at the leash a minute or two into the night's festivities, I suffered momentary doubts as to the viability of our plan.

"Just keep a lid on it, Iffy, will you?" I pleaded. "No spliffs, no lines. No fags even. No stealing alcohol from the bar. No pissing in the corner. No scuffling. No winding up the bouncers. No blatant drug deals."

"You don't ask much, do you?"

"I just ask that you keep it together until…later."

His reply was lost to me, buried beneath the music.

THE LOSS OF ANOTHER POTENTIAL CONVERSATIONAL PARTNER

I was bimbling about, trying to locate the Gaffer, when I clocked Clara. She was deep in conversation with Rotten John, a six foot six ginger-dreadlocked crusty who appeared to be wearing the same threads as when last I'd seen him ten years ago. They had presumably been clothes at one time, but the ravages of the years had turned them literally into threads. Only the multiplicity of layers ensured a complete covering of his skinny frame.

"Enjoying yourselves?" I asked, delivering a peck on Clara's cheek and consigning one hand to be enveloped in Rotten John's filth-encrusted fist. I attempted to pull it back, only slightly mangled, but the big man clutched me firmly in his grasp.

"Y'alright there, John?" I said, and realised that he didn't look alright. He was glassy eyed and a mucusy membrane of gritty white slime coated his top lip. It seemed he was treading the meandering path of the ketamine user these days.

Regretting the loss of another potential conversational partner, I turned to my ex. "And you -" I began cheerfully.

And stopped abruptly. And did a double take and realised that Clara had tears trickling down her face.

I ripped my hand away from Rotten John's monstrous grip. Leaving him standing there, marooned on the dance floor, his red locks glowing like a beacon in the sweep of the lights, I steered Clara to a quieter spot at the side of the room.

"What's up? Missing the old crew?" I figured that her first foray out for a long time was bringing back painful memories of the old days, the ones I still called good.

"I don't know how to tell you this," she said. "It's Iffy."

"What is? What's Iffy? What's wrong?"

I didn't like this. Didn't like the tears, didn't like the tone of voice. Wished I hadn't spotted her and Rotten John. Wished I'd stayed at home. Wished I'd never left Berlin. Wished none of this was happening.

"Fuck, man. I wish none of this was happening."

And that really scared me. Clara was a stoic, a hard-boiled realist, a poker-faced rationalist. She rarely cried in public, and though she often expressed her desire to make the world a better place, she never idly wished for things that couldn't be.

I glanced around me. There he was, the Iffy-boy, doing his Iffy-thing on the dance floor, blagging a can of lager from a stranger, pouring half of it down his throat, spilling some of it down his chest, moving on, chatting, dancing, just as he had always done.

"Clara, please tell me what's wrong," I said evenly.

"He's got the virus.

FEELING AND FEEDING THE WARP AND WEFT

The music continued. A Roland 303 was winding up and up and up and up, a high-hat crashing, a kick-drum spanking over a dirty bassline that wobbled and fizzed through the ether. A strobe light seared my eyeballs. I saw flashes of the party, flashes of my past, flashes of Iffy as he ducked and dived through the party as he had ducked and dived all throughout his life.

"What? Are you sure?"

The party continued. Behind the bar, figures handed out cans of beer and plastic beakers of vodka and orange. In front of the speakers, dancers bustled, romped, bounced and frisked, lost in the perpetual groove.

I saw mouths opening and closing, but I couldn't hear the words. Only the music. Always the music.

I saw Iffy wending his way through the crowd, weaving through the bodies, feeling and feeding the warp and weft of the party's fabric, scattering a smattering of smiles like seeds flying off a dandelion clock.

I saw Clara nod.

Life continued.

But it felt different.

"How d'you know?" I asked. "Did Rotten John tell you?"

"Aye."

I wanted to talk about the fantastic advances in medical science, to laud the progress that had been made in the fight against the AIDS virus. I wanted to hear - even if I had to say it myself - that being seropositive wasn't a death sentence any more. New treatments were being developed all the time. With the right course of medication...

Two things prevented me from speaking.

Firstly, I realised with a thought that slipped into my mind like quicksilver - rapid, heavy, deadly - that except for the bewildering cocktail of illegal highs and lows that he prescribed himself, Iffy wasn't taking any medication.

And secondly, at that moment he was bearing down on and me and Clara, saucily lifting the belly of his tee-shirt to reveal a bottle of vodka that he was cradling like a new-born infant.

Clara lurched away abruptly, clumsily, her crutch clearing a path in front of her, her bony shoulder blades grimly hunched.

"She still got the hump with me?"

"What?"

"Clara. She still got the hump with me? Here, have some of this. Amazing what you can get away with when there's a strobe on the bar. It's all in the timing, you know. Zap! Quick as a flash. Bob's your fucking uncle, my man, and you should invite him round to dinner 'cos the vodka's on us. *Nunc est bibendum, nunc pede libero pulsanda tellus*, innit? Now is the time for drinking, now the time to dance footloose upon the earth. What?"

"I don't know, mate."

"C'mon, it's just a bottle of voddy. The Gaffer can fucking afford it. And speaking of the devil, the man himself has turned up. I clocked him as he came in the door. Did you miss it? With his black shadow, that Andy, micro-managing his every move. Everyone wants a piece of *ze Gaffair* zese days, *mon ami*. He's gonna have one very clean arse in a few minutes, what with all that licking and kissing going on. But it means it's gonna be tricky to get him on his Jack Jones. For delivering the *coup de grâce*."

The words washed over me.

I'm in a forest in the Dordogne. A midnight blue sky

supports a full moon high above the leafy canopy. Our fire releases shoals of sparks that swell and dissipate in the rising river of smoke. Iffy is telling me he never wants to get old. "*Morte magis metuenda senectus,*" is what he says, in one of his beloved Latin quotes. "Old age should rather be feared than death." And it's true, I can't imagine him as an old man. He's vital and spontaneous and raw, youth encapsulated. Then I'm laughing and pouring another glass of pastis and arguing that he'll change his mind when he realises what the only alternative to old age is.

I'm treading footsteps in the sand on a Portuguese beach. The sun bobs below the far-off, liquid horizon. A wave soaks my foot. I hand a spliff back to Iffy, the tangy nip of high-grade Moroccan hashish still in my mouth. There on the continent's edge we have been discussing terminal illnesses. Iffy insists that he would never alter his lifestyle in the hope of living a little longer. It's all about quality, not quantity, he assures me, before adding, "Q*uam bene vivas referre, non quam diu.*" It is how well you live that matters, not how long.

I'm on a traveller site in Dresden and we're trying to fit a new exhaust pipe to Sam Saoule's truck. It's winter and our fingers are cold. The metal is icy to our touch. Every time we exhale, our frozen breath hangs in the air like cartoon speech bubbles. The conversation has drifted and Iffy is spinning out his theory for creating an army of the doomed. He wants to gather together a commando unit of people who know their time is coming - the terminal cancer victims, those with advanced heart disease, the incurables - and meld them into a force with nothing to lose. He wants them to fight for the planet against the corporate bosses and crooked politicians who seem hell-bent on facilitating planetary destruction just so they can make more money than they will ever be able to spend. He says that if you know you're going to die, there's nothing left to be scared of.

And then I was back at the Gaffer's party and Iffy was sliding ahead of me through the crowd and I was thinking that I needed to talk to him. Now. I saw Clara again and wanted to talk to her again as well. I saw Rotten John standing where I'd left him and wanted to talk to him, too.

I saw the Gaffer with his manager and wondered whether I ought to kill him or not.

I had to put a stop to our plan, I realised. I had to call it off, at least until I could be sure that Iffy wasn't on a mad mission inspired the terminal ticking of his body clock. I wanted time to make a decision, to consider and reconsider, to reflect, to assimilate the fact that he was HIV positive. But the music was hammering lumps out of my serenity and everything was happening too fast.

Question Rotten John and see how he'd uncovered Iffy's secret? But I knew that talking to the big man would be like attempting to run a comb through the tangled strands of his dreadlocks - I just had to recall my experience with Juliest in the forest at Jacek's wake.

Get Clara to tell me the story? But where had she got to? Was she still in the building?

Ask Iffy straight up? What's the jackanory, dude? Are you dying? Are you HIV positive? Are you trying to cane yourself to death in a race against the virus where the winner is the one who puts you to sleep forever?

I hastened after him.

A PARTICULARLY TIRESOME BOARD MEETING

"Iffy!" I saw him cock his head, check his stride. "Iffy!"

"'Tis I."

"Have you got a minute?"

"Have I got a minute?" he repeated, looking puzzled. He had every right to, of course. The question was a strange one, more suited to a quiet word in a subordinate's ear at the end of a particularly tiresome board meeting than to addressing a co-conspirator in a murder plot at a rave.

"Er, yeah. Just a few things I've been meaning to ask you."

"I hope you're not ordering a pint of squeamish?"

"No…"

"You mean yes."

"No, I don't. Not exactly."

"Right. Not squeamish - but squeamish-ish."

"No - but, Iffy, mate, something's come up."

"I can hear you squeaming."

"Just fucking shut up, Iffy. Please. For once in your fucking life, do me a favour and shut the fuck up."

It took a while before I realised that he had no intention of replying. "Good. Thank you. Now -"

"Look, is this gonna take very long? It's just I've got things to be getting on with, you know."

I didn't know whether to laugh or cry. My nerves were being tenderised by the blistering techno - great for dancing to when you've got a brain full of drugs; quite distracting, now that I thought about it, when you want to talk about life and death and murder and all that meaningful stuff.

Although a high-decibel background sound track had never

hindered me before.

Iffy, I want you to look inside yourself and tell me if there's anything you think I should know.

Iffy, how long have we known each other? Don't you think we can be honest with each other after all this time?

Iffy, if there was anything wrong - I mean seriously wrong - I hope you know that I'd always be there for you.

Iffy, I've been hearing some pretty crazy rumours about you.

The clichés lined themselves up in my mind, champing at the bit, begging to be set free to gallop rough-shod through the conversation. I had never been much of a TV-watcher, but nonetheless I had seen so many human dramas turned into scripts and played out on-screen that the words that initially came into my head were not my own. I was struggling to find a way to express myself. It was too easy to fall into knee-jerk patterns of behaviour and pre-programmed exchanges, the way, I suspected, that too many people did. Human behavioural patterns were based on mimicry and we were in a *loco parentis* relationship with TV.

"Just bear with me for a minute," I eventually said, despite my best intentions opting for Cliché Number 731, section Tried and Tested, subsection Hackneyed. "I just need to get this straight in my head."

Iffy stared meaningfully at his wrist, the place where his watch would have been had been wearing one.

"We've been hanging out together again for the last few days," I continued clumsily, "since you came to Berlin for Udo's funeral. We've talked a lot, mostly about this whole murder thing. About whether our mates were being offed, and if they were then who was responsible, and what should we do when we find the culprit, *et cetera*, blah, blah, blah. And of course, we've talked about other things in the interludes between the heavy cogitation. We had our usual old light-hearted sessions of banter, and we did our fair share of putting the world to rights. But have we *really* talked?" That one came straight from the Soap Opera Archive, I realised with dismay.

"Is this about me dabbling with the brown? 'Cos this ain't exactly the time and place for a cosy little chat with Mother."

"No. No, it isn't. I don't think so, anyway. Listen, there's been some talk about you…I've been hearing some…stuff."

"Oooh. Tasty bit of goss, was it?"

"No."

"Then let's save it for later, shall we? When we're getting our nails done in the salon?"

"Iffy! Come back here!"

He was gone, melting into the melee like mud in a puddle. I darted after him, pointlessly pirouetting and performing ungainly arabesques as I sought his face in amongst the now densely populated confines of the seething dancefloor. Bodies hemmed me in. I was stuck in a microcosm of my previous existence, surrounded by pilled-up party people.

A thought struck me. Iffy couldn't complete our plan without me. Given the Gaffer's suspicions since he had clocked Iffy trailing him around, I had been elected to administer the *coup de grâce*. For a fraction of a second I wondered how Iffy had talked me into agreeing to that, but it seemed he could talk me into anything if he set his devious mind to it.

And then another thought struck me. I was not, in fact, indispensable as the Gaffer's doom dispenser. Iffy could easily find some other mug to hand over the poisoned chalice.

Where the fuck was he?

And why was the dancefloor emptying?

A SLOW, TECTONIC SLIDE

It wasn't the sort of panicked rush for the exits that a fire sparks off. It was more of a gradual drift; a slow, tectonic slide rather than a volcanic outpouring. Still Iffy-hunting, I turned this way and that, and in so doing found I had more and more space around me. I tried to focus my attention on what was happening. The event was peopled by trendy types and party types, and it was the latter who were growing conspicuous by their absence.

Had they had enough of this plastic sham? All of them? Just like that? Then why were they looking so pleased with themselves? The Gaffer's other guests, the ones who mattered to him, rather than the ones who were there primarily to add some local colour, were oblivious to the trickling exodus, still nodding along to the beat and trying to look like they knew the score.

I became aware of sly grins and knowing glances swooping through the air like swallows on a summer evening. Some snickers, some chortles, some sniggers; a nod and a wink and a dig in the ribs; an underlying, overriding sense of mischief in the air. It was like being back in school again. It felt as though the naughty kids had prepared a nasty surprise for their teacher.

I spied Rotten John looming in the glooming. Despite the mental sludge of however much K he had rammed up his nose, he too seemed clued up on whatever was going down. I hurried up to him, wondering if he was in a fit state to tell me how he had found out that Iffy was HIV positive.

"John, hold on a minute, will you?"

"Party," he mumbled, though whether it was a noun or an imperative I couldn't decide.

"John, listen, will you? It's about Iffy."

"Party," he reiterated, possibly because he was worried that I hadn't fully grasped the full depth and complexity of his argument, but probably because he was out of his box.

Rotten John shambled away. I found myself alone in front of the decks. Well, not really alone. There were still all the critics and corporate muppets and general hangers-on, the groupies and wannabes who had come because tonight this warehouse was the place to be. But all my people had gone.

I had to find Iffy. I had to find Clara. I had to find the Gaffer. And I had to find out what was going on. I might have looked like a particularly - indeed spectacularly - uncoordinated dancer, but in fact I was acting out a scene entitled 'Man Who Can't Make His Mind Up Which Way To Go'.

I headed for the exit, bounding across the empty space of the old warehouse. The bouncers who had made us feel so unwelcome when we arrived were looking on in consternation as a stream of somewhat tatterdemalion but increasingly festive humanity poured out the door and into the yard outside. The stream turned left and disappeared round the corner. I paddled faster and overtook Rotten John.

"Party," I heard him claim - or direct or observe - and I soon realised why.

ELOQUENT IN ITS BREVITY AND INELUCTABLE IN ITS INTEGRITY

Behind me, the Gaffer's event was a synthetic copy of a London squat party. In front of me, in yet another empty warehouse, was the real thing. Those dirty squatting bastards had done it again. They'd taken another building and they'd shoved a sound system inside it, they'd turned the music up, and they were planning on partying the night away.

I had to laugh. I didn't know for sure - it could after all have just been a coincidence that they'd plotted up here on this particular night - but I suspected that the organisers knew exactly what they were doing. They were making a statement. As usual, it was eloquent in its brevity and ineluctable in its integrity.

What it said was: fuck you.

And I had a sneaky suspicion that I knew which sneaky bugger had tipped them off.

I changed tack and headed back against the current. I was greeted by an unguarded doorway and the sight of the two bouncers striding rapidly across the room, one of them barking into his walkie-talkie, the other clearing a path with aggressive thrusts and jabs of his Maglite.

Something was afoot.

When things happen, they happen quickly.

I slipstreamed into the bouncers' wake. They bore down on a doorway and burst through. I tagged along, a rowing boat behind two supertankers. We sped down a corridor, attracting startled looks from the Gaffer's guests who had gathered there to escape the sonic booms of the main room. The rumour that something was happening, that something was wrong, surged along about a yard in front of us, a panic-surfer on the crest of our wave. We came to another door. It yielded.

And the Gaffer was there. Plump. Sartorially impeccable. Surrounded by what passed for his friends these days.

Lying on the floor. Gasping for breath.

Stopping living soon, I presumed.

A CERTAIN KIND OF PARTY

The conclusion I drew was that Iffy had found a way. Like he had joked when he broke the squat next door to the Gaff: says what he's going to do, does what he said he was going to do.

Well, he'd really done it this time.

Our plan - or as I was beginning to think of it, Iffy's mad plan - had been a simple one. Spike the bastard's drink. We believed he had used drugs to kill our other friends, and so we would pay the Gaffer the highest of compliments by imitating his style. From a source unknown to me Iffy had acquired some fentanyl. I had never even heard of it before, but Iffy knew all about it.

The depths of chemical knowledge that some substance abusers cultivated could be impressive, and Iffy's unparalleled apparent ability to analyse the constituent components of any powder or pill was a popular party trick (at a certain kind of party) of his. His reputation as a connoisseur meant he often got his paws on rare drugs.

Fentanyl, then. The scourge of Estonia, Iffy had assured me. A synthetic drug, an opioid of terrible potency; fifty times, a hundred times stronger than a bag of standard street skag. A treatment against the pain of cancer. Killer of more young people than the motor car on the streets of Estonia, where it had come first to plug a gap during a heroin drought, and then simply stayed. Cheap and anything but cheerful. A rarity in the UK, but Iffy had got some.

I didn't know how he had got it into the Gaffer, but it was time for me to make a swift decision.

Not my strong point, that.

I had become persuaded of the Gaffer's guilt, but hearing

that Iffy was HIV positive had put a new slant on that. Everything was not how it had seemed to be. New light was shining in from different angles, and the shadows it cast were dark and confusing.

So. Spill the beans that the Gaffer was overdosing on fentanyl and hope the information saved his life…but in so doing admit complicity…

Or say nothing, blame it on bystander apathy, and let events run their course.

AN IMPENETRABLE FOREST OF WHAT-IFS

I had to admit it: decisions scared me. Dithering came all too easily. Faced with a choice, my mind would attempt to play out all the possible consequences, an endless stream of but-thens, an impenetrable forest of what-ifs, a crippling, paralysing flow of projections and predictions that would overwhelm me up to the point where inertia set in. My life could be defined by the places I hadn't been and the people I hadn't met, the books I hadn't read and the conversations I hadn't had. Every second of every day I didn't do a million things. For everything I did, an infinite amount of things were never done.

But sometimes no reaction was a reaction in itself. Sometimes doing nothing equated to doing something. Letting a playground bully hurt someone, standing idly by while a pub bruiser picked a fight, watching a sex pest intimidate a woman, failing to challenge a racist comment: these non-acts were tantamount to acts of aggression. Burying your head in the sand while pathological corporations violated the planet, keeping schtum as new laws were rolled out to enrich the elite and oppress the poor, blithely accepting that other people could run your life for you. This reluctance or refusal to react could have immeasurably far-reaching, life-changing consequences.

Life-ending consequences.

And as I thought all of this, the Gaffer lay dying.

And as the Gaffer lay dying, I backed out of the room.

Leaving what behind? An atmosphere of agitated panic. A wildly jabbered cacophony of uncertain suggestions hurled at random from mouth to mouth: artificial resuscitation, the

Heimlich manoeuvre, the recovery position, a defibrillator, no, a defibulator, whatever it's called where the fuck do we get one?

Andy, the Gaffer's manager, crouching over the prostrate figure, breathing into his mouth. Some ghoulish fools snapping off some photos on their mobile phones. The Gaffer's breathing getting shallower, ever shallower.

And in that cold little room in the corner of a warehouse, my morals, my innocence, my self respect and the Gaffer lay dying.

MARK SLEIGH

FUSTY ARMPITS AND MUSTY CLOTHES

I stumbled back along the corridor. The temporary excitement caused by the bouncers' hurried passage had faded already, another short-lived titillation soon to be forgotten. I blundered back through the main room. Out of the door and into the cool night air. Around a corner, my shoulder scraping the wall. Legs softening, stomach churning.

An undefined period of time elapsed until a voice that I knew spoke to me. "*Plus ça change*." Iffy smiled as he bent over my trembling figure. In response, a shiver that would have merited a reading on the Richter scale shook through my body.

"Wicked party, eh?" my bosom buddy enthused, as was and ever would be his wont. My stomach spasmed. "Just like old times, eh?" the voice continued. "You in a heap outside the party, covered in puke, retching your ring up. Got hold of some of that MDMA, then, I take it?" My eyelids fluttered, and still Iffy prattled on. "Fucking banging night. Mental stylee. Having it proper large. They're dropping some fat tunes, man. Pucker rig, too, massive link-up. Here, have a go on this." A whisky bottle swung into my visual field. Feebly, I batted it aside. "What you need is a line. Sort you right out. What you want? Got some blinding Lou Reed off Cousin Dave. I won't offer you any K 'cos I know it winds you up. Strictly *ad usum proprium*, the old donkey." I could hear his hands rifling through his pockets. "Pills," he murmured. "Shrooms, trips, more pills. Bit funny, those ones. Got a wrap of chang here somewhere."

His face appeared in front of mine, his eyes popping, his jaw grinding, his grin stretching his cheeks to breaking point, sweat cascading through his stubble.

And of all the myriad ways I could have dealt with the situation - the appeals, the accusations, the questions, the heartfelt declarations laden with loathing and love and all the other fucked up emotions I was feeling - I found myself asking him for a cigarette. He fished a dog-eared packet of tobacco out of a pocket and handed it to me. Giving a hoarse croak of delight, he located his coke stash and cut us out a line each. I turned my head away, and he shrugged and hoovered them both up.

"So what was it you wanted to talk to me about before?" he said conversationally, flicking a filthy finger nail over the flint of his lighter.

I drank deeply of my cigarette, taking a moment to shuffle my thoughts like a drunken croupier. It was time to lay my cards on the table. Beginning with the joker.

"Have you got the virus?"

"What virus?"

"The bad one."

"The bad one?"

"The bad one."

"Have you been talking to Rotten John?"

"Rotten John has been talked to," I admitted, sounding like a government spokesman.

Iffy heaved a sigh up from the depths of his chest and set it loose to seek its fortune. "Rotten John. The big-mouthed git. About as discreet as a teknival in Hyde Park. Should've known the gobshite wouldn't keep his gob shut."

Shit. The last embers of hope faded to grey. "That's a yes, then?"

"As far as Rotten John's concerned, yes."

A flicker of heat in the ashes. "And as far as anyone else is concerned?"

"Well, as far as anyone else is concerned, unless that

particular someone else either squats with Rotten John or has a habit of running to Rotten John and opening their big mouth - no. I haven't got the virus."

If my night had been a rollercoaster instead of a night, thrill seekers from the world over would have been queuing up to get their kicks. Me, I was knackered.

"Explain," I instructed, sending another little sigh out into the big bad world to run free with Iffy's.

"Bit embarrassing, really."

"Surely not?"

"Well, just a bit. See, I kind of owed Rotten John some money or something. Can hardly remember myself now. And, well, I can't precisely recall how it all came about, but somehow we got ourselves into this weird kind of zone where he was under the impression that I was terminally ill and, as such, that it wouldn't really be fair for him to tap me up for my little debt. You know. Funny how these things come about sometimes."

"Hilarious."

"Yeah, well, it's not something I'm proud of. Anyway... C'mon, let's head back inside. On your feet, laddie."

"No," I said. "Wait."

"Tim waits for no-one, my friend."

Why, when he had a mouth - and occasionally a brain - that functioned perfectly well, did he so often insist on talking incomprehensible bollocks?

"What?" I said.

"Tim waits for no-one. Tim Sonik. He'll be on the decks in a minute. Don't want to miss his set, do we? That'd be daft."

Clearly the whole thing was daft. The whole shebang, the whole kit and caboodle, the whole shooting match. Iffy was daft, the Gaffer was daft, we were all completely fucking daft. Humanity was daft. The history of our species was daft, the way we allowed ourselves to be governed was daft, religion was daft, extreme wealth and abject poverty were daft, our consumption of the Earth's natural resources was daft, war was daft, bigotry was daft. The more I repeated it, the more the word daft sounded daft.

And daftest of all? Me, for getting involved.

And once again Iffy was moving. A lingering whiff of fusty armpits and musty clothes, a tiny cloud of tobacco smoke, a sense of befuddlement, a glut of unanswered questions, footsteps fading away...fainter, quieter, gone.

MARK SLEIGH

FUCKING AN ARSEHOLE

Yes, I agreed, I was a little tired. Well, my holiday had certainly been interesting, I conceded. Haha, I chuckled, yes, I did need a holiday to recover from my holiday. No, I indicated, shaking my head, I didn't want any *Vollkornbrot*, tempting though it looked. Damn right, I assented, it was nice to be back home again.

While I had been engaged in small talk in the bakery, it had started raining outside. Head down, I scuttled back to my flat. Once I had set my kettle to do its thing and peeled my sodden sweatshirt off, I turned my computer on. I connected to the internet, logged onto my Facebook page and deactivated my account without so much as a sideways glance at the newsfeed. I then busied myself knocking up a nice breakfast, which I ate at a leisurely pace. I washed it all down with a nice cup of tea and then washed up with the radio on. The rain was beating on the windowpane. I turned the radio off so I could enjoy the sound. The sky was heavy, so low it seemed that I could have reached out and grabbed a handful of cloud. I sorted some records into piles; ones that I would take to the flea-market later that morning, and ones that I wouldn't. The flea-market was in Prenzlauerberg, a nice part of town, so I left some of the hardcore anarchopunk albums on the side and added some nice ambient electro and older hippy stuff. If the rain continued to fall, I probably wouldn't make much money today, but it was nice to be back in the routine. I slapped some new price labels on some of the record covers, reflecting the comparative wealth of the Prenzl'berg citizenry. Later, whilst searching for the keys to my van, I came across an unused SIM card in a drawer, which was nice, and without any hesitation I took the old one out of my phone and dropped it in the rubbish bin. I grabbed a lightweight raincoat from a cupboard and lugged my boxes of records downstairs and around the corner to my van. As I had suspected, the flea-market was a damp squib, but I talked to some nice people and managed to leave with more money and fewer records than I had gone with, which was nice. When I got back home, the pile of dirty laundry in the bathroom needing dealing with. I dealt with it. From my personal collection of records, the ones that I would never sell, I selected Enter The Dragon by Inner Terrestrials, and placed it delicately on my record deck. My neighbours generally liked their music loud, so I had no compunction in turning the volume up. When the track came to an end and the susurration of the needle was blending in with the white noise of the rain, the light was so murky that I was obliged to turn a lamp on. Curling up on the sofa I had blagged the previous summer, I opened the book I had started reading before Iffy turned up for Udo's funeral, and spent the next five minutes trying to find the right page. I polished off a few chapters. As a nice late lunch I grilled some halloumi and ate it on toast with some sliced tomato, black olives, fresh mint and a dribble of olive oil. A bottle of Sternburg beer provided a nice accompaniment. In the late afternoon, with the rain still falling, I settled down to my backlog of internet orders. My work had been put on the back burner while I had been away and I had some catching up to do. It took me a couple of hours to put all the records in parcels and address them correctly, awaiting my next trip to the post office. The day was still far from over, so I applied myself to the tedious necessity of what I generously called accounting - the totting up of how much profit I had made. It was nice to realise that I would be able to pay my rent at the end of the month. My kitchen was a nice place to be, and although I didn't have much of interest in my cupboards, there was nobody to criticise my cooking and I eked out a reasonable repast that I ate alone.

I looked at the time on my watch. It was only eight o'clock.

So far, all things considered, it had been a nice day, all in all, under the circumstances…

And all day long I had Iffy's voice echoing through my mind. ("'Nice?' I fucking hate 'nice'! What sort of a lame-arse fucking adjective is that? Either it's wicked or its pants. Do it because you love it, or hate it and don't fucking do it. 'Nice!' Fuck's sakes, man, were you dropped in a cauldron of blandness as a baby? Get some discernment in your life! Either say that it's having it large, or say that it's complete pony and trap. 'Nice' is for the middle-aged middlemen of the middle-of-the-road middle classes. It's safe and it's boring as fuck and it'll sap your energy and waste your life and make you old before your time, and then it'll send you to your grave with a shedful of regrets and 'RIP - that was nice' engraved on your tombstone.")

After Iffy had left me outside the party, I had got a night bus directly to Clara's flat, collected two hundred pounds and my passport, jumped on the earliest morning train to Stansted Airport and caught the first plane back home. Acting like the bastard spawn of a dog and an ostrich, I scarpered back to Berlin with my tail between my legs and promptly buried my head in the sand. I spoke to nobody. I stayed away from all forms of news media. Sometime soon I would find out what the outcome of the Gaffer's party was, I knew, but I suspected the news would be distressing. Like a slacker with his exam results, or an old man after a medical examination, I foolishly preferred the nerve-shredding torture of ignorance to the certain pain of knowing.

And now, after spending a nice day pottering around, I was going slightly mental.

A cigarette. I remembered blagging a snout off Iffy outside

the party. Maybe this was a good time to start smoking again.

Outside in the rain, I was trotting towards the *Spätkauf* when a small, dark, hooded figure leapt out of a doorway in front of me.

"Island monkey!"

Willy Wanker. The very person I would have most wanted to bump into, had I been a complete idiot.

"Can't stop," I cried, quickening my pace and lengthening my stride.

"Hey, fuck, eh! Ooh, island monkey!"

The thing with the past is that although it's massive, complex and ever expanding, it also has a habit of lurking around near your front door. Willy was high on my list of people I never needed to see again. Accelerating further, I was practically jogging. Willy's little legs proved remarkably swift. Finally accepting that I couldn't very well just run away from him, I slowed to a halt, gritted my teeth and resigned myself to saying, "What's up, Willy?"

"Ach," he spat, "fucking another one dead, eh. Fucking your friend. The Gaffer."

So that was it confirmed. The sixth death from our old sound system. Sam Saoule, Minnie, Jacek, Udo, Allan and now the Gaffer. All gone. With that last death, I hoped the rest of us would be able to live out our lives in relative peace. The survivors: Iffy, Clara and me. Clara, doing good things for needy people. Iffy, burning his candle at both ends. Me, just pottering around nicely and feeling massively guilty.

Willy was still talking. "Always thought he was fucking an arsehole. Bossing everybody around, eh? And then his famous DJ fucking thing. Too good for fucking us, eh? Fuck him. Eh. Fuck."

"Willy," I said. "Give it a rest. Please."

"Fuck, eh," he said, bristling like a tom cat. "You gonna

defend fucking him now? Just because fucking the fucker's fucking dead?"

That was it, I thought, he had finally hit peak Willy. "Leave it," I said. "I'll catch you later."

"Whatever, eh. Fucking peanuts."

My desire for a cigarette having mercifully cooled, I decided to pay Carlo a visit in his bar. Now that I knew the Gaffer's fate, I would need some time to come to terms with the role that I had played in it. A drink would help.

I ran there, noticing as I did so that I was no longer quite as fit as I had been before Iffy had come to see me. I lumbered along the street, my mind preoccupied with the thoughts that I had been suppressing all day. There was just a little room left to chuckle sardonically about the way Willy had got his slang mixed up, saying, "Fucking peanuts," instead of, "Fucking nuts."

SO MANY LITTLE DEATHS

"Ah, my friend!" Carlo called, rising from his stool behind the bar and coming over to hug me. "Who would believe it? The world is crazier and crazier. Crazier and crazier. When will it all stop? Come, have a drink with Carlo. Have two! Have all the drinks you want, and I will have them with you, because today it is another sad day. We are all to die - yes - and before we die we must suffer so many little deaths. The deaths of our friends! Every one a slow death for each of us. Here. Come. Sit down. Drink! It is time for whisky. Only whisky will do in memory of our friend the Gaffer - not the famous Gaffer, no, but our friend, the one we knew. He drank whisky - and we will drink whisky too!"

Good old Carlo. He was as good as his word - his many words - and poured two shot glasses of some whisky that he assured me was the best, the very best, because only the very best would do at a time like this. It was a shame I didn't like whisky, but I elected not to burden Carlo with that information.

I knew a few of the other drinkers in his bar, and they came over and offered some words of commiseration about the Gaffer's death. I realised that I was actually mourning him. I hadn't killed him, not quite, but I had planned his death and I hadn't prevented it, and I was missing him already.

I sat down at the bar counter and put my head in my hands. I wasn't very talkative. Of course, with Carlo that hardly mattered.

"To think - he was here just the other day. Just before you and Iffy came to see me." I smiled a little, the first time that day, because I loved the way he said Iffy: Eeffy. "We knew him a long time ago, didn't we? When we were young - so very young - and life was an adventure. Remember those days? Those nights! Those parties! Oh, the parties we had together! It was our life. Just partying. No bills to pay, no pensions - no bocconcini to order. No plans beyond the next party, no memories from before the last one. But I mustn't make it sound too perfect - oh no, there was stress and problems and all that shit. Of course there was. But still - life was good to us! We made it good. All of us together. Come, more whisky!"

"I'm tired, Carlo." And I was. Tired to my bones, tired to my soul.

"Are you, my friend? But of course. So where have you been? Where did you go with Iffy? And where is he now? Back in London, I am sure, because he does not come to see me in my bar. He lives the good and happy life in London, our Iffy - I know it. We will drink to a long life to our friend - to all our friends! To the friends we still have, to the friends we have lost. To the memories we shared with those friends. To our dead friends and to the memories that have gone - and to the half-memories and the half-stories they left behind. *Salute*!"

And all the time I was bouncing around in a moral maze of my own devising, despite Iffy's assurances that killing the Gaffer had been our only option. I wondered how Iffy was dealing with his own conscience. By burying it under a pile of drugs, I suspected, just as I was determined to submerge mine in a pool of alcohol.

If only the damn thing wouldn't prove so buoyant.

"Fucking peanuts!" I heard Carlo say.

Maybe English, that most modish and flexible of languages, had adopted a new term while my back was turned. First Willy, now Carlo. A peanut butter was a nutter in rhyming slang. I supposed that something had got lost, or at least a little disorientated, in translation, and that my Italian and German friends thought that peanuts meant simply nuts.

The drinking continued. Not at great velocity, but with serious intent. Carlo provided a background monologue about the high times we had shared in the good old days, which was generally the reason I didn't go to his bar very often.

I began to regret the hastiness of my actions in having ditched my Facebook account and my SIM card with all my contacts on it. The expected sense of freedom had not materialised. I wanted to speak to Iffy and Clara, to hear their voices, for them to tell me their versions of the events at the Gaffer's last party.

"Can I use your phone, Carlo? Have you got Iffy's number? And Clara's?"

"*Sì*, of course, of course! I got everybody's number, me. Me, I do not move no more. Here I am, always in my bar - so I need to have people's numbers. They move all the time, like you and Iffy - moving, moving, moving! *Salute*!"

"*Salute*, Carlo. Thanks. You don't mind if I step outside for a minute?"

"A minute? Take two minutes, take ten! Time has no importance here. In my bar there is no time. Look - you see a clock on the walls? A calendar? No! I do not allow it here in my bar. You English, I think - you are the only people who spend time like you spend money. Oh - not you personally, but you English in general. Other nations, we pass time or we give it and take it - only you, you see it as a commodity to spend. Am I right?"

Not really paying attention to whatever he was babbling about, I accepted the proffered mobile and ducked out into the evening air. A few drops were still tumbling from the canopy of lime trees at the edge of the square. The other bars and restaurants were noisy and animated behind their steamy windows but the streets were nearly empty. Lights shone on the cobble stones and reflected off the puddles. A train clattered rhythmically past.

I imagined Clara's phone ringing in her flat in London and I wondered what she was doing and what on earth I was going to say to her.

Ring, ring; ring, ring. Her answer phone picked up.

"Er. Clara. It's me. Just thought I'd. Er. Anyway. You know. That is. I guess. You must be. I know you. I know I. This isn't. I didn't. I don't want. You probably. I don't. Fuck. Call me. Well. If you. Okay?"

With hindsight, I was duty bound to consider the possibility that I had not been at my most eloquent. Also of note was the fact that Clara wouldn't be able to return my call because I had changed my mobile number. Apart from those two salient observations, I felt the call had gone about as well as could be expected.

Next up was Iffy. Ring, ring; ring, ring. Ring, ring; ring, ring. Ring, ring; ring, ring. Ring, ri- "How's tricks, Carlo?"

"Iffy, it's me," I corrected him. "How you doing?"

"A-ha! So I'm not the only one to blag someone else's phone to make international calls. You sly old dog, you."

"Iffy," I said, aiming my conversational arrow at the heart of the target and letting fly, "tell me straight: what did you do at the Gaffer's party?"

"You really want to know?"

"…"

A SEETHING MASS OF ELECTRO-MAGNETIC BIO-CHEMICAL MESSAGES

"I did some Berwick-on-Tweed and a few Jack and Jills, I had a little ride on a donkey, and I saw Adam and Gianluca Vialli. And of course, I drank fifteen cans of Stella."

Oh, that Iffy! What a joker! How he must have made himself chuckle. The twat.

Language and group identity have always been intimately connected, and all communities have a tendency to develop their own lexical idiosyncrasies. It happens within geographical areas, but also within particular trades and professions, and especially in closed environments where privacy is valued, such as schools, prisons and countercultures. Thieves' cant, Cockney rhyming slang, Russian *blatnoy*, Dutch *bargoens*, French *argot*, German *Rotwelsch*, pig Latin, Scouse backslang: all were examples of ways a language could be manipulated in order to separate insiders from outsiders. Mastering the vagaries of any particular slang took time, and demonstrating fluency proved a profound level of immersion. Often the goal was to allow criminals to discuss their business in public without fear of being overheard and understood, though to be fair the degree of cryptographic complexity was rarely impenetrable.

In our particular scene we borrowed words from everywhere, from other cultures and other subcultures. We used lots of rhyming slang, some of it old and much of it invented on the hoof to keep pace with the ever-changing modern world.

Thus, Iffy had just dodged the true nature of my question by wilfully misinterpreting it and listing all the Persian rugs he had done at the party. Some amphetamines, some ecstasy, some ketamine, some MDMA and some cocaine. The fifteen cans of Stella was a cheeky reference to the lyrics of a famous acid techno track in which the protagonist visits his first squat party, takes shitloads of drugs, drinks fifteen cans of Stella and stays till Monday night.

What Iffy had also done was subtly remind me that we were talking on an international phone line, no doubt being snooped on by hi-tech spying software.

"Bit of a shocker about the Gaffer, eh?" he went on.

"Tragic," I muttered, not sure if I meant it or not. "D'you know what happened?"

"Funny you should ask. I take it you've read about it in the papers?"

I confessed that I hadn't, and in response he laughed. A real laugh, the hearty outburst of a man who found something very funny indeed. I felt my upper lip curling up in distaste.

"Yeah," I heard Iffy's voice say, "it was fucking peanuts, man!"

I hastily revised my earlier conclusion that Willy and Carlo had misunderstood the word's correct usage. If Iffy, the ultimate underground insider and slangmaster, was employing it as slang for crazy, it was clearly a kosher expression.

"So that's it, then? Our mission is complete?"

"You could put it like that. It was Anna Phylaxis what done it in the end."

So Iffy had found someone else to administer the fatal dose, I thought.

"Anna who? Is that the Greek girl who used to have dreads?"

There was more laughter in my ear. Then it stopped. Iffy said, "You're serious, aren't you? The Greek girl with the dreads! That's priceless!" And the laughter started again.

It went on for a while, and is it did so my sluggish brain began a laborious process of re-routing and reprogramming. Neurons sent electrical impulses cascading through their axons. Synapses sparked into being. Neurotransmitters were sent spanking into waiting dendrites. My brain became a seething mass of electro-magnetic bio-chemical messages.

Ping!

I got it.

Not Anna Phylaxis, but anaphylaxis.

The Gaffer had died as a result of his peanut allergy.

"Holy fucking moly on a psychedelic pogo-stick!" I exclaimed.

"My thoughts exactly."

"So you didn't…Why didn't you..?"

"Like I said. Some billy, some Gary Abletts, a whole lot of donkey, fifteen cans of Stella, *et cetera*, *et cetera*. I went to see the headmaster, me, and I got well and truly caned. Didn't know what was going on. Hadn't got a Scooby. By the time the mists had cleared, the Gaffer had already taken a ride to the promised land."

"But that's brilliant news!"

"Well, not for the Gaffer, it wasn't."

In my jubilation at finding out that we hadn't killed our old friend, I had momentarily overlooked the fact that he was still dead. "Well, no, not for the Gaffer, of course."

"In fact, as it turns out, I'm pretty chuffed that we didn't get to do our thing. Have you had a chance to have a butcher's at his new manifesto yet?"

"His manifesto?"

"Have a quick shufti at the Gaffer's website, why don't you?"

Back in Carlo's bar, feeling an intriguing mixture of guilt, elation and curiosity, I asked my genial host if I could borrow his laptop to look at the Gaffer's website.

The last entries had been made on the night of the album launch. One was entitled Manifesto.

TORIES IN RAMONES TEE-SHIRTS

I hate orders.
I hate borders.

I believe in my tribe.
I believe in subverts. I hate adverts.
I believe in bringing the vibe.

I hate avarice.
I believe in roots. I hate suits. I believe in seeds. I hate greed.
I hate all injustice.

I believe in unity.
I believe in rigs. I hate the pigs. I believe in riots. I hate diets. I believe in punk rock. I believe in paradox.
I believe in creativity.

I believe we have too much stuff.
I hate lobbyists. I hate selfishness. I believe in LSD not GDP. I believe in altered states. I hate police states. I believe in campfires. I hate vibe vampires.
I believe enough is enough.

I believe in networks.
I believe in cooperation. I hate corporations. I believe in sabotage. I hate espionage. I believe in imagination. I hate mental stagnation. I believe in squatters' rights. I hate vacuous sound bites. I believe in seeking solutions. I believe in minimising pollution.
I hate how debt works.

I hate petty-minded jobsworths.

I believe you should fight for a cause, not for applause. I hate oversimplification. I hate over-complication. I hate following fashion. I believe in pursuing passion. I believe in permaculture. I hate crass consumer culture. I believe in my sisters and brothers. I believe we can all learn from one other. I believe that gods are delusions. I believe masters are illusions.
I hate Tories in Ramones tee shirts.

I hate organised religions.
I believe we can police ourselves. I believe in well-stocked bookshelves. I hate empty houses and evictions. I hate bouncers and dress restrictions. I believe in DIY, not GMO. I believe in respecting the word 'no'. I hate the cult of the celebrity and how it distorts reality. I believe in the underground. I believe what goes around comes around. I believe in keeping an open mind. I believe in being generous and kind. I believe in art for art's sake. I believe in learning from heartbreak.
I hate self-serving politicians.

I believe in beauty, and it isn't for sale.
I hate sexism and homophobia. I hate nationalism and xenophobia. I believe in change, flux and flow. I believe in sometimes letting go. I believe in speaking out and listening. I believe that everyone's good at something. I hate being snooped on, judged and filed. I believe that rivers and forests shouldn't be defiled. I hate tax havens and offshore banking. I believe in summer nights spent stomping and skanking. I hate cognitive dissidence and sophistry. I believe it's up to us to learn from history. I believe in seizing the day and enjoying the hour. I believe in the power of love, not the love of power. I believe the war on terror is a sham. I believe the war on drugs is a scam.
I believe with persistance we will prevail.

I hate the ubiquity of inequity.
I hate the rape of mother earth. I hate how we are labelled from birth. I

hate the tabloids and their harmful lies. I hate antibiotics and hormones in our food supplies. I hate arrogance and pomposity. I hate billionaires who profit from poverty. I believe in civil disobedience and protest. I believe all life is a learning process. I believe in making some fucking noise. I hate elite schools and jobs for the old boys. I believe in the necessity of sustainability. I believe in turning off, tuning out and stopping the TV. I hate how our children are criminalised. I hate how festivals are commercialised. I believe in mutually beneficial exchange. I believe when you're a stranger, people are strange. I believe in non-hierarchical organisation. I believe in moments of silence and contemplation.
I believe in questioning all authority.

I hate being told what to do.
I hate TV executives who control our screens. I hate the promotion of hollow dreams. I believe in sex, drugs and rock 'n' roll. I believe in decks, dogs 'n' socks with holes. I hate the cages forged by wage-slavery. I hate stupidity dressed up as bravery. I hate fear as a controlling mechanism. I believe in fighting all forms of fascism. I believe in targeted property damage. I believe left to ourselves we'll learn to manage. I believe perception is mutable and plural. I believe there's no such thing as normal. I hate all those who prey on the weak. I hate the deceptive banality of management-speak. I believe between black and white are shades of grey. I believe every underdog shall have its day. I believe in friendship and staying in touch. I believe there is a time and a place to turn it up. I hate status symbols for the insecure. I hate the blind acceptance of dogma and law.
I believe in freedom from and freedom to.

I hate that there are so many things to hate when we're all in this together. I believe in acid with techno and techno with acid. I believe there comes a time to stop being placid. I hate the demonisation of refugees. I believe to save this planet we must save the bees. I hate capitalism and the immorality it seeks to hide. I hate nazis, bigots and racists and their fucked-up white pride. I believe there's no government like no government.

I believe in cultivating a sense of wonderment. I believe in good food because you are what you eat. I believe in stopping the city and reclaiming the streets. I hate plastic pop music that cheapens the power of emotion. I believe in keeping the air pure and protecting the ocean. I hate smart speakers and facial recognition software. I believe that the poor should take courage and that the rich should take care. I believe resistance is fertile and we can overgrow the system. I believe the hardest road is the road to wisdom. I believe in freedom of action, so long as it doesn't affect anyone else's freedom of action. I hate it when human contact is reduced to a financial transaction. I believe that all coppers are bastards, but not all bastards are coppers. I believe if we work together, there's no way they can stop us. I believe if you agree with much of this, maybe you too are an anarchist.

I believe in loving and living and sharing and giving before we are dead for ever.

DARK LITTLE LIES

I didn't fall off my chair, because that doesn't really happen. Metaphorically, though, I lay sprawled on my back with my legs in the air.

This latest unexpected development required some sort of explanation. Here was the Gaffer (if his website had not been hacked, hijacked and steered into alien territories by some unknown, swashbuckling cyber-anarchist) seemingly championing our old lifestyle and beliefs at the expense of everything he had apparently become. Either he was lying - or he had been living a truly massive lie for years.

Thoughtfully, he had posted another short essay:

I have been living a lie, it began, conveniently answering my question. *As have most of you who have been foolish enough to listen to my music and support my career as a DJ. Allow me to be honest. Grant me a few more minutes of your time. Put your thinking caps on. Turn the music off. Concentrate. Just for a little while. Then you can either return to your previous existence, or not. It's up to you. You* are *free to do things differently, you know.*

I should apologise. To those of you who genuinely found my music to be as good as the industry hyped it up to be - it wasn't. It really wasn't. It was formulaic tosh. To those of you who sincerely intended donating your hard-earned money to me in order to make my cronies even wealthier - we didn't need it. We only spent it on stupid things. To all of you who actively support the status quo *and see no pressing need to rock the boat or upset the apple cart - I'm sorry, it has to be done.*

It is time for me to tell a story. Are you sitting comfortably? Then I'll begin…

Once upon a time there was a young man. An idealist and a dreamer, he raged against the pernicious global cabal of politicians and businessmen that he thought was sacrificing lives, and indeed destroying life, in the name of profit. He went travelling with a musical collective with the noble aim of spreading the message that another way of life was possible. After half a decade, his sound system hit the rocks and sank. His friends deserted him and he watched as his vagabond's dreams were replaced by the depressing reality of unemployment. For some months he was lost and lonely, cast adrift, a sailor without a ship, a demobbed squaddie, a refugee in a strange land.

One day he got a phone call. An old contact asked him if he wanted to remix a track for release on the B-side of a single. He had no money. He was sleeping on friends' floors, eating out of bins. But he said no. He wouldn't compromise his beliefs. Not for anyone, not for anything.

But his contact called again. And again. And no-one else was calling, and the young man was tired, hungry, cold and desperate. How bad can it be? he asked himself. A few hours in a nice, warm studio, and enough cash to see the month out. All he'd be doing was making music. It's not like they expected him to evict a family from their home, or sell arms to a dictator, or drop a bomb on some strangers in a foreign land. Everyone worked for the Man to some extent; all money was dirty money if you traced it back far enough. Someone was always exploited, the world's resources were always being chipped away at.

So the young man changed his mind. He accepted the offer, signed on the dotted line, dashed off the remix, ate well and slept in hotel beds... until the money ran out. Another opportunity came along and this time the young man didn't hesitate. The A-side was a hit, the remix became a favourite with club DJs, and the offers came flooding in. The young man was a competent DJ/producer, and that was more than enough to permit him to make the kind of music that his backers required. A proposal soon followed to release some of his own tunes. So he kept accepting the wealth and prestige that came his way, and he kept signing the contracts.

Six months later he was told he had a week to bang out another tune. By then his time had become a precious commodity. There were important interviews to give, important parties to attend, important clubs to play at, important people to meet. The manager he had been obliged to hire said *they had to keep the momentum going. It was important. They could not afford to say no to anything that came their way.* With the deadline looming, and the young man exhausted and uninspired, he took the easy option: he rehashed an old favourite, a tune written years before. It wasn't exactly his tune, but he had been there when it was written and he had contributed to its existence, and he felt within his rights to cannibalise it. He reworked it for public consumption, rendered it more accessible, and barely gave it a thought once he handed the finished file over to his team.

How High, as the young man's manager chose to call the track, hit the dance floors of the UK, and a short while later it was picked up by a well-known soft drinks company who wanted to use it as the soundtrack to their latest TV advert. The young man drew the line at this blatantly commercial use of his music, but his manager showed him the clause in the contract that allowed it, and the rest, as they say, is history.

But what about the young man's old beliefs? His fervent anti-capitalism? His strict moral code? His heartfelt understanding of what was right and what was wrong? His mission to do what he could to make the world a better place? Where did all that fit into his new life?

The truth was that he had no time to dwell on the subjects that had previously ruled his existence. During his rare moments of solitude, when he fell to contemplating his life, he told himself the kind of dark little lies that have helped guilty men through the ages to sleep at night. *I spent years promoting the underground scene,* he told himself, *but we reached saturation point. We were preaching to the converted. I don't owe anyone anything. I've done my bit - less than a few but more than most. Let someone else carry the load for a while. I'm not as young as I used to be. My sound system is broken and I don't have the energy to build another.* And so he would finally fall asleep, and when morning came he was busy again, and popular, and respected, and well-paid, and important, and the years passed and he kept signing the contracts, and he kept his doubts to himself.

And now here I am, a young man no more. Here we are, ten years down the line, and I am 'successful' beyond my wildest dreams. And purely because I am rich and famous - not because of what I have to say - I have been allocated a platform to speak from. Millions of people hear what I have to say, safely expecting the same vacuous drivel and trivial chatter that they hear from other 'celebrities'.

Only I've had enough. Eventually, you see, I stopped signing all those fucking contracts. Quite simply, I could no longer live with myself. All those old beliefs of mine had been buried, but they weren't dead, and I was no longer capable of ignoring my conscience. I decided to be true to myself once more.

And here I am.

Please read my manifesto. Feel free to copy it, post it, repost it, stencil it on walls, nail it to church doors, glue it on lamp posts, distribute it as widely as you like. Thoughts are free. Reflect on your life. Re-assess your priorities.

Our society is currently based on greed and the lust for control. Money is the key. Withhold it! Start your own cooperative banks and shops. Trade for services, not cash. Buy locally. Don't buy what you don't need. Waste less. Organise yourselves! Love one another! Police yourselves! Create your own parallel economies based on sustainability and mutual benefit.

Let's begin with one easy experiment in people power. Let's choose one company whose ethical standards have been found wanting by the majority of the population. There are so many to choose from! Should we plump for a bank which launders billions of pounds of dirty money? An oil company that pollutes with impunity? A biotech company that seeks to rule the world? A pharmaceutical company that tried to sue a government for supplying AIDS victims with a cheap generic version of their own patented drugs? The list, unfortunately, is nigh-on endless.

So let's go for something that has to piss everyone off: a hugely profitable multinational that diligently avoids paying taxes. There's no excuse. It's despicable, antisocial behaviour that is depriving us of many of the services we need. Let's kick off with just one of the many, many offenders. And let's make them change their policy...it's very, very easy.

Say, for argument's sake, that we choose a mobile phone network provider. First thing on Monday morning, tell them you want to change provider. When you and a million or two million other people do this, you will be playing them at their own game. Speaking the language they understand: the language of money and profit. They will soon change their ways when they realise that paying their taxes is a better alternative than going out of business.

I'm not talking about armed insurrection here, just switching your mobile phone provider. And then one by one, step by step, company by company, we the people of the world will force the corporations into being more ethically and morally responsible, before finally breaking the behemoths and creating something sustainable in their place.

But back to me and my life...My new album Back To The Roots fulfils the final part of my recording contract. After this I will be free. I will lead the life I want to lead. I have set up my pieces on the chess board of life; now I will play. I am donating most of my money to causes that I hope will further the advancement of justice and equality, and hinder the march of laissez-faire *crony capitalism.*

I know what's in store for me. The vilification. The censure, disapprobation, condemnation and disparagement. The mockery. A world that was prepared to listen to me spout reassuring inanities will turn its nose up at me when I want to get serious. Attempts will be made to dismiss my ideas as the ramblings of a drug-addled, cosseted celebrity who has lost the plot. The journalists and 'opinion-makers' will try to focus on my personality and my lifestyle in order to detract from my message. I will not be taken seriously. My suggestions will be labelled as immature and puerile, the teenage rantings of a grown man who hasn't studied economics or politics, who has neither stood for office nor run a business, and who is therefore unqualified to comment on the 'real world'.

In doing so, they will be diminishing your *right to think, not just mine. The attacks on me will be attacks on you, too. By knocking me, they will be encouraging the belief that I - that you - that we - are not capable of running our own lives. That we must bow to their superior wisdom and defer to their greater knowledge.*

My advice: tell them to fuck off.

Tonight sees the official launch party for Back To The Roots. My new album is just a reworking of an old liveset by myself and some of the other members of my old collective. It is the free party sound. I think it is a thing of beauty, but also of uninhibited joy, righteous anger and shared truth, as should our entire lives be. It was a collaborative effort, as should our entire lives be. Over the past six months, I have visited all my friends who helped produce the original recording, seeking and gaining their permission to use it. The fact that they are all now dead only makes it more important for me to share their work with the world.

Tonight's party is not going to be just another schmooze-in for celebrities and music biz hangers-on. It is an open invitation. You are invited, too! *I want you to come!*

Watch this space for when I announce the location later this evening.

And maybe there will be a little surprise for you in the empty building next door.

You will be hearing more from me. I will milk my fifteen minutes of fame for all it's worth. I do not have all the answers, but I believe that together we can create a fairer, happier, healthier world.

LIFE - SHE IS THE STRANGE ONE

Somewhat self-righteous, self-justifying, self-important and self-centred. A wee bit megalomaniacal and pompous. Nonetheless I had to doff my metaphorical hat to the Gaffer. I certainly hadn't seen that coming.

I thought about my old mate the Gaffer wrestling his scruples into submission for ten long years, and smiled at the thought of them finally rearing up and biting him on the arse. I thought about the slippery slope that he had raced down. It started as a short term solution to a lack of funds and a sense of disillusionment, and the pace grew more frenetic as one tune became a recording contract and one month became a decade.

I knew that the Gaffer wasn't alone in quashing his qualms and silencing his conscience, and much to my astonishment I found myself no longer despising him for having sold out. He had got carried away with the trappings of fame and fortune. He wasn't the first well-meaning person to fall victim to the Sirens of celebrity, to grow to enjoy wealth, or to sacrifice his principles when faced with the practicalities of day-to-day life in a world where, in the Gaffer's own words, all money is dirty money if you trace it back far enough.

Ultimately the Gaffer's underlying sense of decency had won through, and I had to grant him a modicum of respect for that. I certainly wouldn't have chosen to do what he had done, but each to their own. A man who spent most of his time idling about and wishing the world was a better place was in no position to cast aspersions on someone who was trying to change things.

If even a fraction of the Gaffer's army of fans modified their behaviour in the ways he desired, then the world would undoubtedly be a better place.

I had long found it baffling that so few celebrities chose to say anything that I considered worthwhile. Surely, like the rest of us, these people had been born with the cognitive functions necessary to question the misdeeds and crimes of the ruling elite. The world was full of dissenters. Why did such a small proportion of those in the public eye use their position to speak out?

Occasionally a Hollywood star would raise his or her head above the parapet and let fly with both barrels - but they would never dare to stand on the front line. They would criticise the distribution of wealth and power while simultaneously working for the very corporations who were partly responsible for the problem. They were rich enough to never have to work again in their lives, yet continued to prostitute themselves. I could only presume that they were made to believe that they had too much to lose. The houses, the fans, the lifestyle…if they went too far in what they said, they risked having to kiss goodbye to the material vanities and the adoration that they had been taught were an accurate measure of success. And as Iffy had put it, "Once you're in it, you're part of it, and it's in your own interests to serve their interests."

Having crossed the Rubicon, it seemed a shame that the Gaffer was dead now.

Until I remembered that he had slaughtered a lot of my friends.

Which actually no longer made a great deal of sense...

Far from wanting to keep a lid on the sins of his youth, he had elected to shout about them from the pulpit that his celebrity afforded him. He claimed to have secured permission from all our dead friends to use their music.

From what he had written, it also appeared that he was the man behind the squat party next door to his album launch party. A quick glance at some news sites informed me that thousands of people had indeed turned up for the squat party in the building next door to the launch party that night, and it seemed that it was still in progress as I sat in Carlo's bar.

And if the Gaffer genuinely was intending to give away all his riches, there would appear to be little point in killing the others to stop them claiming royalties from his new album.

"Life - she is the strange one, is she not?" Carlo interrupted my thoughts, handing me a glass of something strong, pale and East European. "Just when the Gaffer, he was ready to do something good for the world - it is his time to leave us. Just when he was ready to say *arrivederci* to his shitty manager, he leaves us."

"Yes," I said thoughtfully. "Yes."

"This story with the peanuts…"

"Yes?"

"Just, you know, well…everybody knows he has this allergy. All his friends, I mean. And the Gaffer, he was many things - we all are - but stupid? No. Stupid was one thing he was not - not the Gaffer. Not stupid."

"No."

"He lives, what, forty, forty-five years with this peanut allergy? All his life, the Gaffer, he has this allergy…and then it kills him on the night he wants to start a new life."

"Yes?"

"Just saying, you know. It is fucking strange, no?"

"Yes."

Hot on the heels of the strong, pale, East European something that I had ingested came something strong, dark and Madagascan. The two scuffled briefly in my stomach, then ganged up on the strong, tawny and German something that soon joined them. By the time something strong, transparent and Italian was added, I was on the verge of reaching a new conclusion. I was also on the verge of retching.

"It makes you sick, no?"

"You're not wrong, Carlo."

"No respect." He flicked his fingers at the screen of his laptop. "No privacy, even in death. Who would do such a thing?"

Blearily, I gazed at the screen he was now showing me. It swam into focus, but more like a toddler doggy-paddling than Johnny Weissmuller manfully front crawling. The web page appeared to be from some tawdry celebrity gossip site. The photos were very poor quality, but I recognised the little room in the warehouse where the Gaffer had died.

The first grim, grainy, dimly-lit picture showed the Gaffer sitting on the floor, a look of combined dismay and surprise on his face. He had evidently just hit the deck. The other people in the room were immortalised in a moment of doubt, not yet knowing if they were witnessing a practical joke or a tragedy.

I remembered the idiots I had seen taking photos with their mobile phones. One of them must have sold his images to the website, cashing in on the Gaffer cashing out.

The second photo showed the Gaffer's manager, Andy, crouching down and administering the kiss of life. I stared, recalling the conflicting emotions that had assailed me at the time. I stared more closely, seeing again how panic had let its demons loose among the other onlookers. I stared at the Gaffer's corpulent frame and how it seemed to be struggling against the weight of his black-clad manager, who looked like the angel of death come to harvest his soul.

I stared.

I saw how Andy was cupping his hands around the Gaffer's mouth...Andy, who hated all mention of the Gaffer's days on the road. Andy, whose many riches came entirely on the back of the Gaffer's musical success. Andy, who went everywhere with the Gaffer. Andy, who knew the Gaffer intimately...Who must have known about the Gaffer's deadly peanut allergy.

And slipping out from between Andy's fingers I saw three peanuts.

"Fucking peanuts," I breathed. "The kiss of death."

"I know, I know, the fucking peanuts. I said to myself, Carlo, I said, Carlo -"

"Carlo? Will you shut the fuck up and let me use your phone again?"

"*Si.*"

Once outside, I called Iffy again. I told him about the photo and how it seemed to show Andy in the act of killing the Gaffer.

"Kinell," he muttered.

I told him how Andy could have slipped the Gaffer something that made him feel dizzy. I told him how he must have then taken advantage of the moment to force-feed him some peanuts, knowing it would kill him.

I reminded him that Andy's pay cheques would stop as soon as the Gaffer escaped from his recording deal. That Andy's share of the Gaffer's riches would have been reduced, had the royalties from the new album been split six ways, and how it would be multiplied in the wake of the Gaffer's death. That Andy must have been aghast when he read in the manifesto about the Gaffer's plans to redistribute his own wealth.

I told him that the old friend who had visited Minnie, Jacek and Sam just before they died must indeed have been the Gaffer. I told him that Udo had probably been going to see the Gaffer when he died. I told him that the Gaffer knew that Allan Exit was out and about in Friedrichshain after I had innocently suggested that he come to join his old crew for a drink after Udo's funeral.

I told Iffy that the Gaffer had probably arranged to met them all in order to get their permission to use the old liveset as his new album. That would explain Allan's phone conversations and subsequent missing half hour on the night he was attacked.

I reminded Iffy that everywhere the Gaffer went, his manager went too. Andy could easily have gone back later to have a quiet word with each of our old friends, inventing some excuse that he was coming on the Gaffer's behalf, and he could have killed them so that the Gaffer's royalties would not have to be divided among so many people.

I told him that what we had taken to be evidence of the Gaffer's guilt - the file of photos from our days on the road entitled 'Death of a Travelling Sound System' - must have been a treasured collection of memorabilia that our old friend had compiled, rather than a hitlist he had drawn up.

Iffy told me not to worry.

And I heard that familiar drawn-out rasp of nasal insufflation as he snorted a line. Ketamine, I figured.

I hung up and watched as the rain continued to fall and people dashed in and out of an off-licence and a cheerfully chatting group of students piled into a restaurant and a tired-looking waiter nipped out for a quick smoke and a scruffy brown dog stopped to sniff a lamp post and a cyclist rang her bell and someone dodged out of the way, and the clouds momentarily parted and the moon shone down on me, and I wondered what my friends were doing, wherever they were, and who out there was thinking of me.

SYAD-ASTI-NASTI-AVAKTAVYAH

The Gaffer's manager died a couple of days later. It was generally considered to be an interesting footnote to the main story, that of the Gaffer's early demise.

I read about Andy's fentanyl overdose online, and I made sure I did not think about everything it implied.

I did not allow myself to wonder how it had come about. Nor did I permit myself to remember that Iffy had assured me we needed to kill the Gaffer purely as a pre-emptive act of self-defence, and not out of a lust for vengeance. I did not recall my sense of overwhelming relief when I had realised that Iffy wasn't a killer of men himself.

I certainly did not even begin to think that that fucker Andy, the man who had killed my friends, had got everything he deserved and that the world was a better place without him, and that maybe Iffy was right in saying that the world was sometimes in some places a splendid, glorious cocktail of hope and love, and that at other times and other places it was a foul concoction of hurt and dirt, and what the fuck, Andy dying just meant there was one less evil bastard using up the planet's finite resources.

No, I did not think any of that.

The Gaffer was still big news. His manifesto went viral, but his predictions about how the media would react to his final statements were proved accurate. In light of his decision to give away all his money, the way he had chosen to follow a road less travelled and the unusual circumstances of his death were used to question his soundness of mind. I supposed he had genuinely feared for his life, believing that Iffy was planning to kill him, because he had left a will, it emerged, dividing his riches amongst various anarchist, traveller, squatter, animal rights, human rights, antiglobalisation, direct action, ecological, and generally subversive anti-capitalist organisations, associations and collectives. I imagined posses of lawyers licking their lips at the chance to challenge the stipulations of his last will and testament.

Only time would tell as to whether his legions of fans changed their behaviour at all. I suspected most of them would simply move onto the next plastic music celebrity that the next Andy foisted upon them. A campaign was begun to put into action his ideas for tempering the most egregious excesses of the corporations who were laughing all the way to the off-shore banks. Again, only the arc of the arrow of time would show how successful it would be, although as Iffy liked to say, time flies like an arrow; fruit flies like bananas.

Over the next few days I called Clara's phone with a nagging persistence. When she finally deigned to answer, I forgave her for not responding sooner. She was up to her eyeballs in work, she said - fighting to see that the Gaffer's millions went exactly where he had wanted.

I couldn't resist. "I remember you telling him not to come to you if he needed a lawyer."

"When I bollocked him for not doing something positive with his money and position of influence? I remember that, too."

"Funny he never said a word to any of us."

"Maybe he did to Minnie and the others. Maybe he would've done to me if I hadn't been so shirty."

"Aye..."

"Anyway, I seem to remember some paranoid fucker hiding behind the door with a baseball bat in their hands. So if you want to talk about misjudging your friends, you'd be better qualified than most, wouldn't you? Hmmm?"

As cops went, it was fair. She had me bang all the way to

rights and back. With bells on. I had allowed myself to get swept away by a wave of supposition that emanated from the unfathomable depths of Iffy's ocean of paranoia. We had surfed the whitecapped curlicue, eyes down, concentrating on maintaining our balance, paying little heed to the shoreline that was rushing towards us - until the wave broke and off we tumbled.

Sure, it could have been the Gaffer who was killing our friends - but it wasn't. And I had very nearly believed that Iffy - good old Iffy, poor, fucked-up old Iffy, Iffy the free, Iffy the doomed, Iffy, my one true and faithful friend - was the culprit.

I had come very close to killing the Gaffer myself. Only the ineffable randomness of circumstance had prevented me. The universe and its workings, I reminded myself, were mysterious, indiscriminate and fickle. And that was A Good Thing. It was what our rig - our whole scene - had been all about. Spontaneity, creativity, seizing the day, taking chances, dancing till we dropped, making some fucking noise in the long, dark night.

"There's a saying," Clara was musing down the line, "of indeterminate providence, incontrovertible wisdom and timeless, salient relevance: 'And those who were dancing were thought to be insane by those who could not hear the music.' I couldn't help but -"

"I know!" I said, still thinking about our sound system days. "From the outside, the free party movement must have looked very strange indeed. Lots of freaky looking people basing their entire lives around listening to amplified music. But those of us who went to the parties - those of us who could hear the music - knew it was about so much more. It was about changing perceptions, taking control of our own lives, looking after each other. Living anarchy. But you know all that."

"Sounds like the Gaffer has posthumously rekindled your

passion?"

"I've always been there in spirit."

"Ah, I see. An armchair activist." Before I had time to formulate a rebuttal, she went on: "But that's not what I meant. 'Those who were dancing' - I meant you and Iffy."

And just then my mobile pinged. I put down my cigarette and opened the message box to find a text from Iffy. 'Arriving Berlin tomorrow morn. Is it ok to crash chez toi for a month or two?'

Syad-asti-nasti-avaktavyah, I thought. In some ways, it is, it is not, and it is indescribable.

My finger, bent crooked like a question mark, hovered somewhere above and between the Y and the N on my keypad.

THOSE WHO WERE DANCING

ACKNOWLEDGEMENTS

If you enjoyed this book, please leave a review at
https://www.amazon.com/review/create-review
asin=B087G221JW

Those Who Were Dancing is for anyone who has ever danced in a field and anyone who has ever wanted to make the world a better place. It is also for all the friends I made on the way, including those who are no longer with us.

Enormous thanks to Josh and Antoine for the cover, to Gareth for proofreading, to Chris and Simon for reviewing (and for the music), and to Carmel for being my mate.

Onwards and upwards!